# THE REFUGE

Also by Chaz Brenchley:

*The Samaritan*

# THE REFUGE

## CHAZ BRENCHLEY

St. Martin's Press
New York

Library of Congress Cataloging-in-Publication Data

Brenchley, Chaz.
      The refuge / Chaz Brenchley.
           p.    cm.
      ISBN 0-312-03417-2
      I. Title.
    PR6052.R38R44   1989
    823'.914—dc20                         89-35074
                                                CIP

First published in Great Britain by Hodder and Stoughton.

First U.S. Edition
10 9 8 7 6 5 4 3 2 1

For Jay and for Lellie,
for love and for shelter –
and if that don't spell refuge,
what does?

# THE REFUGE

*It isn't blood he dreams in, and it isn't love he feels; but it might as well be.*

*His name he keeps hidden, and his face. Only his voice is known, and his desires, his demands. His hunger.*

*A creature of self, made in his own image, he values nothing else. He sings in the silence, in the dark, in the heavy rhythms; and his song is all himself. A little of blood, a little of love, and all himself.*

*Fear and anger, too, in equal measure; because he knows they're out to get him. That's why he stays hidden, where they can't get at him. Why he won't move until he has to, until it's safe.*

*Meantime, if they find him, if they want to kill – well, let them try. He'll stop them, one way or another. With a little love, a little blood. Perhaps a lot of blood.*

*So. Blood we got, love we got. What more do we need?*

# PART ONE

*Up and Running*

# 1   Accident and Chance

"The parents of a runaway teenager are to ask the High Court to declare their son a Ward of Court. David FitzAlan is fifteen, comes from Belfast, and is known to be living in an unofficial teenage refuge somewhere in London. He was named recently in a newspaper report about young male prostitutes, the so-called 'rent boys' of Piccadilly and the West End. Mr and Mrs FitzAlan believe that David, who is a Catholic, has given up that life since moving to the refuge; but their hope is that this legal action will force the refuge to hand their son back into their care. It is of course against the law to conceal the whereabouts of a Ward of Court.

"Now, here are the main headlines again . . ."

Joan Horsley snapped the radio off with a convulsive gesture, tipped her chair back and sucked air noisily through her teeth. Then she reached for the telephone handset, where it was lying on her desk; pulled up the aerial and punched a number.

Three minutes later, her chair-legs hit the floor with a crash as she pushed herself up and out of the room. Down the passage, and through the door into the kitchen: where three adolescents were sitting at one end of a long table, passing a cigarette between them.

"*Don't* smoke in the kitchen, please. Colton, you know better than that."

The lean black boy smiled an easy apology, twitched the cigarette from the fingers of the girl opposite and stubbed it out in a saucer. "Sorry, Mrs H."

The girl's lips tightened sourly, but she said nothing.

"And don't glare at me, Nina. I shouldn't let you smoke at all, any of you; so just be grateful there's one room where I do allow it, and don't abuse the privilege, please." Her eyes moved to the third of the group, a boy with vivid blue eyes

and dark hair curling down to his collar. "And you, Davey –
you'd better not go showing your face outside for the moment. All your crows seem to be coming home to roost, and
there are going to be a lot of people looking for you."

Nerves sent his fingers moving to the saucer, to play with
the dead butt as he said, "Something's happened, then?"

"Yes, but I'll explain later, after I've talked to the doctor.
Meanwhile, just stay indoors, please. And aren't you supposed to be washing up the lunch things?"

"Well, yes, I was just . . ."

"Having a post-prandial cigarette. So I observed. But that
particular activity having been curtailed, I would suggest
that the dishes await your attention."

Davey sighed, stood up and headed towards the stacked
sink. Mrs Horsley made for the door again, adding as she
went, "Colton, you're head prefect while I'm gone. Any
difficulties, refer them to Mark, please. He's resting in his
room."

"Okay, Mrs H."

Peter Cole was in a hurry: a nasty, vicious kind of hurry.
Already late for an appointment which had money riding on
it – a lot of money, and just maybe his job, too – he slammed
the car door, flung his briefcase onto the passenger seat and
twisted the key savagely. Made the engine roar a couple of
times in a gesture that was almost reflex, and pulled out into
the stream of traffic with a complete disregard for the
niceties of mirror, indicator, right-of-way.

Like everything else, resting in his room was a process that
called for a great deal of concentration from Mark. He might
read, or he might listen to the radio; but not both, and never
both at once. To go dipping and diving between, the tug of
one thing against the tug of another, and his mind the field
of conflict and the prize . . . Thanks, but no thanks. To be
straight, that was the important thing, to be single-minded –
and never mind a private little grin. Choose a path, and stick
to it. Be careful.

So there he was, lying on his bed with no radio on and no
music playing, actually not even reading, just lying there
with a book in his hands while his eyes moved slowly round
the room.

It was small by any standards, space for a single bed and a chest of drawers and very little more; but he liked that, just as he liked the clean, familiar comfort of the bare white walls. He'd been here more than two years now, and he still hadn't put up a poster or a photograph. He had them, to be sure, and he liked to have them; but he kept them under the bed in boxes and rolls of cardboard. Photographs would stretch the room one way, into memories and dreams; posters would take it the other, through fantasy and imagination. And it was important to him not to allow that, to keep the room small and white, standing four-square to the world, here and now and nothing more . . .

So he lay and held his book, and looked around, content to be here; and below him, directly below, someone shrieked.

Nina. Of course, Nina. Mark felt a surge of tired distaste, and tried to direct it against himself for being so prejudiced, and failed. He just didn't like the girl, that was all. Couldn't. And thank God Mrs H was on duty, so just this once he could ignore her, it wouldn't be him she came to with her sour expression and sullen complaints . . .

But the shriek came again, and was followed hard by a cacophony of voices calling and chairs tumbling and other noises he couldn't identify. It was enough to bring Mrs Horsley down upon them in her favourite role, as avenging angel; but the riot went on, and she should have been there by now, and obviously wasn't.

So at last, reluctantly, he rolled off the bed and went out onto the landing. Leant over the stair-well and shouted, "Oy!"; which made no appreciable difference to the noise-level, probably couldn't even be heard above it, so he had to go down, and don't stop to wonder or worry, just keep moving, straight down the stairs, down the corridor, into the kitchen.

Jane, little Jane was on her hands and knees under the table, in tears. Davey was leaning against the wall, biting the back of his hand, giggling weakly; Nina was on her feet in the middle of the room, scowling indiscriminately, nothing new there; and Colton was trying to pull the cooker off the wall.

"What the hell . . .?"

They all twisted or turned, looked up or round; and

Colton waved his arms wildly. "Shut it, man! Quick!" And when Mark just stared at him: "The *door*, man! Shut the bloody door . . ."

But Davey was already slipping past him to do just that, throwing his shoulder against it to be sure it latched; then the boy looked up at him, still laughing, and said, "Don't panic, Mark, we're only playing hunt the beastie."

And he ran the length of the room, to crouch by the cooker on the opposite side from Colton and peer into the darkness behind.

Mark watched them; listened to the ridiculous come-hither noises Colton was making between his teeth, as if he were trying to tempt an impossibly slender cat out from hiding; and at last put two and two together. He picked up a fallen chair and set it on its legs, stepped around Nina and went to help Jane as she scrambled out from under the table.

"Come on, babe, up you get." When she was on her feet, she headed straight for the boys, or the cooker, or what was behind the cooker. Mark grinned, and followed. "One of your rats, is it, Jane?"

She nodded fretfully, chewing on her lip and rubbing at wet cheeks with a filthy hand.

"I thought Mrs H told you to keep them in your room?"

"I – I know, but I'd had Charlie out for a run, just on my floor, 'cos that box of theirs is ever so small. And then she went to sleep under my shirt, and I thought it'd be okay if I came down for a bit, I thought she'd stay asleep. Only she didn't, she woke up, and I was making coffee, so she just climbed up and sat on my shoulder, that was all, she wasn't doing anything . . ."

She broke off to send a stabbing glance at Nina; and Mark could finish the story for himself.

"And she took fright, did she, and made a run for it?" he said smoothly, not giving Jane a chance to produce a more vindictive version. "Okay, well, all the more reason to keep them upstairs in future, yes? But don't worry, we'll nail her for you."

"Don't hurt her . . ."

"Promise, sweetheart." He saw her looking at her hands, realising how dirty she'd got on the floor; and added, "Just go and get the box, eh? So you've got something to carry her up in? We don't want her making another dash for it, halfway home."

Jane nodded, and vanished at a run. Mark turned to the boys. "Behind here, then?"

"Yeah," Colton grunted, still trying to squint into the gap behind the cooker. "Or underneath, I can't see it . . ."

"Okay, no problem. Davey, you and me'll just pull one side forward, slow and careful, so's we don't squash the poor thing. Colton, you stand by to grab it."

"You're the boss."

Mark and Davey took a grip as best they could on the side of the old cooker, and heaved. Colton crouched like a slip, eyes narrowed and body tense, playing it for all it was worth. Mark caught a sudden glimpse of dirty white fur; and a moment later it was enveloped in two long brown hands, as Colton dived and rolled and came up triumphant.

"Owzat!"

He held his prize aloft, fingers cupped to contain it as gently as he could; and his expression changed from laughing victory to pained surprise.

"Ow! It bit me . . ." He glared through the bars of his fingers. "You little bugger! Do that again, I'll *skin* you, I swear I will . . ."

"Do it anyway, why not?" That was Nina making her contribution, perfectly timed to greet Jane as she hurried back with the rats' wooden box clutched in wet hands. The edge in Nina's voice was aimed at her and Colton both, as she went on, "It's no use as it is, and you could have it for a willy-warmer."

Colton just grinned amiably. "Me, baby? C'mon, it wouldn't fit."

And while Davey relapsed into giggles, and Nina visibly selected another barb from her collection, Colton opened his fingers and let the rat scuttle out into its familiar sawdust and the company of its sister. Then he took the box from Jane, stretched the makeshift wire netting cover tight across its nails, and surveyed the result with patent dissatisfaction.

"It ain't exactly a palace, is it, girl?"

"Well, it's not their proper cage, I couldn't bring that, how could I? It's two feet long! And I couldn't leave them behind . . ."

"Course you couldn't. But you should've said, I could've fixed them up something more comfortable. Do it today, if you like. You'll let me have one of those old tea-chests, won't you, Mark? From the cellar?"

Mark nodded, and was going to offer the use of his tools as well; but Nina got in first, staring apparently into open space as she muttered, "Running away with two rats, for God's sake! Talk about a bloody baby . . ."

Jane flinched; and not for the first time, Mark thought, *She's too young for this. She shouldn't be here, she really shouldn't.*

But young or not, she had her champions – unless it was only that the kids would take any chance to kick back at Nina. Colton's long arm slipped round Jane's shoulders and guided her out into the passage, while he talked of the ratty Ritz he was going to build; and in the kitchen, Davey's soft, scornful voice laid down a gauntlet of his own.

"Baby, is it? It wasn't Jane that screamed. And it wasn't her turned up here with a bagful of stolen booze and her mother's purse. I'd rather rats, myself."

Nina flushed, and Mark broke in hastily. "Leave it out, you two. And talking of screaming, how come Mrs Horsley wasn't down on you like the Wrath of God?" Turning to Davey, because he'd really rather not talk to Nina, and he'd given up trying to hide it. "Any idea where she is?"

"Gone to the doctor's." In this house it was a name as well as a title, all the name they needed. "In a tearing hurry, she was. And she told me to stay inside, you'd better know that."

"Been talking to your newspaper pals again?"

"*No!* I said I'd not do that again, didn't you hear me say it?"

"It would've been better if you hadn't done it the first time."

"I know that. I was stupid, wasn't I? But I don't need you going on at me about it. Right?"

The words were aggressive, but there was more guilt than challenge in his attitude, in his eyes. Mark just nodded, and touched the boy's shoulder lightly.

"Right. I'm sorry."

Davey accepted the apology gravely, as no more than his due; Mark smiled, and went to answer the ringing telephone.

Call it luck, call it fate, call it bloody typical, as Peter Cole himself did; but he'd come the wrong way at the wrong time. He was caught behind a monstrous load too big to be allowed out on its own; and with a police escort front and back, watching precisely for the foolishnesses of impatient drivers, there was nothing he could do but crawl along with his fellow victims, cursing, watching the clock, getting later by the minute.

Until they came to a junction with a minor road, and one of the victims peeled off left, and then another, looking for an alternative route; and Peter made up his mind in an instant, and followed.

Raced down a blessedly empty road, and never mind the speed limit; and turned right, and raced again.

Traffic light ahead, changing too soon from green to amber. The first car got across, and the second; but Peter was third, and the light was red already when he stamped on the accelerator and just kept going.

And Joan Horsley was in a hurry too; she was watching the lights, not the traffic, and lifted her foot from the clutch sooner than she should, and trod on the accelerator. Saw a car shooting in front of her, jumping the lights, and knew she'd miss it, barely; and never thought there might be another coming.

Far too late, Peter yanked the wheel round and stood on the brake. His car skidded and screamed across the junction, while that bloody white Montego estate filled the road ahead, filled the road and the windscreen and Peter's mind as he hurtled into it, crushing the driver's door into the driver's legs –

– and it was that same bloody white Montego estate that emptied Peter's mind of everything, because he hadn't stopped to put on his seat-belt, of course he hadn't, not with that vicious little hurry he was in. So he went through the windscreen in a graceless, sprawling tumble, and down the bonnet of his Rover onto the road. And the two cars were still moving, tangled and mashed together as they slewed across the road and up onto the pavement, and were barely checked in their career by a soft body they knocked aside and left contemptuously in the gutter, the late, the very late

Peter Cole . . .

Mark was busy in the office when Colton and Jane came
looking for him. Nothing important, he left all the major
decisions and problems for Joan, but there was a lot of
minor paperwork he could do to make her job easier. It was
difficult when she was around, there was really only room
for one in the office and delegation was not her strong suit;
she had one of those vigorous souls that fails in its self-
imposed duty if it doesn't leave its fingerprints on everything
within reach. But any time she was out of the house, Mark
would take advantage of her absence to file, to organise, to
answer casual letters and list requirements.

This particular afternoon, he was collating accounts for
the month, matching cheque-stubs against bank-statements
and totting up domestic expenses. Any overdraft at the bank
would be dealt with automatically, there were standing
instructions to that effect; but the doctor liked to be kept
informed about the financial position, and with these kids
around it was just as well to check everything twice. To be
sure, the cheque-books and petty cash were locked away –
but one or two previous inmates could have picked their way
through door-lock, drawer-lock and cashbox while Mark
was still sorting through for the first key.

After forty minutes of figures, he had decimal points
dancing in front of his eyes; so the light tap at the door came
as a relief, pulling him back into a world of people, and he
grinned amiably as Colton and Jane came in.

"Give us the cellar key, will you, Mark, so's we can sort
out a box for the rats? We've been down the road and got
some wire for the front."

Mark nodded, and got to his feet. "Sure. But I'd better
come down with you. I don't know what's in where, and
there'll be murder done if you evict something vital from its
home, just for the sake of a rat-cage."

He lifted a bunch of keys from a hook on the wall and
ushered them out into the passage, locking the office behind
them.

"Best if you work in the garage, Colton," he went on, as
they walked down to the entrance hall and opened the door
onto a damp grey day. "That way the noise won't bother the
others, and you can use my tools if you need them. Should

be plenty of room, even with the Morris in there."

"Yeah, right. That'll be great."

Five stone steps led down from the front door onto a gravel forecourt, divided by low brick walls from its neighbours left and right. To the right of the steps, another narrow flight ran down into shadow, against the front wall of the house. At the bottom was a door, and a small square window. Mark fitted a key into the lock, twisted and pushed.

"Mind your head, Colton," he warned quietly, as the three of them walked slowly forward into darkness. He never felt safe down here even with the light on, the way the joists thrust down from an already-low ceiling; and the black boy was a couple of inches taller than he was.

Reaching up to the left of the door, his fingers found the first of those joists, and the old round light-switch screwed into it. He turned it on and two bare bulbs came to life. About forty watts each, Mark estimated, identifying one of Joan's little economies; but had they been three times as bright, they would only have brought the shadows and dark corners into greater relief. Light was an unwelcome stranger here, and hopelessly out of its depth. Restricted as it is to straight lines and clean angles, light needs space to be effective, it needs room to manoeuvre; and it was allowed none here. Old cupboards and wardrobes blocked it in, sheets of mouldering cardboard soaked it up like water, black-painted walls denied it altogether.

Mark heard Jane swallow convulsively, felt her small body pressing against his side. "It – it's really spooky down here."

"No, it isn't. It's just shadows and stuff, that's all." Colton's voice was self-consciously loud, playing a role; Mark only hoped that Jane was unsophisticated enough to take the reassurance, and never notice the effort going into it. "No ghosts down here, babe. A few creepy-crawlies, maybe; but don't tell me you're scared of spiders, I'll be dead disappointed . . ."

"Of course I'm not," Jane said; and walked ahead of them to prove it. Mark awarded Colton a silent hand-clap, and followed him to where full and empty tea-chests were stacked three high and five wide.

"What is all this junk, anyway?" Colton demanded, after he'd rejected the empty and most easily accessible chests, and they'd begun to unload some of the full ones in their search for sound wood and a solid bottom.

Mark shrugged. "As far as I know, most of it was here when the doctor bought the place. We've never had a real use for the cellar, so there's been no reason to clear it out. We've just added to the garbage every now and then, and left the old Yale on the door, in case some kind-hearted burglar wanted to take pity on us and pinch it all . . ."

"Fat chance, mate." Colton dropped some damp and ancient curtains onto the concrete floor, turned the chest upside-down and punched the base of it. And yelped, and shook his hand indignantly. "That hurt!" He kicked a side-panel, and winced; and examined the chest more carefully. "Here, this one'll do, I reckon. Jane, what d'you reckon to this? Come and have a look, eh?"

No response. Mark looked round, couldn't see her; called, "Jane?"

And was answered by a crashing, reverberant discord that filled his head and his imagination and had them both startling upright, Colton cracking his head on a beam and Mark staring wildly into the shadows.

"Jesus!"

"What the hell was that?"

"God knows . . ."

A girl's hysterical giggle chased through the echoes in an eerie counterpoint, and for a second they were tense and terrified, living in nightmare, horror-movie country. Then there were footsteps, coming in stutters, and that was worse; and Jane appeared, hugging her sides delightedly, laughing in gasps and staggering from one spasm to the next.

Colton rubbed the sweat from his face, glanced from Jane to Mark and back to Jane again, and muttered, "Are you going to kill her, or can I?"

"You do it," Mark said weakly, dropping onto the up-turned chest. "I haven't got the strength."

Colton curled long fingers gently round Jane's throat, and pressed with his thumbs on her windpipe. She screamed and jerked away, all the laughter gone; he stared down at her in confusion, and Mark groaned.

"Easy, Colton. All right, love, he was only fooling. Wasn't going to hurt you." Thought, *He's been here long enough, he should know better.* And thought, *I should've known better, not to encourage him. Some jokes aren't funny, some places.*

But one thing about Colton, he caught on quickly. Standing safely out of reach, he spread his arms wide and said, "Course I wouldn't. Not for the world, Jane, honest." And after a little she stopped trembling, and shook the fear off with a defiant toss of the head

*(and she's getting better, a month ago she couldn't have stood up to her own memories like that)*

and said, "There's a, a piano, in the corner. Come and see."

They went to see, and plinked a few sour notes and crashed some rancid chords to hear the echoes, and wondered how it had ever been brought down the stairs, and why; and after a while Jane looked up at them slyly, and said, "Scared you rotten, didn't I?"

And Colton gripped the back of her neck, and growled; and she didn't even flinch.

"Gee, darling." With a giggle.

"Y'what?"

"That's what I'm going to call it. The Gee, Darling Hotel for Rats."

"Eh?"

"C'mon, Colton! It's a joke, a whatchacallit. A pun. Darjeeling, see? It says Darjeeling, so you sort of turn it round, and it's Gee, Darling. Get it now?"

"Oh. Yeah. Right . . ."

Mark was upstairs when the phone rang, making sure that none of last night's downpour had found its way through the suspect slates into any of the empty attic bedrooms. He heard the shrill tone distantly, and cursed; but he was only halfway down the first flight of stairs when it cut off. He checked his headlong plunge at the landing and went on down more cautiously. In the lower passage he headed for the office door, then remembered it was locked and turned instead towards the kitchen, where the extension was.

Davey was just hanging the receiver back on the wall. He glanced at Mark uncertainly, and said, "I knew you were upstairs, see, and I didn't know if you'd hear, so I thought, better if I answered it, just in case . . ."

"Sure, thanks, Davey," Mark said easily. "What was it,

anything important?"

"Yeah, you could say that." Davey paused, reached into his pocket and pulled out a twisted, tooth-marked pen-top, which he slipped into one corner of his mouth and began to chew. Mark throttled back his impatience and just waited, long familiar with the teenager's urge to dramatise. "That was Joe, he's just been picked up by the shit."

"If you mean the police, say so, will you?" The response was automatic; Mark was cursing in the privacy of his skull, starting to panic, and fighting to keep it private, to stop the panic spreading. He sat heavily on a corner of the table, and wished urgently that Joan would come in. "So what did he say? Exactly?"

Davey smiled; and that was unnerving too, because he looked altogether too knowing like that, as if he could read precisely the state of Mark's mind. "Well, he said they were letting him make just the one call from the station, so he called here. And he said they were taking him back north this evening, and could you call his solicitor. And his mate Andy, and tell him Joe was back inside, and to go visit next Tuesday. And I said he'd be lucky if they let him have a visitor that soon, and he said they could try, anyway. And not to bother about calling his family, 'cos they'd find out from the shit. Sorry, the po-lice."

"Did he tell them who he was phoning, do you know?"

"He's not stupid, Mark. He said he'd been staying with friends, that was all. And he said no one was listening to the call, but we were careful anyway, the both of us."

"Thank Christ for that, anyway. So how did he sound, in a state?"

"Not really." The Irish boy considered for a moment, and went on, "I think he was about ready for it, you know? He didn't want to stay on the run for ever, just to get away for a bit, to get sussed after his mum's funeral. And he'd done that, this last month. And he's got a smart lawyer, he's told me about him, so he shouldn't get more than a bit of remission knocked off for going on the dodge. I don't think he was too upset at all, underneath. Just a bit fed up is all, for getting caught. Down St James's Park, he was," with a flashing grin, "feeding the geese. That's what he said, anyway. But he's a jerk, he was probably doing something flashy to impress some girl, and he impressed the fuzz instead. Do I get bollocked for saying fuzz?"

Mark smiled. "No, you don't get bollocked for saying fuzz. Thanks, Davey. Wish him luck, did you, something like that?"

"Yeah, from all of us. Told him he was a jerk, too, and said we'd be sending a cake."

"What, with a file in it?"

"Nah. Just get Jane to make another like she did last week, he won't need a file. He'd only need to throw it at the wall, it'd bring the whole place down."

"I'll tell Jane you said that."

"Don't bother, I'll be telling her myself."

In the office, Mark took out Joe's file and flicked through it. There was a lot less to read than in some of the others, but every detail was pertinent – solicitor's name, address and phone number, list of convictions, reasons for going on the run written down like a school essay. Joe Barnes was always organised, whatever he did; according to the way he told it, even his criminal career had been carefully planned, likely profits set against likely time behind bars. He maintained that crime could pay, if it were well thought out; and Mark had never argued the case. His role was to be a friend in need, not a missionary.

He grinned, remembering Joe's first contact with the refuge. The boy had phoned from his mother's house, before the funeral that had got him out on compassionate leave; the number had come from another lad at the remand centre, and he was calling to ask whether the refuge could give him a bed, if he slipped his watchdog and came to London?

Mark had choked down a sudden, startled laugh, and said, "Look, we're not in the business of encouraging kids to run away. Particularly not from institutions or the law. We're just here at need, for people who haven't got anywhere else to go."

"Yeah, I know all that. I'm definitely skipping, don't worry about that; I need it bad. Only I don't want to stitch myself up, come down to find I'm out on the streets 'cos no one'll give me a roof, do I? I'd be better off going to Liverpool, I've got a mate there I can doss with. But I'd rather come to you, see? So I thought I'd book in, sort of of . . ."

Mark had been charmed, and in charge with Mrs Horsley off for the day; so he'd said yes, and Joe had arrived that same evening. He'd been a model guest for the last month, settling in quickly and causing no trouble; Mark realised suddenly that he was going to miss the boy.

But they weren't here to provide any kind of permanent home – except maybe for Colton, and he was a special case, already almost more worker than resident. In general, the sooner the kids found a solution and moved on, the better. Mark jotted down a quick précis of what Davey had said about Joe's phone-call, then checked the solicitor's number and reached for the phone himself.

Twenty minutes later, still on the phone, talking to Joe's friend:

"He hasn't got much gear here, but I'll pack up what there is and send it up to you, if that's okay, Andy. Leave it to you to sort out what he's allowed, and hang onto the rest for him, till he gets out."

"Okay, yeah. No problem. Got the address, have you?"

"Yes, it's here. Oh, and give Joe a message for me, will you, when you get to see him? Tell him –"

The door crashed open then, and Davey tumbled in.

"Cops, Mark! Carful, just turning in . . ."

"Oh, Jesus. Andy, I'll call you, okay? Next week . . ."

He was on his feet already as he dropped the receiver, Davey's panic tugging at his own, pulling him halfway to the door before he stopped and turned deliberately to the window, taking time to cover it as he kicked his fears down.

*Be cool, be calm – always be calm. Don't panic – organise!*

He looked out through the blind and saw a patrol car parked on the gravel drive, two officers getting out.

"Right." *Maybe Joe's blown us after all, maybe he hasn't. Take the worst case, assume he has.* "Davey, nip through to the garage, Jane and Colton are there. Let them know, but remember Jane's only a kid, try not to scare her. The three of you may as well stay there; get the back door unlocked, and just make a run for it down the alley if you have to, if the police come looking for you."

"What if they're out there too?"

"Then you've had it, kid. Miracles I can't produce."

Davey nodded, licked his lips, and turned to go.

"Wait up." Mark called him back. "Where's Nina?"

"Don't know. Upstairs?"

The doorbell rang, long and imperative. Mark saw Davey's hands clenching into fists, and tendons standing out like cables in the boy's thin neck.

"Okay, she'll just have to take her chances. There's always the fire-escape, if she thinks of it. Go on, then, Davey, into the garage, quick. I'll bolt the door behind you; and I'll try to give you some warning if you have to run for it."

He pushed Davey gently to get him moving, and they trotted down the passage to the kitchen. The internal door to the garage stood open, the sound of hammering coming through, and a girl's laugh. Davey went in at a run, and Mark slammed the door behind him and threw the bolt across, as the bell rang a second time.

## 2   Baby Blues

"Mandy Thomson, please."

She got to her feet slowly and walked to the desk, a thin, sallow girl in school uniform, with dark hair falling lank to her shoulders and bruised blue eyes behind cheap glasses.

"Room five, Mandy. Doctor Howell."

The receptionist gave her an automatic smile and turned away. Mandy walked down the corridor to the door marked '5', saw the exit just beyond and very nearly walked straight on, straight out, with nothing solved and nothing changed. But she'd delayed too long already, there were things she had to know; and at last she skittered her fingers across the door in a faint gesture towards knocking and pushed it slowly open.

"Hullo, Mandy."

At least he'd checked her name before she went in, he didn't have to glance down at her notes to remind himself; and he was younger than she'd expected, she might have called him sexy a year, six months ago, and giggled about him with friends. Not now, though. Sex wasn't funny any more.

But he looked up at her standing, and smiled, and even now some part of her mind registered a tan and laugh-lines and a cute dimple in his cheek as he said, "Okay, Mandy, so who's been knocking you about?"

She just shook her head, no one; and his eyebrows arched in affected surprise. "You mean they're self-inflicted wounds? They'd shoot you for that, in the army."

"I don't understand."

"Those bruises under your eyes, sweetheart. Want to tell me about them?"

"They're not bruises, not really . . ."

"I know they're not, I'm a doctor. But I'd still like to hear about them. And don't tell me you just haven't been sleeping, there's a good girl." And when she still hesitated, "It's okay to sit down, by the way, I don't mind."

She knew that he was teasing, trying to make her smile, relax a little; and still she sat all in a jerk, rabbit-tense and ready for danger, as she took a breath and told him.

"I'm pregnant. And I don't know what to do."

Her voice was dull, flat, no dramatics. Certainly no tears or panic. She listened to herself saying it, and was satisfied; watched him making a calm little note of it, and felt easier. Not relaxed, there could be no more relaxing now, that was for children; but she'd taken one more step and hadn't slipped yet. She was doing the thing properly, day by day, letting it take over as it should. And it took a little of the pressure off, to tell a doctor; it was an answer of sorts to all the guilt and the worry and the vast, demanding future.

"Are you sure?"

"Yes, I'm sure." Still in that same drab voice; but that was nothing new, nothing special. She spoke to everyone that way. Like talking reluctantly to strangers – which was how it felt, always. Even her oldest and closest friends were so far away from her now, and falling further. "It's been three months now. I did two of those home pregnancy tests, and they were both positive. Besides, you can feel it . . ."

She touched a hand to her abdomen, and Dr Howell nodded.

"I'll have a look at you in a minute, Mandy. You'll have to

give us a sample, too, so that we can make our own tests; but you sound like a sensible girl, so let's just assume for the moment that you're right. You're how old, fifteen, is that right?"

"Fifteen, yes."

"Have you told your parents?"

A slow shake of the head: not defiant, just neutral. "Not yet."

"Would you like me to do that? I will, if you want. I'll probably have to talk to them in any case, so if it'll make things easier for me to break the news . . ."

"No, it's all right. I'll tell them."

"Okay, Mandy, if you're happy to do that. But the offer stands. How about the boyfriend, does he know?"

She didn't answer that, and he glanced at her more sharply. "*Is* there a boyfriend?"

"Not any more. I did, I told him; and . . ."

And there'd been tears from her, and screams, because she couldn't be flat and neutral then, she didn't know how. And he'd been cold and contemptuous, mocking her emotions even as he shrugged off any involvement. Not his responsibility, he said; if she was stupid enough to get pregnant, that was her problem. She should've gone on the pill, stupid bitch. Or just asked him to use a rubber, he might've done that if she'd asked. Too late now, she'd just have to get rid of it. Only he didn't want to have anything to do with it, right? Or with her, either, any more. Maybe if she hadn't bothered him about it, if she'd just got on with it quietly and left him out of it, maybe then he would've gone on with her. Or maybe not. But not now, she'd had it now. He'd had it, up to here with her . . .

And more of that, much more; but she didn't pass it all on to Dr Howell. It was all bottled up now, good and deep, where it couldn't hurt her any more; and all she said was, "We don't see each other any more, we've split up."

"I see. Do you want to tell me his name?"

Mandy shook her head.

"All right. You don't have to. But I'll just warn you now, you'll have social workers asking you the same question, and perhaps a policewoman too. It's a criminal offence, you know, sleeping with a girl your age; and I'll give you my private opinion too, which is that it's a much worse crime to drop her as soon as she gets pregnant. Was he a lot older than you, this boy? Or someone from school?"

Another shake of the head, and she said, "It doesn't matter, does it? It's not important now. I've got a baby, that's what counts. And you've got to tell me what to do."

"I can't tell you to do anything, Mandy. All I can do is give advice. But if you're thinking of an abortion, you don't have to worry about it. I can arrange everything for you, no problem; and you'll only be off school a couple of days, so no one needs to know except your parents . . ."

"No." Her fists were clenched tight in her lap, and all the skin of her face felt pale and tight as she said it again, louder. "*No.* I won't have an abortion. That's not what I mean. You've got to tell me how to look after it while it's inside me, what to eat, what I can't do, that kind of thing. Not to kill it. I won't do that. I *can't.*"

And there was life in her for the first time as she said it, nothing flat or neutral, an urgent, fierce flame that couldn't be questioned or denied.

## 3  Something to Lean On

There were two constables on the doorstep, a burly, middle-aged man and a woman a little younger. The man was apparently fascinated by the brass plate beside the door, gazing at it fixedly and running his fingers over; as Mark opened the door, he looked up and said, "This the Harlborough Institute, is it?"

Which he knew it was already, because that was what it said on the plate; but both constables seemed diffident and awkward, unhappy with whatever it was they had to do. There was no aggression in them, no sense of threat; so Mark only nodded and said, "That's right. Can I help you?"

"Got a Mrs Horsley working here, have you, Joan Horsley?"

"That's right," again. "But I'm afraid she's not here at the moment." Wondering what the police could want with Joan, taking their patent discomfort into account, and deducing bad news of the sort that the police still find themselves called upon to deliver. A relative dead, perhaps? But Joan had no relatives, or none she would admit to. "She could be back any minute, she's been gone a good while now; or I could get her to ring you, if you don't want to leave a message . . ."

"No, it's not . . ." The man shrugged, turned to his companion. She took a step forward, through the door, and then asked permission.

"Look, lad, do you mind if we come in?"

Mark shrugged in his turn, "Sure, if you want," and led them through the hall towards the kitchen. And changed his mind, remembering the kids hiding just beyond, and veered towards the office door; and then couldn't remember what papers were lying around on the desk, what names might be picked up by a casual glance, to ring bells then or later, when they came up in another context . . .

So he took them to the kitchen after all, as being the most neutral and unforthcoming room in the house. He made some noise going in, so the kids would hear, and simply trusted them to keep quiet thereafter. And prayed that Nina would be sulking fiercely in her room, to keep her safely out of the way.

"What's up, then?" he asked, casually picking up a steaming mug from the table and taking a sip, as though it had been his all along. Coffee, white and syrup-sweet – that was Davey, the boy always heaped the sugars in. "What's Joan done?"

He was consciously giving them a lead in, to get them talking, as he often had to do with the kids; and the woman took the chance gratefully. "Nothing. But – well, there's been an accident, I'm afraid."

"Someone's been killed?" He'd been right, then.

"The other driver died, yes. Mrs Horsley was seriously hurt, she's having an operation now, but she should be all right."

Wait a minute. He took a long, slow swallow of the coffee without noticing the taste, and said it aloud. "Wait a minute. You mean *Joan's* been in an accident?"

"That's right, lad." She spoke as if he were slow, or stupid; and perhaps he was, because it was impossibly hard to take in.

"We've been trying to locate her next of kin, to inform them," the man said. "Only this place was the only address she had on her, and the car's registered for here, too."

"She hasn't got any," Mark said abruptly. "Next of kin, I mean. No one she's in touch with, anyway. How bad is she?"

"Pretty smashed up. Legs, mostly, or that's what I heard. I wasn't there myself, we just got it on the radio to come over here and break the news. Friend of yours, is she?"

"Colleague."

*And friend, and family – but that's none of your business, so you don't need to know.*

"What about her husband? We've got her as married." That was the woman, with her notebook out.

In spite of everything, a smile flicked sharply at the corners of Mark's mouth. "Don't ask me, wait till she's herself again and ask her. I'm not going to spoil her fun."

"Divorced?"

"No, she's Catholic. And he didn't stay in the country long enough to petition. But seriously, that's all I'm going to tell you. Ask her, she loves it."

"Well, if we get the chance. We'd probably better check with her anyway, after she comes round. She's in the Princess Elizabeth, by the way – and don't try to visit before tomorrow, because you'd be wasting your time. Lucky if they let you in then."

"Okay, thanks. Um, any idea how long she's likely to be there?"

"Months, from what I heard. I'm no doctor, mind; only legs is like that, they lay you up for ever."

"Oh, shit." Mark picked up the mug and swirled it, watching a mess of undissolved sugar stirring lethargically at the bottom. "Holy – fucking – *shit*."

"Problems?" the woman asked, with the quiet sympathy that invites confidences. Just doing her job, Mark recognised; but, don't try it on me, sister, I'm an expert.

"She's the boss," he said. "God knows what'll happen to the place, with her laid up. I can't run it."

The man looked around him, at the long table and the large kitchen, seats for a dozen and crockery for twice that, just in case. "What goes on here, anyway?"

"Research," Mark said easily, the story long prepared. "The psychology of adolescence. You're lucky, you've hit a quiet spot. We're usually overrun with squabbling teen-agers."

"Research, eh?" The constable grunted, and followed his colleague to the door. "Well, if you come up with any answers, let me know. My eldest is just turned fourteen, and the little bastard's not even human any more."

Mark grinned. "Sorry, can't help. I'm just a dogsbody here, I don't even understand the questions."

He saw them across the hall, and out; stood at the top of the steps while they turned the car neatly in the forecourt, and drove away down the street; then closed the door, leant heavily against it and started to shake.

His world was still shaken and disordered five minutes later, as he made his way back to the office; but at least his hands were steady. Steady enough to punch buttons on the telephone, anyway; and that was all they could ask of him now, all anyone could ask.

The phone had a silicon memory, but what Mark needed now was the one number that could never be stored there. If the refuge were ever raided, there must be no connections made, no clues for the police to follow back to its founder and financer. Because if the refuge were raided, he would open another, in another part of London; and another if necessary, and another, as often as he had to, until his own cover were blown. They had his promise on that; and the promise was enough to buy a guarantee of silence from both Mark and Joan, and every precaution they could take.

So it was Mark's memory that supplied the number, without even a moment's pause for thought. He hadn't needed to memorise it, when he came to work here; it was already a lifebelt to him, a handhold in treacherous seas, and had been for years.

The phone rang briefly at the other end, and was answered.

"Kennedy and Sawyer, reception." A woman's voice, soft and mature, confident and supremely capable. As always, Mark found himself beginning to relax before he'd even spoken, as if competent hands were already reaching out to help.

"Beth, it's Mark Delaney. Can I speak to the doctor, please? Urgent."

"I'm sorry, Mark, he's with a patient." Which meant no, you can't speak to him, not under any circumstances, not till he's free. "But I was just going to call you. What's happened to your Mrs Horsley, do you know? She was supposed to be on her way here two hours ago."

"That's why I'm calling. She had an accident, Beth, she's in hospital. I'm on my own here, and I don't know what to do. I can't cope."

"Of course you can, you fool." Friendly but distant, brusque when she felt the need – that was how Mark had known Beth, any time these last ten years. The whipcrack in her voice was a comfort, a reassurance that not everything was breaking down. *Don't lean on me, boy* – but that in itself was something to lean on.

"One day every week, you cope by yourself," she went on. "So what's different about today, suddenly? I'm sorry Mrs Horsley's been hurt, but that doesn't affect your ability to hold things together."

"But it does, of course it does. Because it's not just today, it's tomorrow and all next week and next month and God knows how long after that! And I'm not up to it, it's not fair to ask me . . ."

"No one is asking you, yet," she reminded him acidly. "One day at a time, boy. You just hang in there until the doctor can talk to you. I'll explain the situation as soon as he's free, and I expect he'll come over tonight. Barring any more accidents. Talking of which, what happened? You'd better tell me, so I can pass it on. He's got a morbid streak of curiosity, that man. Unless it's prurient . . ."

Mark told her all he knew; and was just hanging up when he heard the front door slamming, and running footsteps across the hall. Another door banged in the kitchen, there were voices shouting, yelling his name; and he came out of the office to be confronted by three laughing accusers.

"You forgot about us, didn't you?" That was Jane, squeezing the words out through her giggles. "Locked us in and forgot us. We heard the car drive off, but you still didn't come, so Colton had to go out the back way and run round, to let us out."

"Best for them to stay inside, I thought," Colton added, more seriously. "In case they was still watching from the road. My face don't mean nothing, even to the local fuzz; but Mrs H said for Davey not to go out, and Jane's picture was on the box not so long ago, so . . ."

"Yeah, right. Good thinking, Colton. And listen, kids, I'm sorry, okay? It was just, I had to phone the doctor."

"So what's up, then?" That was Davey, chewing a thumbnail, all the laughter leaving him in a moment. "What did the pigs want, something to do with me, was it? That why she said for me to stay in, because they were looking for me round here?"

"No, I don't know why she said that. I'll try and find out tonight." It was something else to worry about, what could have happened to make Joan go off so precipitously, with such a specific warning to one of the kids. "But the police were here for something different. One of you put the kettle on, will you? I'll go and get Nina, and talk to you all together."

According to the rota, Nina and Joe should have been cooking that evening; but with Joe back in custody, Mrs Horsley in hospital and the whole house in a fluster, Mark was quite content to let the rota lapse. He prepared the meal himself, enlisting the willing Jane as onion-chopper, table-layer and dinner-gong, taking advantage of the chance to give her a quick cookery lesson. He was determined that she should learn to hold her own among the other kids before she left, and the kitchen was a good place to start.

That was assuming she stayed for any length of time, of course. He'd still like to move her on quickly; a twelve-year-old simply wasn't ready to handle refuge life, let alone the world outside. But he couldn't expect her to go back home, to a father who beat her, who'd once strangled her unconscious, and a mother who worked her like a skivvy and starved any rebellion out of her. There ought to be an answer, but it couldn't be found without the help of the authorities; and Lord only knew how they were to achieve that. Joan had refused point-blank even to discuss it, arguing that they couldn't risk the security of the whole refuge for the sake of one girl. It was a moot point whether any official would be willing to treat with them on a basis of total

anonymity; and besides, she didn't trust the Social Services
not to simply bully the address out of Jane, once she was in
their hands. The kid was better off in the refuge than she was
with her family, and for the time being they'd just have to
settle for that.

And Joan was in charge, and Mark only a helper, in his
own estimation little more than a servant in a position of
trust. So he hadn't argued; and now, of course, it was too
late, with Joan in hospital. The doctor would have to take
charge himself, if he couldn't find someone else he could
trust; and if Mark hadn't fought his corner against Joan, he
wouldn't even get into the ring with the doctor.

He sent Jane to do her dinner-gong act, and bring the
others down; and fought hard to contain the panic that
gripped him when she was gone. The doctor had his practice
to run, he couldn't spare time for the refuge; and it wasn't
exactly a post he could advertise. He might have to close it
down temporarily, if he could see no other answer. The kids
couldn't stay here unsupervised, that was obvious. But they
had nowhere else to go – and neither did Mark. No one now
to take him in the way the doctor had, to give him a home
and a life again, and eventually a job, something to do that
was truly worth the doing . . .

The kids came in, talking inevitably about Mrs Horsley's
accident, speculating on what could have happened and
clearly very displeased with Mark for not having got all the
details from the police. Nina surprised him, by being the first
to ask when they could visit.

"Not till next week, probably. I'll go and see her
tomorrow, find out what the situation is. But she's been
badly hurt, she won't want you lot rioting around her."

"One at a time, I meant," Nina said disgustedly. "Not all
together. I'm not stupid."

"No, of course not." A little late, Mark remembered that
Nina's father had been perpetually in and out of hospital,
that she knew far more than he did about the needs and
desires of a long-term patient; and was perversely glad when
Davey interrupted, before he could frame an apology.

"Flowers. We could send her some flowers, couldn't we,
Mark? From all of us. Tomorrow, if you're going in. You'd
take them, wouldn't you?"

"Of course. Glad to."

"Oh, yeah?" That was Colton, snorting sardonicaily at the far end of the table. "How are we gonna pay for any flowers worth bothering about? Any of the rest of you got any dosh? 'Cos I ain't."

"We could always put Davey back on the streets." And that was Nina again in her more familiar role, digging for weak spots, and just digging deeper when she found one.

"Up yours," Davey snarled, stabbing his fork hard into a plate of spaghetti.

"No, up *yours*," sweetly.

"Cool it off, will you?" Mark said hastily. "We'll buy the flowers out of the emergency fund. And one of you had better tell Mrs Horsley about that, it'll make her laugh."

Mark was playing pool when the doctor came. Usually he would leave the table for the kids, and only shoot a few frames solo late at night or in the early morning, when the mood took him; but tonight he was challenging all comers, and winning hands down.

"Just a bloody hustler, you are," Colton said in an aggrieved voice, leaning on his cue and watching Mark clear the table.

"Too right." Davey was sitting on the window-sill, still smarting from three consecutive losses. "There's an idea, now, Mark – why don't you turn professional, and beat people on the telly every night, instead of beating us?"

"Make a fortune, you would," Colton added enticingly. "And there's the bright lights, and the girls . . ."

Mark just shivered, and stepped back from the table so they wouldn't see him shivering. He shook his head free of images

*(bright lights, girls, camera lenses. Reporters and managers, money, pressures and demands; and him alone, webbed in at the centre, where everyone could see him, where everyone could see him shaking . . .)*

and stepped forward again, lined up his shot and sent the cue ball skimming up the table to kiss the last stripe tenderly into the top pocket. The black followed a second later, and Colton grunted, and bent to retrieve the balls and set them up again.

And straightened with empty hands, smiling past Mark.

"Hey, doc!"

And the room was full of noise and greetings, and a small man smiling, touching, talking to everyone, playing pool with Davey before going upstairs to look at Jane's rats in their new domain, Colton trailing behind to receive his due accolade as chief architect and engineer.

Mark went quietly from the games room to the kitchen, made a coffee and a Barleycup and took them through to the office. He sat down and waited; and before long, the doctor came to join him.

To Mark, the doctor looked exhausted as ever, and more than ever like a bird of prey, white hair standing wild like a ruff around his bald crown, and his great beak of a nose thrust forward in perpetual enquiry. The bags were dark under his eyes, and he sighed as he settled into a chair; but his voice was still deep and soft, untouched and caring.

"Well, Mark. How are things?"

Mark gave a tight, edgy shrug. "Not so bad, considering. Everyone's a bit nervy, wondering what's going to happen, but you'd expect that." *And I'm just the same, but you'll expect that too, so I don't even need to mention it.* "I phoned the hospital, and they said Joan's come through one operation okay, but she's due for another tomorrow, so no visitors yet. It's both legs, they said, and her hips as well."

"Yes. I made my own enquiries about that, had a word with the surgeon. He thinks she'll be fit to travel at the end of next week, so I'll make arrangements to have her moved to the clinic."

"What, to Malmebury?" And when the doctor nodded, "I thought you only took psychiatric cases?"

"I do; but Joan's not a case, she's an employee. I'm well equipped to care for her there, better than any NHS hospital; and it's a sorry world if the people who work for me can't have the best of my attention."

"Like I did, you mean?"

"Phooey. All you ever needed was a boot up the backside. And I still owe you one, for what you did to my hydrangeas. I should never have let you near those gardens." The doctor smiled cheerfully, and went on, "So how are you going to cope here, on your own? Any problems?" In a voice which clearly anticipated the answer no.

Mark sat very still for a very long time, while the doctor waited with the patience of a professional. At last, because

the question still hadn't gone away, Mark tried to make it
go. "You don't mean that."

"Yes, I do. Why not?"

"I can't. I just . . . You know I can't."

"No one else can. You know the kids, and the set-up;
you've been here since it started. And there's nowhere else
for these children to go."

It was the same thought he'd had himself, with a different,
a terrifying conclusion. Mark lifted a hand between them,
but not in a gesture, not to hold back the force of the
doctor's argument, it didn't have the strength. He only
wanted the doctor to see how it was trembling.

"Look, that's what . . . I can't. I'm not capable." And in
desperation, "It'll *wreck* me, doctor! You'll have me back at
Malmebury again, and not as any bloody gardener . . ."

"Wouldn't take you, boy. Not at any price. And it won't
be necessary, in any case. You'll cope, because you have to.
They need you, Mark."

There was something terribly wrong about this, because it
was the old, calm voice that had offered strength and suc-
cour for so many years, the voice of the rock he'd clung to;
and now it was throwing him off, throwing him out into the
storm with empty hands.

But because it was that voice, because the doctor had
never lied to him and if he said 'need' he meant it, and
because the kids were kicking up a riot across the hall and
where would they go else to do that, if they couldn't stay
here, where would they be safe?

Because he couldn't in the end do anything else, Mark
nodded, and said, "Yes. Okay. I'll try."

"Good, then. Come on, boy, let's go and claim that pool
table. Best of three, before we turn our attention to young
FitzAlan. We're due for some more publicity there, I'm
afraid; but leave that for now. I want to see if you've learned
anything, since the last time . . ."

White steam and brown skin, scalding hot water driving down her back so hard she could hardly think; and thank God for the lock on the bathroom door, for locking them out and being *alone* for a while . . .

And never mind which God she was thanking, it didn't matter to her. She didn't believe in any of them. Didn't need to. Though it might be useful if she did, just for a while. If she turned Christian, maybe . . .

Tia giggled suddenly, and squirmed against the scorching, solid rod of water. What would they say? – what would they *do*?

Only she knew just what they'd do. Her father would hit her, and start shouting again; her mother would go silent and simply add it to the long list of things she wouldn't talk about; and Uncle Asif would have a serious talk with her, tell her how much trouble she was causing and how it wouldn't do any good, and he'd book the tickets tomorrow to prove it.

No good, then. She had to be careful in her rebellion, or she'd only bring it all down on herself sooner. She scowled, and reached for the shampoo as she moved her head back under the shower. The jet broke and flowed down over her scalp like liquid heat, forcing a soft groan out of her, half pain and all pleasure.

Eyes closed against the water, she worked by touch, shampooing the heavy length of her hair once, twice and a third time (and why not? *They* were paying for the shampoo, so let them pay . . .) before finally letting it fall back, dropping below her waist, the tips of it tickling lightly against her buttocks, shiveringly sensuous.

Another five minutes under the shower, just drifting, letting the steam and the heat and the water push her right out of it all; then she pulled herself sharply back and together, shut the water off and stepped out of the tub.

The bathmat was soaking under her feet, and so was the floor as she walked over for a towel. She'd forgotten to pull the shower-curtains round again. Tough. So she'd get yelled at – so what? She'd survive.

She pressed her face into the warm, thick pad of the towel, then shook it out and started to dry herself as she turned towards the full-length mirror in the corner. She'd had to fight to get that (immodesty, they'd called it; wicked Western decadence they'd meant, only they didn't have the words that she did, not in English, and she didn't, wouldn't speak Bengali); but she'd won for a change, got the uncles on her side for once. That was back when she was fourteen, when they'd still treated her like a little girl and enjoyed indulging her. Before she'd turned into real trouble . . .

The glass was all steamed up, but she gave it a quick rub over and let the towel fall, so she could look at herself properly.

At least she'd stopped looking like a bloody kid. Okay, so her breasts and hips weren't exactly lush (*modest*, she thought, and giggled again); but that was fine by her, she'd rather be trim than blowsy. Slender, like a good Western girl. And the boys seemed to like it that way too, so who was complaining? And her face had lost its roundness in the last couple of years, maturing to match the changes in her head . . .

There was a hammering on the door then, and her grandmother's voice coming through the dimpled glass, screeching in Bengali, ordering her out.

Tia saw her face turn sullen in the mirror, and yelled back in the English her grandmother didn't understand.

"Yes, all right! Give us a break, I'm nearly finished!"

She dried herself quickly, and used the towel to mop the worst of the water from the tiled floor; pulled on the brief bathrobe she'd bought herself with her birthday money, and half hoped she'd run into Grandmother on the landing, just to shock her with a good view of exposed, immodest legs; unlocked the door, and hurried through to chase her sisters out of their bedroom, to try to snatch a little more privacy.

An hour later, Tia walked downstairs in disguise. She was wearing printed silk trousers and top like any dutiful Muslim girl, with a scarf to cover her head and only her hands and feet showing, no make-up. She had sandals on her feet, and no one would object to the red varnish on her toenails. A stud glinted in her nostril, there were rings on her fingers; and her hair was plaited into a single sedate pigtail, and smelling faintly of rosewater.

She swung a bag over her shoulder, checked for purse, cash and ticket, and walked casually into the living-room.

"Are you going out?" The question came slowly, phrased in her mother's painful English; and that was one more victory in the endless war.

"That's right," she said, matter-of-fact, no doubt or question in her voice.

"Where are you going, Tia?" Aunt Panna, from her seat in the corner. She was the best of them, always had been; and she was probably asking out of genuine interest, not because she wanted to stop her going.

Even so, Tia kept her guard up and played it sneaky. "There's a Bhangra band playing in town, Auntie." They'd all know what she meant by that – or they'd think they did. "I know it's not Bengali; but we've got to stick together, haven't we? And it's a cultural event. All the cousins are going, Kumar should be here to pick me up in a minute . . ."

And just then she heard his horn blasting in the road outside, and she could turn and hurry out, gabbling her goodbyes, even saying a polite word to Grandmother in Bengali, knowing that when her father got in he'd be told that she was at a concert of traditional Punjabi folk music. Grinning delightedly, at the thought of the evening ahead . . .

There were six of them squashed into the car – Tia, Kumar, three other cousins and Kumar's white girlfriend, looking anxious and out of her depth, as if she hadn't a clue what she was getting herself into. But then, she probably hadn't. What would she know about Bhangra?

They left the car parked in a back street and headed for the Fairfax, laughing and eager, the boys running and fooling, chasing a tin can along the pavement.

A car slowed right down as it passed, with a skinhead

hanging out of the window, making V-signs with both tat-
tooed hands as he screamed at them.

"Paki bastards! Go home, Pakis!"

Sarah started nervously, and jerked her head the other
way. The others didn't so much as look round, barely stiffened for a moment, so that it was hard to tell they'd even
heard. It was only Tia who turned to glare full in the boy's
face, who drew breath furiously, who yelled back.

"We *are* home! So go fuck yourself, fascist!"

Who ran forward, snatched up the can the boys had been
playing with, and hurled it with all the strength in her arm.
And missed by metres, as the car accelerated away.

"Shit, Tia!" Kumar grabbed her arm and spun her round
to face him. "Do you want to start trouble, is it?"

"I'll start trouble with him, all right," she snarled, snatching her arm free. "That little fucker . . . I was at *school* with
that shit, before Dad sent us private. I'll kill him!"

"Oh, yes. Very tough, aren't you? But you don't start
things when I'm around, right? I'm not fighting your battles
for you."

"I wouldn't ask you to." She said it with a sneer, and
watched it bite; and stalked off ahead, making herself alone
again.

She was a long way in front when she reached the Fairfax,
and joined the queue; and another ten or twelve kids had
fallen into line behind her by the time her cousins caught up.
She ignored them completely, and heard Kumar cursing as
he tagged onto the end of the queue.

Ten minutes later, she handed over her ticket and pushed
her way into the packed hall. It was the heat that hit first,
rolling over her like water; then the noise, separate but
joined, beating through flesh and bone into the very heart of
her. She stood still in the crush of bodies, the chaotic colours
and movement and the heavy, sweat-soaked air; and was
still standing there when the cousins came in behind her.
Kumar and the boys went straight past, but Jaswinder
slipped her arm through Tia's and tugged gently.

"Come on, let's find the loos and get dressed . . ."

So there in the white-tiled toilets, squashed into the space
between cubicles and wash-basins in the company of a dozen
strangers doing exactly the same thing, Tia stripped off her

disguise. The good little Muslim girl was tossed contemptuously piece by piece onto the floor; the printed silks were
replaced with tight blue jeans from her bag, and a skimpy,
glittery red top that exposed her arms, her midriff and her
intentions. The flat sandals were swapped for stilettos that
added three inches to her height. The nose-stud stayed, and
the rings, but there were heavy gold hoops to replace the
discreet studs in her ears, and a dozen slender bracelets to
jingle suggestively on each wrist.

The discarded gear was shoved deep into the bag, and Tia
fought her way forward to the mirrors. All the jostling and
shoving made serious make-up impossible, so she plastered
on glossy crimson lipstick and black eye-liner, and that
would have to do. A few quick squirts of some real scent, to
counteract the rosewater – didn't want to smell like
Grandma – and she was ready, except for her hair. She
rolled off the elastic band that held the ends together, and
worked the plait apart with impatient fingers; then she
brushed and brushed until her arm was tired, until the great
heavy length of it swung wild and free behind her when she
tossed her head. She laughed, and looked around for
Jaswinder; couldn't see her, and shrugged, and went out
alone.

Soul and funk, all the latest mixes, and maybe a thousand
people getting down to the music – girls in saris and boys in
suits and turbans; others in denim, both sexes; all young,
almost all Asian, all of them running with sweat. Someone's
brought a foghorn, and everyone sings along with the lines
they know. And this is only the overture, the warm-up. Wait
for the band – or bands, rather, because three of them will
be playing tonight. And if you're not Asian yourself or
otherwise in the know, if you're not tuned in to Bhangra,
then be ready to be surprised. The name is traditional, and
so was the music, once; but the young have taken it, and
claimed it for their own. It's folk music with a disco mix,
guitars singing with the fiddles and a synthesiser to back up
the accordion.

And the Bhangra beat isn't just a new style of music, it's a
phenomenon. Just watch, as the first band takes the stage –
watch, as the excitement is drowned in pure hysteria. Watch
for the boys dancing dangerously on each others' shoulders,

and the acrobats providing a side-show on the floor with backflips and rolls, surfing on the breakers of sound. And watch for the panties being hurled onto the stage, the girls screaming and stretching to clutch at the singer's groin.

Watch, and wonder – and welcome to Bhangra.

Tia kicked her stilettos off onto a pile by the mirrored wall, with only a passing worry about finding them again at the end of the evening. Then she danced: danced to her reflection at first, dancing out the bitterness and tensions alone and undisturbed, before letting the music spin her away from the wall into the shelter and curious comfort of strangers. This night was a gift to her, a time when she didn't need to be angry any more, when she could lose her life for a while and simply be one in a crowd, no future hanging over her like a sword, just a face among a thousand faces, a body that gleamed in the lights and danced itself to exhaustion . . .

. . . And was still dancing when a pair of hands closed on her naked waist. She jerked away instinctively, or tried to; but skin clung to sweating skin, and there was an unexpected strength in the fingers. She looked round, into eyes on a level with hers; and relaxed, letting the dance drain out and away as she leaned back against his stocky chest.

"Tia, man."

"Hullo, Shahid."

"You look like you could use a drink."

"In this place? Funny, Shahid." Soft drinks only at the bar, as a concession to the Muslims, or their parents; the organisers wouldn't risk half their clientele being banned next time.

But Shahid was twenty-two, a planner, a man who thought ahead. He pulled a half-bottle of vodka from his pocket, and dangled it temptingly before her eyes; and she laughed, and followed the bait across the packed floor to a blessed gust of cold air. There was a fire door standing open, and the bouncer on duty there nodded them out into the back alley.

They sat on a convenient pile of breeze blocks. Shahid took a pair of dark glasses from his shirt pocket and slipped them on, passed Tia the vodka and produced cigarettes and a slim silver lighter.

"Want a tab, then?"

"Yeah, give us."

She smoked because her father forbade it, no other reason. She liked to go home with tobacco – and yes, alcohol too – on her breath, one more small defiance and never mind the consequences.

So they smoked and sipped, and passed the bottle between them; and he talked, and she didn't pretend to listen. At last he dropped his cigarette into a puddle, put his arm round her shoulders and pulled her closer. And after the first shiver of skin on skin, the strength of that arm felt good to lean against, and the warmth of his body good against the cool night. She turned her face up, and saw it twice reflected in the dark lenses that hid his eyes; so it was almost like dancing with herself, almost like talking to herself as she told him.

"They've really done it, the bastards. They've found this boy in Bangladesh, 'very good *family*'," a savage impression of her father's voice, "and it's all fixed up. Dad's taking me out of school at Christmas, and we're all going out together, as a *family*, and I'm supposed to marry this jerk."

"Yes?" There was nothing but amusement in Shahid's voice, but she'd expected nothing more. Shahid's cool was his religion; everything amused him, and nothing made him laugh. "What's his name?"

"Nurul something-or-other, I don't know. I don't care."

"What are you going to do?"

She shrugged. "Not go. I'll just leave if I have to, run off to London or something. At the moment I tell them I'm not going to do it, and then Dad hits me, and I swear at him, and he hits me again. They don't believe me when I say I'm just not going through with it. I guess they think if they can just drag me to Dacca, I won't have the nerve to show them up at the ceremony. I would, though. If I had to."

"Why don't you? String them along that far, then just say no at the altar. Be a laugh, anyway. All their sweet little faces . . ." His spare hand caressed her stomach, and slid curiously up inside her top. "Are you . . .? No, I didn't think you were." He cupped her breast in a cool palm, and said, "Would it help, if we gave this boy's family a reason to refuse you? Say, if you weren't a virgin any more . . ."

Tia snorted with laughter, and pushed him away. "Fuck off, Shahid."

"What's the matter, saving yourself, are you?"

"From the likes of you, yes."

"Ah, bugger." But he was still nothing more than amused, as he folded the dark glasses and hung them by one arm from his pocket, dramatically black against the white shirt. He checked the effect carefully, smiled and held out a hand for hers. "Well, if I think of anything I'll let you know. But I'm not thinking tonight. Let's dance, yes?"

## 5  Story-Time

The judge had been taking evidence in camera all morning. Now his decision was due to be announced in open court. The press and public filed back inside; and Mark went with them, notebook and pen in hand, trying to look like a reporter. As he sat down, he glanced from side to side and decided that it shouldn't be difficult to remain inconspicuous. On his left, a man had calmly taken possession of two ancient wooden chairs, and perched a corpulent buttock on each. He was swathed and rolled in fat, wearing it like something apart from himself, a blanket against the cold of the world.

And on Mark's right a tall girl lounged with her feet perched on the railing in front of them, displaying the impressive length of her legs. She was wearing a red jacket above a short black skirt, green leggings and red baseball boots, the ensemble being topped off with dark shades and a black beret. When she pushed the beret to the back of her head, Mark saw that her cropped hair was a fiery, natural copper.

He smiled to himself, thinking that it couldn't have worked out better if he'd fought for a place between these two. No one would notice or remember his face this afternoon.

The judge had the slurred voice and florid complexion of a heavy drinker, coupled with pendulous jowls and side-whiskers that turned him from a genuine human being into a Dickens caricature. But his mind was sharp enough, even if his speech was slow and deliberate.

He gave a brief summary of the known history of David Anthony Saul FitzAlan: how the boy had run away from his Belfast home at the age of fifteen, and made his way to London; how he had been tempted or forced into male prostitution, for lack of any other way to live; and how his story had come to light through a series of articles in one of the metropolitan daily newspapers. David had been interviewed twice, once while he was still prosecuting his trade in and around Piccadilly Circus – "and you may think it ironic," the judge noted in passing, "that these sordid homosexual transactions were initiated under the aluminium and incorruptible gaze of a statue known as Eros."

The second interview had taken place two weeks later, after David had found support and shelter with an unknown group who claimed to provide a 'refuge' for runaway teenagers. This organisation was in fact operating illegally, and its very anonymity, functioning as it did in total secrecy and from an unknown location, testified to its knowledge of that fact.

These journalistic reports were the first news that David's parents had received of their son's whereabouts and mode of life since he had disappeared from the family home. Mr and Mrs FitzAlan had accordingly come to London to search for him; and having failed in that endeavour, they had now applied to this court to have the boy made a Ward of Court. If this application were granted, then the Crown would become legally responsible for David's welfare; and the people currently sheltering him would be in contempt of court and committing a criminal offence if they failed to come forward.

"At this point," the judge cleared his throat and picked up a sheet of notepaper from the bench in front of him, "I think it appropriate to read out a communication that was hand-delivered to this building overnight, addressed to me personally. It is headed simply, 'The Refuge', and bears yesterday's date. It says this:

"'Sir – this is to assure you of the well-being of Davey FitzAlan, the subject of an application currently before you. Davey has had a medical examination, and is quite fit and healthy; he is well-fed and clothed and has all the necessaries provided. In addition he has the company of people his own age, and he has repeatedly expressed the desire to stay at the refuge for some further time, until he can assume responsibility for his own welfare. He has no wish to return to the care of his family, or to Northern Ireland.

"'Respectfully, the Refuge Director.'

"There is no other signature."

The judge gazed around the court for a moment, while reporters scribbled frantic shorthand, and blessed his slow dictation speed. Then he adjusted his spectacles and went on, "It is of course possible that this letter is a hoax, pure and simple; but I can see no point in such a forgery, and have elected to regard it as genuine. And if it is genuine, it is also an example of outrageous impertinence, both to the judiciary and to the Crown. I would in any case have had little hesitation in granting the application before this court; but this letter has quite decided the matter in my mind. Persons who can be so disregarding of the law and the natural rights of parents can have no claim to be responsible guardians of the morals and welfare of a young and impressionable adolescent. Consequently, David Anthony Saul FitzAlan is hereby declared a Ward of Court. Those persons currently giving him shelter are instructed to bring him forward immediately; and I give warning that I will not tolerate defiance in this matter. Any contempt of court will be dealt with rigorously. In the words of certain fictitious villains from my youth, You Have Been Warned."

He gathered up his papers and departed; and even the hasty shuffling of feet as the court belatedly stood failed to cover the satisfactory ripple of amusement from his audience.

Mark wasn't laughing, as he went with the general rush of reporters, down the marble stairs in search of telephones or taxis. Nor was he watching what went on around him; or he might have noticed the copper-headed girl watching him curiously. He might even have noticed her follow him, out of the building and down the street.

*Always exit on a laugh*, his old mentor had told him, and it was good advice; but the judge wasn't laughing either. Safe in the privacy of his chambers, he pulled off the wig, poured a whisky and swallowed convulsively. Hypocrisy always left a sour taste in his mouth, and he'd really excelled himself today. That crack about Eros, for God's sake! But safety was the prime consideration, now and always; and safety meant never, ever giving the yellow press any reason to pry into his private life. And most particularly never seeming to be at all soft on homosexuality, in any of its manifestations. It wasn't simply for his own sake; for twelve years now, two careers had depended on his maintaining an acceptable public face.

At least, with the rhetoric set aside, his decision had been legally correct. He sighed, and drew comfort from that; and reached for the phone to call Julian, in search of more comfort than he could find there, or in the whisky.

It was a long bus-ride from the court to the refuge, and Mark had left the kids alone too long already; it wasn't fair to dump all the responsibility on Colton.

But nevertheless, with the bus-stop just ahead and a bus already in sight at the end of the street, Mark turned aside suddenly, into a packed shopping-centre. He was going to the hospital tonight; and if Joan were feeling anything like herself, flowers would be appreciated politely, but chocolates would be fallen on with delight. So he dodged from one arcade to the next, looking urgently for a Thornton's or a Maxwell & Kennedy; and ducking and weaving between the jostling crowds, he managed to lose the girl with copper hair, without ever having realised that he was being tailed.

An hour later, she was typing copy onto her monitor at a leisurely rate. Too late even for the last edition of that night's paper, she could take her time, put some fire into the language, try to grab the editor's attention that way.

Then she felt fingers drumming gently on the top of her beret, and looked up to find that she had his full attention already.

"Boss." She smiled, and seized the moment. "A word?"

"Several. And the first innings is mine."

She bowed, and made the gesture graceful even in a sitting position. "Your wish, O Master, is to me as an edict from Heaven."

"Good. My office, then."

He was already turning to lead the way when she twisted calmly back to her keyboard, and said, "Five minutes, okay?"

There was an exasperated noise behind her, but she didn't look round; and after a moment, his footsteps retreated. She grinned secretly, and set to work full-speed on that report. Never mind the fiery language; it'd only be subbed out in any case. And this wasn't the time to take chances with his renowned temper.

So, a hectic five minutes later, she pushed open the glass door of his office and walked in. He glanced up, grunted, and looked back at the paper he was reading. The *London Daily Herald* – their rival, and their major target in the furious circulation war that had been raging for three months now. She craned her neck round, to read the headlines over his shoulder; and he scowled, and tossed the paper down onto his desk.

"Just a small point, Alex, before you raise whatever startling and doubtless innovative idea is currently percolating behind those revealing dark glasses. Oh, you might take them off, by the way. Just while you're in here, if you wouldn't mind."

She took them off.

"Thank you. Now, why have you spent all day at the High Court?"

"I was waiting for the verdict. You know, on the Ward of Court application for Davey FitzAlan."

"Correct. And what time did the judge utter?"

"Two thirty. Ish."

"Right. And what time did you get back here with the glad tidings?"

"A quarter to four."

"Precisely. And that, Alex, is why the *Herald* has two columns of the judge's jests on the front page of its final edition, *and* a photograph, while we have nothing. Not even a statement in the stop-press. What the *hell* were you doing?"

And at last, there was a glimpse of that fabled anger. Just a glitter in the eyes so far, and an edge in the voice; but she could feel the storm building. She perched on the edge of his desk, and said, "That's what I want to talk to you about, squire. It's story-time. *Big* story."

"Explain."

"Think back, O my lord and master. How did all this fuss start? With an article in the *Herald*, right? They did a double spread on rent boys, and this Davey kid was one of the boys they talked to. Just by chance, their reporter bumps into the kid again a fortnight later, and stops to chat – and gets a second story, as the little bugger shoots his mouth off about this refuge place he's staying in. And where are we? Nowhere. It blows up into a major news story, with this High Court nonsense, and there's nothing we can do except tag along and hope people forget it was the *Herald* started it all. And there's a fat chance of that, with them trumpeting it in every issue."

"And even less chance if we don't mention it at all," he added pointedly.

"Don't try to sound mean, boss, it doesn't work. All your teddy-bear qualities come out too strong. And don't interrupt for a minute, okay? Point is, we've got to do something positive on this story, we've got acres of lost ground to make up. And there's only one way to get in the lead."

"Find Davey FitzAlan, I suppose?"

She nodded. "Find the refuge."

"And do it before the police do, and before every other newshound in the city. And I presume you're going to tell me you can do this, if I take you off all other assignments and give you carte blanche and an unlimited budget, am I right?"

She nodded again. "I nearly did it this afternoon, without any of that. Without even trying."

She could have sworn she saw his ears prick. "Explain that."

"If you've read that," she waved a dismissive hand at the *Herald*, "I expect you know about the letter from the refuge director, yeah? Well, they weren't going to send a letter like that without wanting to find out the judge's reaction, were they? At first hand, if they could. So I figured there'd be someone there, from the refuge; and I reckon I was sitting next to him. There was this guy came in with us hacks, you see, notebook and biro, everything; only the notebook was brand new, and I didn't know him, and I don't think anyone else did either. No one was talking to him, anyway. And he sat there all through the judge's speech, and he didn't write a word. Not a pot-hook or a squiggle. He just listened, and leaned forward every time the refuge was mentioned. He couldn't have said it plainer if he'd been wearing a uniform. So I followed him; and he didn't go rushing off to write up copy, either."

"Neither did you."

She ignored that loftily. "He was heading for a bus-stop, I'm sure of that; he was even slowing down, to join the queue. Only then he thought of something else, and dived into a shopping-centre; and I lost him there, it was just too crowded. But I've got the numbers of the buses that stop there, so we can narrow the field by a process of elimination; we won't have to scour the whole city. And I've got another idea, for working undercover if I can't pick this guy up again. So how's about it?"

He looked at her for a long, slow minute, and said, "Yes. But I want results, and I want them fast. Regular reports, too, I want those. Am I clear?"

"Boss, you are the King-Emperor of Fleet Street. The original Great Black Chief. If this weren't a professional relationship, I would kiss you. If the walls weren't see-through."

"Go. Go. Go *now*."

"Can any of you lot cut hair?"

Mark looked round the table, with no expectations. Davey didn't count; Jane just giggled, and shook her head; Colton sighed, and stretched his hands out palm upwards, and looked at them sadly.

"Not so's you'd know yourself afterwards, mate. I tried, once. On my kid brother. Got the shakes. Mum was raving."

No surprises there. It was Nina who startled them, turning back halfway to the sink with the pile of dirty plates in her hands, saying, "Yeah, I can cut hair."

Mark stared at her; she narrowed her eyes for a second, and nodded. "I can cut yours."

"Not mine," he said quickly. "Davey's."

She looked at Davey consideringly, with none of the usual malice. "Yeah. Davey, too. What do you want done?"

"Just make him look different. Or rather, make him not look like this."

He tossed a paper onto the table, that evening's *Herald*, with its two-column report and a photograph of Davey, taken the year before on a family holiday. Colton looked, and laughed.

"He don't look like that anyway, man."

"Near enough, he does. Near enough not to take a chance on it. I don't want him going outside until he's been, uh, redesigned." A glance at Nina, and a smile. "He's in your hands, kid. Anything you want to do."

"Oh, help." Davey groaned, and hid his face behind his hands; and Nina didn't just join in the laugh, she laughed first, open and easy.

"What's the paper say, Colton?" Jane was leaning across the table, straining to read the smudged print upside-down. "Read it out."

"Nah, you." He pushed the paper across to her, stood up and lifted the plates from Nina's hands. "Nice and loud, yeah? I'll do the washing-up."

"It's my turn," Nina said, half reaching to snatch the plates back.

"You got another job, girl." He gestured with his head. "Go check over your customer, yeah?"

"I can't do anything tonight, we haven't got the stuff."

"So work out what you need, or something. I'm doing this."

Mark turned over for the twentieth time, abandoned the dedication that had kept his eyes closed all that time, and reached for his watch on the bedside table. Two fifteen, and he'd come to bed at midnight. The house was quiet; all the noise was in his head, and that was only white noise when you came down to it, pointless and destructive. Worry and panic, chasing each other's tails, getting nowhere.

He sat up and turned the light on, pulled a pillow into place behind his back and picked up the bottle of tablets standing close and convenient, ready with a glass of water. The doctor had brought them round for him yesterday, and pressed them into his hand without explanation.

"I – I don't understand," Mark had stammered, feeling the walls tremble around him, the foundations start to shake. Remembering the days when it was only pills that kept the house from falling down. "You said I was off the medication, unless things went sour again. Five years now, it's been . . ."

"Five and counting," the doctor agreed with a smile. "But they're only sleeping pills. You didn't sleep last night, did you?"

"No. No, I didn't. But . . ."

"And you don't think you'll sleep tonight either, do you?"

"I wasn't going to ask for anything, I really wasn't. Not after five years. I thought you'd want me to get through without."

"I do."

"Then why . . .?"

"Because I don't think you'll use them." The doctor had closed Mark's fingers gently around the bottle, and patted them encouragingly. "Sweet dreams, lad. And keep counting."

And that had been something more to worry about, until at last he understood that it was a gesture of trust, and a challenge. The doctor was very big on turning a small thing into a symbol of something greater.

But this . . . This was like giving a loaded pistol to a child, telling him he could pull the trigger if he wanted to. Mark's hand clenched around the bottle, his thumb strayed across the ridged surface of the plastic cap. Just a quick twist, a swallow, a gulp of water – and goodbye, and hullo. In one door, and out another. Back to the chemical crutches that had held him up for so long; and maybe back to the need for them. Back to the house built on sand.

His mind turned blindly away from that constant fear, and submerged almost gratefully into the immediate anxieties that were keeping him awake. Four people's lives, resting on his inadequate shoulders. Davey and the High Court, the necessity of keeping him hidden with every policeman in the city looking out for him, his face in every paper, on every television bulletin. Jane, and her crying need for another answer, some greater security than the refuge could offer. And Nina, and Colton; and the refuge as a unit, an ideal, a haven that so many kids would need in the future. All of them, faces known and unknown, and all depending on him . . .

Mark turned, and turned again. From one to the other, and back to the first, spinning in circles, trapped and alone. Always that, always alone . . .

His eyes came back to the pills, to the label on the bottle, words that were both a threat and a promise; the key to a gate, and the quiet of a garden beyond. And the house in the garden, with its shifting, shaky foundations . . .

And at last he put the bottle down carefully beside the lamp, next to the glass of water, nice and handy. Turned the light out and rolled over, and went looking again for sleep, on his own, without a helping hand to ease him over.

Coming down far too late in the morning, he found life as usual in the kitchen, Jane boiling the kettle while Colton fed slices of bread into the toaster. "'Morning." He looked round blearily, and said, "Where are the other two?"

"Still in bed, of course. It ain't even ten o'clock yet."

Colton grinned, and added, "Looks like you should go back, and all. Your eyes are *red*, man."

"Can't, there's too much to do." Mark ran his hands down over his face, and went on, "You could help, though, if you wouldn't mind. If you'll do some shopping this morning – the usual food and stuff, and whatever Nina needs for Davey's hair. I got a list off her last night, and we might as well have it ready."

Jane carried two mugs over carefully, gave one to Colton and put the other in front of Mark. "Barleycup, no sugar. That's right, isn't it, Mark?"

"Yeah, right. Thanks, kid." He gave her a smile, and turned back to Colton. "That all right, is it? I'll tell you everything we need."

"Yeah, sure. No problem."

Colton did a round of the supermarket first for the general shopping, then went down the road to the chemist. Nina had demanded a pair of good scissors, turning her nose up at what the refuge could offer; he ran his eyes over the display, and picked out a slim stainless steel pair that looked right. Then he had to find the bleach. That was the tricky one. But he looked around, and saw a young assistant with dead white spiky hair, just showing dark at the roots; and smiled to himself, as he went up to her.

"'Scuse me . . ."

She glanced at him, bored. "Yeah, can I help you?"

"Hope so. I got this problem, see. My girlfriend, she wants to bleach her hair, and she told me to get the stuff to do it. Only, I don't know which kind to get; and she'll murder me if I cock it up, she's dead keen to do it today . . ."

"Okay." The girl led him past racks of shampoo, to the shelves beyond. "What's her natural colour?"

"She's really dark." Then, with a smile, "Not like me, I mean, she's a white girl, but her hair's dark. And she wants to turn it white. Like yours."

"Right, gotcha. Look, this is the stuff I use." She handed him a box. "Only you've got to do it twice, 'cos it'll come out orange the first time, if she's that dark. Straight up, it will." Another box, and at last a flicker round her mouth, and a friendly interest. "And mind she works it in well, both lots, or she'll get yellow streaks in it anyway. Going to help her, are you?"

"Dunno. D'you think I should?"

"Well, my boyfriend always helps me. I like it; you don't feel so daft then, sitting round with a bag on your head. Anyway, he gets off on playing around with my hair, says it's dead sexy . . ."

"Yeah, I bet." He grinned, and followed her to the till; but as he left the store the grin faded, while his mind filled with images. He thought of running his fingers through a girl's wet hair, of rubbing shampoo in under a shower while their bodies jostled together, wet and warm and naked; and felt a longing that was almost unbearable, an abrupt need that jolted through his body like fire.

And had to stamp on it like a fire, like he always did; because there was no way he could run a girlfriend, while he was living at the refuge. There was too much danger in it. If she found out, and talked, she could blow the cover off the whole place; and he couldn't live with himself after that, whatever happened.

So he swung carrier bags from both hands, and whistled softly as he walked along, and tried to think of something else; and his eyes followed every attractive girl along the street, watched the way they moved, talked, laughed together. And he fancied them all, and envied the boys they clung to; and the ones who were alone, his body talked to each of them, said, how's about it, sister, you and me? The blonde on the tottering heels, the black girl in dreadlocks and rasta-colours, the tall girl in the beret and dark glasses, with a glimpse of crisp copper hair beneath. He looked, and yearned, and ached for any of them, all; and told himself that some day, some day soon . . .

Nina had chosen to work in the kitchen, where there was less privacy but a lot more room. Mark had asked the others to keep out for a while, to let her get organised in peace; and soon she had Davey sitting in an old wooden chair, tilted back with his shoulders against the sink while she shampooed him.

Mark watched quietly from the doorway until she had towelled the water out of the boy's hair, and started to comb and cut. Then:

"So where did you learn to cut hair, Nina?"

"I had to." She answered without lifting her eyes from her work, guiding the steel blades confidently through Davey's long dark curls. "There was five of us, remember, and no money to have it done properly, after Dad got ill. Mum was no use, so I just had to learn, or the kids would've looked like birds' nests. And then, I don't know, I liked it. So I started looking at styles in magazines, and trying them out on the kids; and then all my mates wanted me to do theirs like that, so I got loads of practice. I was going to go into it serious, even, after school. Only Dad bloody ruined it for me, didn't he?"

"Come on, Nina love. You can't blame your father."

"Why not? It was him fucking died on me." And for a second she was back to the Nina he knew, vicious and cold. But the comb caught in Davey's hair, and she tugged it savagely, and he yelped; and she muttered awkward apologies and stopped talking altogether as she gave her attention entirely to what she was doing.

But Mark knew the rest of the story already. Nina's world had fallen apart, with her father's slow and painful death; she'd gone with it, and no one had noticed until it was too late, until she was up before a juvenile court on the first of a dozen charges of shoplifting, truancy, assault. At school – when she bothered to go – she was drunken and abusive, so that one suspension followed another. Her friends fell away when the romantic rebel image started to collapse, when she turned on them too; and her mother was too weak to control her. Eventually she'd been taken into care – and inside a fortnight she'd been on the run, coming down to London, sleeping in hostels until her money ran out and then on the street before at last she found her way to the refuge.

Where she'd been the most uncooperative and unpleasant refugee that Mark could remember. Until now, until finally a need in them had seemingly touched a chord in her. And for a wonder, she hadn't even done it to show off; she might be playing to an audience now, as Colton and Jane came in to watch, but that hadn't been in her mind yesterday, when she'd volunteered.

Mark felt that he had a handle on her at last, and a base to work from; and it might be that he could offer her something concrete in return, give her back at least a part of her dream.

But not yet. He'd have to talk to the doctor first, and find out about training courses for hairdressers, what was available and what they asked for. Nina would have no qualifications to offer besides her enthusiasm, which might not be enough; and he wouldn't see her hopes dashed a second time. Better to give her none, than to give and let her lose again.

So he said nothing yet, only stayed with them, and listened to the others talking and laughing while she worked; and notched it up as another minor miracle, every time her lips flicked into a smile.

Nina left Davey a fair length in his fringe, cut the rest short, then shaved it to nothing around the sides and back of his head. When she was satisfied, she said, "Right, that'll do. It's last year's fashion, but there's thousands of people still wear it like this. Makes you look different, anyway."

"Bloody right it does," Colton agreed noisily. "I wouldn't know you, Davey mate. You're almost good-looking."

Davey swung a leg at him from the chair, missed, and said, "Can I go look at it, then, Nina? There's no mirror in here . . ."

"Not yet." She grabbed his shoulders and pulled him back as he moved to stand up. "Not till it's finished. I've got all the bleaching to do first, before you can see it."

"Ah, shit." He ran a hand uncertainly across the velvet stubble on his scalp. "Well, let's have a fag first, eh? Before you start?"

She gave him one of her own, before taking another for herself and turning to pick up a box of bleach, glancing through the instructions. And rules or no rules, Mark let them smoke, and welcome.

Four hours later, with the kitchen windows standing wide against the reek of ammonia, Nina rinsed the second batch of purple gunk from Davey's hair and gave him a final shampoo. Another rinse, a quick rub with a towel and a squirt of mousse; then she combed it through with her fingers, stepped back and nodded.

"That's it. You can look now."

Jane handed him a mirror, giggling and staring; Davey looked, lifted a hand slowly to touch the softly spiked fringe as if to check that it was really his, or really himself that he was seeing, and said, "Jesus."

"Worth it, then, was it? All that moaning?"

"Ah, shut your face, Colton. You'd moan too, with a carrier bag sellotaped over your head and everything on fire underneath." But there wasn't any heat in his voice, and his eyes came back to the mirror. "Nina, it . . . I don't know. It's great."

Privately, Mark agreed with him. The cut looked professional, and the effect of the bleach was startling; people might remember the boy with the dark brows and blue eyes under pure white hair, but they'd never associate him with the media photographs of Davey FitzAlan.

He hoped.

The kids were turning to him now, their eyes demanding an opinion; so he smiled, and said, "Nina, that's marvellous." And added, "Just what the doctor ordered," simply to hear them groan.

"I thought you said it was your idea?" Davey said, flicking the wet towel at him.

Mark laughed, and dodged. "Actually, it was. But I'm not taking any credit. It all goes to Nina." He put an arm round the girl's thin shoulders, and squeezed gently; felt her jump and stiffen, and let her go immediately, knowing how easy it was to push even gratitude too far, too fast.

"Too bad we can't bleach the Irish out of your voice too," Colton said to Davey, parting his friend's hair carefully with his fingers to check the roots.

Davey grinned, and shoved him away. "Och, get away, ye bluidy gorilla," he said, in thick Glaswegian.

There was a moment's silence, followed by a wave of laughter. "Can you keep that up?" Mark demanded.

"Aye, mon, I can that. All day, if I have tae."

"Good. Do that, then. It sounds a bit fake, but no one'll guess there's an Irish voice underneath it. I reckon that's the best we can do for you, Davey. You'll just have to take your chances from here, when you go out."

The boy nodded, losing that cocky grin all in a moment as his nerves came bubbling to the surface again. And it was that same moment that Jane chose to come up behind him and stroke the back of his neck, and giggle, and say, "You're dead clever, though, Davey. Mummy's *good* little white-haired boy . . ."

And he twisted and spun, his face suddenly as pale, as dead as his hair; and caught her with a savage slap that sent her staggering back, and followed with a foot smashing into her side, knocking her sprawling onto the floor. And he might have gone on kicking even then, if Colton hadn't come smashing into him, slamming him up against the wall, "Davey, man, what the hell . . .? She's a kid, she's just a kid . . ."

Nina was screaming, with her hand across her mouth; and then Mark moved, too late,

*(because Colton had already done the first thing, the important thing, he'd stopped it; and that was Mark's job, but he'd been too busy doing nothing, just watching)*

hurrying across the room to help Jane, pausing only for a quick glance at Davey, to see that the madness had left the boy as suddenly as it had come.

"Get him out of here," to Colton, an order that came snapping out of a cold, clear anger; and Mark was only peripherally aware of the two boys leaving, Colton with an arm round Davey that was more supportive now than restraining.

Mark knelt beside Jane where she lay curled on the stone flags, starting to cry, great gasping sobs that seemed too loud to come from her frail body.

"Easy now, kid. Come on, let's have a look at you . . ."

He slipped an arm under her shoulders and lifted her into a sitting position, turning her face up to the light. Her cheek was vivid scarlet, and there'd be heavy bruising there tomorrow; but he couldn't find any other damage, either there or to her ribs where Davey had kicked her.

"I'll ask the doctor to come and check you over tonight, love, just in case. But I think you're okay. Now come on, let's get you upstairs. You'd better lie down for a bit, after you've cleaned up. If you're good, I'll even lend you my radio . . ."

He took her up and got her settled; and came down again to find Nina smoking, in a state of righteous fury.

"That bastard! That little bastard Davey . . . What did Jane do to him?"

"She teased him about his mother," Mark said wearily, dropping into a chair. "That's all. The poor kid didn't even know she was doing it, she thought she was being friendly."

"You ought to chuck him out of here, for that. Let him go somewhere else, he's not safe here."

"None of you are safe, that's why you're here. Look, just let it go, will you, Nina? I'll talk to Davey, he won't lose control like that again. You just mind your own business, right?"

Clenching his hands tight under the table, so that she wouldn't see them shaking.

Alex's feet were hurting, all the muscles in her legs ached from a day of walking, and her eyes were sore even behind the shades, from staring at every dark-haired young man, matching his face against her memory. She checked her watch, and decided that enough was enough, she wasn't going to find him this way. She was fairly confident that she was in the right area now; she'd ridden that bus all round its route and back to the city centre, and this district just felt right. South of the river, about half an hour out of town, a community big enough to swallow a houseful of kids and never notice . . .

But she'd hung around all day and seen nothing, neither Davey FitzAlan nor that guy from the High Court. The failure didn't depress her, though; she hadn't expected miracles. She'd done some groundwork, got to know the area; and if she was wrong, if she was in the wrong place – well, it was only one day gone.

She was heading for the bus-stop, for home and a hot bath, when a voice behind her tugged suddenly at her attention.

"Jesus, man, I never meant it! Not Jane, I wouldn't, not ever . . ."

Never mind the words, was the voice Irish? She thought so, and turned sharply, scanning the street, looking for the boy in the photographs. But there were only two boys in sight, one of them the thin black lad she'd seen this morning; and it was dark curls she was looking for, not the crisp white hair of the other. The black lad caught her eye, and nudged his friend with an elbow, *keep it quiet, strangers tuning in*; but he went on talking, the white boy, and she'd been wrong, her imagination was playing tricks. She must have heard what she wanted to hear; because his voice wasn't Ulster after all, it was Glasgow through and through.

Alex sighed, and went to catch her bus.

Late that evening, Mark sat with the doctor and said, "I told you it wouldn't work. You've got to get someone else in here somehow, for the kids' sake. They're not safe with me."

"Nonsense, lad. Stop wallowing in it, it's not healthy." The doctor shifted comfortably in his chair, and poured himself another finger of malt. "We've had worse fights here, under Mrs Horsley's aegis. Remember Martin Jackson's arm?"

"Yes, but there was no one in the room to stop that. That's the point, I was *there*, and I didn't do a thing, I left it all to Colton, for God's sake . . ."

"And why not? Best thing you could have done, in the circumstances. That left you free to look after little Jane, rather than having your arms full of a crazy Irish boy. And if you're going to be angry with one of the kids, it's much better if you don't have your hands on him at the time, you might do him some damage."

Mark was silent for a moment, watching the light play like fire in the heart of his glass; then he said, "I was angry. I can't remember the last time I felt like that, with everything so clear . . ." And himself cold at the heart of it, like the fire in his glass . . .

He shivered, and put the whisky down on the carpet next to him. It was scary when his mind started to make connections, finding pattern in unrelated things; and he shouldn't be drinking anyway, he was only keeping the doctor company. Making gestures he couldn't afford.

"Did you sleep last night?"

"No."

"Take the pills?"

"No."

"I didn't think you would." And, with a smile, "You're my prize patient, you know, Mark. My white-haired boy."

## 7  Goodbye, Hullo

Kez dug her bare toes into the lawn, through cool grass to the warm earth beneath; she turned her face up to the sun and stretched extravagantly, feeling the pull on every muscle in her body; and laughed, for no reason that she could determine except that she felt like laughing. Then she walked round the corner of the house, treading carefully on the sharp gravel drive, to the open doors of the garage.

Sebastian had been in there for hours now, and he still had his head buried in the engine of his old Mini, with his rear end sticking out too temptingly, irresistibly . . .

Kez didn't even try to resist. She swallowed a chuckle, lifted her arm and slapped him stingingly on his black-denim'd buttocks.

He yelled and came out like a fury, his oily hands grabbing for her; but she was out of reach already, back-pedalling across the gravel, choking with laughter. So he snatched up a ball of rags and chucked that at her instead, and missed.

"What I want to know," she said, retrieving the blackened bundle and bringing it back to him, "is how come the sexiest male bottom in three counties has to belong to my bloody brother? It's discrimination, that's what it is."

He grinned, took the rags and began to clean his hands. She wiped her fingers fastidiously on his singlet, adding one oil-stain to a dozen others. He glared at her.

"You could use your own."

"No, I can't." She giggled. "This one's yours too."

He looked more closely at the baggy T-shirt she was wearing, hanging loose halfway to her knees. "Where did you find that? I haven't seen it for months."

"I pinched it out of the tumble-drier. I knew you wouldn't notice. That's one of the advantages of big brothers." Then she scowled, and added, "It's about their only advantage, when their rotten cars don't work. Haven't you got it fixed yet?"

"Give us time, Kez. Look, I promise, it'll be fixed by this evening. I'll take you into Oxford and lose you, pick you up again later, and Mum'll never know you weren't with me all the time, okay?"

"Magic. Thanks, Seb . . ." She hugged him, oil or no oil; he returned the hug, then looked down at her quizzically.

"Are you wearing anything at all under that?"

"Yes. A pair of panties. Very black, very brief, very sexy. Want to see?"

"Not particularly. And I don't want the rest of the world to see, either – especially not Mrs Billingham. You know the fuss she kicked up when she caught a glimpse of you topless. Can't you put on a pair of shorts, or something?"

"Don't be so bloody paternal. One thing I don't need is a substitute father." Kez stretched again, just to tease, feeling the T-shirt rising up her thighs. "And she'd have to have X-ray eyes, anyway, to see through these hedges."

"She saw your tits all right. I expect you were flaunting them. Look, if you want to be useful, get in and tread on the accelerator, will you? It's the pedal on the right."

"I know which one's the accelerator, I'm not thick."

"'Course not, sweetie."

She snarled, waited till he had his head well in under the bonnet, and leaned hard on the horn.


"Mandy, you look at me when I'm speaking to you!"

Mandy lifted her head, and gazed impassively across the table at her father. There was a real bruise under Mandy's right eye now, spreading right across the cheekbone, from when her mother had lost her temper last night; but even the back of her hand had failed to knock any sense into the girl. This evening it was Mr Thomson's turn.

"Listen to me, love. I don't care how you got into this mess, that's in the past now. But you've got to face facts, Mandy. You're only fifteen years old; you've another year at school yet. And you've no money, and no man to look after you. You're in no condition to bring up a baby. You're just too young. There'll be time enough to start a family in a few years from now, with a husband to help you and a future for the kids. Not now, not while you're still a child . . ."

"I'm not having an abortion." Repetition had worn it to a weary, flat statement of fact with no emotion behind it; but it was still a fact, still something she could cling to, solid and safe. No one could change her mind on that, though they'd all tried: not parents, doctor, social worker, headmistress, no one. They didn't understand, and she couldn't explain, she didn't have the words; all she could do was offer them the fact, and hope that at last they'd accept it. Maybe if she said it one more time . . .

"I'm not."

"You may have to." That was her mother, from the corner.

Rather than look round and meet her baffled, threatening anger eye to eye, Mandy took her glasses off and began to polish them needlessly on her cardigan. It was easier that way; with the room and her parents and her whole life out of focus, it was easier to concentrate on the only thing that mattered now, the life inside.

"No."

"You may not have the choice." Mrs Thomson was on her feet now, striding over to the table, a blurred, jerky figure of menace. "No daughter of mine is going to disgrace me like this. I'll have that – that *thing* got rid of, if I have to go to court to do it."

"You can't!" Mandy jumped up to meet her, wrapping her arms around herself in a protective gesture that was pure instinct. "It's my baby, my *body* – no one can force me to . . ."

"Oh, can't they? I'll tell you this, girl – I'm going to break you down, one way or another. You're not having that baby, and that's flat!"

"Yes, I am. I have to."

Mandy turned, and went to the door.

"Where are you going now?"

"Just out. For a walk."

"Don't be late back." That was her father from his chair, nervous and uncomfortable, wanting no part in any of this.

"I won't, Dad."

And she wouldn't; she'd give them no reason to worry tonight, or to watch her tomorrow. But this last attack from her mother had decided her, finally. Maybe the courts could force an under-age girl to have an abortion, she didn't know.

She couldn't take the risk, at any rate.

So she walked down to the bus-station, found the time-table and pressed her face close against the plastic, because she'd left her glasses on the table at home. It was hard to make out the numbers, especially in the dark; but at last she had them committed to memory, the times of the buses to London. And as she walked back home, she was already packing in her mind, sorting out what she'd need and what could be left behind. She'd leave tomorrow, mid-morning, she could smuggle one big bag out of the house without her mother noticing; and with any luck, they wouldn't miss her till the evening. She'd be in London by then, safe, far away from their needle eyes and murder mouths . . .

"Goodbye, Shahid."

He looked at her in surprise, coupled – of course – with amusement. "You've only just come."

"That's what I've come for. To say goodbye."

"Ah. Well, sit down and do it properly, yes?" He left the room, to came back a minute later with a bottle of white wine and two glasses. "Sit, I said."

Tia shrugged, and sat at one end of the sofa. Shahid drew the cork, filled the glasses and passed one over. "Tabs are on the table there."

She shook her head; he cocked an eyebrow, and reached to take one himself. "No?"

"No. Ta." And even she couldn't have told him why, couldn't have explained that the lesser rebellions were simply lost tonight, like candles in a blaze. She sipped the wine only because it was there and she was thirsty, nothing to do with Koranic or parental prohibitions; and quickly, just to get it said and out in the open, she told him. "I've made up my mind. I'm going, leaving home. Tomorrow." And felt truly committed to it for the first time; because telling Shahid turned it from a plan into a fact, a necessity.

"Running away?" he said, with a stinging smile.

She shrugged. "If you like. Getting the hell out of it."

"What's the rush?"

"My fucking father, what d'you think? It's like he's decided to believe me all of a sudden, about how I don't want to get married. Only he hasn't called the wedding off, or anything like that. He's just sending me over early, with

one of my uncles. We're supposed to be going at the end of
the month; and the idea is, after six months in Bangladesh,
I'll be well broken in by the time they all fly over at Christmas, and I won't make any more fuss about the marriage."

"So you're running away now."

"That's right."

"Well, good luck, baby." With a smile, to say that she'd
need it. "Send us a postcard."

She looked away, pressing the chill of the glass against her
cheek, reminding herself she'd been a fool to hope for
anything more from him.

Then he said, "So where are you going, London?"

"That's right."

"When?"

"Tomorrow."

"Could you wait till Thursday?"

"If I have to, I suppose. If you can give me a reason."

He stood up and went to the window, and let the silence
hang for a minute, two minutes, five; and when Tia's hand
reached edgily for a cigarette, it wasn't any kind of a rebellion at all, she just needed a tab, something to do with her
fingers, a blanket for her nerves.

At last, though, he turned back to face her, smiling. "How
were you going, then? You haven't got any money, I bet."

"Hitch."

"And to live on?"

"Anything I can pinch out of my mother's purse. Dad
keeps his wallet too tight. After that runs out, I'll take my
chances."

"You'll have to. But I can give you a better start. Say a lift
down all the way, and fifty quid cash in your pocket?"

"To do what?"

He shrugged easily. "Nothing. To be a traveller in the car,
that's all."

"That's not all, Shahid. You're up to something."

"Of course. But that's all your part. To sit in the car, and
be driven."

"Hey, you know what, Seb?"

"What?"

"I've got you sussed, mate, that's what."

A quick glance across, before a bend in the lane forced his

attention back to the road. "How do you mean?"

"All this self-sacrifice. Driving your kid sister into town, then looking the other way while I sneak off, and fixing to pick me up again later – it's just cover, isn't it?"

Another, sharper glance, his face set in the shadows. "Cover?"

"Yeah. You can't fool me. You're not doing this out of the goodness of your heart. You're two-timing Annabel, aren't you? You've got some floozy lined up for a sordid evening out, and I'm your alibi."

The momentary tension left him, in a gust of laughter. "Well, I doubt if you're going to spend the evening swapping knitting patterns with a girlfriend."

"Bet your ass, bruv. I'm going out with the second-best bottom in Oxfordshire. But come on, give. Who is she, what's she like? What's she got that Annabel hasn't?"

"Tell the truth, Kez, I don't know yet. I just want a change, that's all, so I'm going fishing."

"Uh-huh. Flaunt the blue eyes and blond hair and see what happens, eh? I still haven't forgiven you for pinching all the beauty in this family, you know. Those lashes are just wasted on a boy."

"Sorry." He grinned sideways at her. "You didn't do so badly, mind. Your turn now. Tell me about this bottom."

She giggled. "It's peachy. Small and tight and – well, just peachy. And it's attached to Jimmy, and the rest of him is pretty lush too."

"Jimmy, eh? How old is he?"

"Twenty-one."

"Cradlesnatcher, then."

She glared at him. "He's my older man. Shut up. And he's a lot younger than you, anyway."

"I'm not looking for a sixteen-year-old. But never mind, you're smart enough to know what you're doing. Is this Jimmy one of the male harem you've been filling the cottage with this summer?"

"No, I daren't. I, um, I don't *think* Mum would approve, somehow."

"Why, what's wrong with him?"

"Nothing. Only, he's a dustman . . ."

Sebastian laughed delightedly. "*Really* a dustman? Kez, you're amazing. I've never even *met* a dustman. Where did you find him?"

"On the back of a dustcart, where do you expect? I met him at a party, one of my mates had brought him along. We aren't all snobs."

"Aren't you? Tell me about it . . . And don't hit me when I'm driving, or we'll end up in a ditch."

Later, as they came into the city:

"Where are you meeting him, then?"

"Down the Plain."

He frowned. "Kez, you will be careful, won't you?"

"Don't worry, I can look after myself."

"Bullshit."

But he drove her across Magdalen Bridge without protest, and pulled up in front of the pub, as requested; and only then added, "I'll pick you up again here. Midnight sharp. And for God's sake stick with this Jimmy character, don't go wandering round on your own. Get him to wait with you, till I come."

"Look, stop hassling, will you? You're beginning to sound like Mum."

"I know, I can hear myself. But . . ."

"But I'm only sixteen, and I'm your kid sister, and you worry about me. I know it." She unfastened her seat-belt, and leaned across abruptly to kiss his cheek. "Thanks, Seb. Have a good time, okay? I hope you find your floozy. And I won't breathe a word to Annabel, honest."

He grinned at her. "Go on, scat. Enjoy your bottom."

"It's not my bottom I'm planning to enjoy, it's Jimmy's."

"Whatever. Don't do anything you'd be ashamed to tell me about, because I want a full report afterwards. That's the price of the lift. And don't forget, midnight on the dot."

"Promise. I'll be here."

She slammed the car door, and watched him drive away; and turned, and went into the heat and noise of the pub, looking for Jimmy.

But disillusion comes easily to a teenager, especially in the small things. And that evening, Jimmy proved himself to be very much one of the small things. He was there with a crowd, throwing darts, playing pool and talking loud. Kez got a kiss and a can of Red Stripe, and the ogling attention of half a dozen strangers; then she sat in a corner, and watched

Jimmy absorbing the nudges and winks, the low-voiced comments that were always followed by a snort of laughter. Watched and saw that he loved it, saw that this was the reason she was here, or half the reason. No doubt there'd be a wrestling session in his car afterwards, his hands inside her shirt and his smoke-stained tongue in her mouth; but this was enough for him for now, to have the casual approval and envy of his mates. *Yeah, right little turn-on, ain't she? Only sixteen, an' all. Still in nappies. Bet you'd like to be the first one in there, yeah? Too late, though, I saw it first. An' I'll get off with her tonight, see if I don't . . .*

It was enough for Kez too, more than enough; the only thing that kept her in her seat was not having anywhere else to go. She tried to persuade herself that this was a romantic and sexy adventure, middle-class girl goes slumming; but even that didn't work. It was just boring and embarrassing, and she wished it was over.

Then the boys started talking about the local rapist, who'd struck six times this year in Oxford and Abingdon and not been caught yet. And that was when Kez decided that it really was over, because they spoke about him almost with admiration, almost with envy.

"Hey, where are you going?" Jimmy demanded, as she stood up and squeezed past him.

"I feel sick," she told him, wondering if maybe he'd make the connection, but not really caring if he didn't. She went to the ladies' toilet, drank a little cold water from the tap, told her reflection that it looked a lot like this fool she knew; walked out and turned left instead of right, down the passage and out into the open air.

Thank God it was a warm, dry night; she hadn't brought a jacket or even a bag, so she'd had nothing to carry out with her, nothing to explain. And never mind that she didn't have anywhere to go, till Seb came to collect her; getting out of there was good enough. She'd just wander round, she didn't know this end of town at all, and it was a lovely starry night for a walk . . .

*And she wasn't the only one who thought so; because he was out too, the man they'd been talking about in the pub. But he wasn't just walking, he was hunting the city. The blood-hunger was on him, hot and heavy, or maybe it was only the ugliness of love turned sick; but whatever it was, it gripped him like a passion. The night and the stars sang in his veins, background music to whatever he did in the darkness. The mood was riding him high tonight; he was aware, strong, powerful, alive to the world around him. The breeze was silk against his skin, he felt every twig, every leaf he brushed against as something sharp and separate and real. His feet could distinguish each discrete ridge and crack in the baked ground beneath his trainers; and the nearby river seemed to catch its breath as he listened.*

*This was right, it was how it should be, everything watching and waiting with him. It was going to be good tonight, he could tell. He could always tell. He pulled a black balaclava down over his head so that only his eyes were showing, took the knife from his pocket and tested the edge with his thumb, stood in the shadow of a tree and waited. Down in the water-meadows, waiting for the night to choose the girl and bring her to him . . .*

Kez walked for a while, until she found a strange little cinema down a back street, converted from an old church hall. They let her in for half price, to see the last hour of a black-and-white French film with subtitles, which was all art and angles, lousy dialogue and no plot.

But that finished at eleven, and she still had an hour to kill and nowhere to kill it; so she let her feet take her again, back to St Clements and over the wide road, into a maze of little dark streets. She followed them down to a children's play-ground, with a belt of trees and the water-meadows beyond; and she was going to go through to throw stones into the river, when she spotted a familiar Mini parked outside a terrace of houses.

She crossed the road to check, even though she didn't need to; and sure enough, it was Sebastian's car. The house immediately next to it had a light shining above the transom, but the front room upstairs was dark, and curtained. Kez chuckled, imagining what might be going on behind those curtains; and murmured, "Yeah, go for it, bruv."

And laughed at herself for saying it aloud, but it had more force that way, even if there was no one to hear. And she meant it just as forcefully as she could. Seb had been going out with Annabel for three years now, ever since he'd come down from Cambridge, and Kez had never understood why. With his looks, and the charm that could still get through to her even after sixteen years of being his sister, he could surely find a girlfriend who'd give back a little more than that frigid bitch. Kez was certain the two of them had never been to bed together, and utterly convinced that was Annabel's fault. It was an insult to the whole Hughes family, herself included, not to go tumbling into bed with its most beautiful member, if you were only given the opportunity. So Annabel had no one but herself to blame, if Seb got his bonking done elsewhere; and more power to his elbow, that's what Kez said . . .

"Or maybe not his *elbow*," she added, aloud again, because there was no one to hear; and giggled, and decided to save that up for the next time she got together with her gang of girlfriends. Come to think of it, she could give them the story of the whole evening, starting with that miserable creep Jimmy; and the icing on the cake would be the look on Seb's face, when he came out, still sweaty from his sordid evening of passion, and found Kez perched on the bonnet of his car, politely waiting . . .

So she did perch, and she did wait; but it wasn't half past yet, and he probably wouldn't tear himself away much before midnight. He only had to drive round the corner, after all; or thought he did. And it was helluva boring, just sitting on a cold car bonnet, watching a door. So after a few minutes Kez slid off again, and went down to the playground. She could see the car from there, and the house; as soon as she saw a light go on, she'd be back there, perching. Meantime, there were the swings.

The thing about swinging, it was easier to think. It made her feel good too, and it was fun; but the thinking was the main attraction. It was as if, diving back into something that was so much a part of her childhood, she could cut loose from the present, and look at it dispassionately.

So she settled into a big rubber tyre and gripped the chains it hung by, kicked off from the tarmac, and let the day drift in review. Inevitably, Jimmy was first and foremost in her mind, the whole disaster of this evening; she'd have cringe-making memories of that for a long time yet. But okay, he was a mistake, forget him. Maybe she'd stick to sixth-formers in future, at least she knew the territory . . .

And that reminded her, as almost everything reminded her nowadays (and this evening was meant to be an escape, only it hadn't worked out like that, it hadn't worked out at all). Her GCSE results would be through soon. And, yes, they ought to be pretty good; she'd been fairly confident after the exams. But it was the way everyone assumed she'd walk them – her parents, the teachers, Sebastian, they were all so *sure*. And the way they talked, about sixth form, A-levels, university, you'd think it was them that were going to live through the next five years for her. They wouldn't even let her choose her subjects without interfering. They didn't call it that, of course, and they wouldn't have understood if she'd accused them of it. They just *assumed* again. English and languages were her best subjects, so of *course* she'd be going into the arts. Won't you, dear? It'd take a stronger will than she could summon up at the moment to fight those assumptions; and she didn't know what she wanted to do, anyway. So she just said yes, of course she would. And cursed herself inside, for a coward and a weakling . . .

A noise interrupted her thinking, footsteps running strongly through the belt of woodland, coming towards her. She tensed in a sudden panic, remembering that she was a girl alone, a long way from the road; and glanced back at Seb's car, hoping to see a light in the house, half intending to run across anyway, so that she could shout if she needed him . . .

But it was too late to move now, as a figure burst out of the shadows between the trees. She just sat very still, letting the slow swing of the tyre die to nothing, hoping he wouldn't see her. She didn't think he had; and that was just as well, because it wasn't only her imagination saying there was danger here. His feet crunched noisily on the loose tarmac, and he slowed instantly to a walk, looking back over his shoulder; and in the light from the solitary street-lamp, Kez caught the glint of a knife-blade in his hand. As she watched, he slipped that into one pocket of the long cagoule he wore; and ripped open the velcro fastening all the way down the front, already pulling it open and shrugging one shoulder out as his other hand jerked the dark balaclava off his head.

The balaclava went into another pocket, the cagoule came off and was rolled into a small, tight bundle; and he was already on his way out of the playground when he stooped to wipe his hands on a tuft of grass, and glanced back one more time.

And saw her.

Nothing moved, or breathed, or lived, except in her; and then it was only a word, a bubble of sound, rising slow and hard and painful in her throat. She tried to swallow it, the word and the fact together; and couldn't, and finally had to open her mouth and let it out, because she was choking on it and her body wanted to live even if she didn't.

Opened her mouth, and let it out.

Said it.

"Seb . . .?"

And it was as if the name broke the moment that had gripped them, because suddenly they were both moving. She was slipping off the tyre, all uncontrolled, staggering to stand up; and he was twisting, turning, wrenching himself away, sprinting over to his car.

"*Seb . . .! Please . . .*"

But he was in and away, racing off up the hill with a squeal of tyres; and for a moment it all seemed wrong, it couldn't have been Seb after all, because he never drove like that . . .

But he never ran away from her either, never wore a cagoule in high summer or a balaclava any time, or carried a knife, or wiped

*(what? something sticky)*

off his hands in the dead of night . . .

And when his red tail-lights were long gone and the sound of his engine lost in the distant traffic, there was only one thing left that she could do; and she wasn't even scared any more, she was only cold, as she turned to do it.

She followed the path back across the playground and into the trees, to find out what it was that Seb had been running from, before he ran from her. What it was he was leaving behind him, marked with his knife and his name. What message he had left her, saying, *I did this.*

On the other side of the trees, long flat meadows ran down through the darkness towards the river; and between Kez and the water, something was moving. Black and shapeless, it humped across the grass towards her, its voice a croaking, bubbling horror with no words in it. Kez did nothing, she only stood and stared, breathing hard and fast, lacking even the air to scream with. At last, almost at her feet, the creature lifted its head; and under long dark hair Kez saw a face pale in the moonlight, a human face, a girl. She dropped to her knees, because her legs couldn't hold her weight any longer, or keep her balance. And now, down on the girl's level as she crawled, Kez could see the rest of it. She could see the black tights torn and tangled around the girl's ankles, the skirt twisted awry over bare legs; the blouse ripped open, and the breasts hanging loose inside; and the dark liquid that came dripping out of the girl's throat, dribbling down onto her hand now as they stared at each other. The girl tried to speak again, her mouth croaked and her throat bubbled; and

*(hullo, Kez. I did this)*

Kez turned her head aside moments before the vomit came spewing up from her stomach, burning in her throat and filling her mouth with sourness.

All feeling came up with the vomit, and lay in pools on the dry dead grass; and when at last she was emptied, Kez could be practical, and helpful, and numb. She peeled off the girl's ruined tights, then stood up and gripped her under the arms

*(and felt nothing, even when the bloodsoaked blouse clung damply to her hand)*

and pulled her gently to her feet. She wadded the tights into a ball and pressed them hard against the seeping slash in the girl's throat, and they made their way back through the trees, Kez as slow and stumbling

*(and feeling nothing)*

as the girl she supported. In silence, sisters in torment, they crossed the playground and the road beyond, and came at last to the terrace of houses. Kez knocked at the first door

*(feeling nothing, though it was light above the transom, dark upstairs)*

and waited, taking all the girl's weight now as she slumped against her, till cautious footsteps came to the door, and a woman opened it, with a man belting his dressing-gown behind.

"Yes?"

"My friend . . . She's been attacked, she needs help . . ."

The woman made a soft noise of horror, and stepped forward into the street. Kez let the girl's weight fall away from her, into the woman's stout arms; and that was enough.

Everything broke then, all at once; and she turned and ran, away up the road with voices calling after her and nothing but terror ahead.

Feeling too much now, too much to bear, she turned blindly away from the lights in St Clements and ran again, up the hill towards Headington. It was quieter here, with a park on either side of the road and no traffic; she slowed to a trot, and above the sound of her own gasping she heard a car behind her, saw the lights of it cutting into the night ahead –

– and saw the lights swerve suddenly, saw her own shadow stark in the centre of the beams, heard the engine racing and the tyres bump over the kerb as it came up onto the wide pavement. She glanced stupidly over her shoulder, and the glare of the headlights shattered her vision, burning closer and bigger and brighter . . .

Her legs jumped before her mind could tell them to, up onto the low wall, flattening herself against the park railings as the car's near side screeched along the stonework. The wing-mirror gashed her calf, and almost knocked her off again; but that simple pain sobered and steadied her, so that she was almost calm as she watched the car, the

*(hullo, Kez)*

white Mini turn in the park entrance ahead, and wait with its lights still pinning her against the railings. She stepped down slowly from the wall, and heard the engine rev viciously; and looked beyond the car, to the park-keeper's house just the other side of the locked iron gate. She drew breath and screamed, and screamed again; and lights showed through the windows as she went on screaming.

Seb dipped his lights twice in a mocking salute, and the car sped down the pavement towards her, just as the door of the house swung open. She jumped up onto the wall again, but this time the Mini missed her by a couple of yards; and for a brief moment she could see her brother's profile through the window as it passed.

"What's going on, then?" The park-keeper stood in his bright doorway, and called out; but there was no one to hear. Seb had gone, driving into his darkness; and Kez was off again, off and running into hers.

# PART TWO

*Travelling, With or Without Hope*

Mark was halfway through polishing his pride and subli-
mation, the Morris Minor in the garage, when Nina came in
through the door from the kitchen.

"Hi."

"Hullo, Nina." He watched her aimlessly pick a spark-
plug off a shelf and put it back down again, and said,
"Where are the others?"

She shrugged. "The boys are playing football out the
front, and Jane's watching some crap thing on the telly."

"And you're suffering from terminal tedium, right?"

Another shrug. "I'm bored, yeah."

"Well, look." An idea had been tugging gently at his mind
for a couple of nights now, and he knew he'd have to do
something about it, because it wasn't going to go away.
"Would you do me a favour?"

"Finish that for you, I suppose. Okay."

He laughed, a bark of genuine surprise. "That wasn't what
I was going to ask, but – would you mind?"

"I said I would, didn't I?" She came back at him aggressively, then half smiled. "I used to do it for Dad, every week.
He liked that, knowing the car was being looked after, even
if he couldn't drive it any more."

Mark just nodded. "Thanks, then. It's really good of
you."

He passed her the cloth, and was heading for the door
when she said, "What was the other thing, then? What you
wanted?"

"Oh. Yes. If the boys come in, can you ask them to keep
out of the games room, please? I'd like a chance to talk to
Jane without being disturbed."

"Yeah, sure. I'll tell them."

"Thanks . . ."

He walked through the kitchen and across the hall with a sense of quiet achievement, hoping that the walls Nina had built around herself were finally being eroded. Then he went into the games room and found Jane on the sofa, perched on the edge and leaning forward, sucking her thumb gently. Mark glanced at the TV screen, and smiled. Gymnastics – a girl who didn't look much older than Jane herself was twisting and spinning on asymmetrical bars, quick and lithe and dramatic.

Mark reached over the back of the sofa, took hold of Jane's fair ponytail and gave it a light tug. She jerked and glanced round.

"Oh – hullo, Mark."

"Hi, brat. Enjoying it?"

She nodded, her eyes already moving back to the TV. "It's wonderful. I'd give anything to be able to do that."

"Sorry, you've left it too late. You have to start when you're about six, to be as good as she is." He gave her a sympathetic grin, as he settled beside her. "It's a tragedy, isn't it? Past it, at twelve years old."

"I could still do it, though, couldn't I? Just for fun, I mean, not for competitions. We did a bit at school, before . . ."

"Before you ran away?"

She nodded, a brief movement of the head, not looking at him.

He watched her biting her lip, and for a second regretted pulling her out of her dreams; then he said, "Listen, can I talk to you, sweetheart? We'll leave the telly on, if you like, but we'd better have the sound down, because I need your attention."

She got up, hesitated, and turned it off altogether. "It's okay, I don't mind."

"Thanks, love. I'll try to be quick. But seriously, Jane, we've got to talk about the future. Make some plans for you. You can't stay here for ever."

She looked suddenly smaller and younger, as she came back and sat next to him, taut and uncertain and afraid. "I – I know. But I haven't got anywhere else to go . . ."

"That's what we're going to talk about, silly." His arm went instinctively round her thin shoulders. "And don't look so scared, okay? We're not going to throw you out. I just want to try and fix up something permanent, that's all; and the important thing is to find out what you want."

"I'm not going home." A sidelong glance, with a wariness in it that cut at him like razors. He saw her hands twisting together in her lap, and reached out to grip them tight, to hold them still.

"I wasn't going to suggest that. Trust me, Jane. Please? It's your happiness that concerns me, nothing else. And I wouldn't dream of sending you back somewhere you were so miserable. Whatever happens, we'll fix it so you don't have to go home. I promise."

She said nothing to that, but at last he felt her beginning to relax, the tension seeping slowly out of her muscles, a physical promise of the trust he had asked for.

"What about Ipswich, though?" Mark asked. She twitched, as though the name alone had power to hurt her; but he went on regardless. "You've lived there all your life, love. Wouldn't you like to be back in a place you know so well? You must have loads of friends there . . ."

"Not loads," she corrected quietly. "Some. I – I'd like to see Ali again . . . But I can't, how can I? There's nowhere for me to go, except back home. I suppose I could stay with Alı for a bit, her mum likes me; but not for good."

"Listen, darling. The point is, kids like you have got to have somewhere to go; everybody accepts that. And if you can't go home, they'll work as hard as they have to, till they find somewhere else for you. But you'll be best back on your own territory, really you will."

She looked at him suspiciously. "Who's 'they'?"

"Your local Social Services. If they'd known the way your parents were treating you, they'd have done something about it ages ago. Then you wouldn't have had to run away at all."

But she was suddenly stiff under his hands again, as she said, "They would've taken me into care, you mean. That's what you mean, isn't it? And that's what you want to do, too. Put me into care . . ."

Mark just laughed, and hugged her. "That's right, love. But don't look at me like I was your wicked stepmother. You've been reading too many comics. It's just what we've done already, taken you into care. The only difference is that here it's unofficial. Your local council can do the thing properly. Legally, so you don't have to be looking over your shoulder all the time. And they could probably fix you up with foster parents, so you'd be living with a family again. A proper family, this time. And you could go back to your old school, and be a regular girl again, not a runaway. You'd like that, wouldn't you?"

"I don't know." Her fingers were fidgeting again; she watched them for a minute, then said, "I think I'd be scared. I mean, if I ran into Mum or Dad, in the streets or something . . ."

"You probably would. Ipswich isn't that big, is it? You'd be pretty certain to bump into them some time. And yeah, you'd probably be scared. You should be, after what they did to you. But that's a part of growing up, sweetheart. Facing the things that scare you. You've run away from them once; and everyone's on your side now, remember that. So maybe it's time you stopped running."

He stood up then. "That's all I wanted to say. Just think about it, okay? I'm not trying to rush you into anything. There's a bed for you here until you're ready to move on, remember that. – Oh, one other thing. Would you like to phone that friend you mentioned – Ali, was that her name?"

"Ali, yes." Jane stared up at him. "Could I, really? I thought it wasn't allowed . . ."

"Stupid. This isn't a jail, you know. The only thing that's definitely not allowed is for you to give her our number, or the address, or the slightest hint about where we are. Promise you won't do that, and you can chat to her as long as you like. Come on, I'll give you the cordless phone out of the office, and you can take it up to your room. No one'll disturb you there. Oh, and don't tell her who else is here, either. Not the other kids, or me, or Mrs H or the doctor, no one. Gossip about us if you have to, but no names, okay? Pretend she's going to be tortured by the Gestapo straight afterwards, and don't give her any secrets."

"I won't, I promise. I'll be ever so careful."

Nina was working hard on the car, and claimed to be quite happy to finish it alone; Mark shrugged and took her at her word, going back to the office to face some of the jobs he'd put aside earlier in favour of the rag and polish. Wondering if Nina was doing him such a big favour after all . . .

Mrs Horsley had initiated the keeping of a loose-leaf daily diary, part record and part opinion; it was Mark's responsibility now, and he knew the doctor valued it, so he brought it up to date whenever he could make the time. Everything the kids did – or everything that he found out about – went down on paper, along with his thoughts, impressions and assessments.

He settled down behind the desk, and drew the fat folder towards him; and was still working on it, painstakingly trying to describe and explain the changes he could see in Nina, when Jane came in with the telephone receiver.

There were tear-streaks on her cheeks, but he'd expected that. He gestured for her to hang the receiver back on the wall-set, then simply said, "Okay?"

She nodded uncertainly, sniffed, and said suddenly, "Mark, I want to go *home!*" Then flinched, as she heard herself say it. "Not – not my parents, I mean . . ."

"I know what you mean, kid. Back where you belong, right?"

She nodded again, more positively. "That's right. Ali said she, she's really missed me . . ."

"I'm sure she has. Now listen, love, I'm not making any promises, because I'm not a miracle-worker, and it's up to your local Social Services department now, how they take it; but I'll get in touch with them straight away, and see if we can set up a deal. All right? Oh, and one more thing. Don't go talking about it to the others, eh? Not till it's fixed up."

She looked at him curiously. "Why not?"

*Because any one of them might go blabbing about it to Mrs H, love, when the doctor takes them down to visit. She won't approve; it's the kind of deal she set her face against when you came here, and she hasn't changed her mind. She'd try to stamp on it, and I don't know what'd happen then. I suppose we'd appeal to the doctor; and if he backed her – well, that'd be it. I couldn't fight his decision. But I'd want to, by Christ I'd want to . . .*

Except he couldn't say that, any of it; so he just said, "Work it out for yourself, sweetheart," and chased her out of the room. He could rely on the adolescent mind to come up with some reason, that was for sure. Probably something totally paranoid, but that was par for the course; and she was a nice kid, she wouldn't let it rankle.

He called Directory Enquiries for the number, waited a minute

*(stiffen the sinews, summon up the blood. But it's only a phone-call)*

and dialled.

"Social Services."

"Hullo. Um, is that the main office?"

"That's right, yes."

"Good. Look, I'd like to talk to someone senior. I don't know how your system works, but I need someone with authority."

"Can I have your name, please, sir? And if you'd like to explain your problem . . ."

"No, I'm sorry, I can't give you my name. But I'm phoning from London, on behalf of a runaway teenager from your area. Basically, the situation is that she wants to come back, but not to her parents. What I'm looking for is just a guarantee that you'll take her into care, and try bloody hard to find her a foster family."

"Oh." A pause, and a tight chuckle. "I'm sorry, I don't quite know what to do about that. I'm kind of new here, and it's not the sort of thing they tell you about at induction courses . . ."

"No, I bet not. Well, look, how's this? If I give you the kid's name and a bit of the background from her point of view, then I'll hang up and give you an hour to pass it along to the right person, and maybe dig up your own files if you've got any. I'll call back later this afternoon, and we can discuss it then. Okay?"

"Er, yes, that sounds fair enough. But look, I really had better have your name . . ."

"Well, call me Mark, then. Just Mark. Now, the girl's name is Jane Tarrant, she's twelve years old . . ."

With time to kill before he called back, Mark sat and thought about what he was doing, how he was taking onto himself more responsibility even than the doctor had pressed upon him; and suddenly, irrevocably, he lost his nerve. You needed a bedrock of certainty to take decisions like this, a confidence in your own judgement that he simply didn't and couldn't have. For a while he had almost forgotten the shifting sands he walked on, almost stepped out strong and sure, and never mind the shuffling caution that kept him safe . . .

Visions filled his mind, of the horrors that lay under that sand, only waiting for a false step to drag him down again; and that froze him, so that for a long time he couldn't move, couldn't even make the decision to put down the telephone that was still in his hand.

He needed help, right now; and because the phone was still right there in his hand, thank God it was easy to find. As the panic drew slowly back, giving him reluctant control of his body again,

*(but not going far, just to coil itself spring-like in the pit of his stomach, and wait for its chance)*

he punched the number that came automatically to his mind, to his fingers.

"Kennedy and Sawyer, reception."

"Beth . . . Can I talk to the doctor? Please?"

"Hang on, Mark."

Twenty seconds of silence, and the doctor's voice came on the line.

"Well, lad? What's the problem?"

"I don't know, Doctor, I, I've done something, and I don't know if it's the right thing, I just don't know . . ."

"There aren't any right things, you fool. There are only better things and worse things. And you're not a total idiot, all appearances to the contrary. Whatever it is, I expect it'll do. Just so long as it doesn't bring the sky crashing down on our heads, I wouldn't worry."

"But it might, it might even do that. If I go through with it, I mean. I don't have to yet, I left myself a get-out; I could just not ring them back, and they wouldn't be any the wiser. But it's too big for me, I can't decide . . ."

"All right, tell me about it."

So he did that, trying to be fair, to point out the pros and cons with equal weight; and he ended with, "So what should I do, doctor? Should I call them back, or what?"

"Mark, my boy, why are you wasting my time? You know what you should do, and I'm not a rubber-stamping agency."

"But I *don't*! I know what I *want* to do, but . . ."

"But nothing. You're the boss there, Mark, until Mrs Horsley comes back; I thought I'd made that clear. If I couldn't trust you to take decisions like this, I wouldn't have left you to meet them. If you're sure that Jane won't shoot her mouth off about the refuge, then carry on; if you're not, you'd better abort it. Up to you, lad."

"But Mrs Horsley wouldn't . . ."

"Mark, you are not required to behave like a clone of Mrs Horsley, fine woman though she is. If you do, I'll be disappointed. Clear?"

"Uh, yes. I suppose."

"Good. Oh, news for you – I'm looking round for someone to come in and help you, even if it's only baby-sitting the place one day a week. At least that'd give you a chance to get away for a bit. Chase girls, or whatever it was you used to do on your days off."

"That'd be good. Thanks, doctor . . ."

He said it vaguely, and was only half aware of it as he hung the receiver back on its mounting. His mind was reeling again, and he couldn't afford to let it; he'd have to be rock-steady and alert, to make that second call. He picked up a pen and began to doodle spirals on a notepad, watching the lines circling in and in towards a centre; then set his thoughts to do the same, with Jane as the centre, the focus of his concentration.

## 9 Poor Little Sister

Dear Jill,

I wish to God you'd been here last night. I never needed anyone so bad; and I'd forgotten you were all away. So I broke in, that's why the kitchen window is smashed. I'm sorry, but don't tell your parents it was me. Please. I don't want anyone to know I've been here, except you.

I can't tell you what's happened, it's just something really awful, the worst thing ever. I couldn't go home, and I didn't have anywhere else to go, except here. I didn't even think about it, really – I was just running, and my feet brought me here. Clever feet. Except you weren't here, no one was. And I was so cold, and frightened, and sick, I just chucked a stone through the window, and waited. And no one came, so I opened the window and climbed in.

I got into your bed for a bit, but it was stupid really, 'cos I didn't sleep. And the sheet and the duvet are all dirty, 'cos I was filthy and I forgot to take anything off except my shoes. Sorry. Can you get them clean without your mum finding out? Try if you can please.

And I feel really bad about this, but I looked to see if I could find any money, 'cos I haven't got any, hardly. But there wasn't any anyway. I think I put everything back the way it was, so I hope no one notices. I'm borrowing that old denim jacket of yours and a pair of trainers, hope you don't mind.

I've got to go away for a bit, to work out what to do. I can't go home, but don't worry, I'll be okay. I'll hitch down to London, we've got a friend there, she'll put me up. I hope. DON'T TELL ANYONE WHERE I'M GOING!

I can't remember when you're coming back, is it next week? I ought to know, but my head's all gone to pieces. I'll try to phone you anyway, even if I can't tell you what's going on. And I can't, honest. I'm not just being sly.

I expect my mum'll get the police out when she realises I've gone, and they may come to talk to you, but PLEASE don't say anything. Sorry to keep on about this, I do trust you really, you're the only one I can trust. But I'm so scared they might bully it out of you, and they mustn't know where I'm going, no one must. DON'T TELL SEB! if he comes asking. Or anyone.

Try not to worry. I'll phone you soon.

Love you

Kez

PS I'm not pregnant, it isn't that. I wish it was.
PPS Burn this note!

Sebastian smiled and crumpled the note in his fist, thinking, *Poor little sister. Poor, trusting little sister. But she shouldn't be so obvious.*

It hadn't taken any great vision to guess that wherever she went or wandered first, she would end up at Jill's; and Seb had remembered that the Dunstons were on holiday, even if Kez hadn't. He'd come hoping to find her still here, sheltering in an empty house, easy prey.

But he couldn't be sure that she wouldn't have gone straight to the police; he could guess, but he couldn't be sure. So just in case, he'd spent the night out of town, hiding the car and sleeping in an old chapel. This morning he'd made his way back on foot. There'd been no watch that he could see on the Dunstons' house, and that suspicious broken window at the back; so he'd climbed in, and found the place empty. And found Kez's note tucked under the collar of a large, stuffed Snoopy on Jill's bed, where anyone coming into the room couldn't possibly miss it.

Too bad he'd missed her here; but still, he knew where she was going. *"I'll hitch down to London, we've got a friend there"* – that could only mean Jenny. And as Kez very obviously hadn't told the police a thing, it meant Seb was free to use his car. Which meant he should get there first. Hitching down wasn't hard, but she'd be lucky if she got a lift straight to Hampstead, and she'd have problems getting across London with no money.

Sebastian thrust the note into his pocket and left the house by that convenient back window, after a quick glance either way to be sure no one was watching from the neighbouring gardens. He closed the window thoughtfully behind him, confident that he'd disturbed nothing inside; Jill or her parents might guess from the evidence that Kez had been there, but they'd have no clues now about where she'd gone.

But then, they wouldn't need clues anyway. Because by the time they came back from holiday, it should be common knowledge where Kez had gone. And what had happened once she got there . . .

## 10   All My Pretty Chickens

"Refuge?" The big man was indignant. "What would my boys be wanting with a refuge? I'm all the refuge they need. A mother hen, that's me. To all my chickens."

He stretched his arms out wide, in demonstration of the shelter they afforded. Alex winced, and trusted that her dark glasses would hide it. She'd get further with this creep if she played up to him, and never mind the embarrassment. But . . .

"Not quite all," she said, hoping he wouldn't take offence. "Davey FitzAlan went to the refuge, Mr Aspinall."

"Ah, Davey!" He sighed deeply, and shook his head; and she knew she'd guessed right. After all, every mother hen has to have a black chicken to get sentimental over, after it's flown the nest . . . "I dunno what got into that boy . . . Not that I'm admitting anything, mind." He changed tack abruptly, with a sharp glance at her.

Alex spread her hands innocently. "It's off the record, Mr Aspinall. Every word of it. I'm interested in my own story, that's all. I don't care what I turn up on the way. I'm just after the refuge. Someone else can have the rent boys."

"Oh yeah, sure. And that was pig-shit fell on my jacket this morning, I suppose. I know you journalists, you'll pick up anything you can grab. And make it stink."

"Trust me, Mr Aspinall. Look, no notebook – and I've got a very short-term memory, I'll forget everything you tell me the minute I walk out of that door. There's honour even in dockland."

"Pig-shit." He shrugged, and took a cigarette out of a
leather case. "But he's yesterday's news, I suppose, that lad.
Dunno what got into him, I swear I don't. Shooting his
mouth off to this hack, then flitting to some hideout . . . Not
that I hold it against him, mind. I don't bear grudges. I'd
find him work if he came back, just the way I used to. You
can tell him that, if you turn him up."

"All right, I will." *And tell him not to be a fool, that there
are better ways to make money than to sell your soul to a
man like this, soft as shit on the surface and hard as a brick
beneath.* "But you haven't any kind of a clue where he might
have gone? Where this refuge is?"

"Not a notion, sweetheart. He didn't confide in me."

"Someone else he might have confided in, then? Any
special friends of his, among your, um, boys?"

He shook his head. "My boys don't make friends. They
just make money." And laughed hugely, and wiped his eyes
with a folded white handkerchief as he went on, "No, but
seriously, I'll ask them, lady. I'll ask them. But you'll have
to offer them something, you know. Some remuneration.
They're sharp lads, they're not going to give something away
when they could sell it."

"Of course not." *And nor are you, am I right?* "I wouldn't
ask them to, Mr Aspinall." She took a purse out of her bag,
and took out a folded wad of notes. "There's a hundred
pounds there. Say if you offered them fifty, and keep the
rest as your, um, commission . . ."

"Well, that's very handsome of you, young lady."

"Not at all, Mr Aspinall. It's a business proposition. It's
only fair to pay you for your time and trouble."

She gave him her phone number at home as well as work,
shook his moist, manicured hand and walked out of the
small office into the porn shop beyond.

And smiled suddenly, between the dildoes and the crotch-
less knickers, wondering how she would explain that hundred pounds to her editor.

*Well, you see, boss, I gave that hundred quid to a fat,
strong, oily man who controls half the rent boys in the West
End; and no, he didn't tell me anything in exchange. Not a
thing. And no, I don't honestly think he'll pass a penny of it
on to any of his boys – sorry, his pretty chickens – he won't*

*even let them know what I'm looking for. But I had to try,*
*didn't I? Just in case . . .*

Laurence Aspinall wasn't the only mother hen she found
that day. Above a cafe close to Piccadilly Circus, a Church
of England clergyman ushered her into a long, drab room
furnished with a table, a dozen chairs, a video game and a
kettle. On the walls, posters warned of the dangers of AIDS
– Use A Condom! Don't Share Needles! Don't Swallow
Sperm!

Four of the chairs were occupied, boys and young men,
mid-teens to early twenties. They sat listlessly holding plastic
beakers of coffee, eating their way through a packet of
ginger nuts, talking softly or letting the silences stretch.

"We've been running this centre almost a year now," the
Rev Michael Coles said cheerfully, too loud. One of the
boys glanced up, looked at Alex with a long lack of interest,
and turned away. "We're open twenty-four hours a day, and
I like to think we provide a useful service. A lot of the lads
come here, to get off the streets for a while. They don't
really have anywhere else to go, you see, that's the wicked-
ness of it. So we do what we can, and I think they appreciate
it. I hope so. Of course they *say* it's only to sit down and
warm up – 'between tricks', is how they put it – but I like to
think it's more than that. We can at least offer some stabil-
ity, you see? A safe haven in the storm."

"A refuge," Alex said politely.

"Exactly so. A refuge, yes."

"Actually, it's another refuge I'm really looking for. This
is very interesting, and our editor may well want to do a
feature – perhaps in the Sunday edition one week. But I
expect you read about the High Court decision earlier in the
week, making Davey FitzAlan a Ward of Court?"

"Davey, yes. I hope he's all right. I've been quite worried
about him. All that publicity can't be a good thing, you
know. Can it? And not knowing where the boy's hiding . . .
He was one of our regulars, for a time. Before he disappeared. I do wish he would come forward. I'm sure something could be worked out . . ."

"You don't know where it is, then, this refuge he's supposed to be living in?"

"I'm afraid not, no. I'd heard nothing about it, before this week."

"Ah, well. Look, is it all right if I talk to the boys? Davey must have got the address from someone."

"Yes, of course. Go right ahead, ah, Miss Holden. I hope one of the lads can help you; it can only be a good thing, if Davey is found. And perhaps, a small article, it might be of great help to us, you know, so perhaps a mention . . ."

"I'll do my best." She smiled at him, refused a coffee and went to sit next to the youngest of the boys.

"Hullo." His eyes flicked towards her, flicked away again, incurious as a lizard. "My name's Alex Holden . . ."

"Yeah? So what?" His voice was sullen, and wary. "Social worker, are you?"

"No, nothing like that. I'm a journalist."

"You look like a social worker."

"Do I?" She chuckled. "Is that a compliment?"

"Nah."

"Ah, well. Don't worry, I'm not. I just want to talk to you, that's all."

"What about?"

"Well – did you know Davey FitzAlan, when he was around?"

"The Irish kid? 'Course, we all knew him." But he said it with a sneer, which made her change her next question suddenly, made her ask:

"Didn't you like him?"

The boy shrugged. "Couldn't take it, could he? Shot his mouth off to the papers, so there's twice as many pigs on the streets now and the tricks are all scared off, and then the little rat does a bunk somewhere. Shits on us and scarpers. See?"

"Yes, I see. You don't know where he is now, I suppose?"

The boy shook his head, and looked away. "No."

Alex didn't believe him, so she went on asking questions about Davey, trying to find out if he'd had any other friends or contacts that the boy knew about, where he might have heard about the refuge. She met nothing but a blank wall, though, of ignorance or refusal; and while she was still knocking her head against it, the other youngster got up and left. He was just a year or two older, perhaps seventeen; and Alex cursed mentally as he picked up a leather jacket from a chair by the door, and loped off down the stairs. The centre's other two customers were both over twenty; and though she would talk to them, of course she would – just in case – it was the kids who would know, if anyone did.

She left half an hour later, no better off than when she went in; and as she crossed the Circus, she spotted a leather jacket, a head of straight blond hair, and recognised the boy she hadn't had a chance to speak to.

But now wouldn't be a good time to interrupt him. He was talking to a man with a crewcut and a Zapata moustache, with gold glinting in his ears, with a T-shirt that proclaimed he loved New York; and as she watched, the two of them walked off up Shaftesbury Avenue together.

*Alex, my girl, know what that was? That was him turning a trick, that was. But never mind him, concentrate. Davey FitzAlan. The refuge. Question: how are we going to find it? Answer: go underground. We could chase round like this for ever, and not get anywhere. Or rather we couldn't, because the boss would pull us off pretty damn quick, and put us back on the bloody women's page. So . . .*

## 11 Somewhere Central

Nina and Davey had been picking at each other for an hour or more, caught together in the kitchen as Davey cooked and Nina washed some clothes. Mark could hear them clearly from the garage, where he was back working on the car, finding it easiest to think while his hands were busy;

*(and it was strange, that, because he'd been so careful for so long never to do more than one thing at once, never to risk that tug in his mind, one side to the other, that used to send him staggering blind between, into darkness)*

and their voices jarred and disturbed him, when he needed quiet to feed his concentration and keep him steady. At last he went through, and said, "Turn it off, you two. Give us a break, eh?"

Nina transferred her glare to him, and he could see a retort rising to her lips; but Davey got in first, tossing him something from the draining-board, white and warm and damp, and saying, "Here, wipe the oil off your fingers, Mark mate."

And he caught it automatically and started to clean his hands without thinking; and Nina screeched, "You shit, Davey! You filthy fucking shit!" and slapped the boy, viciously hard, with fingers crooked to rake her nails across his cheek. Davey twisted away too late, spun back all fists and fury – and this time there was no Colton around to break it up, so Mark had to move fast and did, dropping whatever-it-was onto a clothes-horse and sprinting over, three quick paces, to grab a shoulder of each and wrench them apart.

"What the *hell* is going on with you two?"

Davey breathed hard, said nothing; Nina tried to kick him around Mark's legs, and panted, "That was my best T-shirt! Filthy fucking queer . . ."

Davey jerked free at that, the nail-scratches flaming red across his white cheek, and tried to get at her again; Mark grabbed at him wildly, caught a handful of his shirt and shoved hard, sending the boy staggering back against the wall.

"That's *enough!* You hear me?" They were words out of his childhood, school stories and adventure thrillers; but they seemed to work. Neither of the kids moved, or so much as looked at each other; they were both staring at him, anticipating trouble. He let Nina go, and she pulled her blouse straight with a wrench that could have torn a seam.

Mark knew what Mrs Horsley would have done now; she would have sat the kids down at opposite ends of the table and stood in judgement over them, demanding the story, waiting coldly through their silences until she was rewarded with muttered accusations and recriminations from both sides. But

(*"you are not required to behave like a clone of Mrs Horsley"*)

Mark couldn't play the schoolteacher with any conviction, and he had too much on his mind now to be bothered with trying. So he glanced over to the cooker, where a pan was sizzling, and said, "Davey, you'd better do something with those onions before they burn. Snap it up."

Then he took Nina's arm, feeling it taut and trembling beneath his fingers, and steered her over to the clothes-horse.

"Your T-shirt, was it, love?" He picked it off the wooden rail and shook it out, looking at the smeared oil-stains across the white cloth.

"It's the only decent one I've got. Was. It's ruined now. That bloody . . ."

"Drop it, will you? Look, I'll tell you what." He glanced at the clock – half past four, time enough. "I'll give you some money from the kitty, and you can go buy yourself a new one, all right? Run and get a jacket or something, I don't trust the weather."

When she'd gone, he turned to Davey. "You didn't have to do that."

A shrug. "She's been riding me all bloody day. Fucking cow. Just because I. . . because of what happened with Jane. It's none of her bloody business."

"No, it isn't. But that's no excuse, Davey. I'll talk to you later, right?"

Right now, he had to get some cash from the office; and as soon as he'd dealt with Nina, he ought to phone Ipswich again. His contact there should have finished her meeting by now, should have got the authorisation she was seeking. But his hands were still filthy with oil. He looked at the smeared T-shirt he was still holding, shrugged, and wiped off the worst of it, tossing the T-shirt through the open door into the garage before moving to the sink and the tin of Swarfega.

A casual, practised glance around told Nina that the assistant was busy at the till, and no one else was looking in her direction. Her arm oh-so-accidentally brushed half a dozen T-shirts off the pile she'd been going through, and onto the floor at her feet. She tutted, and crouched in the aisle to pick them up; and stuffed two quickly into her carrier-bag, before folding the others neatly and putting them back. She wandered through the store for a minute or two, stopping to look at this and finger that; bought some lipstick and an aerosol deodorant out of the tenner Mark had given her; made her way outside with never a look back over her shoulder.

That was good, two shirts for the price of none; and what

was better, she could ride the bus into town, buy some cigarettes and get right away from the house for an hour or two, and still have a couple of quid change to satisfy Mark. Mrs Horsley wasn't soft like that, she would've told Nina how much she could spend and raised hell if she'd gone a penny over; but Mark was different, you could push him and get away with it.

"Umm. Mark, I don't quite understand your role in this business. What exactly is your current relationship with Jane?"

Mark grinned, at the suspicion in her voice. "It's all very innocent, Mrs Burroughs. I stand *in loco parentis*, if you like; I'm feeding the kid, clothing her and keeping a roof over her head. That's all."

"I see. And what is she doing to repay you, what's her side of the bargain?"

"Oh, she cooks a bit, cleans a bit, watches telly a lot. And mucks out her pet rats, I'm very strict about that." Silence from the other end, so he added, "I'm not her pimp, if that's what you're worrying about. She doesn't have to earn her keep here, that way or any other."

"Mmm. Well, if all that is true, why won't you give us your full name and address?"

"There are reasons for that; and I'm sorry, I'm not even going to tell you the reasons. You'll have to trust me, I'm afraid, the same way I'll have to trust you. That's one thing I'm going to insist on, Mrs Burroughs; I want your promise that if I do hand Jane over to you, you won't ask her questions about me, or anything she did in London. She's only a baby, and you could probably bully it all out of her, if you kept at it; but it'd tear her apart, if you made her break faith with us."

"Ah. Yes, I see. Look, Mark, I think we'd better meet, to discuss this face to face. Will that be possible?"

"If you can come to London, yes. I expected that. You'll want to talk to Jane too, I imagine?"

"Oh, yes. Certainly I'll want to speak to Jane. Well, shall we fix a time and a place, then? Somewhere central, if that's convenient . . ."

She was reading the notices outside a theatre on Charing

Cross Road when a voice behind her said, "Hey, Nina! Long time no see. How's tricks?"

She turned round to see blond hair, a leather jacket, a mocking smile. "Hullo, Secky," she said, not even trying to sound pleased to see him.

He laughed. "Still at the ref, then?"

"Yeah."

"How's the old bat?"

"Mrs Horsley's in hospital. She had a smash-up, in the car."

"Too bad. I always said she was a lousy driver." He looked around, started to walk away, then turned back. "Hey, listen. Pretty little Davey-boy's still hiding out with you lot, right?"

"Yeah."

"Well, do me a favour, eh? Give him a message from me." And Secky smiled happily. "Tell him that favourite trick of his, the thin guy with the glasses? Tell him he tested out positive, last month. Davey'll understand. Tell him I had it from Stand-Up Joe, so it's real. That's all."

And Secky went on his way, laughing.

Twenty minutes later Nina found a cafe, bought herself twenty Silk Cut and a cup of coffee, and sat down by the window with her mind still on that odd encounter. Ordinarily she wouldn't dream of doing any favours for Secky, of all people; but whatever it was that message meant, she was bloody sure it wasn't good news for Davey. Secky had been too eager, laughing too loud. He and Davey had never been friends – hell, Secky had never been friends with anyone – and right now, Nina was only too glad to pass on anything that would bring Davey down, the little shit . . .

So whatever it was about, she'd be sure to tell him. And to get the message right, to be sure it bit deep.

She took a cigarette out of the packet, and realised she'd forgotten to get any matches. Cursed, and glanced at the girl on the other side of the table.

"Haven't got a light, have you?"

The girl looked at Nina, blank-eyed behind her glasses; then she shook her head, just as slowly, and turned away to gaze out of the window again.

Nina sighed, and went back to the counter for a box of

matches. Returning to her seat, she saw the stuffed sports bag and the plastic carriers piled on the seat next to the girl, and for a moment

*(struggling off the bus with everything she could carry, everything she couldn't bear to part with; looking round helplessly, streets and cars and people, strangers, not a friend in the world; walking till she couldn't walk any more, then finding a cafe to hide in, forcing a coffee down her tight throat to stop herself crying)*

she was back in her own past, seeing herself in this girl's empty stare.

Two and two made four; and one of the girl's hands kept straying across her stomach, like stroking a cat under her skin, and two fours are eight, and Nina couldn't just let her sit there until she was thrown out, to spend the night on the streets.

"What's your name, kid?"

That same slow stare; then the girl's lips parted, and twitched, and shaped a word.

"Sorry? I didn't hear."

"Mandy."

"Run away from home, have you, Mandy?"

A long pause, and a fractional nod.

"It's all right, I'm not going to turn you in. Are you pregnant?"

"Yes."

"Got anywhere to go tonight?"

"No."

"I didn't think so. Look, don't go away, okay? I've just got to make a quick phone-call."

The girl's head jerked upwards, the first sign of life that Nina had seen in her. "Who are you phoning?"

"I said, didn't I? I'm not going to turn you in. I'll just call the place I'm staying, and get the okay to take you there, right? I'll tell you, kid, meeting me's the best thing could've happened to you tonight . . ."

Jenny Wright designed and made jewellery in a Hampstead flat, one of a dozen in a large converted house.

The communal doorway was protected by an entryphone system; and when Sebastian rang Jenny's bell, after parking his car in a back street ten minutes' walk away, he got no answer. Fair enough; Kez could hardly have beaten him here, and if he couldn't get an answer nor would she.

On the other side of the street was a fenced-in area of grass and trees, a garden for the residents. The gates were locked; but a quick glance from left to right, and Sebastian stepped onto the bonnet of a parked car, to the roof, to the cross-bar that topped the iron railings, and jumped down inside. He found a bench that gave a perfect vantage point, affording a direct view of the doorway between the trees. The book making an awkward bulge in his pocket was an old leather-bound copy of Thomas Browne, when he pulled it out to check; he smiled and settled back happily, glad of something to read that would be more than camouflage, an unalloyed pleasure for his eyes to return to time and again, as he alternately read and watched, watched and read . . .

Kez looked out through the windscreen of the Volvo, with the blue sunstrip constantly fooling her eyes, making her think the sky was clear overhead when it wasn't. When it was grey, like the streets and the pavements and the concrete and the suits were grey, like the taste of fear in her mouth. Grey and gritty, coating her mouth and her stomach and the inside of her skull.

The man driving the car was an odd one, small and spectacled, with greasy hanks of hair spread across his bald scalp from one ear to the other. He spoke so softly she could barely hear sometimes, and he kept flicking his tongue out to wipe little bubbles of saliva from his lips; he was dead creepy, the kind of guy she'd never dream of taking a lift from, ordinarily.

*(And wouldn't need to, because there was always Seb, wasn't there? Always Seb, to be a guard against creepy men, to give her lifts and keep her safe . . .)*

But then, she'd never dream of being this desperate, either. Ordinarily.

Mr Jackson was a businessman, with calls to make; and they'd barely got onto the M40 outside Oxford before they were turning off again, heading for Princes Risborough. "I hope you're not in a hurry," he'd said; she'd done her best to smile, and shake her head.

In the end, they'd taken all day over it. He'd bought her lunch, and she'd helped him carry boxes of stuff into offices and out to the car. Told him lies, and slept a little; and pretended to sleep, to give herself a chance to think.

But now they were here at last, just turning into the Mall; and he was indicating and pulling over, even while he shot her an anxious glance.

"You're sure you'll be all right, Joanne? I don't like it, leaving a youngster like you alone in the big city."

She eyed him warily for a moment. Was this where the creep made his move, shouldering the nice guy aside? Trust was in shatters at her feet, and all men were suspect. But he seemed genuinely concerned and nothing more, keeping his hands to himself and only his eyes on her. So she smiled,

*(and she was getting better at that, it was just muscle control, after all)*

and shook her head meaninglessly.

"I'll be fine, Mr Jackson, ta. I'll meet my friend out of work, like I told you. Plenty of time."

"That's all right, then. As long as you're going to be with someone."

"Oh, yes. Don't worry about that, I'll be with someone."

Only she wouldn't, and he was right to worry. Because she'd been thinking hard, behind closed lids; and it hadn't taken much of that to make her realise how stupid she'd been. Seb was a smart guy, and he knew her inside out. Chances were he'd guess sooner or later where she went last night. And go there himself, see the broken window, follow her in – and find the note. She was bloody lucky he hadn't come during the night some time, and found her.

She had to assume now that he knew where she'd been heading; and what it all came down to was that she couldn't go to Jenny's any more. She couldn't go anywhere near Jenny.

Which left her with nowhere to go. Probably the best thing would be to jump on a bus or a train and get right out of London, if Seb was looking for her there; but she had no money, and no way to get hold of any.

So she smiled brightly as she stepped out of the car, slammed the door confidently, waved through the window and stood watching until the car had disappeared into the busy traffic around Buckingham Palace.

And looked round helplessly, took a step one way, two steps the other, half made as if to cross the road, changed her mind, turned a full circle . . .

Seb had time to read his way through *Religio Medici* and get well into *Urne Buriall* before his vigilance was finally rewarded; and even then it wasn't the figure he was looking for, not his slender sister ringing the bell. Jenny was home at last. He watched her plump figure climb the steps and disappear through the door; then got to his feet, clambered over the railings and trotted across the road to ring her bell again.

"Yes, hullo?" She answered immediately, the voice breathy and long familiar.

"Hullo, Jen. It's Sebastian Hughes."

"Seb! Whatever are you doing in town?"

"Coming to see you, sweetheart. So are you going to let me in, or shall we just chat through this machine?"

"Sorry, ducks. Come on up . . ."

A buzzer sounded and he reached for the handle on the heavy door; but as he gripped it, a hand tapped his shoulder.

"Excuse me, I'd like a word with you."

And

*(she's gone to the police after all, they've put my face and name up on the news bulletins all day, the whole country's been looking for me)*

his hand sweated and slipped on the brass handle and the buzzing stopped and he couldn't open the door, no escape there. So he turned round, tense and ready, and the old bat with the plummy voice didn't look like trouble, but there were enough people on the street to join in and hold him if she screamed . . .

"That garden is private property, young feller," she said firmly. "And don't tell me you had any right to be there, I saw you climbing over the railings. Now what were you up to?"

"I – I'm sorry." The tension flooded out of his muscles all in a moment, found nowhere to go and backed up into pools and puddles in his mind, hiccups of hysteria that he had to swallow and keep swallowing, like a car-sick boy trying not to vomit. "I've been waiting, you see, and there wasn't anywhere else to sit down . . ."

"Waiting for whom?"

"Jenny Wright, in 1b. She's been out all day . . ."

"Oh, you're a friend of Jenny's?" That, apparently, was different. "No, she would have been giving her workshop today, you see, at the summer school. I expect she's just back now, though, is she?"

"Yes, I saw her. That's why I climbed out of the garden . . ."

The old woman smiled at him approvingly, and fished a bunch of keys out of her bag; but before she could unlock the door, it buzzed again, loud and long.

"Jenny's getting impatient." Seb pushed the door open, and held it for his interrogator; but rather than follow her into the lift, he turned left towards the stairs. "It's only one floor, and I'd rather walk."

"I should hope so, at your age." She gave him a cheerful wave, as the lift doors closed between them; Seb closed his eyes, clenched his fists and pushed her face and voice and life to the back of his mind, to be reconsidered as and when necessary. He had enough

*(more than enough, too much)*

on his plate already. But he couldn't afford to forget her . . .

Jenny was out on the landing when he reached it, looking for him.

"What happened to you?"

"Met an old lady at the door, who didn't like me climbing in and out of your sacred garden. Short, stout, dressed like nothing on earth."

"Sounds like me."

"White hair, and murky brown eyes. *Nothing* like you, Jenny love."

She laughed. "Must have been Mrs Richardson in 2b, then. Everyone else in this place is slim and beautiful. You know, the kind of slim that costs a hundred a week."

"So what's your excuse? You'd never notice it."

She boxed his ears, and he hugged her, laughing.

"Same old Jenny. Violent as ever."

"I've had twenty years of cheek from you, young Sebastian, and I think you're getting worse. Come inside, anyway. Mix me a gin, while I take my coat off; and if you can still remember how I like it, I'll give you a sneak preview of my new collection. How's that?"

"Sounds good to me, Jen. If I get to mix one for myself at the same time."

"Daresay you're old enough. I won't tell your mother if you don't."

"How's my god-daughter, then, Seb lad? What's Kez up to?"

*(I don't know, and I wish I did. She should've been here by now.)*

"God knows. Worrying hell out of Mum probably, that's her usual game."

*(She's probably frantic by now, with both of us gone and not even a note to tell her where. Unless Kez has phoned her, of course. Or gone to the police.)*

"Of course it is, it's a duty incumbent on all teenagers. You did enough of it yourself, in your time. Now then, lad. What do you want to eat? We're not going out, so don't try to talk me into it. You're not fifteen any more. Don't mind treating a schoolboy, just to watch his eyes bulge, but damned if I'll buy good cooking for an unemployed lay-about. Have to make do with what's in the freezer. Come and pick."

He stood and watched her rummage in an ancient chest-freezer, and said, "For God's sake, Jen, why don't you get an upright?"

She snorted. "Only exercise my waist ever gets, this is. Bending and stretching, it's good for me. Better for you, though. Have a dig in this corner, will you? I can't see whether that pack's green beans or peppers, and it's frosted in so hard I can't get it loose . . ."

At ten o'clock, Jenny put the news on; Sebastian watched from the kitchen doorway, while his hands stroked a short-bladed Sabatier cook's knife across a steel.

Jenny hit a button on the remote control, and the volume increased; then she glared over her shoulder. "What are you doing that for? Makes a hell of a noise."

"Bullshit. You just like complaining, that's all. And I'm doing it as a favour for you. If you're going to have decent knives, you could at least make an effort to keep them sharp. This poor thing's got no edge on it at all."

"I do try, but I can't do it. You'll have to show me how, before you go."

"Pleasure."

And he went on drawing the blade gently down the steel, until, just two minutes into a report on the Oxford rapist and his latest victim, Jenny pressed another button and the screen went blank.

"Too depressing," she announced. "I don't want to know. Still play chess, Seb?"

He nodded, put the knife and the steel away and fetched the board for her, and set the pieces out; and could have kissed her for turning the news off when she had, before they could go naturally on from one story to another, from a rapist to a vanished schoolgirl, and her vanished brother.

By midnight, Jenny was in bed. Seb unfolded the sofabed in the living-room, and spread out the sleeping-bag she had produced; but he didn't undress, he simply kicked his shoes off and stretched himself full-length along the mattress, tucking his hands behind his head and staring at the fresh white paint on the ceiling.

Kez wouldn't come now. Something must have happened, between Oxford and here; and he couldn't count on its being something fatal to schoolgirls. Safest to assume that she had after all gone to the police; and if that were true . . . Well. The game was over, that was all, or greatly changed.

*(But that wasn't news. The game had changed twenty-four hours ago, in a playground in Oxford – and what the hell had Kez been doing there, anyway? Just sitting, swinging, staring*

*at him . . .)*

He shook his head sharply, angry with himself. Never mind why, the game had changed, that was all. He'd been playing by different rules for a full day now, and it was time he settled down and got comfortable with them.

So. If Kez had gone to the police

*(and play it like she has, it's the only way)*

they'd be keeping her somewhere, keeping her safe. Nothing he could do about that.

But Jenny . . . Well. Jenny would learn something from her morning paper, be it only that Seb and his sister were missing from home; and even if he were long gone by then, she'd be straight on the phone, telling the police where he'd been, putting them on his trail. And he couldn't afford that. It was no good trying to keep just one step ahead, he'd trip up some time and they'd be on him. That was inevitable.

So he stood up again and got undressed slowly, methodically, folding his clothes one by one into a pile, until he was naked; then he left the living-room and went into Jenny's bedroom.

By way of the kitchen.

He closed the bedroom door behind him and turned on the light, not wanting to blunder about messily in the dark. Jenny had heavy curtains over her windows, which was all to the good; no danger of a nosy neighbour seeing anything.

She slept heavily, noisily, more animal than human in this state, with her mind stolen out of her and nothing left but the massive body collapsed under the covers. Easier to think of her like that, to dissociate this

*(too too solid)*

flesh, creature of flesh, from the Jenny of his memory, friend of the family, bringer of gifts and good cheer throughout his childhood, first adult friend in adolescence.

But she wasn't cooperating, wasn't making it easy for him. Rolling over in bed, throwing an arm across her face against the light, peering up from its shadow.

"Who's that, Seb, is it?"

"Yes, dear. It's me. Who else?"

"Well, what's up?" Then, as she saw him properly, saw him naked: "Seb, what are you up to?"

"Oh, don't worry, darling. You're not about to be seduced. This is just so that I don't get blood on my clothes."

"Seb, I don't –"

And she never did, she never got the chance even to know, let alone to understand. Unless her mind could move vastly faster than her body, unless her watering, myopic eyes could make out details of skin and steel as Seb dragged the duvet off her bed and spread his fingers across her face, cupped the heel of his hand beneath her chin and pushed hard.

Unless in some brief, curious separation of herself, as if her mind were still not fully back from sleep, not yet absorbed into her body, a little voice could whisper,

*he's going to kill us, Jenny. We used to cut his meat up for him, and now*

and now with her head forced up and back into the pillow, Seb stabbed the knife into her exposed throat and tugged, dragged it down until her gullet was ripped open from the chin to the breastbone. And Jenny couldn't scream then, she couldn't even breathe; all she could do was froth and bubble, and flounder from side to side across the wide bed.

And all Seb could do was stand and watch, see her tossing and turning and dying for him, his friend; and understand at last how greatly, how very greatly the game had changed.

## 13  *Head Prefect*

Colton came breezily downstairs and into the games room, to find Mark sprawled on the sofa, watching late-night snooker on the television.

"How's Jimmy White doing?"

"He's losing. Seven-three."

"Shit. How's about you turn that off, then, and give us a game of pool?"

Mark turned his face up wearily and said, "Sorry, Colton, I'm not up to it tonight. I'm shattered."

"Yeah, you look it." Colton perched on the arm of the

sofa and scowled at him. "Jesus, man, why ain't you in bed already? I'll do all the locking up and stuff, you know that, you can trust me. And you ain't no use to anyone like that."

"You sound like the doctor," Mark grumbled, pulling himself upright.

"Maybe that's 'cos we both talk sense sometimes. Go on, sod off."

Mark levered himself slowly to his feet, and said, "I'd better check on Mandy first, see if she's settled for the night."

"Too late, mate, I done that. She's a funny one, Mark. Sitting on her bed, she was – not doing nothing, just sitting. I said wasn't she tired, and she said no. So I bullied her a bit, said it was one of the rules that she should've been in bed by midnight. And then I said it'd be better for her baby if she got some sleep, and that got her moving. I checked, and she was in bed ten minutes after."

"That's fine, Colton. Thanks. I'd better look in on her, though, just to say good night."

"Oh yeah, and wake the kid up. Terrific. Why don't you leave it till breakfast, and say good morning instead?"

Mark's lips twitched into a smile. "You know, sometimes I wonder which of us two is running this place. Good night, then. And don't worry, I'll leave Mandy alone."

Colton watched from the foot of the stairs, until Mark had turned the corner; then he went back into the games room. The snooker was too depressing, so he shifted through the channels till he found a horror film, and settled back happily on the sofa.

Half an hour later, he heard the telephone distantly between the screams of the heroine and the crescendos of the soundtrack. Given half a chance, he would have left it; but the office was directly beneath Mark's bedroom, and Colton didn't want Mark dragging himself out of bed again to answer it.

So he cursed, got reluctantly to his feet and walked through to the extension in the kitchen, glancing at a clock on the way. One o'clock, near enough; who the hell would be ringing at this kind of time? Some kind of emergency, it must be. He might have to wake Mark up after all . . .

He picked the receiver up, praying hard for a wrong number; and said, "Hullo?"

"Hullo. This is the Samaritans calling. I'm sorry to be telephoning this late, but I have your number here as a place where teenagers can find a bed for the night, is that right?"

Shit. Colton punched the wall, and gave up on God, not for the first time. The guy just didn't *listen*. "Yeah, that's right." The woman on the other end had been very careful not to say 'refuge', and so was he. She probably knew bloody well that she was phoning the house that had been in the papers all month, but if she was willing to be tactful, that suited him. "What's your problem?"

"I've got a runaway here, a girl of sixteen. She says her name's Julie, but I'm not sure that's true. Anyway, she called us an hour ago, to ask if there was anywhere she could go, where she wouldn't be asked questions. I told her to come here in the first instance, just to get her off the streets; and if necessary, I'll take her home with me tonight. But we're not supposed to do that, and in any case it's obviously not a permanent solution. Then I remembered we had your number here, so I thought I'd ask if you could find space for her."

Shit again. *Double* shit. He couldn't make decisions like this, it was well out of his league. He ought to run upstairs and get Mark, right now. But . . . Hell, they had plenty of space, and he knew what Mark would say. Or thought he did.

At any rate, he knew what questions to ask. "How is she, is she high, anything like that?" If the girl was on drugs, he'd have to call the doctor; but he'd rather do that than wake Mark up. Maybe he should do it anyway . . .

"No, there's no sign of it. She's tired, and very distressed about something; but she's keeping it all bottled up. She won't talk at all. I'd say that what she needs more than anything is a place where she can feel safe for a few days. I think she's very frightened."

Colton sighed, ran his fingers through his hair, thought, *help, I shouldn't have to do this, it isn't fair*: and said, "Yeah. Okay, we'll take her, for tonight anyway."

"Oh, splendid. Thank you very much. Now, can you come and pick her up? I can't leave the office, and I don't want to send her out to find you on her own."

"No, don't do that. I'm not allowed to give you the address anyway." Which was the closest either of them came to admitting that the refuge operated outside the law. Colton would have to make it clear to the girl, once he'd collected her; but from the sound of it, she wouldn't worry about that. "Tell me where you are, and I'll come round."

Thank God (and maybe the old bastard was paying attention after all), the address she gave wasn't too far away. And thanks again, big fella, he knew the street. "Okay, look. I'll be there in about half an hour, right? Give or take."

"You can't make it sooner?"

"No, sorry. The car's off the road, see." Which was true enough; one car was a wreck, a write-off. And never mind that he couldn't drive. No need to mention that.

"All right, then. I'll expect you in half an hour. What's your name, please?"

"Colton. Just Colton."

"Fair enough. And I'm Margaret."

Whatever it was that Margaret had been expecting, to judge by her expression it wasn't a skinny black boy on a skateboard. He switched off his Walkman and pulled the earphones off his head, while she stared; then he grinned, and said, "I'm Colton. Honest."

"I believe you, I recognise the voice. But . . . did you have to bring that?"

He picked up the skateboard and swung it over his shoulder, as he followed her up the narrow stairs to the Samaritans' office. "It's quicker than walking. And it's not half as suspicious as running. I figured you wouldn't want me turning up with half a dozen cops on my tail. Nor would what's-her-name, probably."

"Julie. No, I suppose not. But frankly, I'm a little reluctant . . . Are you seriously in charge at your, ah, house, Colton?"

"No, not seriously." Time to be honest. "But the guy who runs it is knackered, and I knew he'd say yes anyway, so I said it for him. And I'm not exactly one of the kids either, if that's what you're worrying about. Not any more. I just live there now. Kind of head prefect, that's what I am."

It was Mrs Horsley's expression, not his own; and it meant something to Margaret. Two of a kind, her and Mrs H, he'd sussed that on the way here. She nodded and relaxed, even smiling a little as she led him through a room where two blokes were sitting patiently beside silent telephones, down a corridor lined with filing cabinets and into a small kitchen.

A girl was standing by the sink with a mug in her hands, staring at the dark space of the window; from the expression on her face, she wasn't even seeing the brick wall two yards beyond, but something far further off, far more threatening.

"Julie, dear . . ."

The girl jerked, and turned to face them. Long brown hair fell across her face, and she tossed it back with an automatic flick of her head. Colton caught his breath, looked her up and down with all the eager haste of an adolescent,

*(good figure, great legs, amazing cheekbones)*

checked to see what colour her eyes were –

– and crashed. Like running into concrete, that was. Because they weren't any colour at all, they were just dead. And she wasn't just a white girl, she was *white*; and the reason her cheekbones looked so great was because her eyes were sunk right into her skull . . .

And he wanted to apologise, and realised only just in time how silly that would sound, because they wouldn't even know what he was being sorry for.

Margaret explained quickly who he was, and the girl didn't look surprised at all to be picked up by a black boy with a skateboard. Colton had the feeling that nothing was going to surprise her tonight, nothing could get deep enough to touch her like that. She might want to hide out at the refuge, but inside she was hiding even from that, hiding from the need that made her hide . . .

"Sorry, but we got to walk back," he said softly. "The skateboard ain't big enough for two."

And she just nodded, accepting it at face value, or maybe not even hearing it, only nodding when her instincts told her to.

They said goodbye to Margaret and walked off through the orange glow of street-lights. Colton didn't try to talk, or to get her talking; but he watched her carefully, and saw how she startled at every car that passed, and kept looking back to check the street behind them.

After a while, he said, "Hey, listen, you better wind down. Or hide it, anyway. Any cop sees you jumping about like that, he's going to stop us for sure. And I can't risk being picked up, even if you can. I got a record long as your arm, with a broken probation sitting on the bottom of it."

She heard that all right, looking up at him with big, frightened eyes. "I'm sorry. I'll try. But . . ."

"But you're scared. Someone's after you, right?" She turned her head away, and he chuckled. "It's okay, it ain't nothing new. But listen to this. If there are any cops around, they see two nervy kids, they'll stop us, yeah? But if they see a couple of sweethearts, that's different. It's legit to be out at two in the morning, if you're in love. So . . ."

He shifted his skateboard to the other shoulder, and draped his left arm loosely round her neck.

"How's this, okay?"

He could feel every muscle in her tense up, and saw her mouth turn thin and hard, as if she wanted to shrug him off, to fight and kick and scream if she had to, to drive him away; but she only nodded tightly, accepting the necessity.

"Good girl." He loped along beside her, adjusting his pace awkwardly to hers,

*(no practice, walking with girls; but I'll get it)*

and said, "So what's your name, anyway? Never been this close to a girl without knowing her name."

*(Never been this close to a girl, full stop, but I ain't telling you that.)*

"Julie. She told you that, Margaret did."

"Oh, right. Julie. Yeah."

*(Well, it was worth trying. You'll come across eventually, kid. Everyone does. Almost everyone.)*

At half past two, Colton unlocked the door and led her into the hall, touching a finger to her cold lips for quiet.

"Don't want to wake Mark up," he whispered. "Sleeps with both eyes open, him. 'Specially since Mrs H went to hospital."

The girl – okay, call her Julie, if that's what she wants – didn't show any curiosity, didn't ask who Mark was or Mrs H or why she was in hospital; she only stood there, silent and dead-looking, waiting. Colton scratched his head, wondering if maybe he should wake Mark up after all; but it was too late now, she was here, and the morning would be soon enough to tell him.

So he said, "D'you want a drink, or anything to eat, stuff like that?"

Julie shook her head.

"Okay, then, I'll take you straight upstairs. You'll have to sleep in one of the attic rooms, and it'll be a bit rough, 'cos I can't dig sheets and stuff out at this time of night. But we'll fix you up comfy, one way or another. Come on – and tiptoe, yeah?"

He led her up to the first floor, pointing out which was his room, just in case; and then up again, a second flight and a second landing, past Jane's door and into the front bedroom. There was a bedstead and a mattress, an empty wardrobe, nothing else; but Colton left her for a minute, and came back with a pillow, a pile of blankets and his favourite rugby shirt.

He dumped it all on the bed, picked up the shirt and said, "Um, you got nothing with you, so I thought, maybe you'd like this for a nightie, sort of. Should be big enough. Only, I'll take it away if you don't want it, no sweat, it was just an idea . . ."

And there was just the hint of a smile tugging at her mouth as she reached out for it, held it up shoulder-height and watched the hem fall to her knees; and a trace of life in her voice, as she said, "Thanks, that's nice of you."

"Keep you warm, anyway. That's the main thing." He turned away, and started fidgeting with the blankets. "Are you going to be okay like this? I thought, you could make a sort of nest, like . . ."

"Yes, I'll be fine. Really."

"Right, then. You know where I am, if you need anything; and don't get the wrong door, or you'll give Mark the shock of his life. And the, the toilet's just at the bottom of the stairs. Oh, and listen, don't come down in the morning, eh? Not till I come to get you. If that's okay . . ."

She nodded, and half smiled again. "Yeah, that's okay."

"Great. Ta. See you in the morning, then . . ."

Back in his own room, he set the alarm in his watch for seven o'clock. Julie sure as hell wasn't going to sleep much, and he didn't want her sitting up there alone for hours with no breakfast, not even a drink, and nothing to do except stare at the blank walls and think, and be afraid . . .

But as it turned out, he didn't sleep much either; and he was wide awake when the alarm went off, beeping persist-

ently above the soft music from his radio. He groaned,
fumbled to turn it off, and swung his long legs out of bed.

He dressed quickly, and headed for the bathroom; and he
was just coming out when he heard Mark's own alarm clock
ringing, through his bedroom door. Colton went downstairs,
chewing his lip thoughtfully; and in the kitchen, he took two
mugs down off the shelf, thought again, and added a third.

He made two coffees
*(and God knows how she likes it – white no sugar at a
guess, but take the Sweetex up in case, they can slip in a
pocket easy)*
and a Barleycup, left the latter on the landing outside
Mark's room, knowing he wouldn't be out of bed for
another quarter of an hour at least, and went on up.

He knocked awkwardly with his free hand and put his
head round the door, ready to duck out quickly if he had to.
Sure enough, Julie wasn't asleep; she was sitting up on the
bed, huddled in the blankets and hugging her knees, with
her hair half across her face. But she lifted her head at his
repeated knock, brushed the hair back with the heel of one
hand and said, "Hullo, Colton. Come in."

"Er, ta. If you're sure. Um, I brought you some coffee.
Didn't know how you liked it, but there's Sweetex, if . . ."

"No, I don't. Thanks anyway." She took the mug and put
it down on the floor; he perched himself on the edge of the
bed, forgetting embarrassment, picked it up again and
passed it back to her.

"No, drink it now. You're gonna need it."

Ten minutes later, Mark was just thinking about getting
out of bed when there was a light, familiar tap at the door.

"Yeah, come in, Colton."

And Colton did come in, with a steaming mug in one hand
– and leading a strange girl by the other. Pale and pretty,
barefoot, wearing nothing but that old rugby shirt Colton
was so fond of; Mark blinked, and wondered, and finally
just waited, accepting the mug in silence. Colton fidgeted,
and drew the girl further into the room so he could shut the
door behind her; then he took her hand again, looking as if it
were as much for his own comfort as hers.

"Mark, this is Julie. She, uh, she needed somewhere to go
last night, so I fetched her here. I know, I should've told

you, but, hell . . ."

## 14   Over the Rainbow

*Ten o'clock,* Shahid had said. *Be outside Fenham Foods, with your gear. Not too much, mind. One bag. And dress Western.*

Not that she would have dressed any other way, or ever would again. She'd had it with Islam. So she was there fifteen minutes early, standing between the bollards with a black leather hold-all at her feet, wearing jeans, sweatshirt, stilettos. She'd pinched the bag from her uncle's shop yesterday, and stuffed some random clothes into it, perfumes and make-up, not much else. She had twenty quid in her pocket, that she'd lifted out of her mother's purse that morning, and some jewellery that might be worth something, might not.

It wasn't the best place to wait, with people she knew going in and out of the shop behind her; but when they spoke to her she smiled brightly, and said she was waiting for a lift, a friend taking her to the Metrocentre for a morning's shopping. The bag held clothes that didn't fit her any more, that she was going to pass on to a cousin she was meeting there.

At ten past, a battered old Citroën 2CV came round the corner and drew up next to her. She swallowed a giggle, staring at it in disbelief. It looked as if it had been cannibalised from three or four cars, with the doors and wings all in different colours, orange and blue and green.

The driver was an Asian boy, nineteen or twenty. He leaned across the passenger seat, unlocked the nearside door and pushed it open.

"You Tia, are you?"

"That's right."

"Okay, get in."

She chucked the bag over onto the back seat, sat down and pulled the door shut. He drove up onto the West Road, turned right past the hospital and went north at the roundabout.

Tia frowned. "Where are we going, then?"

"Gosforth, first. And don't ask questions, right?"

She shrugged, and settled back in her seat.

He turned off Gosforth High Street into a wide road with large detached houses standing secluded in their own gardens. He stopped under the shadow of a tree, sounded the horn, and waited; and after ten minutes of silence, a grey car pulled out of a drive just behind them. A Nissan Bluebird; Tia knew those, because her father had driven one before he'd graduated to Mercs. It flashed its lights twice, and the Asian boy put the Citroën into gear and drove off with the Bluebird following at a short distance.

"Now listen," the boy said. "I'm Mahmed. We're going straight down the motorway to London; and if we get pulled over by the cops, your name's Aysha, got that? I don't want them coming at me later, asking questions about you. So you're Aysha, you're my girlfriend and we're going down to Southall to stay with some people. You don't know them, so you don't need to worry about their names. It's a last-minute thing, me taking you along."

"Got it. But what's it all about, then? What's in this car?"

"I told you, don't ask questions."

"I've got a right to know, haven't I? If it's drugs or something, I could end up in jail too. I want to know what I'm risking."

"You're not risking anything. There's nothing in this car, just us."

"Pull the other one."

"It's true. We're innocent, see? That's the point. Two kids going to London for a week, to have some laughs with friends. And that's it. So just relax, right?"

He turned the radio on and the volume up, not subtle at all.

The radio worked erratically, giving them bursts of static punctuated with bursts of music, either too loud or too quiet; but they listened anyway, because it saved them having to talk, or confront the silence. Tia fiddled with the tuning, and smoked, and watched the Bluebird sitting grey like a shadow in the wing-mirror.

After an hour on the motorway, the Bluebird's reflection was replaced with another car, a big Range Rover with police markings. Mahmed grunted and drove steadily on, sparing one single glance for Tia.

"Remember. You're Aysha, you're my girlfriend."

"And we're going to stay with these people in Southall. I've got it."

The police tailed them for five minutes, before drawing alongside and gesturing them to pull over. Mahmed shrugged, waved in acknowledgement and drew up on the hard shoulder. The Range Rover stopped just ahead of them, and two officers got out.

Mahmed walked down to meet them; Tia pushed her door open and stood up, stretching with relief after the cramped ride. Then she got a cigarette out and lit it in the shelter of her cupped hands, and watched the Bluebird gliding past in the middle lane, fast but legal.

The police kept them for fifteen minutes, asking questions, checking the car over, searching it and their bags. Tia followed Mahmed's lead, taking it all sullenly but without complaint; they stood together while the cops went through their things, and she played up to the role he'd assigned her, slipping her arm loosely round his waist and resting her cheek against his shoulder. He was stiff and unresponsive, which only added a scornful contempt to the antipathy she already felt towards him; it was a relief when they were finally permitted to go, and they could fall back into their antagonistic silence.

They passed a sign announcing motorway services, ten miles on. Tia was dying for the toilet, but she wasn't going to ask Mahmed to stop; and she didn't need to, because when they came to the slip-road he pulled onto it without reference to her.

There were plenty of empty spaces in the car-park, but Mahmed drove up and down the aisles without stopping, until he finally found what he was looking for; and Tia wasn't too surprised when he parked just three cars away from the grey Bluebird.

"Twenty minutes," he told her. "And don't be late, right? If you're not here, I'll just go, and you'll be stuck here. And you won't get paid, either."

Tia nodded, and went off to find the ladies'. Then she headed for the refreshments, saw Mahmed there ahead of her, and took her coffee and sandwich deliberately to another table.

If Mahmed was waiting for a signal, she didn't see it; but after a while he got up and left the building. She followed him back to the car, and as they made their way down onto the motorway again, she saw the Bluebird once again in the wing-mirror.

*Don't ask questions* – but she didn't need to now, she could work it all out for herself. And it all added up to something very interesting: something that made her keep her eyes wide open as they picked their way through Highgate streets, and stopped at last in a road that wasn't too different from where they had started in Gosforth, except that the houses would cost four or five times as much.

The Bluebird passed them now, turned up a drive and vanished into a garage. The door swung down automatically behind it.

"You wait here," Mahmed said abruptly. He got out of the car and walked up the drive to the garage, hesitated for a second, then tapped at the ridged metal door. A voice yelled something indistinct; he called back, too softly for Tia to hear, and went round the side of the garage, out of her sight.

She waited patiently for ten minutes, doing nothing except to note and memorise the number of the house; then Mahmed came back, with an envelope in his hand.

"Forty quid, right?"

"Fifty, Shahid said."

Mahmed scowled, but took five ten-pound notes out of the envelope and passed them across to her. "That's it, then. Tara."

Tia didn't move; after a second he looked at her and said, "You can get out here."

"No way."

"Eh?"

"You're not dumping me like that. I'm not a bag of garbage, for you to chuck out on the pavement. And I've got nowhere to go, I don't know anyone in London. I've never been here before."

"Tough shit. That's your problem."

"Yours, too. I'm not getting out of the car, see? You've got somewhere to stay tonight. Not in Southall, I bet, but you're going somewhere. And you can bloody well take me with you."

"Fuck off, man! Go on, get the hell out of it. You've got your money, and that's it."

"Oh, yeah? So what are you going to do, drag me out? I warn you, I'll scream if you try it. I'll scream my bloody head off. And your bosses in there won't be too happy, you kicking up a fuss right by their front door . . ."

"Oh, shit. Shit, shit, *shit!*" He ran his hands slowly down over his face, then glared at her. "All right, then. I'll take you to my girl's, where I'm going. You can sleep on the floor. But just one night, right? After that you're out, and you can scream just as much as you fuckin' well like, nobody'll pay any attention round there."

Which was probably true; because his girlfriend lived in a squat, in a row of condemned houses waiting for demolition. The terrace stood like an island in a sea of rubble; Mahmed left the car in the road and led Tia over heaps of broken brick and concrete, to the one door that wasn't nailed up.

"Christ," she muttered, following him into darkness. "All the comforts of home."

"If you don't like it, fuck off."

But she followed him instead, up the stairs to a room lit by fire and candles, boards over the windows and a dozen people sprawling on cushions on the floor.

"Mahmed!" A short, blonde white girl jumped to her feet and picked her way between the bodies. Tia watched as they kissed, seeing the firelight glinting off a ring in the girl's nostril.

Then his head jerked in her direction. "I brought her along, just for tonight. Got nowhere else to go, so . . ."

"Yeah, sure." The girl smiled at her. "Hi, I'm Taff."

"Hullo."

They made space for her on a cushion by the fire, a bottle of wine came from one direction, a joint from another; and she thought, *what the hell am I doing, with this bunch of hippies?*

And answered herself; or had it answered for her, in Mahmed's voice.

*Nowhere else to go.*

Sebastian spent the whole day in Jenny's flat, alternating between times of frenetic activity and times of sitting very still indeed, waiting for the eyes of the world to move on. That was what it felt like, that there was a single unified gaze out there like a beam of light, searching, searching. It was paranoia pure and simple, he knew that; there was only one girl who could put a face and a name to him, and she wasn't searching, she was running. But even so it was hard, very hard to stay calm, to stay indoors.

But the flat should be safe, for the moment at least. Jenny lived alone, and privacy was – had been – important to her; no one was going to walk in without an invitation. He shouldn't be disturbed here until people actually started worrying about her; and if he were careful, he could delay that for some few days.

The first priority was not to be seen around too much himself, not to attract the curiosity of the neighbours. So he stayed inside and away from the windows, fixing meals from what he could find in cupboards and the well-stocked freezer.

And the second thing was to keep her friends and contacts at a distance, and try to prevent them getting anxious or suspicious about her absence, her silence, her unanswered door.

Fortunately she had an answering machine next to the telephone, and there was a choice of half a dozen different tapes with various messages on. Sebastian played them all through, and found one that was perfect. That went back into the machine; and so made Jenny an accessory after the fact in her own murder.

"Hullo, this is Jenny Wright. I'm sorry, darlings, but you've missed me good and proper; I've taken myself off to the country for a week or so. Isn't it bliss, being self-employed? Leave me a loving message when the beep goes, and I'll get back to you some time in the not-too-distant. I promise."

Meanwhile there was Jenny herself, or what remained of her. She couldn't safely be smuggled out of the flat and dumped elsewhere; but while Sebastian had no objections in principle to sharing accommodation with a corpse, she couldn't very well be left to suppurate quietly in the summer heat of the bedroom.

There was an obvious, easy answer to the problem, though; and Sebastian could see the luck running for him, strong and clear, in the way that Jenny had prepared even for this. He emptied that old chest-freezer in the kitchen, and distributed the contents between the fridge, the work-top and a black bin-liner, depending on his taste.

Then, with the curtains pulled, he peeled off all his clothes again and went into the bedroom. Jenny's body lay sprawled on clotted red-brown sheets, naked and open and terribly empty; Sebastian swallowed against the smell, and turned his head away from the uninhabited eyes, his mind from the night before and his making them so. Bringing death into the equation had changed everything, and not only for Jenny.

*Rigor mortis* had been and gone, so that when he lifted her in his arms she hung slackly, like something that had never lived. He carried her through and folded her awkwardly into the freezer, and didn't laugh, didn't find it funny till well after the lid was shut.


*He sleeps, much of the time. He hides in his dreams.*

*You can't blame him, really. She certainly doesn't. There isn't a whole lot else for him to do. Except talk, of course. He talks to himself all the time, and she catches only the fringes of that, like rumours of war, a constant mutter of shells just over the hill. Like looking out through a window, and seeing storm.*

*Sometimes, though, he talks to her. Then she listens, and does more than listen. She does what he wants. Gives him what he asks for, every time, no question.*

*And sometimes he talks in his sleep; and that's the worst, because she hears the words and doesn't understand them, can't connect them to anything in the world she knows.*

*Asleep, he's as restless as he is awake, lashing out in or against his dreams. Sometimes he hurts her, but she never tells him so. She just keeps quiet.*

*He's afraid, she knows that; and she knows why. It's death that stalks him and sends him running, the fear of death that rolls him over in his sleep and makes him kick like a puppy at something he can't even touch.*

*And there's nothing she can do, except run with him. She tells him that he's safe with her, again and again she tells him; she's his promise, his guarantee of safety. Of life. A hostage to his fortune.*

*But he won't listen. Or if he listens, he won't understand; or if he understands, he won't believe. He just huddles in the dark, and screams his fear at her; and she listens, and fears with him, with the single-mindedness of possession, of being possessed.*

*If it isn't love she feels, it's something like it. A good imitation. And it'll sure as hell do. It'll have to, because it's all she's got.*

*All he's got, too.*

# PART THREE

*Other Days, Other Faces*

"Julie? Can I see you now, please?"

She nodded and got to her feet, letting her magazine drop back onto the sofa. Colton was a few feet away, fixing a new tip to a pool cue; he looked up too, but Mark met his gaze coldly, and turned away without a word. He was furious with the boy, for bringing Julie here without permission. He'd broken one of the most sacred rules of the refuge, by doing it on his own initiative; and even if Colton wasn't strictly one of the kids any more, he wasn't staff either, not by a long way.

It wasn't really the security risk that angered Mark so much; there was no question but that he would have said yes himself, if he'd still been up when the Samaritans had called. What rankled was that he was certain Colton wouldn't have done it off his own bat, if Mrs Horsley had been around. *The offended pride of usurped authority*, the doctor had called it on the phone that afternoon; and maybe he was right. Probably. But labelling an emotion couldn't affect its potency, however neat and accurate the label. Mark still felt angry with Colton, and was very willing that the boy and the rest of the kids should know it.

But that shouldn't, mustn't affect the way he treated Julie now. He took the girl through to the office, and cleared a chair for her; then he sat down himself.

"Okay, then, Julie. Just a few questions, nothing to worry about. Everybody goes through this. Just relax."

Julie nodded cautiously. "What do you want to know?"

"Well, your full name, first of all." He watched for the usual hesitation, and saw it. "Look, love, it won't go any further, I can promise you that. But you've got to trust us, or we can't help you."

"All right, then. Julie Marchant. Julie *Ann* Marchant."

"That's fine. And how old are you?"

"Seventeen."

"Uh-huh. Where have you come from, Julie?"

"Canterbury."

"Canterbury, got it. Now, would you like to phone home, just to let them know you're all right? You mustn't tell them where you are, but then, I don't suppose you'd want to, would you?"

A single shake of her head said no to both questions: she didn't want to ring home, she didn't want to tell them where she was.

"Would you like me to do it, then? They must be worrying about you, and even a phone-call from a stranger is better than nothing."

"No. Please. I, I'll write to them or something. Just not yet, that's all."

"That's fine. We've got stamps and envelopes and stuff, you only have to ask for them." He tilted his chair back against the wall, stretching his legs out under the desk for balance. "Now comes the difficult bit. Do you want to tell me why you left home? You don't have to, but we can't really help much unless we know. Most of the kids tell us sooner or later – in fact everyone does, sooner or later. No pressure, but I'd like to know now, if you feel up to talking about it."

"Not much to talk about, really," Julie said with a shrug. "Only, Mum went off with some other man when I was a kid, and Dad brought me up. And, he's just married again, and I don't get on with my stepmother, not at all. We're always fighting, and I just, I couldn't cope any more, I'd had enough. So I left."

It was a familiar story, as far as it went. But . . . "Colton tells me you didn't bring anything with you? Not even a change of clothes?"

She shook her head. "It was kind of a spur of the moment thing, you know? I just jumped on a coach and got the hell out of there."

"Mmm. Well, we'll sort out some clean clothes for you, for as long as you're here. That's no problem. But if I were you, Julie, I wouldn't count on staying here very long."

"You mean you're going to throw me out?" A sudden edge in her voice, that made him look at her sharply. There was a panic there, hidden deep but nonetheless real and active; and it seemed out of proportion to her problem. But then, so was everything else she'd done, running away with nothing, going to the Samaritans in the dead of night. Or put it another way, it was classic teenager.

"No, love, of course not. Stick to the rules, and you're welcome here for as long as there's a bed. We've never chucked anyone out yet, and I'm not going to start with you. All I meant was, you don't really need us, except maybe in the short term, while you get yourself sorted out. Look, you're seventeen, that's old enough to leave home legally; you didn't have to run away, and you don't have to hide. If you want to stay in London, you can find yourself a room in a hostel or something, sign on, start looking for a job; no one's going to pick you up and drag you off home. Or you could go back to Canterbury and set up home on your own account, share a flat with a friend, something like that. Your parents couldn't force you back into their house, even if they wanted you."

"Yeah, I guess. But . . ."

"But it's all a bit scary, right?" Mark grinned at her. "I know. It scared the shit out of me, when I left home."

*(Except I didn't, I still haven't. But never mind that.)*

"But just think about it, okay? That's all I'm saying. Get it straight in your own head, what you want to do; then come and talk to me again." Then, with an effort, seizing hold of his anger and setting it deliberately aside: "Talk to Colton first, if you like. He's got a head on his shoulders, that boy, and he knows London better than any of us."

Even as he said it, he admitted wryly to himself that he was only giving official backing to the status quo; Colton had adopted Julie from the moment he brought her in, and had rarely been seen more than ten feet away from her since. With the anger put aside, he could smile about it, remembering how he'd behaved the same way with his own first admission, a girl he'd found in the streets and brought to the refuge. Caren still phoned him occasionally, and had sent him photos of her boyfriend and baby.

Mark knew precisely how Colton was feeling; and he wasn't surprised when there was a sharp tap at the office door half an hour after Julie had gone, and the black boy came in seething.

"Mark, you ain't being fair!"

"How do you mean?"

"Taking it out on Julie just 'cos you're mad at me, that's just shit, man."

"I'm not, Colton. I'm not taking anything out on Julie. I am mad at you, you're right about that, mind."

"You bloody are! As good as told her she'd have to move out bloody quick, that's what you did. And you never done that with anyone else, so . . ."

"So you're jumping to conclusions. Sit down and listen for a minute, kid." And when Colton stayed on his feet, every muscle wire-taut and trembling, "Go on, for God's sake sit *down*. You can beat me up later, okay?"

Colton lowered himself cautiously onto the edge of a chair. "Okay, I'm sitting down. Now what?"

"Now you listen. And I mean *listen*, not argue."

"Okay, I'm listening."

"Good, thanks." Mark picked a pen off the desk, twiddled it between his fingers, and said, "Julie doesn't need to be here, Colton. That's why I talked to her about moving on."

"Oh, great. Where the hell else is she supposed to go?"

"She can go anywhere she likes, that's the point. Legally she hasn't run away, she's just left home; and –"

"She's only sixteen."

"No, she isn't. She's seventeen, she told me just now."

"The Samaritans said sixteen."

"Well, she ought to know her own age. And anyway, she's not on the run from anything, the police don't want her . . . The point is, she's not desperate, Colton mate. She doesn't need a refuge, she just needs somewhere to live. And we're not a hotel, we're a last resort. I'm not asking her to leave, so you can calm down on that score; but as soon as I can, I'll make arrangements for her to move on. She just needs to get away from her family, that's all; and there's a dozen ways for a teenager to do that."

Colton shook his head slowly. "That ain't right, Mark. None of it. If you'd only seen her, when I picked her up . . ."

"Yes, but I didn't see her, did I? You smuggled her in."

"Yeah, all right, we've been through that. But honest, Mark, she was so *scared* . . . I dunno what it is, but she's on the run from something, right enough."

"Not according to what she told me."

"Could be something else, though, couldn't there? Something she didn't tell you?"

Mark shrugged. "I suppose there could be, yes. But she knows we can't help her if she keeps things back, I told her that. And all I can do is go by what she told me, that's how we run this place."

"Yeah, I know." Colton looked at his long fingers for a moment, watched them picking at a mole on his palm; then he said, "Hey, Mark. Fancy a couple of games of pool tonight, then? Best of three, maybe?"

Mark's first instinct was to say yes, his considered response to say no, to rub his anger in. Instead, he temporised. "I thought you said you weren't going to play me again, after last time?"

"Ah, I was just mouthing off. Anyway, I figured, maybe if you stomped me into the ground like you usually do, maybe you'd talk to me again afterwards, you know?" He glanced up quickly, and added, "I'm sorry, I am. I still reckon I was right, mind; but I won't do it again, honest."

"I know." And it was a relief to smile, to let the anger vanish, because it had no place between two of the doctor's fosterlings; and a relief too to be able to trust his instincts. "Best of three, then. But I warn you, no mercy. I'll take you apart."

"I know. You always do. Bugger."

But that last was said with only a smile, not the grin Mark would have expected, and not the relief that should have been mutual; and Colton's obvious preoccupation lasted right through the evening, so that he didn't even give Mark a run for his money.

By midnight, everyone was in bed, except Colton – or so he thought. He was fooling around at the pool table, with his concentration shot to hell and nothing going down, when the hall floor creaked in warning, an announcement of company.

And his concentration was back one hundred per cent, all in a moment; because it was Julie who slipped through the half-open door, barefoot and hesitant.

"Colton, can I just put the radio on, just for a minute, to hear the news?"

"'Course you can. I'll even shut up knocking balls about if you like, so's you can hear."

She smiled and shook her head, and tuned the stereo to Radio Four. She wanted the full bulletin, then, half an hour of it; Colton smiled to himself, *you ain't that clever, girl*, and went out to the kitchen.

Five minutes later, he came back with two mugs of coffee, gave her one, and watched. She wrapped both hands round it for warmth or comfort, and it was a warm night; but didn't drink a sip until the programme was over. Then she lifted her head, and frowned at him.

"What are you staring at?"

"You." He gave her a moment, then added, "You weren't on it, then? The news?"

She didn't jump, or startle; but the mug slipped awkwardly in her fingers, and half the coffee slopped onto the floor.

"Me? Why should I be on the news? I was, I was just interested, that's all. Find out what's happening, you know?"

"Sure. Play pool, do you?"

"A bit. My brother . . . But hadn't I better get a cloth, to mop this up?"

"Nah, don't bother. It'll dry. No one'll notice, come morning. Come on, how's about a game, then? I'll spot you two balls, to make it fair."

For a second, a smile touched her eyes. "You might regret that . . ."

And he did regret it, despite having all his concentration back full strength; he regretted it deeply, when Julie was lining up on her last ball before the black, while he still had three on the table. Then he said:

"Tell me about your brother, then. I didn't know you had a brother –"

– and she miscued dreadfully, sending the cue-ball screwing off behind the black, missing her ball altogether.

"Two shots to me," Colton said cheerfully, stepping up to the table. "So what's your brother's name, then?"

"Er, Terry."

Colton smashed one of his balls into the bottom pocket; the white ball rocketed off the balk cushion and finished up at the top of the table, in perfect position for his next shot.

"Uh-huh. And how does he get on with your step-mother?"

"He, oh, he's a lot older than me, he doesn't live at home. I guess he doesn't really know her . . ."

"Right."

Another shot, another ball into a pocket; and again, and then there was only the black to go, and it went, clean as anything.

"Set 'em up again, eh?" Colton said, fishing for a cigarette. "You can have your revenge. Only this time you don't get spotted nothing."

"Pig."

She started to fish the balls out of the trough they rolled into; he went to help, and said, "This brother of yours. Where's he live, then?"

"Oh, in, um, in London."

"Well, couldn't you have gone to him first, when you went on the dodge? How come you ended up at the Samaritans, wouldn't he have you?"

"He . . ." She stood very still, half bent over with pool balls in her hand, and said, "Please, Colton, can we not talk about my brother? *Please* . . ."

"Okay," he said equably. "Let's talk about you, instead. And I'll start, shall I? Like this. I dunno who you are, or what's going on with you, but I bet your name ain't Julie, and you ain't from Canterbury. You ain't seventeen, even. And you ain't on the run from no cruel stepmother, neither. It's something else, right? But there is something; 'cos the one thing I'm sure about you, girl, you're scared as shit. Even if you have been hiding it ever since you got here."

Very, very slowly, she straightened up; and she opened her hands above the table, to let the balls drop out.

"Bullshit. What are you talking about? I don't know. Come on, whose turn to break?"

"Yours."

*More ways than one. 'Cos you can hold out for a bit if you have to, if it's really that important; but I ain't going to let you be chucked out of here, girl. You wouldn't be safe, I know that much. So I got to break you, somehow . . .*

## 17   Sitting at the Feet of Eros

The girl was sitting hunched in the doorway of an empty office-block, five minutes from Piccadilly. Her arms were wrapped tight around her legs, her cheek resting on one knee, while she gazed listlessly out at the steady flow of early-morning traffic.

She was wearing a torn and sleeveless leather jerkin over a filthy T-shirt, old jeans and ragged tennis shoes, no socks. Her hair was dark and spiky with dirt as much as setting gel, and yesterday's mascara was streaked around her eyes.

She looked cold, exhausted, lost; and above all, young. Too young, much too young to be so numbed and helpless, to be shivering alone in a London doorway at eight o'clock on a summer's morning.

The passing constable looked at her once, and his mind said *junkie*; and he might have left it at that, walked on and left her alone, because he'd passed half a dozen addicts already that morning, and he knew he'd see dozens more around the Dilly before his shift was over. It wasn't that he didn't care; he was still too young himself, too thin-skinned to see addicts as simply another policing problem. But there were just too many of them; and manpower was too short, crime levels were too high, there was too much else needing doing. *If you catch 'em using or dealing, then bring 'em in; otherwise leave 'em to the do-gooders.* That was the standing instruction.

And he would have left this girl as he had left so many others, if he hadn't looked again, and seen no needle-tracks on her bare arms as she stretched forlornly in the sunlight. This time his mind said something else, saw her youth and misery and said *runaway*; and there were plenty of those as well, but at least he wasn't under official orders to ignore them.

So he stopped and went back; and she looked up as his shadow fell across her eyes. For a moment, an odd little half-smile flickered at the corners of her mouth; then she turned her head away, staring down at the cracked marble tiling she sat on.

"What's your name, kid?"

"Alex."

"Alex what?"

"Holden."

"How old are you, Alex?"

"Seventeen," she muttered, with quick defiance. He looked at her thin body and smeared make-up, and said, "Bullshit, Alex. Come on, seriously now. What is it, sixteen?"

She just shrugged.

"So what's your address, then, Alex?"

"I'm staying with friends."

"Your home address?"

"Who cares? I've left home."

He sighed, and took out his notebook. "Alex with an 'e', is it?"

"Yeah. Why do you want to know?"

"Well, I'll tell you, kid. You may be telling the truth about your name; but if you are, that's the only truth you're telling me. I don't think you're seventeen yet, and I don't think you've got anyone to stay with. I think you've run away from home, and you're living out on the streets. Where did you sleep last night, one of the parks?"

She ignored the question, and squinted up at him distrustfully. "What are you going to do?"

"Call a car," he said, reaching for the radio clipped to his jacket. "They'll take you down the station, and a WPC will have a chat with you there. Don't panic, no third degree or anything; if you're lucky, you might even get a hot breakfast."

The girl sighed, and said "Bugger it." And it was odd, but all the dead hopelessness seemed to have gone out of her voice, and she was smiling, no, grinning as she got lithely to her feet with none of the adolescent gawkiness he would have looked for.

She was tall and easy, no nerves, as she said, "Don't do that," and reached into her back pocket to pull out a plastic-covered card. He looked at it, saw the name she'd given him and the letters NUJ; and she said, "I'm sorry, I suppose I've been wasting police time or something; but you're not going to arrest me, are you? I'm a journalist, working under cover."

"Working on what?"

"A story. But do me a favour, and don't ask. And if you see me around in the next few days, look the other way . . ."

She was standing ten yards downwind of a hot-dog stand, counting change in her hand, when a voice behind her said, "What's up, kid, you hungry?"

There was a man standing at her shoulder: thirty-odd, shades, black leather jacket and peaked cap, 501s and Italian shoes. She looked at him, labelled him, nearly told him where to go; but

*(stay in character, Alex girl. Even with creeps like this)*

in the end she just nodded, and waited.

"Short, are you?"

Another nod, as she clenched her fist over the coins.

"Well, I could just give you what you're short of," he said, jingling cash suggestively in his pocket, "but tell you what, I've got a better idea. There's a Wimpy down the road, let's go and eat in the warm, eh? My treat."

"Why?" That was well in character, to be sullen and wary, suspicious of charity.

"Because I don't like eating alone, and you don't like being hungry. Do you? You can't afford to be proud, kid, you'll learn that soon enough."

Time to give in; so she shrugged and nodded, slouched along beside him with a bubble of laughter swelling in her throat and wondered what it was he wanted to sell – drugs? her body? both?

It didn't take long to find out. Sitting hunched over a hot chocolate and a cheeseburger, while he sat back and smoked and watched her eat, she saw a Chinese boy get up and pick his way between the tables. He'd had his eye on them since they came in; but when he reached them he paused as if surprised, as if recognising Alex's companion all in a moment.

"Oy, Tod. I got a complaint. I got a dose off one of your girls last month, and I've been in and out of the clap clinic ever since. I want a refund."

"Sod off, Johnny. You couldn't afford one of my girls."

"No, that's right enough. Worth a try, though. See you around . . ."

The boy winked at Alex, and she gave him a thin smile back, to let him know the message had got through. Then he left, pulling a harmonica from his pocket as he went.

"Stupid git." Tod scowled, and turned his attention back to Alex. "Listen, kid, are you open to a business proposition?"

She might have said yes, she might have had to, to stay in character; but Johnny had given her a cue she could follow, and it would be as well to pick it up. With her editor's two-week deadline looming, she didn't have the time to chase up blind alleys.

So she looked away, and mumbled, "I'm not a whore."

"Sure you're not. And I'm not a pimp."

"That's what that bloke said you were."

"Johnny Chin? He's just a pain in the ass. His sense of humour's going to get him into trouble one of these days. But never mind him. All you've got to worry about is where your next meal's coming from, and where you're going to sleep tonight. And I can help you there. I've got this room you can have, I'll take you there right now. It's got its own shower, loo just down the hall, everything a girl like you could want. And you'll get three meals a day, and pocket money on top."

"Oh, yeah? For what?"

He shrugged. "This and that. A bit of waitressing, maybe a bit of entertaining if you can sing or dance. We'll talk details later. It's just keeping the customers happy, that's all; and the customers like to see pretty girls about the place, that's why I'm talking to you."

Alex shook her head, hard. "No. I'm not a whore."

"Look, I told you . . ."

"Yeah, but I don't believe you, see? I believe that Johnny boy, I reckon he was dead right about you. And I'm not interested."

Tod's expression didn't change, as he stood up and tossed a card onto the table. "You will be, after you've starved a couple of nights. When you change your mind, give me a ring."

*Tod Hunter*, the card said, with a phone number beneath; nothing else. Alex pocketed it carefully, against a future need, and took a cheerful bite of cheeseburger. At least she'd had lunch bought for her; and this was all very educational, even if it wasn't getting her anywhere. Yet.

When she left, she followed the strains of a distant harmonica, and found Johnny busking in a subway, with a hat upturned at his feet. She leant against the wall a few metres away and watched him, and watched the pedestrians who hustled past, or paused to toss a coin into the hat, or stopped and listened for a while before moving on.

After a while he stopped playing, pocketed the harmonica and picked up the hat; then he glanced at Alex, and beckoned her over with a grin and a jerk of his head.

"You got away from Tod okay, then?"

"Yeah, no trouble. I wanted to say thanks for tipping me off, that was nice of you."

"Pleasure. I don't like Tod. He's a bastard to his girls. He's got half of them hooked on smack, just to keep them quiet. But I'll give you a job if you're short."

"Oh, yeah? Doing what?"

"Bottling."

"Y'what?"

"Passing the hat round. I'm going up the arcade, now the sun's out. Get a bit of a crowd together, then you go round with the hat, and I'll split it with you. Deal?"

"Deal."

They made forty pounds in two hours (and there was another article there, perhaps – about the more innocuous ways kids find to make money on the streets); then Johnny called a halt, before the banks closed. He changed the coins for notes, and pressed three fivers into Alex's hand.

"Oh, that's not fair. You did all the work." *And I don't need it, I'm only playing.*

"No, you're a good bottler. Been lucky to make twenty without you. Take it."

She took it.

"Ta, then."

"Where are you staying tonight? And don't just shrug at me, I want to know."

"So do I. I haven't found anywhere yet."

"Thought not. You'd better come along with your Uncle Johnny. I'll fix you up."

Just for a moment, hope flickered into life; there had to be some kids on the street who knew where the refuge was, and Johnny seemed like a good bet. But then he added, "It'll cost you, mind," and that killed it. The refuge couldn't charge.

"Where, then?"

"Same place I stay. Sort of a hostel. Most of us are on the dole, but they don't ask questions, just take your money and squash you in three to a room."

"How much?"

"Tenner a night, cash, if you're passing through. But you get breakfast. It's the best deal you'll find."

Alex felt that she ought to say no, and go on looking; but she was tired, and her feet were getting blisters, and she just couldn't be bothered tonight. So she followed Johnny onto a bus and out to Streatham, to a terrace of tall houses; paid her ten pounds to a fat Irishman, and was allotted a bottom bunk in a back room. She and Johnny had pie and chips for supper, and watched a flickering black-and-white television till eleven o'clock, when the Irishman turned it off and told them to go to bed.

She was up at seven the next morning, well ahead of the pack, fighting hard against the temptation of spending a further pound on a shower. Soap and hot water were a delightful daydream, shampoo was a promise of heaven; but staying dirty was in the script, so she settled for cleaning her teeth and simply scratching her itching scalp.

Last night, she'd agreed with Johnny to go bottling again; but the job had to come first. So she slipped out of the hostel before he was up, leaving a note with the Irishman that said little more than thanks and goodbye, and headed back to the West End.

And once there, and thinking *homeless, penniless,* thinking *runaway,* the tides took her as they take all the homeless and penniless, all the runaway kids in London; and she found herself back in Piccadilly, sitting at the feet of Eros. One of a pack, the world-weary, the frightened, the rebels: but it was a pack of loners, each of them hugging themselves and their secrets, giving nothing away and selling only what they had to to survive.

Easy to become one of them for real, sitting in the sunshine with cold stone beneath her and the roar of traffic all around – easy to forget her job and just let time and ambitions drift away from her, to hold on to nothing but her name and the immediate demands of her body.

But easy or not, she didn't make it, quite – because she saw a blond head go past, with a leather jacket beneath, and her reluctant mind made connections just in time. He was one of the rent boys from the centre, the one she hadn't had a chance to speak to – the one she'd seen later making a pick-up. Sorry, turning a trick.

He shouldn't recognise her, the way she looked now; so she watched him, and blessed her luck as she saw him settle just ten yards away, with tobacco and Rizlas. She took a chance then, and ran across the road to an off-licence to buy a can of lager; but it paid off, because he was still there when she came out, just lighting up.

She pulled the tab off the can, took a swig and went over to join him.

He glanced at her and away again, totally uninterested, until she said, "I'll trade you."

He turned back, puzzled. "What?"

"Half of this, for a fag." She hadn't smoked for five years, but she'd take a chance on that, too.

"Okay."

"Only you'll have to roll it, I don't know how."

He nodded, pulled out a paper and added a pinch of tobacco. *Mean bastard*, she thought cheerfully, watching him roll it thin and tight; then they swapped, cigarette for lager, and she lit up as he drained half the can in two long swallows.

"What's your name, then? I'm Alex."

"Secky." He held on to the can, took another gulp.

She let the silence sit between them for a minute, then said, "Listen, you don't know anywhere I could stay tonight, do you?"

And felt another surge of hope as he smiled, and said, "Maybe."

"Yeah? Where?"

And felt it die again, when he said, "Depends. Got any money?"

"Some. Why?"

"'Cos it'll cost you."

"Fuck that. I shelled out last night, I'm not doing that again."

"Not for the bed, that's free. Long as you like. You just have to tell them you're on the run, that's all."

"What's the money for, then?" Holding her breath.

"Me. For the information. The address."

*Mean bastard.* She fought to hide her excitement with a scowl, and said, "How much?"

"Twenty quid."

"Sod off."

He just shrugged, and drank again. She reached into her jacket pocket and pulled out what Johnny had given her yesterday. "Look, I've got fifteen. You can have that."

He held out a hand for the money, checked it and said, "Okay. Got a pen?"

She wrote the address he gave her on the palm of her hand, and asked, "What kind of a place is it, then?"

"A refuge, they call it. A bunch of creeps run it, but they'll take you in, no bother."

She snatched the can out of his hands and drained it, a silent toast to herself; and walked off singing, to find a phone and call her editor.

## 18 Faith

It was just eleven o'clock as Mark and Jane walked over Waterloo Bridge towards the Hayward Gallery. He'd spent the last hour window-shopping with her, trying to calm her down; but now she was walking slower and slower, watching her feet scuffing the pavement.

"Nothing to be scared of, love," he said quietly. "We're only going to talk."

"I know." But her hand slipped unexpectedly into his, and

he could feel it trembling. He gripped it securely, trying to will some warmth into her cold fingers, making a silent promise to her not to let go until she wanted him to.

A woman was waiting in the gallery entrance, taking a step towards them as they approached. Mark registered short dark hair and fashionable glasses, stylish but comfortable clothes; and he transferred Jane casually from his right side to his left, so that he could shake hands without having to let her stand alone.

"Mrs Burroughs, I presume?" And when she nodded, "I'm Mark, and this is Jane."

"Pleased to meet you. Hullo, Jane." She winked cheerfully at the girl, and produced three entrance tickets. "We don't have to look at the pictures, they're all peculiar in here. But it's a good place to talk, and we can get coffee and doughnuts inside. Oh, and before I forget, Jane, I went to see your friend Ali last week, and she asked me to give you these." She produced a brown paper bag, and held it out. Jane let go of Mark's hand to take it cautiously, peered inside and giggled suddenly.

"Sunflower seeds!"

"For your rats, she said. Did she mean rats?"

Jane nodded. "Charlie and Bobbie. Only they're both girls."

"Well, of course. I had a gerbil called Jeremy, once. She was a girl, too. I'm afraid I've got a confession to make, though; I stole a handful out of that bag, to nibble on the train. I love sunflower seeds. I might have eaten the whole half-pound, except that there was this gentleman in a business suit sitting next to me, who wasn't at all amused. He kept coughing and huffing, and glaring at me as he brushed bits of shell off his trousers . . ."

An hour later, when they left the gallery, Jane was confident enough to walk on the far side of Mrs Burroughs as they saw her back to the tube station; and her hands were too full for her to hold onto Mark, even if she'd wanted to. As well as the sunflower seeds, she was carrying a book Mrs Burroughs had given her, teenagers' own stories of life with foster parents; and she'd bought some postcards from the gallery, to send to Ali and other friends in Ipswich.

After taking delivery of the sunflower seeds, it seemed,

Mrs Burroughs had spent some time talking to Ali's parents, to get an independent view on Jane's home life before she ran away; and what she'd heard from them had convinced her. Now Jane was totally sold on the idea of foster parents, and nothing remained except to locate a suitable family, and complete the formalities. Mark had Mrs Burroughs' promise that she wouldn't rush into it, she'd take her time to find the right people; and in the meantime, she was happy to leave Jane in his care, even without any way to contact him.

Back at the refuge, they found Colton sitting on the stairs, jumping to his feet as they walked in. Mark read the signs – *message, urgent, action required* – and sent Jane off to find the others.

"Go on, go and break the news. No need to keep it quiet now, it's all fixed up bar the shouting."

When she'd gone, he cocked an eyebrow at Colton. "What, then?"

"There was a phone call, while you was out. Remember Taff?"

Taff. Small girl, dirty blonde hair, ring in her nose. Dedicated anarchist, who'd stayed with them a month or so, then moved on to a commune or a squat or some such. Done her best to convert them all to veganism; she'd even sworn at the doctor, on account of his wearing leather shoes. Nice kid, though.

"Yes, I remember Taff. Don't tell me, she's out on the streets again and she wants to come home." And welcome.

"Nah, not her. She's fine. Only, there's this girl turned up at the squat, she's Pakistani and her dad's fixed up a marriage for her back home, some bloke she's never even met. And he wouldn't listen when she said she didn't want to, so she just ran away. Taff says they can keep her there for a bit, only she thought she might rather come here, so she rang up to see if there was room."

"There's room. What did you say?"

"Just we had space, but she'd have to ask you. She's going to ring back this evening."

"Thanks, Colton." *For waiting, for not going round to get her straight off* – only he didn't need to say that aloud, it was implicit and understood in the smile they swapped, the jerk of his head that brought Colton following him down the passage and into the office.

"Going to take her, then?"

"Yes, of course, if she wants to come. You know that."

"She'll want. Taff didn't say, exactly, but I sort of got the idea this girl ain't too happy at the squat – and they ain't too happy with her, either. Like they were fighting all the time, something like that."

No surprises there; if she'd been brought up a Muslim, she'd probably find an anarchist squat pretty hard to take, however Westernised she thought herself. Mark sat down behind the desk, ran a quick check-list through his mind of the things he had to do that evening, and groaned.

"Look, Colton, would you like to go and fetch her tonight, if she does want to come? I'm getting swamped here, and I'll never catch up otherwise."

"Yeah, sure. If I can find it. I dunno where Taff lives."

"Neither do I. But don't worry, you'll find it. Have a bit of faith, boy."

"Yeah, right. Faith."

Jane was still talking excitedly about her future when they all crowded into the games room after dinner, to watch television. Nina scowled, and turned the volume up pointedly; but Jane took no notice, she just went on talking.

". . . and Mrs Burroughs says there's a gymnastics club in town that I could join, she's going to find out all about it for me . . ."

"For Christ's sake cut it out, will you?" Nina snapped, hunching closer to the screen. "We're not interested, get it?"

"You speak for yourself." That was Davey, back in his old role as Jane's champion, trying to redeem himself. He crossed the room to sit beside her, and she hardly flinched, almost managed to smile. "I want to hear it. It's more interesting than bloody *Coronation Street*, anyway."

"'Course it is. It's real, innit?" Colton joined in from his perch on the pool table; and when Nina looked round for support from the two new girls, she didn't find it. Both were sitting in corners: Mandy quiet and still on an old upright, hands on her stomach and her head down, seemingly unaware that there was even anyone else in the room; and Julie crouched on the floor, in the shadows, arms tight round her knees and eyes jerking round the room again and again, from face to face to the window, to the door, watching everything and trusting nothing.

Nina hissed resentfully, *thanks for the support, sisters*; and Colton said, "What's the matter with you, anyway? Ain't you glad that Jane's getting sorted out?"

"The only thing I'm glad about," in a clear, vicious voice, "is that those fucking rats'll be going with her. It's disgusting, keeping rats in the house. We're lucky we haven't all got the plague off those flea-ridden things."

"They're not flea-ridden!" Jane protested furiously. "They've never had fleas, I'm dead careful about that . . ."

"Ah, don't you listen to her, sweet, she's only jealous." Davey smiled awkwardly, and said, "Have you told them yet?"

"Told them what?"

"That you'll be moving on soon. Rats like to be kept in touch, you know. In fact, they have to be. You can't go until the decision's been ratified, now can you?"

Colton groaned, and Nina yelled for silence; but Jane was all giggles and forgetfulness, and Davey lost his caution as he got to his feet. "Come on, then, let's go and rattle their bars, see if they get ratty."

"Can't, they've only got wire netting, and it doesn't rattle."

"Rats. We'll just have to feed 'em sunflower seeds, then, and watch 'em get seedy . . ."

They left the room laughing, easy with each other for the first time in days. Then Colton heard the phone ring, and stop ringing; and a few minutes later Mark called him out of the room.

"You still on to fetch this girl from the squat?"

"Yeah, sure."

"Good. Her name's Tia, and they're expecting you. Now, it shouldn't be too hard to find; you probably know the area already."

Mark gave him detailed directions; and as soon as Colton had them fixed in his head, he collected his jacket and, on an impulse, put his head round the games room door.

"Julie, fancy a walk? I've got to pick this girl up; and you haven't been out all day, so I thought, maybe you'd like to come along . . ."

Julie shook her head, hard and definite.

"Oh. Okay, then. If you're sure . . ."

And Colton went alone, telling himself, *It's not you, boy. She might've said yes if things was normal. She's just scared, that's all, too scared to go out, even; and Mark's wrong about her, I know he is . . .*

"Here, give us that."

Colton held out his hand, as they stumbled side by side across the rubble; and the girl passed her bag over with a grunt. He swung it up onto one shoulder, and reached out with the other arm to help her as she slipped on a loose brick.

"Tia, is it?"

"Yeah, Tia." She pulled free of his grasp when they hit the pavement; but that was okay, she didn't know him from Adam, no reason why she should want to stay close.

He had reason enough to regret it, though, looking at her now in the light of a shop window. He hadn't seen anything hardly in the squat, with just a few thin candles burning and the fire down to a glow; long hair and a slim figure, that was all he knew. And a chilly atmosphere, that told him both sides were glad she was leaving. Taff had been the only one to bother with a goodbye, and she'd been pretty surly about it.

But now he looked at big, dark eyes, soft skin two shades lighter than his own, a nose with this sexy little gold stud in it; and he thought, *Jesus, I'm glad you're not going to marry that dildo in Pakistan. Marry you myself, given half a chance . . .*

"Funny place, was it, the squat?" he asked, in a hurry to fill the silence. Some people could read silences like a book.

"Funny? It was fucking *weird*, man." There was a rich, rolling scorn in her voice, that she made no effort to hide or disguise. Colton got the impression that maybe she hadn't tried to hide it back there either, which would explain the atmosphere as she left. "All these bloody hippies, smoking dope and dropping acid, and *talking* – talk talk talk, all the time, never doing anything. Christ, I'm glad to be away from there."

They walked for a minute or two without speaking; then she said, "So tell us about this refuge place, then."

"Not much to tell. It's a big house, you'll get a room to

yourself; three meals a day, all that kind of stuff, and you can stay as long as you like, pretty much. They won't throw you out till you got somewhere else to go, anyway."

"Yeah, that's what Taff said. But I don't get it, it must cost a fortune to keep it going. Who runs it, anyway?"

"The doctor." Even before Mrs Horsley had her accident, there had always only been one answer to that question. She and Mark might run it day to day, but the refuge was the doctor's and that was that.

"What doctor? What's his name?"

"Don't ask that, not ever. He's just the doctor, that's all."

Back at the refuge, Mark took charge of Tia, getting her settled into another of the attic rooms. With the responsibility gone from him, Colton drifted uncertainly from room to room, until at last he found Julie standing at the window on the landing, with her cheek against the cool glass and her eyes closed, hiding in the light. And his responsibility for her was something solid and real and continuing, something that Mark couldn't touch, could neither sanction nor deny; so Colton whistled softly, not to frighten her, and touched her on the arm.

Her eyes opened, slowly focused.

"Hullo, Colton."

"Hullo, Julie." He said it as flatly as she had, mimicry without mockery; then he smiled. "Fancy a game of pool before bed? No one's on the table, I checked."

"Okay, then."

He sensed that what enthusiasm she could whip up wasn't so much for the game, as for putting off the time she had to go to bed; from the look of her she wasn't sleeping any more than Mark was.

But let that go, for now. As long as she wanted to stay up, he was happy to stay with her; and the pool was only a device for him, too. Tonight, he was determined, she was going to talk.

They played two games, and won one each; then, setting the balls up for the decider, he said, "Taught you how to play, did he, wosname, this brother of yours?"

He remembered the name well enough; Terry, she'd called him. But from the look on her face, she didn't; so he let the silence sit for a moment, and went cheerfully on.

"You were dead funny about him, the other night. Like you couldn't even bear to talk about him. What's up, have a row, did you?"

"Yes, I suppose." She muttered it to her cue-tip, and wouldn't look at him. "It's private, though. All right?"

"Yeah, fine. You break."

*More ways than one.*

There was a steady stream of people looking in to say good night, Mark almost the first and Davey the last; and after the Irish boy had clattered his way upstairs, Colton potted the black once more (four-three in his favour, skin of his teeth), and leant his cue against the wall, stretching long and slow.

"That's enough, my eyes are going."

Julie didn't argue, she simply nodded and helped pull the cover over the table.

"I ain't tired, though, just knackered," Colton said reflectively. "You going to bed, or what?"

She shook her head, and he thought, *no, 'course you're not. It's dark up there, ain't it, girl? And you're scared of the dark.*

"Good," he said aloud. "Let's talk, eh?"

"What about?"

"Same as last time. You. The way I remember it, I called you a liar, and you changed the subject bloody quick. Do you want me to run through it all again? 'Cos I could, I've got a bloody good memory. Give it to you word for word, if you like."

A jerk of the head, *no, not again, leave me alone*, and she turned away; but he was wired up to fight for it tonight, to get the truth out of her one way or another, any way he had to. So he dodged round her quick, and blocked the door before she could get away; and said, "No, wait. Don't run out on me. Please?"

She hesitated, then turned again and went to the window. He followed her, awkward and unsure.

"I don't get this, really I don't. Why don't you trust us? And how long's it going to take, before you come clean?"

"I don't know. I just can't, that's all. I do trust you – I mean, I trust *you*," and her hand found his unexpectedly, clung to it. "I do. But, I just can't talk about it . . ."

"Sure you can." He took a deep slow breath, finding himself in sudden confrontation with his own ghosts; and another for the touch of her against his palm, slender bones beneath cold skin. "Listen, it's easy, once you start. I should know. Anyone told you how come I ended up here?"

She shook her head.

"Okay, listen up and I'll tell you myself. It's a long story, mind, so we might as well get comfy."

He led her over to the sofa, still holding her hand,

*(not daring to let go, in case it looked like a rejection; and not wanting to anyway, because it felt so good, never mind whether it helped her or not)*

and they settled down side by side. He loosened his grip experimentally, just in case; but she hung on tighter, and that was enough.

"One thing, though," he said softly. "What's your real name? You can tell us that, can't you? I won't pass it on, if you don't want me to."

She bit her lip, and brushed long hair back off her face; and said, "Kez. Kez Hughes. Keryn."

"Hi, Kez." For a minute, maybe more, he said nothing else, simply sitting and looking at her with a half-smile on his face, holding her hand.

She shifted restlessly, said, "What now?"

"Eh? Oh, nothing. Just, I was thinking. I like your friend Julie – but I'd rather talk to you."

"Well, go on then. Say something."

"Yeah, well. I almost killed my stepfather, see? That's what happened to me. I was fourteen, and I got in from school, and my kid sister was crying upstairs, in the bathroom. She was eleven then, too big to cry without a reason. So I went up, and my stepfather was in there with her, and he'd got all her clothes off, and he was – well, *playing* with her, like she was a big doll. Sticking his fingers into her, while she stood there and cried. And I had this cricket-bat with me, right there in my hand it was; and I didn't even think about it, I just went for him. And I was, I was going to kill him. There was blood all over, and . . ."

And he broke off suddenly, because he could feel her trembling beside him; and all the fear was back in her face again, out of hiding and running rampant.

"You don't want to hear this, do you?"

Her head jerked from one side to the other, all she could manage in the way of a negative.

Colton put his free arm tentatively round her shoulders. She leant against him, shaking, and he had to tighten his grip simply to stop her falling.

"What is it, Kez? Come on, you got to tell me now. Is it the blood, or the sex thing? Something's started you off." And when she still didn't or couldn't answer, he said, "Or is it both? Kez, why really won't you talk about your brother?"

After two nights of exhausted unconsciousness, Mark had just about caught up on his sleep ration; and now it was playing games with him again, dodging and dancing around behind his eyes, teasing and tempting and sliding away from his grasp.

At two o'clock he gave up for the moment, pulled a dressing-gown on and went downstairs

*(only remembering about the doctor's pills halfway down, and shrugging the thought off before he reached the bottom, no trouble)*

to get a drink. There was a light still on in the games room; and when he looked in he found Colton and Julie on the sofa, his arm round her shoulders and his cheek in her hair.

"Colton . . ."

He looked up with no guilt, nothing furtive about him; and maybe Mark was jumping to conclusions, because the boy's face was sombre and serious.

"Mark, can you sit down a minute? You ought to hear this. It's okay if I tell him, ain't it?" he went on to Julie. "He's got to know, but you ain't got to go through it all again . . ."

The girl's expression was hidden by long falls of hair; but she straightened up suddenly and brushed it all back, to show Mark a face that might have been sculpted in stone.

"It's all right, Colton," and the voice was stone too, or porcelain, perhaps – clean and white and hard and ready to shatter any time. "I'll tell him. It's my story."

When the story was told, Mark sat quiet for a long time, well out of his depth and scrabbling desperately in his mind for some solid ground to start from. Finally he gave up, and passed the buck weakly back to Kez.

"So what do you want to do now?"

Kez only shook her head, drained; it was Colton who answered for her. "She wants to stay here. You can't make her move out now, not with that bastard out there somewhere, looking for her . . ."

"No, of course not. That wasn't what I meant. You're welcome to stay, Kez, for as long as you need us." And he knew they could help her, too, while she was in their care. Her pain was deep and all-consuming, but they'd faced such extremes of pain before, and helped kids over or around. Hell, he'd walked that journey himself, he knew every step of the way. But for once that was the lesser concern. "But you ought to go to the police, love. He's got to be stopped."

"I can't."

"Well, it's your decision; but . . ."

"I know. But. Only I've been through all the buts, over and over; and I still can't. I've got no evidence anyway, just what I saw on a dark night, my word against his; and even if that was enough, I don't think I could stand up in court and say it. *My brother's the Oxford rapist.* No. I just couldn't. He's my *brother*! I hate what he's done, but . . ."

But. Whichever way they argued it, they kept tripping over that same small word, and ending up back where they started, at the heart of uncertainty.

In the end it was Colton who found a way out for them both, proposing a compromise that left Kez out of it altogether and committed Mark to no more than a phone-call. It was shifting the buck again, and little more; but it was good enough, for that time of night and that particular situation. If it didn't work, they'd just have to talk again.

So Mark went off to the office, to look up the number of the Oxford police; and he left Kez and Colton as he had found them, with her curled up tight against the boy's side, clutching one hand fiercely in both of hers. His other arm was around her shoulders and his cheek against her hair, his face betraying only a determination not to move before she did, before she wanted him to.

## OXFORD RAPIST – MAN SOUGHT

### By Our Crime Correspondent

For over a year, Oxford women have been terrorised by a series of vicious sex assaults. At least seven girls have been attacked and brutally raped by a knife-wielding madman.

But in a startling new development this morning, the Thames Valley police have taken the unusual step of issuing the name and description of a man they wish to question in connection with the case.

Sebastian Hughes is twenty-four years old and six feet tall, with blue eyes and short blond hair. He is slim and well-spoken, and may be driving a white Mini, registration number VPG 312A.

Superintendent David Chisholm said, "A man telephoned us in the early hours of this morning, with information concerning last week's attack on Anita Shapworth. He didn't give his name, but said he was calling on behalf of the girl who found Anita, helped her to safety and immediately disappeared. We don't know who that girl was; but Sebastian Hughes' younger sister Keryn has been missing from home since the night of the attack, as has her brother.

"Following that telephone call," the Superintendent went on, "enquiries were made at the Hughes' home in Oxford-shire; and we are now looking for both Sebastian and Keryn as a matter of urgency. I would stress that Sebastian is almost certainly carrying a knife, and may be desperate enough to use it. He is regarded as extremely dangerous, and members of the public could be risking their lives if they attempted to detain him."

The *Evening Star* has obtained a recent photograph of Sebastian Hughes and his sister, known as 'Kez'. If you think you have seen either of them, you should phone the police *immediately*.

Sebastian knew it all already, long before he slipped down to pick up Jenny's evening paper from the hall. He'd caught it on the one o'clock news, seen his own face staring back at him from the television screen, laughing at him. It was a photograph taken early that summer, with his arm looped oh-so-casually round his loving sister's neck,

*(and too bad it couldn't be like that again, just for two minutes, Kez within his reach and her neck there, ripe for the wringing)*

and both of them laughing at the camera lens, at their camera-crazy mother. And how she must be hating her life now, and her children, for bringing all this down on her: the panic of two disappearances, and then a dawn raid from the police, questions and accusations and a demand for photographs . . .

But Sebastian had no sympathy to spare, not even for his unintended victims, not even for family. No sympathy, and no time; because it wouldn't be long before some busybody reported his car, parked in a cul-de-sac half a mile away. And once the police turned their attention to London in general and Hampstead in particular, they'd be ringing Jenny's bell in no time at all. That was what Hampstead meant to the Hughes family, after all – Jenny, and Jenny's hospitality. They'd be round before you could say Sebastian Hughes, to break the door down and drag him away . . .

Except that he wasn't going to be dragged, because he wasn't going to be here when they came. And he wasn't going to leave any evidence behind him, either. That was something to be remembered, after all; they still didn't have any direct proof, they couldn't have. There'd only ever been the knife he used, the balaclava to hide his face and the cagoule to keep the blood off his clothes; and he'd never taken them into the house. They lived in a carrier bag in the boot of the car, always; and now that carrier bag was lost in a black bin-liner at a motorway service station between Oxford and London. No reason to suppose they'd ever find that.

There was always biological evidence, of course, when and if they did pick him up: genetic fingerprinting, blood and semen samples, all of that. But even if they'd managed to collect samples from some of his

*(clients, call them clients)*

it might not stick, if there were nothing else against him.

And there wasn't anything else. Nothing definite, nothing to say *guilty*.

Except, of course, dear little sister. And dear little sisters could be silenced, if they could only be found in time. Found before the police found them, or him.

Kez hadn't even blown him herself, that was the curious thing. She must have taken shelter with some guy, who'd phoned in for her; from the sound of it, she was hiding from himself and the police both. Which suited Seb fine, because at least it gave him a breathing-space. There was still hope that he could get to her first, before she even gave her story to the police, let alone repeated it in a court.

But first things first – and the first thing was to get the hell out of Jenny's flat, without leaving anything behind that could incriminate him. He was sorry now that he'd given in to the giggle, and put Jenny into the freezer; that was just helping to preserve things for the forensic labs. Still, he could do something about that before he left.

First, though – not knowing how well fingerprints might survive fire – he pulled on a pair of Jenny's rubber gloves and went through the flat with a cloth, wiping all the paint-work he could reach, all the furniture, every smooth surface that might hold a print. Then, with one eye on the clock and the other on the fire escape, just in case his time was out already, he opened the freezer lid to have a look.

And the luck was riding with him still, good and strong; because he'd forgotten to switch it onto 'Freeze', and Jenny wasn't frozen, only stiff, with a skin of ice. So he built a careful bonfire in her bedroom, carried her through and laid her on top of it like a guy. He had to take a minute out then, leaning against the wall with his eyes closed, running a hand down over his sweating face, breathing hard against a sudden attack of the shakes. The next move was out beyond the door; and there were too many people out there, too many eyes – windows like eyes, and lights like eyes, and even the bloody *stars* would be watching and maybe shuffling themselves around when his back was turned, to spell his name across the sky . . .

But he couldn't hide any more, he had to get out and be doing; and he had eyes too, he could stare them all down if he had to. Stare the stars out of the sky.

He ran quickly from room to room, turning on every gastap in the flat: four rings, the oven, all the fires. Then he lit the bonfire under Jenny, and left her.

He opened the flat door cautiously, just an inch, and listened for noises on the landing. Nothing; so he slipped out, pulled the door quietly shut behind him and hurried up the stairs, to 2b.

A finger on the bell, and wait,

*(gloved hands in pockets, feet shuffling on the carpet, head down and huffing, like a man in the cold at a bus-stop – waiting, and very much in the cold, never mind the weather)*

footsteps on the other side and the door pulled confidently open, just a moment's pause before a smile touched the old woman's face.

"I remember you, young feller. You're Jenny's friend, aren't you? The one who climbed over the railings."

"That's right." Smiling easily, with the charm that was second nature. "And you're Mrs Richardson. I was wondering,"

*(wondering too late, because he should have checked it with Jenny long ago, shouldn't have to do it now)*

"is Mr Richardson at home?"

She chuckled. "No good to you if he was, lad, whatever you want him for. He's been dead twenty years."

It was presumably conventional regrets she paused for then, perhaps embarrassment she was looking for on his face; but if so she must have been disappointed, finding nothing but relief.

"That's good, that's very good."

Out of the cold and into the fire; and his hands, nowhere near his pockets now, his hands took her hard by the neck, closing her throat off, sealing her life inside with its bedmate death. She kicked and flailed, staggering back into the flat, bouncing off one wall to the next. Sebastian used one foot to push the door shut behind them; then he simply kept his grip and his feet and went with her, until at last she stumbled and dropped, and was nothing but dead weight on his arms. He let her fall and followed her down, keeping up the pressure for certainty's sake.

And when he was certain, he went through her pockets, through her handbag, through her flat: taking all the money he could find, turning on the gas-taps, starting a blaze in the bedroom.

Out again and down the stairs, quick but careful, and please let's not meet anyone now – and oh how that luck was strong, taking him down and out and away from there, no trouble.

## 20   Legitimate Behaviour

Alex paused on the corner, telling herself it was just for a final check, nothing to do with nerves. She had her street clothes on again, so she knew she looked right; and she was still filthy, even after a day talking to her editor and making her own plans, even after a night spent in her own flat, her own bed.

She had a carrier bag with her now, stuffed with a few more old clothes, no problem there; and she'd left her NUJ card at home, not to be caught out before she was ready. She was only taking one chance, with a camera and two rolls of film wrapped in a sweatshirt at the bottom of the bag; but she had to risk that. She could hardly bring a photographer in with her. And at least it was the kind of camera a teenage girl might well carry, simple but not too cheap, last year's Christmas present from her parents or a working boyfriend.

So. *Off we go, then, Alex girl.*

But it was still a long pause and a deep slow breath before

she walked on down the street; and she still walked slowly, looking round her, stopping by a tree at the pavement's edge to run her hand over the rough bark and trace some carved initials with a fingertip. Telling herself that it was legitimate behaviour for a runaway with sore feet, who was bound to be nervous, of course she was . . .

*Cairey Grant plc*, *Amersham Electronics*, *Davis & Davis plc* – it seemed the whole street had been annexed by overflow businesses avoiding city centre prices. The large detached houses were company property, the new-registration Volvos and BMWs were company cars, even the trees in the gardens were company trees; and she didn't see how a teenage refuge could possibly hope to hide in such an alien environment.

Until she found the right house, and saw that it had a sign of its own. There was the street number, repeated on both left and right corners, for her to check against the address on her palm; and underneath THE HARLBOROUGH INSTITUTE, and a logo made up from the initial letters H and I, intertwined.

She looked up and saw a teenage boy moving behind a window, and knew she'd come to the right place. And decided as she made her way up the gravel drive that they were no fools, this lot. Make it look and sound official enough and few people would ever ask or even wonder what the Harlborough Institute was, what it actually did.

Presumably that was a question they had a nice pat answer for, in case anyone ever did ask; but one thing was for sure, they wouldn't need it much longer. Not after her story hit print . . .

Alex smiled to herself, *intrepid reporter risks all to bring you the TRUTH!* – and ducked her head quickly to hide the smile from any inquisitive eyes at the windows. She trudged on slowly, limping a little and watching her torn canvas shoes kicking through the gravel, well in character.

The drive opened out into a wide area in front of the house, room to turn a car. The house itself was three storeys of Victorian brick, all bay windows and gables, and a slate roof; Alex saw concrete stairs going down to a cellar door, an iron fire-escape clinging to one side wall, and on the opposite side a more recent addition, a garage with folding wooden doors.

The front door was an imposing affair, at the top of a short flight of stone steps. Alex chewed a knuckle hesitantly, then dragged herself up it step by slow step, not acting at all.

To the left of the door was a brass plaque with the same information as the sign at the gateway, street number, name and logo, nothing else. To the right was an old-fashioned bell-push.

Committed now, Alex put her thumb on the button and pressed it almost jauntily, almost as a challenge to her own nervousness. This was a job, nothing more – and it was the job she wanted, digging out secrets, telling the world what it needed or wanted to know. And in this case, cocking a cheerful snook at the police and the courts, who had been looking for the refuge for months and getting nowhere; and giving an explosive V-sign with accompanying raspberry to the rest of her profession, as she scooped every paper in the country and most particularly the *London Daily Herald* . . .

She waited for a minute, two minutes; and was about to ring again when the door opened, and a man looked out at her. Middle twenties, five-ten, dark curly hair neither fashionably short nor fashionably long, just scruffy . . . Alex's hand clenched in a private celebration; it was the same guy, the man from the High Court who so obviously hadn't been a journalist. That made her right twice over – once that he was worth following and checking up on, and again that she could find the refuge anyway, without him. Find him.

The refuge worker

*(too young to be the boss, surely?)*

asked what she wanted, while his eyes scanned her face, her clothes and her carrier-bag and knew it all already. And answered a vital question in the process, because he obviously didn't recognise her. Not yet, anyway. Not too surprising; all he would have seen in court was beret and sunglasses, and maybe a flash of copper hair. Oh yes, and plenty of leg. Cool and confident and trendy, and nothing like the frightened, filthy teenager who was on his doorstep now.

"Please," she said. Passed a dry tongue across dry lips, and tried again. "Someone said I could get a bed here. I haven't got any money, but . . ."

"You don't need money." He looked at her a moment longer, with a hint of a frown that clearly wasn't aimed at her, not personally; then he looked past her, down the drive; and at last he stepped back, and smiled.

"Come on in, love. What's your name? I'm Mark."

"Alex. Alex Holden." No point lying about that, no one was going to recognise it.

"Okay, then, Alex. We're going to have to have a talk a bit later," and again that quick frown, and an anxious glance through the door to something out there, in the world, "but never mind that now. What would you like first, coffee and something to eat? Or a bath? Or just a bed to crash on?"

She bit her lip savagely, and whispered, "A coffee. If that's all right . . ."

"It's what we're here for, kid. Come on through to the kitchen."

She followed him across the parquet flooring in the hall, down a corridor and into a roomy kitchen. There was a lean black boy perched on a long wooden table, tapping ash from a cigarette into a saucer; he blew a careful smoke-ring, smiled at the guy – Mark –

*(Mark who? Find out)*

then glanced at her with a friendly curiosity and maybe something more, an adolescent's sexual interest.

"Colton, this is Alex."

"Hullo, Alex."

She half smiled, well into her role. He grinned, stretched and got easily to his feet, while Mark went to fill the kettle. Alex hadn't seen any signal pass between them, but Colton had apparently got the message; he reached out a hand for his cigarettes, then checked himself and left them on the table.

"Help yourself, if you want one." He gave Alex a cheerful wink, dodged around her with a deliberate sway of the hips and went out. She watched him go, thinking *I've seen you somewhere before, too*; but left that for the moment, as Mark said:

"Sit down, Alex, before you fall down. You look knackered."

"Yeah." He wasn't wrong there; she'd hardly slept at all last night, familiar bed or not. She slumped into a wooden chair by the table, and

*(stay in character, as long as you can)*

reached for a cigarette.

Colton went into the games room, where Jane was struggling over a thousand-piece jigsaw on the big table. Mandy was sitting on the other side, probably supposed to be helping; but she wasn't even looking at the pieces, just sitting with her hands folded protectively across her stomach, guarding the life that was growing inside. Colton thought suddenly that he'd never seen her sit any other way, except when she was eating; but thought maybe it was natural, maybe you just couldn't think of anything else for long, when you were pregnant. 'Specially if you were pregnant and panicking, no boyfriend and no home, no obvious future. And it seemed to follow naturally from that to wonder how it would feel for him, to be a father; and he thought he'd like it, sort of. Not yet, sure, but some time. Only he'd do it right, be sure she wanted it too; and he'd never treat her like poor Mandy had been treated, never just dump her. Whoever she was, he'd give her a home and a future, love her and the kid too, love 'em half to death . . .

He grinned, shook his head, and looked around. Nina and Tia were on the sofa, talking about something or other, and Davey was at the pool table, playing himself. That was all of them,

*(except for Kez, and he knew about her)*

so he shut the door and said, "Listen, don't nobody go into the kitchen for a bit. Mark's in there with a new girl, and he'll want to talk to her."

"Her at the door, was it?" Davey asked. "So where's she come from? I've heard no one on the phone today."

"I dunno. Mark didn't mention she was coming, so I don't reckon he knew. Maybe she just turned up. Anyway, she's here."

Jane turned round. "What's she like?"

"Dunno, I only saw her for a second. Tall, skinny. Looks like she's been sleeping rough for a week." He hesitated, then added, "Tell the truth, she looks like she does smack, or something. Sort of pretty, though."

*(Dead sexy, he'd bet, if she did herself up a bit. But not his type, not with her hair chopped short like that. It might be trendy, but he liked it long, to run his fingers through and watch it fall. He'd kill, for a girl with hair like that. Like Tia. Or Kez. 'Specially Kez . . .)*

And as if he'd spoken her name aloud, Nina glanced up and said, "Where's what's-her-name, Julie, Kez, whatever? Lost her, have you?"

"No, I ain't lost her. She's upstairs. In her room." Asleep, he hoped, because she sure as hell wasn't sleeping at night. He'd taken one look at her this morning, and told her to go back to bed. And she'd gone, too, except *I don't want to be alone*, she'd said; so he'd gone with her, stared out of the window while she'd undressed, then held her hand till she dozed off. And even then he'd sat for a long time with her slack fingers linked with his, just watching her, really churned up inside. She was still wearing his rugby shirt for a nightie, though he knew Mark had offered her a real one out of the cupboard; and that got to him more than anything else, sometimes. Like it made him responsible for her. Scary, that was. But he didn't tell her, because she'd probably only laugh at him. He'd never heard her laugh yet; and when he did, he couldn't stand for it to be like that, not at him for being stupid, making things up . . .

So he'd sat quietly, mulling it all over in private, in his head, until she turned over in her sleep and her hand pulled free of his. Then he'd slipped out of the room and come downstairs, lit a cigarette and sat smoking in the kitchen, wanting to be alone.

But Mark and the new kid, Alex, had disturbed him; and now he had to face Nina's mocking voice, saying, "So how come you're not up there with her? Thought you had a new job, her shadow."

"She's in bed."

"Like I said. How come you're not with her?"

He wanted to hit her, for that; but he wasn't Davey, he'd never got into a fight at the ref yet and he bloody well wasn't going to start now. Not with Mark and the doctor both trusting him, so that he was practically doing Mark's old job now, with Mrs H in hospital. He forced a smile, said, "She didn't ask me. Anyway, it's against the rules."

"Oh, yeah. Dead hot for the rules, you are."

"'S'right."

He turned his back on her then, and went to the pool table. "Game, Davey?"

*Got to do something, just till Kez comes down. Then yeah, I'll be her shadow, long as she'll have me . . .*

". . . And, I don't know, I just couldn't stand it any more, not with both of them on my back all the time, so I just thought fuck it, I'm off. Came down last week, I've been sleeping in bus stations, stuff like that . . ."

Mark made a soft noise in his throat, calm and encouraging; then he stood up, reaching to take her mug. As he passed behind her on the way to the sink, he dropped his free hand onto her shoulder. She flinched, and pulled away.

"Don't touch me!"

He stopped dead, and she could guess easily at his thoughts from the expression on his face. He was wondering if that was just a nervous reaction, or something more; and he had to make the right decision now, that was crucial. She'd nudge him if she had to, but it'd be so much better if he got there all by himself . . .

In fact he was there already, saying gently, "You've been moving stiffly ever since you arrived. I thought maybe it was only the sleeping out, but . . . Your dad beat you up, did he? Or your mother?"

"Both of 'em," she muttered. "All the time. But I'm okay."

"The hell you are, if it hurts for me to touch you. I'll get the doctor to come and have a look at you this evening."

"What doctor?"

"Just the doctor. Like Doctor Who, you know? He doesn't have a name. Not in here. But he'll help, I promise. Now listen, just one more question, all right? And this one's important. I've got to know how you found out about this place, where you got our address from."

"Why's that matter?"

He half smiled. "Because whoever it was gave it to you, they shouldn't have. Not that we don't want you here, love, you're very welcome. But no one's supposed to go giving our address out, even to kids who need it. There's a system, and everyone knows they should phone here first. Then we would've come to pick you up. So who was it, Alex?"

"What, so's you can bollock him, you mean?" She shrugged listlessly. "You're welcome. Guy called Secky, down Piccadilly. And the bastard didn't give me the address, he bloody sold it to me, didn't he? Fifteen quid it cost me, all the money I had left . . ."

At lunch, meeting the rest of the refugees over sausages and beans, Alex remembered where she'd seen Colton before. She heard an Irish voice, and thought, *Davey FitzAlan*; and saw a bleached head with dark roots just showing at the shaved sides, and remembered the two boys together in the street, when she'd been scouting the bus-route just on the off-chance. So she'd been that close, even then. *It's a miracle this place has stayed hidden as long as it has. That's three ways I could have found it. What the hell have the police been up to, all this time?*

Not that it mattered, what the police had been up to. They were too late now, that was the important thing; and even more important, so were the other papers. She'd get her story in before the weekend, even if she stayed two or three days here. And she'd have a by-line, and probably interviews on radio or TV when the other media picked it up, and the law came following . . .

But never mind daydreams, she was supposed to be working. The most useful thing right now would be getting to know the kids; but her adopted persona prohibited too much open curiosity. So in the main, she stayed quiet and simply listened, and looked at their faces.

Most particularly, she looked at the girl with the long brown hair and the pale face, who ignored her food and watched the windows; and she listened to Colton, who was sitting next to the girl and alternately bullying and cajoling her.

"Come on, Kez, you got to eat, girl. You ain't nothing but bones anyway, and you ain't gonna go all wotsit on me, anorexic, I ain't gonna let you . . ."

It wasn't a difficult equation, even for a cub reporter off the social pages. Kez went into Keryn, Keryn *Hughes*, once with nothing over; and that face went very well with another, because the two of them were all over the front pages and the news bulletins. And it was that second face that Kez was looking for so urgently, that she kept expecting to see at any window . . .

*Safe? Oh, no. Safe he isn't, not what you could call safe. But he's getting there. He's working for it.*

*Or – like now – it's her that does the work. He lies curled in on himself, in the dark, and calls her name; and as always, she's there to listen, to do what he wants. No questions.*

*So she stands for a moment, sees stairs rising in front of her, hears nothing but his voice still in her head, a scream in a whisper. And she goes up.*

*And when she gets there, when she gets inside – it's only imagination, of course it is, because she knows he isn't really standing behind her, hot eyes watching, hot breath on her neck. But all the same she feels it, feels him, the breath and the eyes, the fear.*

*And oh yes, he's right to be afraid, because there's danger here; danger that greets her – them – with a scuffle, claws on paper, rasping like a cat's-tongue echo in her head. But you don't need to be scared, we're not in nightmare country here. Not yet. It's her that has the nightmares. And him too, she thinks, only she doesn't know that for sure. She can't dream his dreams for him, and he doesn't talk about what happens when he sleeps.*

*She steps forward, and caution gloves her hands in a carrier bag for safety, got to be safe. Got to be canny. She's walking on wires here; and if she falls, so does he . . .*

# PART FOUR

*Lips Do More Than Smile*

Mark sat in the office, grinding a biro slowly between his teeth and trying to organise his thoughts. There was something he wanted to say about Alex, in the daily diary; and he had to make sense of it somehow in his head, before he could make it sound sensible on paper.

Her story was perfectly believable, almost run of the mill for the kids they dealt with; and he didn't disbelieve it. His feelings weren't strong enough for something as definite as doubt. There was just an air about her, a sense of objectivity as she talked to him, as if at the same time she were surveying her own performance, and finding it good. Or maybe it was only that she occasionally looked so much older than sixteen, when he caught a glimpse of her face in profile, or when he'd watched her watching the others over lunch . . .

But all the kids looked and acted older than they had any right to, every now and then. Just as they looked and acted so much younger, too, on occasion. Perhaps he was only imagining things after all, jumping at shadows. And perhaps there was a reason for that.

He closed his eyes, and saw the shadows creeping up into his subconscious, sneaking in when he wasn't looking, terror coming in on tiptoe. If it started with something simple, old eyes on a young girl and a face behind her face, so what? It didn't have to end there. There were plenty of places it could go, plenty of routes. The world was full of 'em, roads and tracks and pathways, teasing and tempting and just a step away. And above and beyond them all was the easiest of all, the highway to destruction, loud and fast and clean, tyres screeching and the horn blaring and here we go, join the crowd, off and away . . .

And perhaps because his mind was halfway there already, looking down into a chaos where such things were com-

monplace, he barely reacted to the first scream, only taking
a moment to be sure, to be glad it hadn't come from his own
mouth. But the second one brought him suddenly back to
himself, his present self, who didn't scream without warning
or cause; and the third had him on his feet and running for
the door.

He found the kids packing into the hall, while the screams
echoed around them; Colton in the lead, anxious and disturbed, with Kez close behind him, snatching at his hand,
genuinely frightened. After her came Davey and Mandy,
both of them jumpy and on edge; and then Tia and Nina
together, walking slowly, making it clear that it was only
curiosity bringing them out, not concern. Alex was last,
running through from the kitchen, pushing her way to the
front and looking suddenly – again – a lot older than her
years.

"Where's Jane?" Mark demanded sharply.

Colton shrugged, Davey shook his head; Mark turned
towards the stairs, and had just started up them when the
screams cut off abruptly. He heard running, staggering footsteps overhead, and checked himself; and seconds later Jane
answered the question herself. She hurtled round the landing, blind and driven, so unlike herself that he wouldn't have
known her if he hadn't been looking for her. Behind him,
someone cried out and choked it off again, all in a moment.

Then she came tumbling into him, not seeing him at all,
not seeing anything except maybe the horror that had
started all this, somewhere behind her eyes; and it was all he
could do to keep his balance against the crashing weight of
her panic. For a second they swayed together on the stairs,
his arms tight around her and her feet still trying to run, to
escape; then he pulled her down, going with her with no
thought in his head except to hold her still until the panic left
her. And if it seeped through some emotional osmosis into
him, if it kept its shape and coherence – well, that was part
of the job, what he was here for. He could handle it, better
than she could. He'd had the practice, after all.

So he guided her head onto his shoulder, eased her gently
until she stopped fighting, stopped being all elbows and
sharp edges and turned instead into a small and frightened
girl. Until the panic was gone

*(and not after all absorbed into himself, but simply dying*

*somewhere between them, to leave him still clear and quiet, still in control)*

and there was nothing left in her but tears.

Looking up, he saw the other kids still standing, watching, uncertain and afraid. There was no hope yet of getting any sense out of Jane, with the sobs tearing themselves so painfully from her throat he was surprised not to see gobbets of blood freckling his shirt. He lifted a hand to beckon Colton, to ask him to take a look upstairs, and see if he could puzzle out what this was all about. But Colton had an arm round Kez's shoulders now, and his other hand was gripping both of hers; and Mark thought, *she won't go with him, she's too scared*, and *he won't want to leave her, not in that state*.

So he let his hand fall back onto Jane's shoulder, and held her close a minute longer, until the worst of the shakes had left her. Then he called them both over, Colton and Kez together; and said, "Can you two look after Jane, while I chase up what this is all about? Don't ask her any questions, she's not ready to talk yet. Just do what you can for her, yeah?"

"Uh, yeah. Sure . . ." Only Colton looked anything but sure, reaching a tentative arm down towards Jane. Kez gave him a glance that was almost a smile, "Here, I'll take her," and pushed him lightly out of the way. Mark stood up, lifted Jane to her feet and gave Kez a nod of approval as she slipped an arm around her.

"Manage?"

"Yes. Of course."

Jane's knees sagged suddenly, as if to test her; Kez simply shifted her grip and took the younger girl's weight easily, no trouble.

"Thanks, Kez. I'd take her into the kitchen if I were you, keep the others out and make her a coffee . . ."

Kez nodded and started to make her way across the hall, supporting Jane all the way and talking to her in a low undertone while Colton followed, his hands making gestures towards helping which his body didn't or couldn't follow through. Mark watched a moment longer to be certain, then turned the other way, towards the landing and the floors above, whatever it was that lay up there. There had to be something, Jane wasn't normally the hysterical type; and he had to find it, face it and somehow make it safe. The world outside was bad enough, for these kids; the refuge had to be just that, a place of shelter and safety, or else it failed, *he* failed. He failed both the kids and the doctor, and he wasn't sure which was worse . . .

He started up the stairs, going slow, not knowing what in the world he might meet up there, only that it couldn't be worse than some of the things he'd met before, not possibly. He'd seen the worst the world had to offer, and survived it; so there was nothing to be afraid of,

*(except falling back, seeing it all again; and he wasn't going to do that, no way, he wouldn't let the doctor down like that)*

was there?

He reached the first landing and turned onto the next flight of stairs without looking back, going quicker now, remembering that he had a role to play for the kids' sake. Big Mark, the boss, who wasn't scared of anything because there was nothing to be scared of. Fast and confident, that was the way to play it; and he played it that way for half a dozen steps, so that they could hear him down in the hall –

– and stopped suddenly, his hand snatching at the banister, because the kids weren't the only people who could hear things, and he was hearing something himself now. He was hearing footsteps that weren't his own, light but urgent,

*(fast and confident, you could say)*

and it was just as well the kids couldn't see him now, couldn't see his face turn pale and the sweat break out across his brow, in the half-second it took him to realise that it was all right, they were coming from below. Just one of the kids following him up. Nothing to worry about.

He turned and looked back, ready to tell whoever-it-was to get the hell back down there and keep out of this, expecting Nina or maybe Tia. But it was Alex who turned the corner below and came up to join him, a weirdly adult-looking Alex who seemed for a moment as if her borrowed clothes and clumsy make-up and maybe even her whole damn lanky body were just a costume she'd put on for the day. Mark closed his eyes,

*(careful, now. Don't see things that aren't there. You don't do that any more, remember?)*

opened them again and she was still there, giving him a half-smile before her eyes moved on to the corridor above, the open doors and the shadows beyond.

"What d'you think then, Mark?"

*Even your voice is older now, that's what I think.* But he shelved that with a determined effort, left it on one side to tell the doctor when he came, see what *he* thought. "I don't know. But there's something, there must be. Jane wasn't faking."

"So what do we do, look in every room?"

For some reason he didn't challenge that *we*, or the assumptions behind it. Something up there was going to be bad, he was certain of that; and he was simply glad of the company.

"No, we'll go straight up to Jane's. That's what it sounded like, that she was right at the top. If there's nothing there, we'll work our way down."

He led the way down the corridor and up the final flight of stairs to the attic, taking the last few steps at a run. The door to Jane's room was standing wide, like a welcome, *come and see*; Mark drew one quick breath and walked straight in, with Alex just a moment behind him.

And in hat room, he found an answer – and for a long minute couldn't see any of the questions that came with it, he couldn't see anything except Jane staring, screaming, running, couldn't feel anything except a shadow of the terror that must have seized her, crushed her, torn her through to the bone . . .

At last, there was something else to feel, which was Alex's hand on his arm, a grip too tight to be the simple attention-getter it was pretending; and something else to see, which was Alex's face paled with shock, turning to him, or maybe

*(more likely)*

simply turning away from the rest of it, the walls of that room.

"Mark . . . Mark, what *is* it?"

"Rats," he said wearily. "Like it says on the door there, yeah? Two pet rats, Jane loved the little buggers . . ."

*Loved*, past tense; because she surely didn't love them now, she just screamed and ran from them, and why not? It made better sense than what he was doing, gazing – gaping – at white walls splattered with red, at bits of bone and shreds of fur smeared across furniture and bedding, at a tea-chest smashed and tangled with wire and scattered across a carpet thick with sawdust, nothing like a hotel now.

At the word 'RATS' written thickly on the door, written bloodily, written in the death of what it spoke of: because it wasn't hard, it was horribly easy to imagine a hand gripping a pulped body

*(Charlie or Bobbie, it didn't matter which)*

like a fat felt-tip, maybe squeezing, wringing it even, to get out a little more blood as it was dragged across the paintwork, leaving a foul trail of letters where it passed . . .

"Christ." Alex let go of his arm and stepped gingerly forward through the mess towards the open window. Following her with his eyes, Mark saw broken glass on the floor among the sawdust and the splintered wood; and relief washed through him, clean and sharp, as she leaned out and said, "The fire-escape ends right outside here, did you know? Must be how he got in. Broke the window, stuck his hand through, twiddled the latch and Bob's your uncle."

And thank God for Bob, however sick an uncle; at least he lived out there somewhere, in the big bad dangerous outside world, at least it wasn't one of the kids did this . . .

Alex drew her head inside, straightened up and shivered as her eyes roamed the room and came back to settle on his face again, seeking refuge. For a moment she looked young again, the way she ought to look, young and scared; but it was only a moment before her face fell into its new, mature lines. As if that was the natural way for it to be – and now he could look at her with at least something settled, one mystery gone and the threat of panic receding, he thought he saw something familiar in that face. Or the face and the hair together; because she'd had an hour in the bathroom that afternoon, and with the dirt washed out of it her hair was crisply copper, and trying to ring a bell or two, somewhere in his head.

"But who the hell would do something like this?" she demanded, waving an arm to gather in all the mess she didn't want to look at. "What kind of sicko is going to break into a house in broad daylight, just to kill a couple of rats?"

"I don't know, love." But it wasn't just to kill; and this was important, it had to be. The intruder hadn't simply killed, he had destroyed, and made a point of the destruction – written it in red, in blood and bone.

They held each other's gaze a second longer, as if each was looking to find something in the other, some understanding of what had happened, or only a little strength to help them cope with the aftermath. Then – whether they'd found it or not – they turned eyes and minds back to the chaos. This time, Mark spotted something white

*(but pink too, and red in places)*

and plastic half-buried in the sawdust on the floor. He bent to pick it up, carefully between finger and thumb; and found himself holding a supermarket carrier bag turned inside-out, smeared and stained with blood. Dangling from it, with one leg caught in a fold of the plastic, was the tail and crushed hindquarters of one of Jane's rats. He flinched, dropped it again and gestured towards the door.

"Come on, Alex, let's get out of here."

"What are you going to do," she asked, picking a path back towards him, "call the police?"

"To this place? Don't be silly, sweetheart. I'm going to call the doctor."

## 22  Daylight Ghosts

Colton couldn't remember the last time the doctor had come before nightfall. Yesterday it would've been weird to see him bustling in at four o'clock; but not today. At least it made sense, which was more than any of the rest did, the really weird stuff. Jane flipping her lid like that, scaring the shit out of everyone (and 'specially Kez, who'd been *shaking* till Mark gave her something to do, looking after Jane, she was all right then), and something up in Jane's room that she wouldn't talk about and Mark wouldn't say what, he'd just locked it up and left it. Him and Alex – and that was another weirdie, what was going on there. Something about Alex; Mark kept looking at her dead odd, like he wasn't sure what he was seeing.

But however weird things had got it didn't matter, not any more; 'cos the doctor was here now, and he'd straighten it all

out. That was what he did, straighten people out, and problems, even your pool game if you were going through a bad
patch, missing everything . . .

Colton grinned at himself, *yeah, sure, boy, life's just one
big game of pool, and the doctor's Fast Eddie*, but laugh if
you like, he still meant it. Something happened, and the
doctor came, and it all got patched up double quick.

Funny how helpless he'd felt, though, when it was all
going on. He wasn't usually like that; a month ago, he
would've gone running upstairs straight off, to check what
had happened and make sure there wasn't anyone up there.
Then he'd be right down again, to take Jane off of Mark and
get her settled.

They were a good team in an emergency, him and Mark –
or they used to be. Not any more, though, it seemed like. It
was Kez that had changed everything; he'd known things
were different with her around, only he hadn't realised how
much different until it all blew up this afternoon.

He couldn't have gone upstairs to check out what had
scared Janey, even if he'd wanted to; not with Kez hanging
onto his hand the way she was, gripping like murder and
shaking all the way up her arm. And he hadn't even wanted
to, really, not if it meant leaving her behind.

But he still should've gone and looked after Jane, without
Mark having to ask; only he didn't think of it, it was like he
couldn't think of anything except Kez. And then when Mark
did ask it was Kez who took charge, while Colton just let
her, standing round like a spare prick at a wedding . . .

But he'd got it sort of figured out now, or thought he had.
If he wasn't just making excuses for himself. Thing was,
what Jane had needed was cuddles and comfort, and he
hadn't exactly run out of those, not exactly; but he'd been
giving it all to Kez, everything he had, and it was hard to
focus in on what someone else was needing, all of a sudden.
And he would've felt dead funny doing it in front of Kez
anyway, picking Jane up and hugging her the way he
should've, the way she needed to be . . .

But anyway, all that was over now. The doctor had come
round as soon as Mark phoned, and Jane was tucked up in
Mrs H's old room now, right out of it, from a jab the doctor
had given her. Mark and the doctor were in the office,
talking with the door closed, making it obvious they wanted

to be private; and the kids were all under orders not to go up to the attics. So the rest of them were kicking around in the games room, gabbing about what was going on. Kez had sat in with them for a bit, listening and not saying anything; then she'd come through to the kitchen, for some peace. And, of course, Colton had come with her.

And now she sat astride one of the old uprights, with her arms crossed across its back and her chin cupped in one fist, while Colton perched on the table behind her and massaged her shoulders gently, working his thumbs into the tight, tense muscles and feeling there wasn't anywhere, not any-where in the *world* he'd rather be now than right here, and not a thing else he'd rather be doing . . .

Kez closed her eyes and sat up straighter, leaning back into the insistent pressure of Colton's fingers. She could lose herself in this, it wouldn't be hard; the boy had magic in his hands, and she could almost feel her personality starting to crumble like stale bread as he worked on her. There was something beyond pain in it, when he caught a stiff tendon between finger and thumb, and kneaded it like a string of dough; something beyond pleasure, when he slid soft finger-tips up her neck and sent them probing under her hair, setting her whole scalp tingling . . .

Oh yes, she could lose herself all right – but she couldn't lose Seb. That was the bugger factor that kept her trapped inside her skull, that kept her muscles tight and terrified. Seb wasn't simply a past horror, something she'd run from. It wasn't that easy. He'd done something special to Kez, sealed himself in there with her, *here I am and here I remain*; so that it wasn't just her dreams that were haunted, she carried him with her as a daylight ghost, hearing his foot-steps in every corridor and his voice behind every door. Seeing his face at every window; and wondering, always wondering who else was seeing it too.

Like Jane, for instance. Had it been Seb who'd gouged and splintered his way into her life today? That had been Kez's first thought, when Jane's screams filled the house: there was terror abroad, therefore Seb was here, he'd found the refuge. A equals B, no problem. And that thought hadn't gone away, even after Kez had talked to Jane. She hadn't got much out of her, only that someone had broken into her room and killed her pets; but if it wasn't Seb, it could have been. And that thought was enough: enough to keep her stiff and shaking, to carry her beyond the reach even of Colton's magic fingers.

Nina sprawled herself out more comfortably on the sofa, one eye on the telly and the other on the chair where Davey had been sitting. Her left hand was picking idly at the hole in the sofa's padded arm, where the stuffing was coming out, and her right hand was holding a cigarette; and she could feel a smile teasing at the corners of her mouth, reflecting the content that was seeping slowly through every inch of her body.

Behind her, over by the pool table, she could hear Tia still talking about Jane, talking to Mandy – or talking *at* Mandy, anyway, because that kid wasn't saying much, she never did. Maybe Tia thought she was talking to Nina, too; but Nina wasn't listening, she was too busy enjoying what the others had just missed.

It was a bit odd, how she hadn't remembered to do it before – or maybe it wasn't, because she'd met Mandy in that cafe straight afterwards, and bringing her back to the ref had been even bigger, important enough to make her forget all about the other thing. Mark had been dead pleased with her about that; and that had been important too, for a while. Only it hadn't lasted. He'd got too tied up with the new kids to be bothered with her. And she couldn't keep it up for long anyway, the brown-nose act. What was the point? Like Tia said, it didn't get you anywhere.

And just this afternoon, in the middle of all that panic, she'd caught sight of Davey jittering in the hall, shit scared he'd looked, the little jerk – and then she'd remembered Secky, and his message. And his vicious little smile, when he'd given it to her.

The message was still sitting in her head, word for word, ready to be picked up and passed on. And that was just what she'd done; she'd waited for the right moment, when she could get Davey alone, and then she'd simply picked it up and passed it on.

*Hey, Davey. Message from Secky, he just wants you to know something. He said to tell you that favourite trick of yours, the guy with the glasses, he tested out positive last month. Secky said you'd understand. He said he had it from some guy called Stand-Up Joe or something, so it was real. That was it, okay?*

And maybe it wasn't okay for him, but it was great for her, just standing there watching the little creep jitter and jerk, shit scared all over again . . .

*Ask the doctor!*

But he wasn't going to do that. No way. Not even with the guy just downstairs in the office, talking to Mark. No, he was just going to sit up here in his room, *hide* up here, and wait for the horrors to go away.

But they weren't going to do that, either. No way. Not these horrors. He could sit and wait, sit and hide for weeks, for months, for *ever*, they'd still be hanging in there with him, dancing in his head, laughing, *hullo, Davey lad, we're still here, and isn't this fun?*

Fun for Nina it had been, that was for sure. He could still see her face when she'd told him, her smile – and Secky's smile like a ghost behind hers, his voice like an echo in hers as she said it. Really enjoyed themselves, those two had. And the funny thing was, he didn't give a fuck about that, he didn't have it to spare. They could laugh all they liked, it wasn't even going to reach him. The horrors laughed louder, that was all.

And there was only one way to shut *them* up; which brought him back to

*(ask the doctor!)*

what the hell was he going to do?

And for tonight, at least, there was only one answer to that, because he couldn't ask the doctor, he just couldn't. So he'd sit here and sweat, sit and hide with the horrors, sit and *think* . . .

But thinking meant remembering, too – remembering a guy in glasses. And Christ they were sweet, some of those memories, sweet enough to shake him, even now. Julian had always had somewhere to go, a room in a hotel – not like the cheap bastards who just wanted a quick fuck in a back alley and give you a fiver for it, take it or leave it. The first time he'd had a bottle of wine up there too, but Davey had hardly touched it, and he'd learned from that; next time, there was the wine for Julian and a couple of cans for Davey.

And he was always happy to talk, Julian, always interested. It wasn't nerves or embarrassment or anything, not like some of them, the ones who just wanted to talk to save them getting their trousers off – *not just yet, sweetie. No hurry, is there? We've got all evening. Tell me about yourself* . . . Julian just liked to talk; in the shower, in the bath, in bed, wherever. Before, after – during, if there really wasn't any hurry. Take it slow and playful, and chat while they played; and only one rule, that they never talked money till it was over, clothes on, ready for the street again.

And

*(oh!)*

the pleasure of it, hot and sweet and melting – now *there* was a place to hide, if you like . . .

Mandy sat against the wall by the pool table, on the wooden upright that made her back feel less achy, and let Tia's voice just ride over her. She didn't want to be here; she wasn't interested in what Tia was going on about, what could've made Jane throw a fit like that, and she wasn't interested in what was blaring out from the telly, some boring old film. She slipped one hand under her swelling belly and stroked it lightly, just wishing that she could go to bed and curl up around the curled-up life inside.

But she couldn't go up to her room, Mark wasn't letting anyone into the attics at the moment; and she had to stay up for a while longer anyway, she had to see the doctor.

It was the responsibility, that was the worst thing about carrying another life around inside her. The rest didn't matter, the sickness and the feeling heavy all the time, the way her back ached, and her feet. She didn't care about any of that. But she'd been dead scared at first, when she'd heard those screams echoing round the house this afternoon; and that couldn't be good for her little one, to have her heart pumping like crazy and all that stuff, that adrenalin being shoved out into her bloodstream. The baby had to share her blood, she'd read up on that and she knew all about it; and she just had to talk to the doctor, to be sure that she hadn't done it any harm.

And there were other things she'd read about, scans and stuff, that pregnant girls needed; she wanted to talk about all of that, too. Okay, so she couldn't go to an ordinary hospital for it, she knew that; but the doctor would know somewhere she could go, where they wouldn't ask questions. He hadn't done anything yet except take her blood-pressure and listen to her heart, feel her abdomen. He had to get her a proper check-up soon, he just *had* to . . .

Pretty soon, Tia got tired of talking to the empty air. She wasn't getting any response from Mandy – no surprise there, the kid didn't seem to have a brain to respond with, just a waistline that got bigger every time you looked – or from Nina, who was miles away, daydreaming about something that kept making her smile. So she bummed a tab instead, and turned her mind to something even more interesting than Jane's hysterics, and much more urgent.

Money was Tia's major problem now. She had a guaranteed roof over her head, she had meals provided, and she'd brought enough clothes with her to get by. But a girl needed cash, to have a good time; and from what Nina had told her today, the pocket-money Mark doled out every week wasn't going to be enough to keep her in make-up and fags.

There was no point being in London, if you didn't make the most of it; and that meant she was going to need something big, some long-term source of real money. That wouldn't be easy to organise. She had an idea about it, which could be really profitable; but it wasn't exactly safe. In fact, it was bloody dangerous. She'd be risking everything she'd gained at the refuge, and a whole lot more besides. It'd take a lot of thinking out, and some careful planning to make it work; but she had plenty of time for that, and the nerve to carry it through. That was something she'd learned, that you had to take risks to get anywhere. She'd done it once already, getting the hell away from home, and she'd wound up here at the refuge; but one thing was for sure, she wasn't going to stay here too long. She'd just use it as a base till she got set up, it'd be really handy for that; then as soon as she got things moving, she'd be off.

The refuge grapevine had slipped up, just a little. Missed something important. It was true, Mark and the doctor were closeted in the office with the door closed; but they weren't alone in there. Alex was with them.

Feeling schizophrenic, Alex was. Partly it was like being back at school, called into the head's study to explain some particularly juvenile practical joke in an embarrassed mutter, flushed and fidgeting, with two pairs of censorious eyes fixed on her across a wide wooden desk. And at the same time she felt like a blackmailer with all the aces, cool and in control, the power of the press wrapped around her like a protective cloak. *I can expose you, fellas. Tell your whole story in print, and you can't stop me.*

That was what she was here for, after all. That was the job. It was what she'd trained for, what she'd always wanted to do. Investigative Journalism, with capital letters: getting out there, digging around under cover, finding out about matters of public concern and telling the world. Exposing them.

But now she was here and it was happening, it wasn't just a daydream any more; and it didn't feel so good. It felt like blackmail.

She pictured what would happen if she went ahead and printed the story: squads of police and social workers descending on the refuge, everyone taken away and the house closed up, the kids sent back to the homes they'd run away from, or else taken into care or custody, Mark and the doctor in court. All that was bad enough, because she liked these people, and she didn't want to do them that kind of damage. And then she thought again about what it would mean to have the refuge gone – what it would mean to next year's runaways, all the dozens or maybe hundreds of kids out on the street with one avenue of escape cut off, one shelter gone.

*Listen, kid, are you open to a business proposition?* Tod's face and voice, coming back to her. *This and that . . . Just keeping the customers happy . . .* She'd been able to say no, but real runaways weren't so lucky. And if the refuge weren't here, more of them would be saying yes to people like Tod Hunter or Laurence Aspinall. *I'm all the refuge they need. A mother hen, that's me. To all my chickens.* Teenage prostitutes, rent boys, God knew what.

But these were all private thoughts, and not for sharing. What she needed was time, to look at them carefully and make some kind of balanced judgement; but time was just what she didn't have, because she was here and now, just where she'd wanted to be, *doing my job and won't the boss be pleased with me?*, in a room with two of the people she'd be hurting if she did her job. Scrabbling desperately in her mind for some instant solution which might obviate a little of that pain, trying to be sober and sensible and adult about it, when she really wanted to kick the furniture and protest that it wasn't *fair*, it wasn't meant to be like this . . .

Keeping quiet, and letting the others do the talking for a while. But it seemed like it wasn't easy for them either, because they were dodging the issue too, or at least setting it aside for a while, now that they'd had the basic facts from her. Trying to deal with one crisis at a time. And Christ knew, they had enough on their plate already, with that sick mess upstairs in the attic; they didn't need her barging in, threatening the whole set-up.

". . . We'll have to move the kids right out of the attic," Mark was saying. "I mean, Christ, have you thought what might've happened if he'd found Jane *in* there when he bust in? Jesus . . . But then it was the fire-escape he came in off, not the roof, and half the rooms in the house have access off that thing. He could get in anywhere, if he comes back. And we don't know that he won't, whoever he was. We don't know why he came in the first place, we don't know *any-thing*. And what the hell are we going to tell the kids? They're supposed to be *safe* here, for God's sake, and there's some crazy bogeyman out there who may be showing up at their window any night now . . ."

"One thing at a time," the doctor said, cutting in smoothly

as Mark wallowed dangerously near panic. "Set an agenda,
lad, and we'll go through it point by point. Okay?"

"Okay." But there was something more that passed between them then, an unexpected half-smile from Mark and
something close to a wink from the doctor, that Alex saw but
didn't understand. As if this were an old game – or no, more
than a game, an old and familiar way of dealing with crises.

Mark pulled a sheet of paper across the desk towards him,
picked up a pen and scribbled, chewed the end for a moment
and scribbled again. After a minute, he looked up and said,
"Jane."

"Right." And there was something there too, in the doctor's tone of voice – as if it were some kind of test, and Mark
had just passed with flying colours. "What are we going to
do about Jane? That's your province, lad, you're the one
who's sorting out her future for her."

"This is different. She's going to need help, doctor . . ."

"So help her."

"Help from you, I meant. It's too big for me."

"She's not sick, Mark. Shocked, frightened and upset,
yes; but I've done what I can for the shock, and the rest is up
to you. You know her better than I do, you've been living
with her all this time. Come on, boy, it's your agenda. She's
your priority. So what's she going to need?"

These waters were still deeper than Alex could understand – or maybe they just stretched back out of sight, into
some country she had no knowledge of. For a second, she
wasn't sure if Mark was going to laugh or throw something.
But she had her own ideas of what Jane would need most;
and when in the event he did neither, only answered the
question, she found herself nodding, thinking, *He's no fool,
that boy. He understands.*

"She needs to get out of here," he said simply. "As soon
as possible – tomorrow, if we can fix it. The best thing we
can do for her now is find somewhere else for her to go."

"Yes. What's your contact in Ipswich up to?"

"She hasn't found a foster home for her yet, so far as I
know. But I think she may be our best bet anyway. They
must have somewhere they can put her in the meantime, and
she'll go willingly enough now. I think she'd go anywhere."

"Right." The doctor glanced at his watch. "Too late to
phone her now, but you can do that first thing in the morn-

ing. Tell her as little as you have to, but get her moving."

"Will do."

"Jane should sleep right through tonight, after that jab I gave her. But you'll have to do something with her tomorrow morning . . ."

"Yeah." Mark frowned. "Best thing would be if she stayed in her room, but she'll need someone with her. That'll be a full-time job, so I can't do it. I'd ask Colton, he's the obvious one; only he seems to have adopted Kez for the duration, and both of them might be a bit much for her."

"I'll do it." Alex had made the offer almost before she knew she was going to speak at all; it came automatically, and seemed almost inevitable.

To her, at any rate. Not, apparently, to Mark; he glanced at her coldly

*(and that hurt; and that wasn't fair either, she wasn't supposed to get hurt, it wasn't in the job description)*

and she could see him getting ready to say no, and more than no; to say, *what the hell makes you think you're going to be here tomorrow?*

And she wouldn't have had an answer, couldn't even have explained why she wanted to be, except that Jane would need someone and she wanted to help. As compensation, maybe, for the trouble she was bringing with her; or maybe it was simpler than that, maybe she just wanted to be needed.

Whatever the reason, Mark didn't get the chance to turn it down. The doctor nodded almost idly, as if it were a matter of no great importance, and said, "Yes, that'll be best. Thanks, Alex. What's next, Mark?"

Mark hesitated, on the verge of arguing; then he shrugged a sullen acceptance, shot Alex another glance of bitter dislike and looked down at his list. "Where the rest of them are going to sleep tonight. I'm not having any of the kids in the attic, that's definite. I'll move up there myself, that'll make one room available; but they'll still have to double up, unless we bed someone down in the games room. They might prefer to share anyway, for the company."

Alex listened to him working the problem through aloud, finding his own solutions while the doctor did nothing but nod; and she thought, *I don't know what this agenda game is, but it works. Ten minutes ago he was in a real stew, he*

*couldn't have coped with any of this; now he's doing it all.*
*And getting it right, I reckon . . .*

Her mind had drifted away from following what Mark was actually saying, and she was taken by surprise when the doctor turned to her.

"Alex? Would you mind sleeping in one of the attic rooms tonight?"

She had a sudden memory of Jane's room, of the blood-smeared walls and the pulped bodies, the wreckage and the sheer hatred

*(no, worse than that, the twisted sickness)*

that had created it. She shivered, imagining a shadow falling across a window, the glass exploding inward, a body forcing its way inside –

– and caught Mark's eye on her, straightened in her chair and said, "No, of course I don't mind. That's fine."

"Good, then. That's settled, I think, Mark. Next?"

Mark was still watching Alex. He grunted, jerked his gaze away and glanced at his list. "Next? Oh – yeah. Next is a nasty idea. Has it occurred to you that it might not have been a random psycho that broke in? That it might've been someone who knows us? Someone who's been here, say – one of the kids we couldn't help. Someone with a grudge."

"Someone like Secky, you mean?"

"He knows his way round here, after all," Mark said, arguing his case. "The fire-escape and everything."

"Yes . . ." The doctor pursed his lips consideringly. "He wouldn't know Jane's room, though, would he? He wouldn't know Jane, he'd left before she arrived here."

"No, but it might not have been aimed at Jane specifically. If he'd only wanted to smash the place up a bit, to get at the ref in general, he'd head for the top of the house anyway, because no one was likely to be up there that time of day. Finding the rats there would just be a bonus. And the word on the door, *RATS*, it could be his idea of a joke . . ."

"Perhaps. But I don't think it's safe to assume anything at this stage, Mark."

"Maybe not, but that's not the point. What I'm getting at, if this nutter is someone who knows us, he may keep coming back – and we *can't stop him*. Even if we catch him in the act. What are we going to do, turn him over to the law? We're blown, doctor. That's the only assumption we can make."

"So what are you suggesting?" the doctor asked, in a voice that said he knew already.

"That maybe it's time to move. Or start looking, at any rate." Then he jerked a thumb towards Alex, and added, "And it's high time she wasn't in here any more. We can't trust her, and I don't want her listening in. We've probably said too much already, I expect it'll all be in the papers in a couple of days. I mean, hell, with her here we're blown anyway, never mind the nutter."

Alex shifted unhappily in her seat, helpless even to protest in the face of so much anger. After all, he was probably right. He ought to be. She should blow them sky-high, make the boss happy. But . . .

"Let's not be precipitate," the doctor said, stepping in again. *Love you, Doc.* "All Alex has told us so far is what she came here to do, not what she's actually going to do. But, Alex, I think Mark's right. We'd better put you on the agenda now."

*On the spot, you mean. Hate you, Doc.* But he was right, damn him, they both were. It was fair. It just meant that she'd have to make the decision now; and she wasn't *ready* for this . . .

She uncrossed her legs and hitched herself further back on the chair, ran a hand over the short hairs on the back of her neck, took a breath and blew it out again; and said, "Christ. I don't know. I mean, I just don't. I don't *know*. Like, I don't want to spoil things for you here; I think it's important, what you're doing. Now that I've seen it. Only, my job's important too, you know? What am I supposed to do, tell my editor yes, I found the place, and no, I'm not going to write about it? I'd be out on my ear. I'd probably never work again. And it's not just having the job, either, it's doing it that counts. I think people have a right to know what's being hidden from them; and it's my job to find out, and tell them. That's what journalism ought to be. It's not always like that, I know, but when it is, I think it's worthwhile."

"Uh-huh. So you think it's worthwhile to splash our address across your front page, do you? Just because it's a secret?" That was Mark, of course, coming on hard. "It hasn't occurred to you that maybe some secrets are worth keeping, you little shit-digger? That maybe what they're hiding is more valuable than your fucking job satisfaction?"

"As a matter of fact," she bit back, "I'm beginning to wonder if this place isn't more valuable than my whole fucking job. 'Cos that's what's in the balance here, remember? So why don't you just go and have a nice wank, while me and the doctor talk like grown-ups?"

And anything might have happened after that, and she wouldn't have cared too much if it did; but they were interrupted by a quiet chuckle, cutting between them more effectively than any shout could have done. They both swivelled indignantly round to glare at the doctor, who grinned back at them, quite unabashed.

"Oh, don't stop, children. Not on my account. I'm enjoying myself hugely."

"I bet you are, you old bat," Mark growled. "But this isn't a bloody joke."

"No, it isn't. However, if you two would like to stop abusing each other and just think for a minute, there is a solution to all this. One which does not require you to be at each other's throats, entertaining though that is."

"Yeah? What, then?"

"Work it out for yourselves. It's a test."

And with that, he sat back and smiled inscrutably. Alex decided that Mark was right about one thing, at least – he *was* an old bat. For all that he looked like a vulture, with that fluffy tonsure and the great beak of a nose . . .

But, a solution? If he could find one, so could she; and sure enough, she did. Knowing that it was there, that the thing was not after all hopeless, she found it quickly. Except that . . .

"You mean, I could publish the story without the details? Just talk about why the kids are here and how they're looked after, and keep the address quiet?"

The doctor nodded. "And their names too, no need to shout those around. But there could even be advantages for us, in having it told from our side. Public opinion could be a useful weapon, as and when the authorities do find us. They're bound to sooner or later; and probably sooner, we've been lucky to get away with it as long as we have. But you could do us some good by sowing a few seeds now, get your readers thinking that the refuge is fundamentally a good idea . . ."

Alex nodded thoughtfully, already rewriting in her mind. "Yes, I could do that. If my editor'll let me. It's difficult, though. If the police really wanted to find you that bad, they could take us to court . . ."

"I know." The doctor's smile stretched a little wider. "But that's all right, isn't it? You make a brilliant speech from the dock, defending a journalist's right to protect her sources; then you do a month or two in jail, and come out to find every newspaper in Fleet Street wants to give you a job."

"Dockland."

"I beg your pardon?"

"Dockland, not Fleet Street. No one's in Fleet Street any more. And it's all right for you to smile, you wouldn't be the one doing time."

"If you do the dirty on us, I would be. It's you or me, sweetheart; and I'm too old and frail."

"Hell you are," Mark said, glowering at him. "Do you good." But his eyes came back to Alex, with no fight left in them; and it was that mute appeal that finally decided her.

"What the hell, let's try it. *If* I can get it past my editor."

## 24  Pleasure

Colton was a bit surprised to find himself still in his old room, after all the switching around. That was down to Alex again; Mark had moved her up into the attic, so that Kez could have her room. He was glad about that, because it meant Kez was just down the corridor, and he didn't have to worry about her so much; but even so, he wondered. He'd been expecting to end up with an attic room himself. He was the oldest, after all, and he was a bloke.

But it was just a part of Alex's weirdness, that Mark treated her like an adult. Like the adult she looked like now. There was a story there, and he'd get it tomorrow. Mark wasn't going to keep any secrets from him.

And he was just as glad, still to be here. It would've been kind of flattering, to be asked to move up for a bit; like a recognition that he really wasn't a kid any more. But he'd lived in this room for three years now, and it was more than just familiar, it was a part of him, almost. He'd painted the walls himself, and chosen the colour first; he'd swapped the furniture that was in here for stuff he wanted from other rooms; he'd bought the duvet cover with his own money, he liked it so much; and they were his posters on the wall, his clothes on the floor, all his gear scattered around. He *belonged* in here, and he'd never felt like that before, anywhere . . .

"Home sweet home," he said aloud; and grinned, as he pulled his sweatshirt off and tossed it over the back of the chair. But however much he laughed at himself, it was still true.

He stripped off the rest of his clothes, and left them lying by the bed, as usual; they'd do for tomorrow. Except maybe the socks. He'd have to watch that; Kez had spent half the evening sitting on the floor with her back against his legs, and if she was going to make a habit of it

*(please?)*

he didn't want his smelly feet chasing her away.

He took a moment to look down at himself naked, and grimaced. Too bloody skinny, that was his problem. Maybe he should exercise, or something. He was fit enough, but he couldn't half use a few muscles. Well, he'd think about it tomorrow. At least he had the privacy of his room, if he decided to have a go. There was no way he was going to do it in public.

He slipped under the duvet and reached down to turn on the ghetto-blaster on the floor. It was tuned permanently to Capital Radio, and music pounded out to fill the darkness. He jerked the volume down quickly to a near-whisper that wouldn't disturb Mark – no, Mandy it was now – next door, and lit a cigarette; and lay on his back to smoke it, with the ashtray on his chest and his free hand tucked comfortably behind his head. He watched the smoke eddy in the red glow from the fag's burning, and thought about Kez.

When it had burned down to the filter, he stubbed the cigarette out, put the ashtray back on the floor and turned over onto his stomach, tucking his feet over the end of the mattress so he could lie full stretch, leaving the music playing. He always slept with the radio on, liking to drift away in the not-quite-silence, and wake up to a companionable voice in the morning.

And he was just starting to drift, following the music down into half-dreams, when he heard a soft noise that brought him abruptly back with a jerk that was almost painful. That was the bottom of his door rubbing across the carpet as someone pushed it open, it couldn't be anything else. He stared into the dark and saw something darker, a shadow in the doorway; and tasted fear like something sweet and furred and foul

*(dead rats)*

in his mouth, choking him, filling his throat with bile.

Heard a voice, barely a whisper, calling his name: "Colton? Are you awake?"

Tried to speak, and almost vomited; swallowed urgently, once and a second time, sat up and tried again.

"Yeah . . . Yeah, I'm awake. What's up, Kez?"

"Nothing, only . . ." She took one small, slow step into his room, and stopped again. "I can't sleep, and – I'm sorry, I'll go away if you want, but . . ."

"No, come in, it's all right." Pulling the duvet quickly up to cover his chest, in a rush of embarrassment.

She edged inside and made her way slowly over to his bed without saying anything more, her feet fumbling their way through his scattered clothes; and as she stood just a foot away, her face unreadable in the shadow, his mind shied away from the important questions and the possibilities that underlay her coming to him like this, finding refuge in a stray thought: *She's still wearing my shirt. Must be getting pretty smelly by now, girl. But that's okay, that's fine by me . . .*

But she went on just standing there, and he knew that if he reached out to touch her

*(if he had the nerve, which he didn't)*

she'd be shaking; and he couldn't just let her shake, he had to say something, he had to help.

So he said, "Look, d'you want to talk? 'Cos that's okay, no bother. Just give me a minute to get dressed, and we'll go down and have a coffee, and . . ."

"No, that's not what I . . ." She chewed her lip, there was

just enough light for him to see that; then she said quietly, "What I'd really like, I'd like to get in there with you. I'm *scared*, Col . . ."

"Oh." *Play it cool, boy. Happens all the time, right?* "Yeah, sure, Kez. Come on in . . ."

He scrunched up against the wall to make room for her in the narrow bed, and lifted up the corner of the duvet, and hoped it didn't look stupid, like a guy dashing to open a door for a girl who could quite easily open it herself. She slithered in to join him; he pulled the duvet tight around her, and never mind if that left his own back bare against the wall.

He put his arm awkwardly round her, trying to keep the rest of his body right back out of the way, not even touching her, so's she wouldn't think he was making any kind of pass. But that wasn't right, it wasn't what she wanted; she put both arms round his chest and pressed tight against him, with her face in his neck and her long legs wrapping themselves around his, skin on skin and nothing between them anywhere except the soft warmth of the rugby shirt. And yeah, it was getting smelly all right, smelling of her, warm and sweet and wonderful . . .

And, yeah, she was shaking. He didn't have any choice now; he hugged her hard, pressed his cheek against her hair and wished he'd shaved that morning. And felt dead mad with himself for thinking stupid things like that, when she was in a right state; but it wasn't his fault, you couldn't stop thoughts sneaking sideways into your head, however worried you were. Like he couldn't stop the electrics chasing all over his skin, that left it feeling so *alive*, so aware of every little twitch and shiver in Kez's body, and half ready to match her twitch for twitch. Like he couldn't stop the breath catching in his chest when she shifted her head a bit, so that he could feel her breath warm and moist on his collar-bone; couldn't stop that tight, hot feeling growing in his stomach and spreading down to his crotch, couldn't stop . . .

*Oh Christ, no! Don't get a hard-on now, you wanker! Think of something else, quick . . .*

And he did try; but it wasn't easy, when he hadn't been thinking of nothing except Kez ever since she'd turned up here, hardly, and the hem of the rugby shirt was tickling his willy like an invitation, *come on in*, and she was pressed so close against him, sort of soft and firm both at the same time, and nothing like how he'd imagined, and he wanted to do it so fucking *much* . . .

He just had to get her talking, that was all, take his mind off of it, fast; so he opened his mouth, and desperation put the words in.

"So what's scared you, then?"

It was a stupid bloody question to be asking anyone to-night, especially her; but at that, it was better than his prick sticking into her belly, stiff as a root, asking questions of its own. And that was going to happen any second now

*(don't even think about it . . .)*

if this didn't work.

But it did work, because she pushed away from him sud-denly, to lie on her back and stare at the ceiling; and he could have sobbed with the relief of it, if it didn't hurt so much, if he didn't want to pull her back. If he didn't hate himself for the tension he could feel in her, that he'd put there with that godawful question. She'd come to him to hide, and he'd let her down. Just because he couldn't control his bloody body, she wasn't soft and shaking any more, she was

*(yeah, stiff as a root)*

facing the darkness, her hand like a claw on his chest and her voice like steel, hard to hear above the music.

"My brother," she said; and he wanted to say, *I know, come here, don't talk about it,* but it was too late for that now, too late to do anything but listen. "And, I don't know who it was broke into Jane's room, but it could, it could've been him. And I was lying there in bed, in the dark, and I couldn't stop thinking about him, wondering where he was, if maybe he was outside somewhere, watching the house, waiting to come back. And, I know this sounds stupid, but I turned the light on and it was still dark, I could *feel* the darkness right there in the room still. And the fire-escape goes right outside the window in that room, and I thought of him climbing up, knowing where I was, standing right out-side there, watching me through the curtain; and I couldn't stand it. I was going to scream, or something. Or go crazy. So I came to find you; and even just walking down the corridor I was frightened, that was dark too and I didn't know where the light was . . ."

"I'm sorry," he said, and didn't care whether she knew or

not, what he was apologising for. "Look, d'you want the light on in here, would that help?"

"No. Really. It's dark anyway, out there; and it'd feel like, you know, a lighthouse or something, telling him where to find me . . ."

"It probably wasn't him, you know. Broke into Jane's room, I mean. Just some crazy."

"I know that. He doesn't know where I am, he can't. But it doesn't matter who it was really, it *could've* been him, and that's all that counts. Does that make any sense?"

"Nah," he said, meaning yes. "It's crazy. But it's okay, everybody's crazy here."

He heard half a chuckle lose itself somewhere in her throat, and scored one point to him; then saw her head turn away, scanning the window, the corners of the room, all the darkness inside and out.

"You don't want to go back to your room tonight, do you?" he asked, just to get it straight. "Not even if I came and sat with you, till you fell asleep?"

"No. Please . . ."

"Sure. But look, you come over to this side, right?" And he slipped an arm underneath her ribs and rolled her across his body, taking her weight onto himself for one sweet second while he wriggled over, then easing her off again so that she lay between himself and the wall. "Now you know you're not going to fall out, even if I toss around in the night. And nobody's going to get at you either, 'cos they'll have to come through me first. Okay?"

"Yes." And she was almost laughing at herself, at her own fears

*(and score ten for that, boy)*

as she said, "Thanks, Col."

"Pleasure." And he meant that all right, as she snuggled up against him, head on his shoulder and hair all over the place. Her arms came more loosely round his chest, sending stray shivers up his back as her fingers brushed over ribs and spine and came to rest. This time, thank God, he'd had the sense to bring his knees up a bit, to give him space, to keep his erection private if he got one.

*(And yup, here it came, right on time.)*

She didn't like it, him being so unfriendly with his legs. She fidgeted a bit, fought him knee to knee; and with a bloody great boner sheltering between his thighs, it was instinct or something like it that sent his hand down to ward her off. It settled on her hip, found it naked and jerked away; and ventured back again, to pull the rucked-up rugby shirt slowly down like a curtain across her skin

*(and oh, the feel of her against his palm, the way he reckoned silk must feel, or ought to, only better)*

while she settled and lay still.

"That's nice, Col," barely whispered above the radio.

"Yeah. But, Kez, do me a favour?"

"What?"

"Don't call me Col."

"Why not?"

"Dunno. Don't like it, that's all. Never did."

"Oh. All right, then. Silly."

And was it just accident as she nestled closer, or was that a hurried, momentary kiss on the point of his collar-bone? He didn't know, and wasn't going to ask.

They didn't talk after that, and soon he felt her slowly relaxing into sleep. At least he could give her that. Himself, he wasn't planning to sleep at all. Good bodyguards stayed awake, right? Not that he thought anything was going to happen; but he could be wrong, and if he was he wanted to be awake and ready for it.

And anyway, he didn't want to sleep. He was quite happy, lying here with Kez in his arms, listening to the radio. Sleep'd only get in the way, he might forget this was real and think he was only dreaming.

But he did sleep eventually, sliding into it unawares; and he went with a private grin on his face, thinking how turned-around Kez made him. Like, here he was with a girl in his bed, first time ever – and he'd been fighting so hard not to get an erection, even, just in case she noticed. Crazy, or what . . .?

And he woke again after an hour or two, with his face in her hair and her hair in his mouth. He teased it out with a finger, trying not to disturb her; and then couldn't resist running it through his hand, all the glorious long length of it

*(and maybe this was what silk felt like, and her skin was something else, maybe even just her skin and not like anything else in the world, he could believe that)*

slipping through his fingers like a daydream.

And she did wake up then, a soft grunt in her throat and her hand moving halfway to her head, sliding across his ribs to get there, her eyes opening cautious and curious.

He watched her focus and remember, saw her relax, all the caution burned away in a moment; and something bubbled into life deep inside him, came bubbling all through him, something deeper than content or happiness or any words he knew.

"Sorry," he said.

"'S'okay." She smiled softly, sleepily, and all the bubbles burst at once, little flowers of pain that made him shiver with a violent delight.

Then her hand moved on, up over his shoulder; he felt her fingers digging into the tough curls of his hair, and didn't dare move a muscle, not even his eyes. They stayed watching her lips, and read the words with a baffled joy.

"You're lovely," she said, and he saw her say it. That was all, and it wasn't *I love you*, it was a long way from that; but it was enough, Christ, it was more than enough.

## 25    *All in the Mind*

*Safety*, Seb thought, *is a boarding-house in Gravesend*; and grinned, and stretched himself out on the bed, gazing through the window at the pale morning sky beyond. It wasn't true, of course, but that didn't matter. Safety was being careful, doing things right. And at the moment, the right thing was being here, in a cheap and seedy room, taking it day by day and moment by moment. Feeling safe, *acting* safe, that was the important thing – not giving anyone the chance to wonder if maybe he wasn't safe.

*Safety is all in the mind.* He tried that, and found that it fitted better; but he didn't like it as much. It sounded chancy. Minds were subtle, dangerous things to depend on, too apt to change without notice.

Best not to go into it too deeply, perhaps. Not at the moment. Best just to settle for what he had, four walls and a door he could lock, and a landlord who wouldn't bother him, who would never think to connect one of his lodgers, his safe and predictable guests

*(it's a good job, isn't it, Mr Burton, working for the council? A social worker, a good, safe job, yes. And you'll only be staying a month or two, you say? Yes, I quite understand. That's fine. A lot of my guests are only here temporarily, while they find a place of their own. I like to see young men getting settled. Now there's to be no cooking in the rooms, I hope I've made that clear. It's not safe. I don't mind you bringing in a carry-out, but please keep your door closed, and put the rubbish out into the back yard, if you don't mind. The smell, you see . . .)*

with a police hunt, a photo on the telly.

Seb's watch beeped an alarm at him, and he rolled casually to his feet. Eight thirty; time to go. Time to pull on his jacket, lock his door, shimmy down the stairs and out of the door, to keep up the fiction of a regular job.

There was a mirror in the corner, above the wash-basin; he caught a glimpse of his moving reflection and was jerked to a sudden stop, taken by surprise once again by a face he didn't know. He'd dyed his hair in the showers on Waterloo Station, and it was oddly disorienting to look at himself and see chestnut instead of blond; but that was only the lesser change. He was losing weight fast, and it showed above all in his face, in the angular cheekbones and jutting jaw. *Losing all your pretty curves, Seb mate,* he thought, moving closer to the mirror to check the roots of his hair. *Still, it's useful. It's safe. And thin faces are in this year. As always.*

He put on a pair of sunglasses to hide his eyes

*(blue eyes and brown hair weren't safe together, they were too interesting. And thank God it was a hot summer, no one would think twice seeing a man in shades)*

and went down and out into the street, taking the stairs two at a time and the hall in three quick strides.

It was going to be another hot day. Yet another. Maybe he could skip the library, and stay out in the sun – or then again, maybe not. It was a matter of eyes, when you came right down to it. There were more eyes in the streets, in the

parks, than there were in the library; and eyes were dangerous, they might remember and make connections.

*Just because you're paranoid doesn't mean they're not out
to get you. They are.*

So he'd stay with the library, thanks. For the moment. He
could top up his tan on Sunday, if the weather held.

He went into the bakery on the corner to buy a couple of
ham rolls, one for breakfast, one for lunch; and found himself queueing behind a couple of girls. They were talking
about lectures, and essays; but those were clues he didn't
need. They were all too obviously students, from their
clothes, the folders and books thrusting out of shoulder-bags
designed to carry things with fewer corners, the general air
they had of living in a world of different priorities. For a
moment

*(Rebecca)*

Seb felt a pang of something more than memory, the
burning touch of a life-shift lived again, fresh and hot as the
first time, as every time since. Wondered where Rebecca
was now, if she'd been following the news: if she'd been
surprised to see his picture in the papers, hear his name.
And found the answer ready and waiting for him. No, she
wouldn't be surprised, how could she be? Not surprised, not
shocked. Shaken, perhaps – *so many others, and so much
worse* – and distressed for sure; but it'd make more sense to
her than to anyone else. She'd come closer to understanding.

Her face hung in front of his eyes, her voice filled his
mind, so much more than memory. The skin pale and filthy
with smeared make-up, tear-streaked, and *It – it's all right,
Seb. I understand. I guess. But – just go, will you? Please?
We'll talk later. Not now, I can't . . .*

"Yes, love, help you?"

He found himself at the counter, with his palms sweating
and no idea why he was there. He looked round blankly, felt
the stirring of hunger in his stomach, and remembered.
Laughed through a tight throat, and said, "Sorry, miles
away, I was. Two of your ham rolls, please. Oh, and a carton
of milk."

He paid the woman, and remembered as he did so how
low on cash he was running; and seized on the worry about
that as a welcome relief from the almost-physical haunting.

*Go away, Rebecca, I've got more important things to think about.*

He was going to have to do something about money, by the end of this week. No friendly bank-accounts now to keep him supplied as needed, no cash-cards to feed him fivers out of a slot and simply record an overdraft in green figures on a VDU. No indulgent mother to pay off said overdraft and slip him a little more; not even the fortnightly giro from the DHSS, which had never been nearly enough. Life was on a strict cash basis now, that was one of the greatest changes; and he needed to find a source.

Circumstances more or less ruled out any honest job. Even casual labour in a cafe or such would leave him open to too many questions, too close a scrutiny for comfort. That, of course, left crime; and he walked down the road chewing on a ham roll and considering the options. There was straightforward mugging,

*(but not rape, oh no, no sexual assault)*

he could certainly mug for a living if he had to. But he could probably do better than that. A mug's game, that was, pun very much intended. Burglary held more attraction, and probably carried no greater risk; or he quite fancied himself as a con man, if he could work out a viable scam . . .

A twenty-minute stroll brought him into the centre of town with no decisions made; but that was all right, he didn't need to act yet. Day by day and moment by moment, that was the way. There was still time for some other, unexpected solution to turn up; and if it didn't, well, he had no objection to bopping a few old ladies on the head to stave off insolvency while he worked out something more clever.

The library didn't open till half past nine, so he killed time with a coffee in a department store brasserie and a browse through their book section until ten, so as not to be found waiting on the doorstep, attracting attention. Then he made his way there, and ran straight upstairs like any other research student to claim a table in the reading-room.

He marked out his territory by throwing his jacket over the back of a chair, and went slowly downstairs again, to find something to read. All the newspapers had been claimed by the first-comers; he'd pick them up later, one by one, and check each for any mention of himself or Kez. That was the most productive thing he could do at the moment, stay out of sight and simply keep in touch. He couldn't make any long-term plans until the heat was off, until he was just another untraced and half-forgotten fugitive, not *news*; but in the meantime he had to be ready to respond to new developments, whether that response be running again or something more positive.

For the thousandth time he wondered where Kez could be hiding, and whether he stood any chance of finding her before the police did. Not so long as he was hanging around here, that was certain; but after the idiocy of leaving his car on full view in Hampstead, London proper was simply too dangerous for him. Especially as he had no more clues than anyone else now, where Kez might be. For all he knew, the note he'd found that night might have been an elaborate bluff, designed to bring him down here while she fled to the other end of the country. She wasn't stupid, after all; she could well have guessed that he'd follow her to Jill's house fairly smartly.

But she shouldn't have been thinking that clever, the state she must have been in. *Poor little sister*. No, he still felt safe assuming that she *had* come to London, and had simply thought better of going to Jenny. She was holed up somewhere in the city, somewhere among eight million people; and the chances of his being picked up there were far better than his chances of finding her. At the moment.

So, at the moment, he'd stay out of town. Wait, and watch. And pass his time with books . . .

At first he moved among the non-fiction shelves; but his eye fell on *The Psychology of Rape*, and he found himself turning his back and walking quickly away even while he smiled at himself for over-reacting. Six months ago he would have taken the book down and flicked through it, finding at the least some amusement in a professional analysis of his supposed motives. He might even have borrowed the book if he'd found it in Oxford, taken it home and read it properly, and either admitted its truths or laughed at its fallacies. But not now. *Too close to home* was his first thought; and then, *No, not that. The opposite. Home is safety, in any reasonable definition, security unchallenged; and I'm too far away from that.* It wasn't funny any more.

So he ended up in the fiction section, and thought himself

safe there. Until an old favourite turned treacherous on him, and laid him open to his ghosts again. Habit led him to D for du Maurier, thinking of *The House on the Strand* if it was in, or *Rule Britannia*, books which he knew well, which he could trust. But what he found instead was

(*Rebecca*)

*Rebecca*; and he left it alone, of course he did, and pulled a couple of others off the shelves almost at random, Ronald Firbank and E. F. Benson. Carried them upstairs, and took them to his seat; opened one or the other, and tried to read.

And saw nothing but a face framed with sandy-brown hair, a face that changed and changed again within that frame: that twisted easily

(*or was twisted, and how easy that twist had been*)

from a smile to a sob, from warmth to fear.

*Rebecca, get the hell out of my head!*

But she didn't or wouldn't or couldn't; and Seb found himself deep in the psychology of rape after all, deep in the bitterness and exaltation of something that should have been his first love affair and wasn't, not by a long chalk.

## 26 . Not That Easy

Colton's universe had shrunk alarmingly, holding nothing now except the bed, and himself, and Kez. He supposed vaguely that his room was still there surrounding them, and the refuge around that, and London further out, and the rest of the world in widening circles beyond; but he couldn't see or feel any of that, he couldn't believe in it. He didn't have the space. He was just lying there with her sprawled loosely against him, supporting her with an arm that had gone dead long ago, dying for a piss and feeling wonderful. He watched her through the thick grey light, and felt her breathing, slow and steady and easy, and didn't want her ever to wake up. This was enough for him, and he was terrified of losing it.

At last she did, though, she stirred and shifted and lifted her head an inch. Her eyes met his, through a curtain of hair; he held his breath, and saw a half-smile touch her lips before her head dropped back onto his shoulder again.

"Hullo, Col."

"Hi." It was a word that was more than half a sigh, as all his air escaped him in a rush. She chuckled, and snuggled closer; and he found a little life in his right arm after all, just enough to tighten it around her narrow shoulders as he said, "And don't call me Col."

"Sorry. Forgot."

"Yeah." ·

They lay quietly for a minute, while his fingers played with a fold in her

*(his)*

rugby shirt; then,

"What time is it, Colton, d'you know?"

"Hang on."

He let his left arm slip out of bed and fumble across the carpet, till his fingers found the strap of his watch. Picked it up, and held it in front of his eyes so that he wouldn't have to move his head even half an inch, and break its tenuous contact with hers.

"Yeah, it's twenty to eleven."

"Bugger."

"What?"

"I said bugger."

"Yeah, I heard. What's up, I meant."

"Well, everyone else is, by now." With another chuckle; and, *Score plenty for that, boy. She couldn't have made a joke last night. Not if you'd paid her.* "So I suppose we should too, and I don't want to."

"Me neither." Tightening his grip again, to hold her still in case she tried to move.

"Won't they come looking for us, though?"

"Not yet. There's no rules about it, now Mark's in charge. Mrs H used to be quite strict about bedtimes and getting-up times and stuff, but Mark don't give a toss. He might come and have a look in an hour, in case we're ill or something, but there's no panic about it. Hell, Davey never gets up before twelve."

"Good." And this time it was her arm that wriggled itself

tighter around his ribs, making the breath catch in his throat in a fresh panic, *stay cool, baby, don't get excited for God's sake, can't hide it now.*

And more than anything else it was the growing warmth in his groin, the threat of last night all over again, that gave him the nerve to say, "Tell you what, though, Kez, I've been thinking . . ."

"Oh, yeah?" Her voice was lightly teasing, wrapped around a giggle. "When did you find the time for that, then?"

*The last couple of hours, while you was sleeping and I was holding you. Only I ain't telling you that, girl.* "Just now. I mean, I know I ain't smart, but I do think sometimes, you know?"

"Hey." She did move now, propping herself up on one elbow to face him directly, brushing her hair back out of the way. "I was only kidding, okay? Don't take me seriously. It's just, I don't know, a knee-jerk reaction, being snide like that, it doesn't mean anything. We used to do it all the time, me and . . ."

And she cut herself off dead; and because of everything – because of how scared she was, and because he wanted to help her, and because he was getting an erection again in spite of everything, because her breast was brushing against his chest, because of the way she was hanging over him – he finished it for her. "You and your brother."

Not a muscle in her moved, but he sensed her going suddenly stiff inside, pulling away from him. For a second he didn't know what the hell was going to happen; but then she spoke softly and clearly, said "Yes, me and my brother," and added, "Fuck you, Col, did you have to make me say it?"

"Gonna make you say a whole lot more than that, girl. And don't call me Col." She didn't respond to that, so he went on quietly, "Thing is, Kez, I know why you're so frightened of him, and I ain't saying you're wrong; but, I don't know, it scares me, just to see you that scared. It ain't healthy, you'll make yourself sick. And I was thinking, maybe it'd help if you talked about it. About him. I know you don't want to," as she stiffened again, and this time physically, so that he could feel her muscles tense against him, "but how's about doing it anyway? For me? Just see if it helps, like, you can stop if you want, I just think you should try, that's all . . ."

He ran out of words then, couldn't do anything except hold her, and hope that he was right, that he wasn't going to scare her away and blow everything. The silence seemed to drag on for ever; but at last she sniffed, shook her head and said, "Yes. Okay, I'll try. I've got to face up to it some time, I suppose; and if I can't talk to you . . ."

She left that sentence hanging; but even as it was, unfinished and uncertain, it brought the bubbles back for Colton, making him feel unbelievably special.

Only then her hand moved slowly across his chest, tracing a line like fire on his skin; and she said, "I can't do it like this, though. Not in bed."

"Why not? Best place for it, I reckon. Nice and comfy," and never mind that he was going to wet the bed soon, "just the two of us . . ."

"That's the *point*," she said, making her hand into a fist to thump his ribs with, to hammer it home. "I don't, I don't want *him* here too, getting between us . . . Does that make sense?"

"Nah, it's crazy." Meaning yes again, and knowing she'd understand. "What d'you want to do, then?"

"I don't know. Get dressed, have some coffee. Have a pee," she added with a smile. He laughed and hugged her, and wondered how she could say that, so casual; because he couldn't have said it to her, no way.

"You go and get some clothes on, then," he said, "and I'll make the coffee. Bring it up here, shall I, so we can be private?" And when she nodded, "Your room or mine?"

"In here." She was definite about that, turning to look round the walls in a way that brought them back into Colton's shrunken universe, made it that bit bigger. "I like this place, it's dead right for you."

"Yeah." And if he'd liked it before, he loved it now, wouldn't change a picture or put up so much as another postcard without her approval.

She moved suddenly, decisively, slithering across him and sitting full on his stomach for a second while she swung her feet to the floor and stood up. He caught a momentary glimpse of one buttock before the shirt fell down to cover it, but was too busy to think about it, grabbing the duvet as it fell away from her and pulling it up to cover himself. She looked round, saw him clutching it to his chest, and giggled.

"'S'all right for you," he said hotly, "you've got a nightie on, you're decent."

"So are you, stupid. Even with no clothes on." She reached out a hand to touch his face; then snatched it away and almost ran out of the room. He watched the door swing shut behind her, and felt her leaving like a pain below his ribs, sharp and lasting.

But at least it solved one problem. He'd been in a fret earlier, about what if maybe he had to get up first. Underwear was the thing. He couldn't have gone prancing naked round the room looking for a clean pair of underpants, he just couldn't, not with her watching. But if he'd done the easy thing, grabbed yesterday's out of his jeans and pulled them on quick, not giving her anything except a sneak view of his bum, she might've thought that was really yucky. Girls could be funny about things like that, wearing yesterday's knickers . . .

But she was gone, and he had to be moving. He rolled out of bed, reached for his clothes – and checked, went to the wardrobe and dug around for a clean pair of underpants. Just in case. Socks, too – and what the hell, while he was there, a fresh T-shirt and his other pair of jeans. Give her a treat.

He left his room, finding that without Kez beside him his old universe was still there, just as he'd left it last night; ran downstairs and had that piss at last – and giggled in the middle of it, and almost missed the bowl, thinking of her doing the same thing in the upstairs bathroom. Then he went into the kitchen, said a quick hi to the others, and got two mugs out of the cupboard. Put the kettle on and found the coffee, spooned it out, and felt them all watching him, all those curious eyes. Looked over his shoulder, and no, they were just chatting, ignoring him. Except they'd probably all turned away that second, just before he looked . . .

*Paranoid, that's what you are, Colton mate,* he thought; and felt dead proud of himself for remembering the word. *Yeah, paranoid. They haven't got a clue.*

He strolled over to the window and looked out, whistling under his breath, waiting for the kettle to boil. Felt those eyes again, and checked the reflection in the glass. Yup, paranoid, that's all it was.

Except then the kettle did boil, and he made the coffee, sloshed milk in and carried the mugs to the door; and Nina was watching him all the way. That wasn't paranoid, he caught her at it. Met her eyes, and saw her smile; and got out of there quick, before she could say anything. That wouldn't stop her talking, of course, but at least he wouldn't have to hear it. And maybe the others wouldn't listen, if he wasn't there looking all guilty and embarrassed. Maybe they'd just put it down to her nasty tongue, nothing in it, just Nina trying to make trouble again . . .

He carried the mugs down the corridor to the hall, and almost walked straight into Mark.

"Whoops! Careful, kid. You spill it, you clear it up."

"Yeah, right, sorry. It's okay, didn't spill . . ." He glanced up at Mark's face and down again, felt panic opening like a flower in his guts, *Christ, what would he say? If he knew we'd spent the night together? What would he* do? Said, "I, um, I met Kez upstairs, coming out of the loo. Said I'd take her, you know, a coffee, she don't eat breakfast . . ."

"Good, thanks, Colton." Mark sounded like he wasn't listening to a word. "Listen, Jane's staying in her room this morning, okay? I've told the others. She's all right, but she'll be leaving us this afternoon, she's going back to Ipswich. Alex is with her now, and it'd be best to leave them be for the moment; but don't worry, you'll get a chance to say goodbye to her, before she goes."

"Oh, right. Okay." He should have been full of questions, he knew that – where was she going, who was taking her, what was the hurry – but Kez was still there in his head, still filling it. The smell and touch of her, the taste of her hair in his mouth, the ghosts and fears behind her eyes . . . He just didn't have the room for anyone or anything else yet.

Getting to his room at last, Colton nudged the door open with his hip and found Kez in there already, sitting on the bed hugging his pillow and chewing a corner fretfully. He put the coffees down carefully on the floor and sat beside her, his arm finding its way almost automatically around her shoulders as he said, "What's up, anything?"

She nodded, and went on chewing. Moving slowly, he peeled her unresisting arms away from the pillow, teased it from between her teeth and tossed it behind them, then pulled her close. Her teeth closed on his T-shirt. He grinned, then felt the sharpness of her bite on the muscle of his shoulder, sending a jolt right through him. His grip on her tightened instinctively, and, *watch it, girl, or I'll bite you back. And Christ knows what'll happen then, and so do I, I reckon; but I dunno if it's what you need, so just, just watch it, okay?*

Aloud, he said, "What, then?"

"Went out of here without looking, didn't I?" she mumbled, against his neck. And yeah, she was fretting, but she was almost laughing too. "And I ran right into that Alex girl. She must've seen which room I came out of. And me with just that shirt on, just out of bed . . ."

"Oh, fuck. *Fuck* it. That's trouble. She's in dead thick with Mark, she'll tell him, sure as anything."

"I don't know, Col. Ton." The last bit added with half a giggle. "I mean, she didn't look shocked, just a bit surprised. And I might have imagined it, but I *think* she winked at me. Maybe she just had something in her eye, but I don't think so. I didn't stop to ask, though, I just ran . . ."

"Yeah, right." He shrugged, and felt his shoulder rub gently against her hair. "Well, just have to see what happens. They can't do anything except bollock us, they ain't gonna throw us out. And we didn't, you know, do anything, anyway. You just needed company, that's all. Mark'll understand."

Kez snorted. "You think he'll believe that?"

"Well. He might."

"No chance," she said flatly; but she said it smiling. And bit his shoulder again, so that he almost said it aloud. *Watch it, girl, or we will be doing something.*

He let go of her, to reach down and pick up the coffees. She took one, wrapping both hands around the mug and staring down into the steam. He sipped from the other, and said, "Come on, then. Tell me about Seb."

"I can't."

"You got to, Kez. I thought we was straight on that. You *need* to."

"I'm not arguing. But I don't know how. I mean, what do you want to know? He's my brother, that's all. He's twenty-four, he went to Oxford, he's tall and blond and dead good-looking. But you know all that, you've seen the papers. And that picture of us."

"Yeah." *And if you think he looks good, you should see yourself, girl. There was both of you in that photo. Try looking at it through my eyes.* Colton still had it, torn carefully out of the paper and preserved in his wallet, for taking out and looking at, the times when he was alone. He'd thought of cutting Seb out of it, but there wouldn't be much left after that, it wouldn't last long. So he'd kept it whole, and just tried not to look at Seb. Except he thought it meant something, that he couldn't see Kez without seeing her brother too, his arm round her shoulders, *gotcha*, and that sly grin on his face.

"Okay, so say I haven't read the papers. Just pretend, right? Say I don't know nothing about it."

"You'd be the only guy in Britain who didn't."

He reached for his cigarettes, and didn't say anything.

"Well, I'll try. But I don't know what."

"Like they say. Start at the beginning. When you was kids."

"We never were, really. Not kids together. He's eight years older than me, remember. And my sister Judith was six years older than him, even, so she was almost grown up when I was born."

Colton nodded. He'd seen Judith on the telly news a few nights ago, her and Kez's mum sitting on a sofa, and it was dead hard to believe she was really Kez's sister. She'd looked so old, and not just because she was worried. They'd been making one of those tearful appeals people did, *Seb . . . Kez . . . wherever you are, whatever's happened, come forward and let us help, we can sort it all out somehow . . . It's the only way . . . We love you both . . .* Colton had been alone in the games room for once, having torn himself away from Kez and a kitchen poker school both, to do his quiet watch-dog act, keeping in touch with what the world knew. He hadn't told Kez; she'd only get upset, and it wouldn't do any good. She wasn't going home until Seb was found, that was the only thing she was definite about. She wasn't going any place he could find her. And Colton had his own angle on that; he wasn't going to *let* her go anywhere, unless he was sure it was safe. And that meant she wasn't going nowhere without him.

"What about your dad?" he asked. "I ain't heard nothing

about him."

"You haven't been reading the papers properly," Kez said in a dull, flat voice. "They've all run that little story, as a bit of extra juice to pad the pages out. He left home while Mum was pregnant with me. He said he was going to find lodgings in Oxford, so's he could still be near us; only he didn't, he just disappeared. They think he probably left the country, went off to Canada or Australia. None of us has heard a word from him since."

Colton scowled, and wished someone had thought to let him in on that. They wouldn't, though; why should they? They wouldn't know he'd missed it, and wouldn't know he needed it.

Nothing he could say now, though; too late for sympathy, and no point in apologies. That was an old, familiar pain he'd stirred up there, and it wasn't nothing to what he was going to do, what he was doing now.

"So who looked after Seb, while your mum was having you?"

"Judith. It was a long job, too, because Mum was ill for ages afterwards. It was really chancy, having another baby at her age, and she only just got away with it." Then, with a tired smile, "I don't suppose Judith was much good at it, though. She's never been what you might call maternal; and she was what, fourteen, she had her own life to live. Seb didn't talk about it much, I don't think he liked to; but he did say she left him alone a lot of the time. And they've never really got on that well since. I guess it changes things a lot, when your sister's suddenly acting like your mother . . ."

"Must do, yeah."

"I don't think he had a lot of friends back then, either. He never has had, really; but it was worse then. I remember him saying once, he said he was too clever and too fat to get on with other kids."

"He ain't fat, Kez. Not in that photo, he ain't."

"Not now, no. But he was when I was young, I can remember that. I used to tease him about it, when he'd been getting at me."

"What, bully you much, did he?"

She shook her head, with a hint of a smile. "No. It's not that easy, Colton, really it isn't. I've been looking back, over and over, I've hardly done anything else since I got here; but there's nothing I can put my finger on, and say that was where it started, and it grew into – into what he is now. No, he never bullied me. He was sweet as pie – my wonderful big brother, you know? Ever since I can remember. We fought, sure, but just brother-and-sister stuff, it didn't mean anything, it couldn't touch the way I felt. I didn't just love him, I worshipped him, almost. Especially when I got a bit older, it was even better then, because he burned all that fat off, and I could boast to all my friends about how wonderful he was and I knew they wouldn't laugh. I was so *proud* of him, you wouldn't believe . . ." Her voice caught then, and he reached for her hand without even thinking about it, folding his fingers into hers.

"What about him, though, what was he up to? What about girls, many of them?"

"No. None at all, that I can remember. Not till he went to university." She was frowning now, wrestling with her memory, trying to make sense of it all. "It's odd, that, you'd think they would've been flocking round him, wouldn't you? A guy who looks as good as that . . . And he's not gay, either."

*Well, no,* Colton thought and didn't say. *You can be sure of that.*

"But he just never did have girlfriends. Not that he brought home, anyway, or talked about. And he would have told me, we were really close. Talked about everything. I thought."

Her voice didn't die away, it cut off dead, leaving her stranded some place terrible, by the bleak, hopeless look in her eye. Colton gripped her hand tight, *hang on to that, kid, I'll pull you through somehow, I swear I will,* and nudged her back on track.

"He had a girl at college, though, did he? You said it was different then."

"For a while. I liked her a lot. I remember he brought her out to meet us a couple of times, at weekends. Rachel, or something – no, Rebecca,

Rebecca didn't make sense. That was what shook him, and did more than shake him – what shook his whole world, the world he saw.

Christ, she was a woman, wasn't she? Or a girl. Female. And if anyone understood females, it should be him. The house – his past – was bloody full of them, after all. Mum, Judith, Keryn – sorry, Kez.

And the thing about females, the rock-solid fact that underlay all his understanding, was that they didn't leave you in any doubt. One way or another (and they all had their own separate ways: Mum ordered, Judith organised, Kez either demanded or wheedled, depending on how grown-up she was feeling) they let you know what they wanted. And got it, sure. A lifetime of experience had taught him that, you gave them what they were after, or they'd very lovingly take it out of you in blood. One way or another.

And that was why he kept tripping up, with Rebecca – because even after knowing her for a full year, he still couldn't make out what she wanted. He couldn't get a handle on her at all, there was just nothing to hang on to. It felt like trying to fish shards of shell out of a raw egg; he'd grab and grab, and the more he grabbed the more she slithered away, slipping out of his grasp just when he thought that at last he had her, at last he could make some sense out of her.

It wasn't right, it wasn't *kind*, when a guy only wanted to know where he stood. But she was still doing it now, still slithering. He'd taken her out for the evening, and wasn't even sure if he'd got that right; as usual, she hadn't thrown out so much as a hint of what she wanted to do, she'd just left all the decisions to him. Smiled, and said yes, and gone along. She'd seemed happy enough, yes; but then, she always did. That didn't help, it didn't tell him anything.

And now she was sitting quietly on her bed, smiling, not saying anything, just
– slithering –
watching him while he walked, fidgeted, checked the titles on her bookshelves, wondered what to do.
– *Coming up?* she'd said. And, *I've got coffee.*
And did it mean anything, the way she'd put her hand on his arm, as she'd said it? Christ knew. And did it mean anything, that she hadn't made a move towards the kettle, that she was just sitting
– on the bed –
and watching? And smiling?
He wanted to shout, to scream, to shake her, *Tell me what you want!* But that was a common feeling by now, a classic, and he'd learned to avoid it. Not to escape, no, it'd be back; but it could be dodged, for now. All it took was action. Shift the scene, and see what happens next.
So he sat down abruptly next to her and put his arm round her, taking another step in the dark. Thus far, the ground was at least familiar; this had happened before. He knew the way her slim shoulders fitted into the crook of his arm, the way her sandy-brown hair floated across his cheek as she turned her head, the way her smile looked in close-up, with her lips half parted and the white teeth not quite straight behind.
He lowered his head to kiss her, to dodge the questions again and hide that haunting smile; and met it instead with an extra dimension, physical and solid against his mouth. It wasn't Rebecca he was kissing, even as his tongue touched fleetingly against hers, it was only her bloody smile. And was she laughing at him, at his confusion, was that why her mouth was opening wider like an invitation, just to let out a silent belly-laugh? Could be, Seb, could be.
He gripped her tighter and thrust his tongue deep into her mouth, seeking nothing but the source of his uncertainty, wanting nothing but to dig it out and destroy it. He felt her arms curl tight around his neck, but knew it for only a response; as always she was a measure behind him, following, going along.
Breaking away for a snatched breath, his eyes went questing across her face and found nothing but that smile, lurking in her eyes now while her mouth poised, open and wet and

waiting. He could almost hate her sometimes for being so different, so wrong. For leaving him flailing in uncertainty,
*(unsafe)*
so blind, groping and grabbing in the dark.

It was nothing but her body that he held in his arms, he knew that much. Not her mind, soul, spirit – call it what you would, that was
– slithering –
far out of his reach, watching, waiting. No doubt smiling.

His hand fumbled awkwardly with the buttons of her blouse, easing it open far enough to slip inside and cup her breast against his palm, searching for a signal. Her head dropped against his shoulder, showing him nothing but a heavy fall of hair.

Fighting the words out through a tight throat, he said, "Rebecca. Do you want me to stop?"

And still got nothing but a brief motion of her head against him, which might have meant yes and might have meant no.

He thrust himself away from her with a spasm of helpless anger, stood up and pulled his shirt off over his head. She looked up at him and smiled, and
*(following, copying, saying yes)*
began to untuck her blouse.

His shoes, and hers; trousers, skirt, underwear; and they stood naked, facing each other, a yard apart.

"You're lovely," he said, meaning, *Help me. Guide me. Show me what you want. Give me some certainty. You're a woman, it's in your gift, and I'm drowning here.*

And she smiled and shook her head, meaning, *No.*

And
*(God, if she'd only come to me, take a step, just reach out a hand, she doesn't have to talk)*
she didn't move, so he had to. He stepped forward and put his arms round her waist, feeling the soft weight of her breasts against his ribs, and warmth contained in a cool skin.

She took her cue from him as ever, wrapped her arms about him and settled her head against his chest, still following, still that beat behind.

Even now she wouldn't give him the sense of direction – of being directed – that he so badly needed. The anger snapped back into his head, just strong enough and hot enough to carry them both over to the bed, to push her down onto the duvet and pull him down after; and a stray thought slicked his mind across like oil on water, saying, *Anger could do it all, if you'd let it. You could ride the anger, and the anger could ride her.*

Only that wasn't what he was here for, nor what he was hungry for. He let it slip and run, and for a moment felt himself abandoned, naked and defenceless. But God, she was here too, and as naked as himself. This must be what she wanted, he could surely count on that.

So he took his weight on his elbows, and felt himself hanging, caught by the moment. He looked down at her, searching her eyes and lips for even the whisper of a word; and saw nothing except that haunting smile.

Haunted, he buried his face in her hair and tried to take it for a 'yes', her usual quiet acceptance; and tried to pretend that he wasn't more than lost here, that he wasn't crashing, falling, dying. Tried, and failed.

The failure was proved and brutally underlined by his treacherous body, by his penis hanging limp and ignorant between his legs, not going anywhere. He yearned and strained, tried to force it into life, closed his eyes and made believe he was only wanking, nothing different from any normal night; but the panic-measures were ritual and hopeless, and he knew it. Only the panic was real.

Any minute now, he knew, even as he clutched and grunted, as his head swam with despair; any minute now, she was going to do it, at last and far too late. She was going to take the initiative, and love it. He'd hear her voice, *Seb, it's all right. Just relax. Lots of boys can't, the first time.* And she'd ease out from under him, he'd feel her fingers in his hair, gentling his head down onto her shoulder; and he'd open his eyes to find that smile just inches away, filling his mind and his future, day by day and night after long, bitter night . . .

And with that vision in his head, searingly bright, he took the only other path he could, the one that led away from everywhere. He abandoned his choices, and let the anger in; and did more than let it, he called it, urged it, whipped it on.

Riding the anger, he had a lot more than an erection to show Rebecca; and he let her have it all, plunging and thrusting, digging deep. If he couldn't catch hold of her this way he could sure to God crush her, and there was a certainty in that which would do more than satisfy.

He heard her sobbing, crying, "No, Seb, no," and knew that for a victory, and surged again. And smiled, content with the thought that she wasn't smiling now.

Later, after he'd left her,
*(It – it's all right, Seb. I understand. I guess. But – just go, will you? Please? We'll talk later. Not now, I can't . . .)*
he watched himself in shop-windows on the long walk home, looking for the change; and found it. It was there in the way he walked, the way he held himself, even with no one but himself to see. It wasn't sex – Christ, you couldn't even *call* that sex, what he'd done tonight. He'd fucked her, sure, but that was different. Sex was fumbling and uncertainty, worrying beforehand and living with it afterwards. Fucking was simple, straightforward, stronger.

And it was strength he could see in his reflection, in every sweet, shining window. He wouldn't even need the anger next time, he could do it now. He knew how. He was finally just beginning to understand himself, what he had and what he needed. Strength and power, an awareness of power within himself, yes, that was it,

## 28   Reasons to Stop

that was it, Rebecca. I wish she'd lasted. Funny girl, though – dead quiet, you know? She hardly talked at all, that I can remember. Though maybe she just never got the chance, with us around." A brief smile touched her face, and was gone. "I used to reckon Seb was only going out with her because she was such a change from us bossy lot. She was really keen on him, though, you could tell. She couldn't keep this smile off her face, every time she looked at him. I remember that."

"So what happened?" Colton asked, as Kez lapsed into silence.

"Don't know. He never said, really. And I didn't like to ask. If he didn't want to talk about it, I didn't have any right to press him. They just split up, that was all. I remember, I asked him on the phone one night, how she was; and he just said he wasn't seeing her any more. Maybe it ended badly, and that put him off trying again, because I don't think there was anyone after that, till Annabel. Not that he let on about, anyway."

"Who's Annabel?"

"She turned up his last year at university, and he's been going out with her ever since. She lives in Oxford, see, so it's easy. Couple of nights a week, they see each other. Used to." With a shiver which sent her burrowing against him, looking for shelter. "I never understood what he saw in Annabel, but that could be just prejudice, 'cos I didn't like her that much. I think she was too much like Judith. Bossy elder sister, you know? But it wasn't ever one of the great love affairs. He never even stayed overnight; and so far as I know they didn't have any plans to live together. I used to think Annabel was holding out on him, until he got a job and started to do something with his life. She used to get at him about that, I heard her. Just like the rest of us." Colton couldn't see her face now, but he heard her snort into his sweatshirt, and could picture another quick, bitter smile fading fast. "Me, too. I used to bully him something rotten. It seemed such a *waste*, a clever guy like that, kicking around on the dole. But he was happy, I suppose. He had his, his *interests* . . ."

And now the shivers set in for real, shaking her hard; and Colton couldn't stop them, even with both arms wrapped hard around her. *Time to give over, boy. Dunno if it's helped or not, but that's enough. More than.*

He shifted his grip, and lifted her easily onto his lap; said, "Christ, girl, you don't weigh nothing, you know that?" and simply hugged her, tight and tender, waiting for a reason to stop.

Finally Kez gave him one, gripping his wrist with light fingers and turning it to read the face of his watch. "Colton, do you think we could have the radio on, just for a bit? I'd like to catch the news . . ."

*You want to know if Seb's on it, right?* Aloud, he said, "Sure, no problem," and reached one hand down to flick the switch, keeping a firm grip on her with the other, just in case. And was glad he had; because yeah, there was Seb all right, top billing. And the news he brought with him was enough to make Kez do more than shake . . .

"The Metropolitan Police have now released the names of the two women found dead after the explosion and fire in Hampstead at the weekend. They were Mrs Grace Richardson, a sixty-eight-year-old pensioner, and Miss Jennifer Wright, a jewellery designer, aged forty-two. Both bodies were severely burned in the fire, and identified only through dental records; but the police believe that both women died before the fire was started. A murder enquiry has been launched, and any member of the public with information is asked to contact the Incident Room at Hampstead Police Station. Although the police are keeping an open mind at present, they have pointed out that Sebastian Hughes, the man being sought in connection with a series of rapes in Oxfordshire, was known to Miss Wright, and that his car was found half a mile from her flat. The search for him is now being concentrated in the Greater London area.

"Other news: the Duke and Duchess of York have made a surprise visit to Northern Ireland . . ."

Colton snapped the radio off again as Kez pushed suddenly, savagely away from him and walked blindly to the window. He wanted to go after her and couldn't, after being so deliberately turned away from; and had to accept that there was a limit to the comfort his arms could offer her, and she was well past that limit now.

Alex had always been good with kids – drawing them out, relaxing them, cheering them up. As the eldest of four, with two working parents, she'd had to be. But two hours with Jane had exhausted her, and she was only too relieved when Mark came in at half past eleven to take over. It was as if Jane had forgotten how to smile, almost how to talk; and Alex had never had to deal before with a girl so damaged, so nearly destroyed. She'd been driven to talking about herself, talking fast and almost at random of her own childhood in the New Forest, of ancient trees and wild ponies,

*(and ponies are okay, just, but for God's sake don't mention pets)*

of her twin devils of ambition and curiosity leading her into her current job via university in Brighton; and finally ending up with the true story of how she'd come to the refuge. That had at least evoked a little interest; Alex got the impression that in more ordinary circumstances, Jane would have been thrilled to discover a journalist

*(spy)*

living among them in disguise, and doubly thrilled to be the first of the kids to learn the truth.

But circumstances weren't normal, and it was bloody hard work simply to keep talking, to drive out the dreadful silence that lurked behind Jane's eyes; and all in all, Alex had never been more glad to see anyone than when Mark appeared in the doorway and beckoned her out.

"How is she?" Last night's hostility seemed to have been forgotten this morning, or at least overridden by more urgent concerns.

Alex shrugged. "Not good, but you'd expect that. She'll be okay. Kids are tough, you know? She just needs time, that's all. And something else to think about. I did my best, but she wasn't even listening half the time." *Or not to me. Listening to her rats, that's what she's doing in there. Hearing them die.*

"Yeah, right. Well, look, you take a break now, you've done enough. I'll go in and tell her a bit more about what's happening, and what she should expect back in Ipswich. Get her worrying about that instead," he added, with a grin where the malice was totally and obviously fake.

"Fine. Anything else I can do?"

"You can explain yourself to the others, if you want." Another grin, more malice measured out by the spoonful. "And if you wanted to be really useful, you could put some sandwiches together for lunch. I sent Tia and Nina out to the shops, so there's plenty of bread; and we've got cheese and eggs, and some tinned stuff. Just make twice as many as you think nine people could possibly eat, and tell 'em if they want more they can do it themselves. Then sit back and watch 'em do it."

"Right you are, Mark." She smiled back, *I don't know if this is pax or just a truce, but either way I like it better than what we had last night,* and went downstairs.

A quick scout through the kitchen cupboards produced oil and vinegar and mustard, and a couple of tins of tuna; Alex chuckled cheerfully, rolled her sleeves up and was just going to start work when she noticed the phone on the wall. *Get it over with now, girlie. Might as well.*

Picked the receiver up, and dialled her editor.

". . . I see, Alex. And just what happens when they take us to court, and require us to reveal the address of this place?"

"I go to prison for contempt, of course. What else?"

"And quite right too, you are very contemptible. What concerns me more is that I could very well join you."

"No, you couldn't, they don't have blokes in Holloway, they'd get mobbed. And anyway, you just have to plead ignorance. I'm the secretive type, see. I didn't give you the address."

"You didn't? So what precisely is it that I copied down in what is manifestly my own handwriting, onto the sheet of paper I have in front of me now?"

"Well, I don't know, boss. What did you copy it from?"

"The palm of your hand, as I remember."

"Oh, well, in that case it must be my gran's address in Brighton. Can't think why you've got that, you might as well tear it up, yeah? Gran wouldn't like to be bothered by a lot of reporters, she's entitled to her privacy."

"Alex, the first rule of journalism is that no one is entitled to their privacy."

But she heard tearing noises coming down the phone; and hung up, satisfied, while he was still tearing.

Ten minutes later, Alex was stirring tuna into a bowl when she heard footsteps in the corridor, and the kitchen door was pushed open. She looked up, and smiled.

"Hullo, Mandy. Lunch'll be ready in a minute. Come and taste this, tell me what you think."

Mandy walked over, peered into the bowl and shook her head. "No thanks, I'd be sick."

Alex laughed. "It's a good thing you're pregnant, kid, or I'd belt you one. But I'll do you something else, if you like. What do you fancy?"

"I'm not hungry."

"You may not be, love, but I bet your baby is. You've got to eat."

Mandy considered that, and nodded. "Cheese and Marmite, then. Please."

"Cheese and *Marmite*? Are you sure?" And when Mandy nodded, "Yuck. But go on, then, find us the Marmite."

"It's in that big cupboard, on the top shelf. I can't reach."

Alex made a face at her, got a solemn little smile in return, and went to the cupboard. While she was scrabbling among the jars on the top shelf, Mandy suddenly addressed a statement to her back.

"You're not sixteen. I don't care what you say, you're *not*."

Alex checked, and looked back over her shoulder at the younger girl. "No," she said quietly, "you're right. I'm not."

"What are you, then?"

She didn't mean in age, and Alex didn't pretend to misunderstand. "I'm a journalist."

"What are you doing here?" Mandy's hands gripped the edge of the table, so tight that Alex could see her knuckles turning white, even from the other side of the room.

*Looking for a story, kid. And you're it. And you know it, right? That's why you're scared.*

She found the Marmite and turned, with the jar in her hands and an easy smile on her lips. "I'll do you a deal, Mandy. There's the bread, and there's the margarine; you know where the knives are, and the plates. So sit yourself down and get busy, and I'll tell you all about it, okay? You spread, and I'll talk."

Nina and Tia drifted in together at half past, to see what was cooking; Alex distributed coffee, sandwiches and information, then asked, "Do you know where the others are? The boys, and Kez Hughes?"

"I know where Colton is, right enough," Nina said, with a sneer. "He'll be with Kez."

"Right." Alex remembered seeing the girl slipping out of Colton's room that morning, all legs and shirt and startled guilt, and suppressed a smile. "So where's Kez?"

"Dunno. Where Colton is." The two girls giggled, and Alex sighed heavily.

"Great help, Nina. Thanks. What about Davey? Either of you?"

Nina just shrugged, *couldn't care less*; Tia shook her head. "He was around earlier. Went out, I think. Didn't say where."

"All right. Never mind. It's his problem, if he misses lunch."

"One of his problems," Nina said, and giggled again, alone this time. "Hey, are you going to write about me, for this paper of yours?"

"Maybe. No names, though. Just the reasons you left home, and something about what you want to do for the future. I'll talk to you about it later, after things have settled down a bit." Then an idea struck her, watching them chew their way through a pile of sandwiches. "I wouldn't mind a photo now, though. Not your faces, we'll keep this anonymous; but a view of the kitchen with you lot sitting at the table like this, nice and atmospheric . . ."

"Not me," Mandy said abruptly, from her seat at the other end. "Please. I don't want my picture in the paper."

"All right, love. No pressure. How about you two, any objections?"

Nina shook her head immediately; Tia thought about it, and shrugged. "I don't mind."

"Great. Hang on, then, I'll get my camera."

Alex ran up to the attic, and dug around in her carrier bag until she found the camera; then, on the way down again, she stopped on an impulse outside Colton's door. No voices, but that didn't mean they weren't in there. She grinned to herself, and moved a half-step away; but curiosity took her back, to tap lightly on the panelled door. No squeaking springs, either, and if her own bed last night was anything to go by, that meant they weren't actually bonking at the moment, whatever else they might be doing . . .

"Yeah, who is it?" Colton's voice, sounding almost relieved, as if the interruption were something to be welcomed rather than resented. Alex pushed the door open, and looked inside.

They were both there, all right: Colton sitting on the bed looking miserable, and Kez on the floor under the window. Alex didn't have words to describe the way she looked – though 'suicidal' came closest to it, with her haggard face and eyes like wounds, the way her hands were clutching her knees hard and still visibly trembling.

Alex wondered whether to ask what was wrong, and decided against it. Best just to leave it for the moment, they probably wouldn't appreciate her interfering. She'd mention it to Mark, and keep an eye on the kid herself, see how she was looking by the evening.

"Lunch," she said briefly, casually, as if she'd noticed nothing. "You two coming down?"

"Yeah." Colton got to his feet, giving her a quick, grateful glance, *thanks for getting me out of this*. Then he turned to Kez. "Come on, eh?"

Kez just shook her head listlessly. "I don't want any."

"Yes, you bloody do." Alex could sense Colton's urgent relief at having something to *do*, some reason to move himself and to get Kez moving, as he crossed the room in three long strides, grabbed the girl's wrists and pulled her almost angrily to her feet. He shifted his grip then, holding her tight around the waist as if afraid she'd just flop down again without his support; and that same fiery near-anger was in his voice as he hissed, "You got to fight that fucker, girl. It don't matter what he's done, you're still the one who can put him away, right? So you can't just give up and fade away. You got to eat."

"I'll throw up," she muttered; but her eyes were fixed on his in some exchange that was worth a lot more than either of them was saying, and Alex watched quietly from the doorway as her hands moved up his back to his narrow shoulders, and clung there.

"So throw. 'S'okay, I won't be mad. I'll even clean it up. Just so long as you *try*. You're so bloody thin, it's scary."

"You can't talk. Bloody skeleton, you are . . ."

And then her head thrust itself into his shoulder, and her fingers tightened like claws; and, *time to go, Alex. Curious is one thing, but voyeur's something else, something nasty.*

They followed her down a few minutes afterwards. Colton had lost that look of trapped misery, and exhibited a certain proprietorial smugness as he guided Kez to the table with a hand on the small of her back. Alex winked at him, and passed over a plate of sandwiches.

He took one, peeled back a corner and peered suspiciously.

"That ain't cheese and pickle."

"Well done, you noticed."

"So what is it?"

"Try."

He nibbled cautiously, and blinked. "Wow."

"Tuna mayonnaise."

"Tuna what?"

"Mayonnaise. Home-made, I might add. With my own fair hands."

"Oh, right," he agreed. Alex turned back to the kettle, and heard him whisper urgently to Kez. "Tuna *what?*"

"Mayonnaise, you dope. Like salad cream, only nicer." There was the suspicion of a giggle in Kez's voice, which was presumably what Colton had been working for; and when Alex glanced back, she saw the girl reaching for a sandwich herself. *Gold star for you, Colton boy. Couldn't have done it better myself.* In fact, she thought, he was probably the only one who could have done it at all. It was fascinating to watch how this place worked. The crisis might be exaggerating all the relationships, drawing them in richer colours, but that only made it easier to see the patterns. She felt a sudden spasm of regret, that she would only be here a day or two longer; and shook her head angrily, to get rid of it. She was here to work, to find the story, and that was all. She couldn't afford to be sentimental about these kids. Professionals didn't get involved.

She built up a stack of sandwiches onto another plate, and looked around. "Mandy, you finished, love?"

Mandy nodded quietly.

"Good. Run upstairs with this lot, will you, and take them to Mark and Jane? Tell them I'll be up with coffees in a minute."

"Mark don't drink coffee," Colton put in. "Only Barleycup. In that tin there, you make it the same. And Jane likes tea."

Alex made a face at him. "Okay, tell them that, then. Barleycup and tea, on the way."

She felt Colton's eyes still on her while she filled the kettle, and was sufficiently tuned in to recognise that for the near-miracle it was, that he could be curious enough about her to take his attention away from Kez for a while. But there seemed to be a touch of resentment in his voice too, which she couldn't account for, when he finally asked,

"What is it with you, Alex? You act like you're working here, and you've only been around since yesterday. I don't get it . . ."

Alex sighed, perched herself on the table and started to explain, for the fourth time that day.

Jane came downstairs at two o'clock, moving slowly and gripping Mark's arm like an invalid. In his free hand he carried a pathetically small case, everything she called her own. She was leaving with less even than she had brought, down by two pets and a lot of trust.

Alex had been heading up to her room to make some notes, remind herself that she was working; but she checked when she saw them, and gave the girl a smile.

"You off, then, Jane?"

Jane nodded distantly. Mark guided her to a chair in the hall, then joined Alex to say, "Would you mind phoning for a taxi, while Jane says goodbye to the others? We're going to Euston Station. From the Harlborough Institute, remember, and they'll need the street number."

"Yes, sure. You're not driving her yourself, then?"

"No. I'm not driving her myself."

Alex was bewildered by the harshness in his voice. "Sorry," she said defensively. "I just thought it might be better, that's all."

He sighed, and spoke more gently. "You're right, it would be better. But I can't drive."

"Oh. I thought . . . That car in the garage, the Moggy Thou, someone told me it was yours . . ."

"It is. But I don't drive it, I haven't got a licence."

She sensed his determination not to explain further, and decided not to push it. But, "I could drive it, if you like. Save taking a chance with a smart taxi-driver."

Mark held her gaze for a moment, then nodded. "All right. Thanks. The keys are in the office, I'll just get them for you. Stay with Jane for a minute, will you?"

Shortly afterwards, Colton folded the garage doors back and beckoned Alex out. She drove slowly onto the forecourt, feeling her way in the unfamiliar car, and found that the kids had come out in a pack to say goodbye, or simply to watch the proceedings.

She pulled up and jumped out, playing chauffeuse for all it was worth, opening the rear door with a bow in Jane's direction; but it all went for nothing, because Jane wasn't even looking, she was running suddenly across the gravel to give Colton a hard little hug.

"You will write to me, won't you?" she pleaded. "Promise you'll write . . ."

"Yeah, 'course," he mumbled awkwardly, barely loud enough for Alex to hear. "Tell you what, I'll phone you, okay? Send us a number, and I'll phone . . ."

She nodded, accepting that; and looked around, still in the protective circle of his arms. "Where's Davey? I want to say goodbye . . ."

"Dunno, he hasn't been around all day. I don't think he knew you was going today. I'll tell him to write you, shall I? He'll be dead pissed off, missing you."

Jane nodded, and stood unexpectedly on tiptoe to kiss his cheek. "'Bye, then . . ." She sketched a vague wave to the others, the ones she didn't know so well, or knew and didn't much like, and came over to the car. Mark followed with her case, and Alex slammed the door on both of them with a flourish.

It had taken Davey all morning to find out where he should go, and another hour to get there; and even then, he couldn't simply walk in. Physically it was only a door with a stone surround, set into a brick wall; but in reality, in his head, it was so much more than that, it might as well have had stained teeth, cracked and bleeding lips and an ulcerous tongue to lick them. The windows above might as well be eyes, mocking his fear and waiting with all the patience of the utterly certain . . .

At last he did it, though, he pushed the door open

*(reading the notice on it one more time, the name and the times of opening)*

and walked in. There was a corridor inside, another door labelled 'Reception and Waiting Room', and posters on the wall, more reasons to hesitate, to delay; but this time he just kept going, in through the door and up to the desk, get it over with.

The receptionist was a woman in her fifties, with greying hair and a white coat. She looked at him as though she knew everything already, except for his name; and she probably did, it wasn't difficult.

But all she said was, "Yes, can I help you?"

Davey rubbed the sweat from his palms onto his jeans, and said, "Is this where I get the, you know, the Aids test?"

"That's right." She picked up a pen and reached for a form, while Davey's eyes wandered restlessly around the room. There were chairs set against two walls, half a dozen of them occupied: one girl in denim shorts and long sleeves, and the rest of them young men. He thought he had never seen a roomful of people so still; they sat with their bodies slack and their eyes empty, nothing to do but wait. He shuddered, and turned gratefully back to the receptionist as she spoke.

"Can I have your name, please?"

"Michael. Michael Hanlon."

"Thank you. Have you been referred to us by your GP?"

"No, I just, I just came . . ."

"That's all right. I'll need your doctor's name, though, in any case. We prefer to send the results to a GP, so that he can advise the patient if any further steps are necessary."

Christ. "I, um, I haven't got a doctor. Not in this country. I'm Irish, see, I've only been here a month."

"I see. In that case, if you'll just give me your address for now, we'll arrange for the results to be sent directly to you. But I do advise you to register with a doctor locally. It's easier for everyone in the long run."

He barely heard that. His head was thick with the acrid smell of fear, cutting even through the inevitable disinfectant; his hands gripped the edge of the table, and he said, "How long does it take, then? For the results?"

"Three weeks, usually."

"Christ." This time he couldn't keep the swear word inside. "I thought, someone said you could do it straight away, that I'd only have to wait a bit here . . ."

"Oh. Yes, we can run the test immediately, but only if you're in a position to pay for it. That's a service we offer to our private patients. Otherwise, if you have it done on the NHS, you have to wait."

Wait like the others, with dead eyes and no movement, no priorities – but wait for weeks, not hours. He couldn't do it, he didn't have the strength; and he didn't have an address to give them, anyway. She knew what he was, might be only a moment from guessing who. He didn't dare tell her where to find him.

"How much does it cost, then?"

"One hundred pounds."

"Jesus, how am I supposed to get that much?"

*The same way you got the virus, dear.* Her eyes said it, though her mouth didn't. Her fingers tapped the pen on the form she'd begun to fill out, and she said, "I'm afraid that's the fee. We can't offer a reduction. What do you want to do?"

"I don't know. I, um, I'll think about it. Come back later . . ."

And he walked out blindly, his feet scuffing the floor, feeling for solid ground.

## 31  *A Little Knowledge*

"I don't know what you're talking about."

"Yes, you do," Tia said quietly, fighting to keep her voice sounding confident but not cocky. She was taking a hell of a chance here, and she'd have to watch herself. "I'm talking about a little Citroën that you paid for, to act as a decoy; and a grey Bluebird that followed it all the way down from Newcastle."

"A decoy, and a Bluebird. Well." The man she was talking to pursed his lips thoughtfully, and reached for his cup. Tia tried to hold his gaze, and couldn't do it; her eyes jerked away of their own accord, and focused instead on the clock in the corner. Twenty to five; she'd been alone in this room for over an hour, before he'd finally come home. *I have to see your husband,* she'd told the woman who answered the door. *Business, it's important.* The wife had asked no questions, she'd simply shown Tia in, and left her. Waiting had been the hardest thing, harder even than ringing the bell in the first place; an hour was plenty of time for her nerve to betray her, to slip away and leave her edgy and afraid.

But the waiting was over now. He'd arrived at last, small and self-controlled, speaking perfect English, full of danger. He sipped at his tea, and said, "Why should I do this, then? Why should I pay money for a, what did you call it, a decoy?"

"Because of what was in the Bluebird."

"I see. And what was that?"

"Heroin."

The word fell heavily between them, like something crude and solid, and distasteful. He blinked, and sipped; and said, "That is a dangerous allegation, little girl."

"I know. And my name's Tia."

"Indeed. Tia. Do you have any evidence?"

*I know the number of the Bluebird, mate. And the Citroën. And I know where that boy Mahmed hangs out when he's in London. Come to that, I don't suppose Shahid would hold out for long, once the police got to work on him. So yeah, I know enough to break up your little ring, even if I couldn't put you away with it.*

"No," she said, "but I wouldn't want any, would I? I'm not here to blackmail you."

For a second he almost looked surprised. She forced a smile, and said, "I don't think it'd be exactly healthy, would it? If I did?"

"No," he agreed, "it would not. But health can be elusive, even for girls who do not blackmail. Even a little knowledge is dangerous."

This time it was his turn to smile, powerful and easy, as she gulped air down a dry throat.

"My friends know where I am," she said hastily.

"If I believed that, I might be very angry with you." He wasn't smiling now. "Little girls who blabber addresses and such – well, they do not live very long."

"No. No, of course not. I was, I was bluffing, you frightened me . . ."

"So. Now tell me. If you are not here to blackmail, which is very sensible of you, then what do you want?"

"I want to work for you." He said nothing, and she went on, "Just as a courier, that's all, nothing important. I only want to earn a bit of money. I was thinking about it, see, and I thought, if I dress up Muslim, no one's going to suspect I'm carrying drugs. I could deliver all over London for you, if you wanted. And I've got a great place to stash the stuff, if you need it any time. Guaranteed safe . . ."

It wasn't lack of sleep the previous night that sent Colton up to bed early that evening. True, he was shattered, but even physical and mental exhaustion couldn't usually drag him upstairs before midnight. And it wasn't lack of company either, though Jane had gone, Mark was closeted in the office with Alex again, and Davey was in a weird mood, not talking to anyone. That still left the other three girls; but Nina was just a pain in the arse, Mandy never spoke unless you bullied her into it, and Tia – well, she might be sexy as hell, but he just didn't like her much, somehow.

There was nothing he wanted to watch on telly, but it wasn't even that which took him off at ten thirty. On a normal night he would've been quite happy fooling around on the pool table, practising sneaky shots and dreaming of being talent-spotted

*(oh, yeah? How? He never played anywhere except here)*

by one of the big managers, and making a fortune on the snooker circuit.

No, it wasn't any of that. It was just that Kez had gone half an hour earlier, kissed him a quick good night and slipped away; and he wanted to be there, in bed ready and waiting, just in case she needed him again. Just in case she came.

She hadn't said anything, and he wasn't really expecting her. Not after what he'd put her through that morning, she'd probably be scared of him doing that again, rubbing her face in what she'd come here to get away from. Besides, she'd settled down a bit during the day, she wasn't so nervy now. Chances were she'd snuggled down in bed and was fast asleep by now.

But he went anyway, just to be there; and listened to the radio, and waited for sleep, and knew that it wouldn't come for hours yet, no matter how tired he was. Because he was waiting for her too, and he couldn't sleep until he knew for sure that she wasn't coming.

He heard a floor-board creak in the passage outside his door, and nah, it wouldn't be her, just one of the others on their way to bed; but –

– but his door swung slowly open, and it was her, a shadow against the light outside; and her voice was like a shadow too, calling.

"Colton?"

"Yeah. Come on in."

She slipped inside and shut the door; and this time she didn't need to ask, he was already shifting over to make room for her.

"Been keeping it warm for you," he murmured, lifting the duvet again on a welcoming arm. She chuckled, and sighed a little as she settled against him. He brushed the hair lightly back off her face, and said, "How are you, then?"

"Okay. Better than last time. But, I don't know, I was getting a bit spooked. The curtains are dead thin in that room, and the moonlight was making shadows, and – oh, I just missed you, that was all. The bed was too big, or something." She rubbed her cheek against his bare shoulder, then kissed it briefly. "You don't mind, do you?"

"Stupid." His hand found hers and moved on, pushing the cuff of the big shirt up over her elbow, so that he could stroke the fine hairs on her arm. He felt her shiver and caught it from her, and hugged her tighter to kill it.

"Tell you what, though."

"What?"

*Careful, son. Keep it casual.* "Like, if this is going to be a regular, maybe I'd better get some pyjamas. I mean, you got a nightie . . ."

"We can fix that, Col. Ton. I just didn't want to scare you, that's all." Sat up, and pulled the shirt off over her head with two tugs and a wriggle. Tossed it onto the floor and cuddled up to him again, skin on skin. "How's that?"

He took a deep breath, settled his hands carefully on her back,

*(warm and smooth, ribs hiding under a layer of softness, and Christ he was* dying *here!)*

and said, "Scary."

"I know. But don't be. And stop trying to squirm away from me down there, I know you've got an erection." Another giggle. "I'd be upset if you didn't, okay? But I'm not going to"

*(rape)*

"*seduce* you or anything. So just relax. Right?"

"Right."

# PART FIVE

*Comfortable Bodies*

Mark was just about to spread marmalade on his breakfast toast when Alex reached around from behind him and snatched it away.

He blinked at her indignantly. "Do you mind?"

"Sorry, but I had to snatch. I don't like marmalade." She crunched buttered toast, and smiled sweetly; and went on, "Have you got the key to Jane's room? 'Cos I'd like it, please."

"Yes, I've got it. But you're not going to write about that."

"Censorship, Mr – what is your surname, anyway?"

"Delaney. But don't print it. And you can call it what you like, you're still not going to write about that mess."

"I hate censorship," she said mildly. "But actually you're right, I'm not. I'm going to clean it up."

"What?"

"Well, someone's got to do it. You're busy enough already, and you can't ask any of the kids. So that leaves me, doesn't it?"

Mark frowned, and shook his head. "I can make time, if necessary. But I was thinking of Colton, he's old enough to handle it."

"Maybe he is, but he's got his hands full"

*(and I just might mean that literally)*

"with Kez. So come on, don't be difficult. I want to earn my keep."

She bit and chewed defiantly, and held one hand out. After a pause, Mark fished the big bunch of keys out of his pocket, sorted through them slowly and finally twisted one off the ring. He dropped it into her palm, and said, "There you go, then. But I'll be up to help you later."

She nodded, and closed her fingers around the key. "Fine.

See you up there."

She swallowed the last piece of crust, thrust both hands into her pockets and danced towards the door. Mark watched her go, wondering; and turned back towards the grill.

Mark usually liked to be well visible in the mornings, to see each of the kids as they came down, in case of problems. Today, though, he decided they could look after themselves for once; and after spending half an hour on the phone in the office, he ran up to the attic and into what had been Jane's room.

Alex had already cleared up the broken glass and plywood,

*(and the rags and tatters of rat-flesh)*

throwing it all into a black bin-liner. She was working on the walls now, with a sponge and a bowl of cold water. She looked round as he came in, and said, "Well, I suppose I'm getting somewhere. Turning red streaks into pink stains, anyway. And at least the smell's gone. There's something to be said for broken windows, they do let the air in. But these walls are going to need repainting, before anyone can sleep here. I don't know what to do about the bedclothes, whether to try washing them or just chuck them out. And the carpet'll need some serious going over, we'll have to hire something stronger than a vacuum . . ."

Mark looked at her, and tried very hard not to sound aggressive or challenging as he said, "We?"

She shrugged. "We, you, someone. What's the difference?"

"The difference is that you don't live here, Alex. The difference is that you're just a journalist looking for a story; and you're not acting like one. And I'm sorry, but that makes me suspicious."

"I'm not looking for a story, not any more," she reminded him quietly, while her hands went on working. "I've found one. This place is my story. And the more involved I get, the better the story's going to be."

"Even so. You should be downstairs writing or asking questions, not up here acting like a housekeeper. It's very good of you to do this, but it isn't going to get you anywhere with the kids. And they're your story, surely."

"Yes." She regarded him speculatively. "You sound like you want me down there being the good reporter. That's a change of tune, isn't it, from two nights ago?"

"I just want you out of here," he said. "I'm sorry, but you're dangerous. And I want to limit the damage."

"I know. I accept that. I think you're wrong, mind; I reckon it'll help you if anything, if I do it right. Public opinion – like the doctor said, it's a useful weapon. And I can give it to you, I can win them over. But I do understand how you feel." She frowned, then fished in the bowl of pinkish water and drew out another sponge. "And I was working, as it happens. Being a good reporter. I was getting it all straight in my head, figuring out how to approach the story. But you did say you'd help; so why don't you get busy on the door, and we'll talk while we scrub? I know a fair bit about the kids now, but I'm quite ignorant about Mr Mark Delaney. Tell me about you and the doctor, how you ended up here."

Mark took the sponge and the opportunity to turn his back on her, picking his way carefully from one sentence to the next. "I've known the doctor a long time now. Since I was a teenager. He was, I suppose you'd say a family friend. He gave me my first job, working in the gardens at – I'm sorry, I'm not going to tell you the name of the place, but he has a private clinic in the country, in a converted manor house."

"Malmebury," she said cheerfully. "I know, Colton told me."

"*Shit!*"

"It's all *right*, Mark. I don't know where the bloody place is, just the name. Oh, I suppose I could find out; and once I'd done that I could get the doctor's name, no trouble. That's what you're afraid of, right? But I'm not going to do it. I'm quite happy to have a mysterious anonymous doctor-figure, readers go for a bit of theatre in a story. And for the hundredth time, I'm not going to blow this place, if I can help it. I wish you'd try trusting me for a change, it'd be a lot easier for both of us."

He didn't respond to that; and after a moment he heard Alex sigh behind him, and say, "Go on, then. What happened after you were a gardener?"

"After that? Oh, I came here. I've been here since it

opened. Before it opened, in fact; I did most of the work to get the house ready. Mrs Horsley was always going to be in charge, but the doctor wanted someone else here to take a bit of the pressure off her, and I – well, I wasn't really a very good gardener, so . . ."

"I see. Here's a question for you, though, Mark. Who's going to take the pressure off you, now you're running the refuge single-handed?"

And he had no answer to that, except to sponge more vigorously, and wait for the question to go away.

Which it did; she took his silence for the more-than-hint it was, and talked of other things, books and films, nothing he had to be wary of.

But questions are sneaky by nature, they can double back and surprise you when you're not expecting them. Sometimes they can even throw up their own answers, like a challenge.

Mark was cooking that evening, letting the rota lapse for a few days until things settled down, when Alex came into the kitchen looking for him. She had paint on her jeans, and in her hair; she'd dug a tin of white out of the cellar during the afternoon and disappeared upstairs again, claiming that those pink patches were still on her mind.

"Finished?" he asked.

"First coat, anyway. It'll need two, to look halfway decent." She dropped into a chair, stretched her legs out with a grunt. "I like painting, usually. It's therapeutic, you know?"

Mark nodded. He did know. He'd painted every room in the house, during the weeks before the refuge was officially up and running; and there was a simple physical satisfaction in the work, with the results clear and obvious on every wall.

"But it's different, up there," Alex went on quietly. "It feels like I'm sticking plasters on a cut that's still bleeding. I slap the paint on and watch it dry, and I can still see every bloody stain afterwards, seeping through the white. It's in my mind more than on the wall, I know that; but knowing it doesn't help, I still see it."

"Then don't go back," Mark said. "I'll do the second coat tomorrow."

"Thanks, but that wouldn't help. I'd still see it, in my head. Besides, I'm a great finisher. Hate to leave things half done." She tried to grin up at him, nonchalant and competent, mocking herself; but didn't make a very good job of it. All she did was confirm a suspicion of Mark's that he'd held all day, that he really didn't understand her at all. He shrugged, and reached for the kettle.

"Well, we'll see how it goes. Do you want a coffee?"

"No, ta. What I really want is a drink. Several drinks. And it occurs to me, Mark mate, that it wouldn't do you any harm to get a pint or two down your neck. Fancy joining me?"

"I can't." He didn't know which surprised him more, the invitation or the blind lack of imagination which could produce it.

She looked past him at the bubbling pots, and snorted. "After dinner, I meant. Wouldn't want to drink on an empty stomach."

"It's not that. I can't."

"Why not?"

"For one thing, I don't drink."

"Not ever?"

"Not ever," conveniently forgetting the occasional nip of whisky with the doctor. Mark would rarely break the rules for him, and certainly not for a girl he barely knew.

"Well, you can come and watch me drink, anyway. Save me doing it alone."

"No, Alex. I *can't*."

"Why not, damn it?" She was almost shouting now, and he saw at last how important it was to her, to have company tonight; and almost regretted that he had to refuse. "You've got to get out of this place some time, boy. Why not tonight? Just for an hour or two, I'll drink fast."

"Alex, listen to me. You said it yourself earlier, I'm alone here now. It's my responsibility, this house and every one of the kids; and it's just two days since we had some lunatic breaking in. I can't leave them alone tonight. Suppose he came back?"

"Suppose he does. What are you going to do, put him under citizen's arrest?"

"That's not the point." Mark only knew what he would do if he came back to more broken glass, and more blood. What he would feel.

"All right. But Colton can watch out for them, he's a big

boy now."

"Not big enough."

She scowled, and he thought he'd won; but then she got to her feet with a jerk, grabbed his arm and pulled him over to the phone.

"The doctor, ring him up." And when Mark hesitated, "Just do it, will you? Please?"

Then she turned her back, so that he couldn't even suspect her of watching what number he dialled. Mark added a degree of desperation to his measure of her need, and phoned the doctor.

Alex took the phone as soon as he was through, and said, "Doctor? It's me, Alex Holden. . . . No, I'm fine, thanks, but it's been a rough day, and I reckon we just need a bit of time off, me and Mark both. Only he won't leave the kids on their own, as long as there's a chance of that freak coming back; and I can't argue with that. But he really does need the break, so . . . Oh, will you? That's magic. Thanks, doctor . . ."

She hung up, and grinned aggressively at Mark, and got it right this time. "He says he'll hold the fort, while we're out. He was coming over anyway, he said, so it's no trouble. And you can't grumble at that, can you?"

"No," Mark said lightly, "I can't grumble at that."

And, *damn you, doctor, what are you throwing me into now?*

## 34  *Finally Feeling Grateful*

Tia could probably have borrowed money for clothes from her new employer, or claimed it as an advance payment, an earnest of his good faith; but she had decided it was better not. She had no more illusions about him than he had about her, and she would tread as wary as she could, cat-cautious and asking nothing until she'd earned it.

So she'd asked Alex instead, that morning. "Just a lend, to buy some material with. I'm sick of jeans."

Alex had looked surprised, said, "Why don't you ask Mark?"

*Because he wouldn't believe me, would he, after I told him how sick I was of everything Asian?* "Because he might think I was trying to scrounge. Like, waiting for him to say don't worry about paying it back, you know? It's different, if I borrow it off you."

She'd laughed then, and reached for her purse. "No, it isn't. I've still got fifteen quid of the refuge's money, Mark gave it to me when I came, to cover what I paid Secky for the address. When he still thought I was one of you. You can have that, and welcome; and if you want to pay it back, give it to Mark. But I won't tell him if you don't."

Tia had spent the afternoon and the money in Lala's Sari Emporium, choosing a length of peach-coloured 'silk' that had never seen the backside of a worm. She'd added thread and a cheap pair of sandals, and still got change.

And now she was in her room with the refuge's old, cranky sewing machine, finally feeling grateful for all the sewing her mother had forced her to do. Running up a kameez was no problem, she could have done it with her eyes shut; and indeed her mind was a long way off, barely aware of her fingers' working. She spared a quick smile for the irony of it, the certainty she'd had when she came to London that she'd never wear Muslim clothes again, but her attention was fixed on the future, the vast and profitable future.

Davey left the refuge soon after dinner, edging out when no one was around. He took a bus to Chelsea, walked for five minutes, and pressed a bell at the door of a large Edwardian block of flats.

After a moment, the intercom crackled, and a voice said, "Yes?"

"It's Davey, Mr Aspinall. Davey FitzAlan."

"Davey boy! Anyone with you, any friends?"

"No, Mr Aspinall. Just me."

"Come up, lad, come on up."

The security lock buzzed. He pushed the heavy door open and went inside, running quickly up three flights of steps and along the corridor at the top, feeling himself in the grip of something more than nostalgia, a salt current that sucked and dragged at him, pulling him back and down, no escape.

He paused in front of a panelled oak door, ran sweat-slicked hands through his cropped hair, and knocked. He heard footsteps on the other side, heavy and unhurried, the echo of a dozen memories, a dozen visits here. Then the door opened, and Laurence Aspinall was smiling at him, as he always had smiled.

"Davey." A fat, strong hand clasped his shoulder and drew him inside. "You're looking good. I like the hair. Very pretty."

Davey said nothing, and the big man took him down the passage

*(past the bedroom door, and another memory there, cold sheets and a heavy body. Mr Aspinall liked to test his boys personally, before offering them to his clients)*

and into a small sitting-room.

"Well, sit down, Davey boy, and tell me what I can do for you."

Aspinall poured himself a whisky, added water, and smiled benevolently down as Davey perched himself on the edge of a soft settee.

"I need some money, Mr Aspinall."

"We all need money, Davey. You wouldn't be asking me to give you some, now would you?"

*Why not? I made you plenty. And you'd never notice a hundred quid* . . . But Davey knew his man too well to beg, and didn't have the nerve for blackmail. He shook his head, and said, "Not for nothing. I'll earn it."

"Oh, well, that's different, lad. If you're ready to work again. I like that. It's funny, I'd always hoped you'd come back to me. I like my lads to know they have somewhere to turn."

"I'll do anything, Mr Aspinall."

An eyebrow lifted curiously in the big, smiling face. "You must need that money bad, boy. Very picky, you used to be. Very troublesome, sometimes."

"I'm sorry, Mr Aspinall. But really, I'll do anything."

"How much do you need, then?"

*Don't tell him.* But Aspinall just waited, the soul of patience; and at last Davey said, "A hundred."

"That much, eh?" The smile stretched into a grin, and Davey thought, *He knows. I'm not the first; and he knows the price of everything, Mr Aspinall.* "Well, it'll take time, lad. You'll have to work for it. Business is hard at the moment, the police are being very difficult. But I can help you, I'm sure. I wouldn't turn one of my boys away." He pursed his lips, and sucked air slowly in through his teeth. "When do you want to start?"

"As soon as you like, Mr Aspinall. Tonight, if you want."

"Right, then. I've got a couple of customers coming in for a special at ten o'clock. They wanted two boys, but I could only offer them one. It's worth fifteen quid to you, if you'll make up the pair."

Davey nodded. "Anything. I said. What is it?"

"Spanking. And such. You never did any of that, did you? But it don't matter, they'll enjoy someone fresh." He glanced at a clock on the mantelpiece, and chuckled. "You'd better get over there sharp, lad. They won't be nice to you if you're late. Not nice at all . . ."

There were two bell-pushes set in a brass plate under the porch of the house in Croydon. The upper one was labelled 'Visitors', the lower 'Servants'. Mr Aspinall's little joke, that was; it had originally been on the door of his Chelsea flat, but he'd had it fitted here six months ago, when he bought the house. Or when his partner bought the house, rather, from the safety of his home in the Bahamas. The law wouldn't find it easy to prove anything against Laurence Aspinall.

Davey pressed the lower bell, and heard the buzzer sound in the hallway. 'Visitors' got a two-tone chime; and joke or not, there was trouble if a boy pressed the wrong bell.

He stood back under the porch light, to let himself be clearly seen through the spy-hole in the door. There was the sound of shooting bolts, and the door swung open.

"Inside, Davey. Quick."

"Hullo, Mike." The lad who let him in was nineteen or twenty, one of the oldest of Aspinall's employees. You didn't have to be young, to be a rent boy – Davey had met men of thirty or more who were still working the streets, and living well – but Aspinall specialised.

"You on the door now, then?"

"That's right." Mike smiled tightly. "Big promotion, eh?"

"You get to keep your trousers on. What happened to Steve, did he quit?"

"Not exactly. Steve got clever, thought he could blackmail the Slug. You know, give us money or I'll talk to the cops."

"Jerk."

"You said it. Hard to talk, when your jaw's been smashed with a baseball bat. They picked him up in the street; and he got smart then, told the cops it was a hit-and-run or something. That was two months ago, and he's still in hospital."

No, the law wouldn't find it easy at all, to prove anything against Laurence Aspinall.

Mike glanced at the clock, and said, "You'd better go on up and get ready, Davey. They'll be here in ten minutes. Front room. And try and keep the noise down, eh? Busy night tonight, and the other customers like it quiet."

Davey nodded, wondering just what was in store for him – and realising that Mike knew, and didn't want to say. That had been a warning and an expression of sympathy both, as much as any rent boy was going to give another. It was a job, and nothing more – but sometimes it was a very bad job indeed.

Upstairs, he found the other boy already sitting on one corner of the king-sized bed. Davey didn't know him, but that was no surprise. Davey nodded a greeting, and said, "How long is this going to be, then, do you know?"

"Two hours, they're paying for."

"Shit." It'd be almost one o'clock before he got back to the refuge. Mark'd be wild with him. And the doctor was coming tonight, too, and he never stayed that late. "How much are you getting for it, then?"

"The usual. Twenty."

*I knew that bastard would milk me, when he knew how much I was after. He'll get another couple of nights out of me that way, fuck him . . .*

Davey nodded, and looked around the room; and saw the selection of canes and leather belts neatly arrayed with a single worn plimsoll on a chest of drawers beside the door. There would be tubes of KY jelly in the top drawer, he knew, and a choice of condoms. It was a house rule, that condoms were worn on all occasions; if a client refused, he would not be invited back.

*Too bad you didn't carry it over to your private clients, Davey.* Too late for regrets now, though, or recriminations. And it didn't matter anyway, he wouldn't have it. He felt fine. He just wanted to be sure, that was all . . .

He looked at the canes again, and licked his lips nervously as he heard the soft double-chiming of the 'Visitors' bell, heard voices on the stairs, coming up.

The doctor had arrived at eight, and promised to stay till
midnight. With so much time at their disposal, Alex had
insisted on going first to her flat, to dump the old clothes
she'd been wearing and remake herself in her own image.

They'd made their way slowly back towards the refuge,
from pub to pub; and now Mark looked at her, saw dark
glasses and a dark beret, and felt himself teetering dangerously from one image to the other. He saw the confident
journalist he'd sat next to in court, remote from him, the
professional he could never trust; and at the same time he
saw the girl he was slowly getting to know. And it was more
than that, even, because there was an edge of attraction that
cut at him when she smiled, and slashed deeper when she
asked him the questions he didn't dare to answer. The force
of her curiosity had struck at him again and again through
the evening; he sensed her desire to penetrate his secrets, to
understand him, and knew it for what it was. Attraction is
double-edged, it can cut both ways. Again and again he had
met it with silence or fast footwork, or in the last resort a
plain, obstinate denial; and watched her bleed.

Now she slipped her arm through his, feather-light and
laughing, and said, "So tell me, Mark. Why don't you
drink?"

Lies came easily to his tongue, and flippant rebuttals; but
he rejected them all, and asked quietly, "Do you drink when
you're driving?"

"No. Of course not." She scowled, not understanding,
expecting another stone wall; and he surprised her with
another question.

"Why not?"

"Well." She frowned for the words, and found them. "It's
a matter of responsibility. To yourself, and to other people,

I suppose."

"That's right. And if I drink I'm not being responsible. To myself, or anyone else."

"Ah," she said lightly, either the alcohol or some belated sensitivity drawing her sharply away from his intensity. "Can't take it, eh?"

"That's right, Alex," he said again. "I can't take it."

"Okay, so try another one. Why don't you drive?"

"Would you drive while you're drinking?"

She considered that for a moment, then swung the bag she was carrying up onto her shoulder, and punched him quite hard below the ribs. Then she grinned, and tightened her grip on his arm.

"I like you, Mark Delaney. You're slippery as shit, but I still like you."

"You're drunk," he said quietly.

"That's right. In whatsit thingummibob. Vino veritas, that's the stuff."

"Probably." He looked down at her – just an inch or two, she stood almost his own height – and asked deliberately, "How's the story coming?"

"All right, I take it back. I don't like you. At all."

He waited, and when she said nothing more he pressed her. "Your editor must be getting impatient. You're a professional, it's not going to take you long to run up a few thousand words. Do it tomorrow, could you?"

"I've just packed enough clothes for a week."

"I know, I saw you do it. That's why I'm asking."

"Sod you, Mark. I can stave the boss off for a while, with the promise of something big. And – I *like* it at the ref! I like the kids, I like talking to them, I like being useful. Christ, I even like you, when you're not being a pain in the arse."

"You can come back and visit. Always assuming we're still there."

A pause, growing into a silence; and at last, "All right. I'll do it tomorrow, and get the hell out of your hair. Happy now?"

Another question he wasn't going to answer. But he touched her fingers with his, and said, "Thanks, Alex." He was glad, eager to be free of her, both for the refuge and for himself; but he also knew the threat that lay within that freedom, both for the refuge and for himself.

Back home – and feeling a curious comfort even at the word, after seeing where Alex lived and being reminded that people did that, they lived on their own, no cushion between themselves and the world – Mark was pleased to find no one up except the doctor. With it settled between them that she would leave tomorrow, he was keen to stretch out this time with Alex for as long as he could, to see if he could build on the rapport that was growing between them, that felt so strange to him.

"Enjoy yourselves, then?" the doctor asked.

"Mm-hmm." Alex hooked a chair from the kitchen table with one foot, and dropped into it, stretching her long legs out across the floor. The doctor reached across to lift the sunglasses from her nose, peered at her eyes for a moment and let them drop again.

"I see you've been keeping up the traditions of your profession, young lady."

"Want to smell my breath?"

"I just have."

She laughed, and waved two fingers cheerfully in his direction. Mark grinned, and went to fill the kettle.

"Kids been behaving themselves, doctor?"

"More or less. I'm a little concerned about Davey."

"What's he been up to?"

"I don't know. He isn't in yet."

"Shit." Mark turned from the sink, leaving the tap running. "When did he go out?"

"No one's very sure. He hasn't been around all evening; I think he must have gone out before I arrived, or I should have seen him."

"Didn't he tell anyone where he was going?"

"Apparently not."

Mark paced fretfully across the kitchen floor, thinking aloud. "What's the time now, nearly midnight? It's not like him, he doesn't usually go out without a reason. But he's been very quiet the last couple of days. I think that break-in scared him badly. And we've had kids run out on us before . . ."

"If he's gone, he hasn't taken anything with him," the doctor said quietly. "I checked that. And he'd be more likely to talk than run, don't you think?"

"Okay, so what else? He could have been recognised and picked up somewhere; he wouldn't phone us with the police hanging over his shoulder. Or he might have been in an accident, he could be in hospital . . ."

"Mark." Alex got to her feet in one sudden movement, grabbed his shoulders and his attention. "Mark, just slow down, will you? He's fifteen, he's in London; he could just as easily be at a late-night horror movie. It's nothing to panic about yet." She steered him towards her chair, and pushed him into it. "You sit there and keep quiet, I'll make the coffee."

"Barleycup for me." That was automatic now, almost instinctive, fighting even through his anxiety.

"Barleycup. I remember." She levered the lid off the tin, sniffed, and pulled a face. "Why do you drink this muck, anyway? No, don't tell me, let me guess. Coffee's bad for you, right? Like alcohol?"

"That's right."

"And driving cars?"

"People get killed in cars."

She snorted. "People get killed crossing the road."

"Sure. But what is it kills them?"

He watched her shaking her head, making the connection but not understanding.

Then the doctor stood up, and lifted his coat off the back of a chair. "I'll be off now. I expect Alex is right, and Davey will turn up soon; but I suppose you'll be waiting up for him, Mark?"

"Yes. Of course."

"Well, phone me if he's not in by two, and we'll think again. All right?"

Mark nodded. The doctor said a quick good night, and left them; Alex sat down on the other side of the table, reached across and squeezed Mark's hand gently.

"Stop worrying, you. It'll give you wrinkles."

"It's my job. Someone's got to worry about these kids."

She smiled. "Point taken. But there's no need to go overboard. Do you play cribbage?"

"Afraid not."

"Don't be afraid. I'll teach you. There must be a pack of cards in this place somewhere."

"Dozens. But you don't have to stay up."

"Phooey to that. I'm not going to bed yet, I'm too pissed. And I'm not leaving you down here on your own, to work yourself into a state over that boy. Where are the cards?"

"Eight."

"Fifteen, for two." She grinned at him, and added the points to her score.

He grinned back, and put down another card. "And another seven, for what's that, twenty-two and a pair."

"Two to you, smart-arse." She picked up the pen again, then stiffened. Mark was already getting to his feet; he'd heard it too, the front door closing softly, and light footsteps in the hall.

He almost ran out of the kitchen and down the passage, with Alex just a step behind. When they reached the hall, Davey was already halfway up the stairs. He turned reluctantly to face them, came slowly back down; and Mark said, "Davey, where the hell have you been?"

"Just out." His voice was sullen, and he spoke to his feet rather than to Mark.

"Till one in the morning? We'd have been phoning the hospitals in another hour!"

A quick shrug, a muttered, "Sorry."

"That's not enough." Mark's relief was doing the traditional thing, turning to anger. "I want to know what you've been doing."

Davey jerked his head in a quick negative, said nothing.

"Listen, I don't want to run this place like a bloody boarding-school, but it's not a hotel either, you can't just traipse in and out when you feel like it –"

He broke off abruptly, as Alex's hand closed on his shoulder. He could feel himself trembling against her grip, and knew that she could feel it too.

"Mark. Leave it till the morning. You'll wake everyone else, yelling in the hall like this; and by the look of him, Davey needs sleep more than he needs shouting at."

Her words cut through his anger, and brought home to him just what was happening. He'd never lost his temper with one of the kids before, and had always sworn he never would. He hadn't thought he still had a temper; he'd believed it lost with his teenage, with so much else.

He thrust his hands deep into his pockets, so that Davey at

least shouldn't see them shaking. Then he looked at the boy's face with a sharper focus than his anger had permitted him, and saw what he should have seen before – the darting, nervous eyes, the sheen of sweat on his skin, the suspicion of a bruise on one cheekbone.

"Yes. All right. Go on, Davey, get up to bed. I'll talk to you tomorrow – and don't worry, I promise not to shout."

Davey nodded, a long way beyond smiling, and turned to the stairs again. Alex swung an arm, and helped him on his way with a friendly slap on the buttocks; and Mark's eyes widened, seeing the boy flinch, choke back a cry, grab the banister wildly to keep from falling.

"For crying out loud, Davey – what's the matter with you?"

"Nothing." But he had to swallow twice before he could get the word out. "Just – just leave me alone, right?"

And then he was off and running, stumbling up the stairs and out of sight.

Alex and Mark abandoned their game by mutual consent, and headed for bed; but Mark was still half-dressed when there was a tap on his door, and he heard her voice call his name.

"Yes, what is it?"

She put her head in. "Just to say, don't be too hard on Davey tomorrow. I stopped outside his door on my way to the loo, and he's crying in there. Whatever's wrong with him, he doesn't need you coming the heavy on top."

Mark ran a hand wearily through his hair. "Shit. Right, thanks, Alex. Don't worry, I'll let him off easy. Try and get him to talk, that's all, find out what he's got himself into this time."

Ten minutes later, Mark made his way softly down to Davey's room, figuring that the tears should be gone by now, and the boy might find it easier to talk in the dark; but his knock produced no response, and when he pushed the door open he saw Davey sleeping, his pillow hugged in both arms, for whatever transitory comfort that could give.

Alex spent the following morning in her room, nursing a hangover and scribbling, she said; and she left straight after lunch, saying goodbye to the kids with a hug for some and a smile for others, a few whispered words for Kez and Mandy.

Mark went out to the doorstep with her; she swung her tote bag higher onto her shoulder, and grinned at him.

"'Bye then, fella. Look after them."

"I will."

"And look after yourself, too. Don't go driving or drinking, or doing anything dangerous."

"No. I won't."

"Right, then."

And before he could anticipate, she grabbed the back of his neck, pulled his head closer and kissed him.

"Ta-ta," she said, turning and walking quickly away across the gravel. He stood and watched from the doorway until she was out of sight beyond the trees; then he swung the big door closed and walked across the hall to the office, shut himself in and tried to concentrate on the paperwork.

But his eyes kept turning inward, and he couldn't settle; he couldn't even find his usual escape, in worrying about the kids. Alex's arrival had done more than shake the fragile security of the refuge with the mingled threats and promises of publicity. For the first time in years, he'd been thrown together with a girl close to his own age, and the contact had affected him more deeply than he'd been prepared for. Last night particularly, all that talking, the flows and currents of the evening taking him unexpectedly close to revelations he didn't want to make, then twisting him away so that all his attention fell on her – and there was danger there too, in her long legs and copper hair, in her green eyes and her ready smile . . .

Mark dropped his pen and propped his head in his hands, staring unseeingly at the papers in front of him. *Don't go doing anything dangerous*, she'd said; and then she kissed him, like an open invitation to disaster. She wouldn't understand that, of course. She wouldn't expect a man his age to be frightened of a simple physical attraction, and terrified of anything more. How could she, when she didn't even understand about the little things, the not drinking or driving? She'd been laughing at him about those – nothing malicious, just teasing, because she didn't understand.

At last he gave up trying to work, and wandered through to the games room. Colton and Kez were there, playing pool; Mark watched for a while, then joined in, played each of them and lost to each. "I don't believe it," Colton said. "You throwing 'em deliberately, or what?"

"No. I wouldn't do that."

"Well, you're ruining my reputation as a picker. I been telling this girl you're the best potter since Jimmy White, and you go and blow it . . ."

"Sorry, Colton. I can't concentrate, that's all." He leant his cue against the wall, feeling an urgent need to get away from it all, if only for an hour; and found that what had been impossible last night was easy today. Thought, *Christ, Alex, what are you doing to me?*, and said, "Look, can you keep an eye on things for me for a bit? I won't be long, I'm just going for a walk."

"Yeah, sure. 'Course." Colton frowned, as if recognising the strangeness, the stress in him. "You all right, Mark?"

"Yes, I'm fine. I need some air, that's all."

Walking helped, as it always had. Alone and away from other people's needs and demands, he could focus more easily on his own, the private checks and balances that kept him stable in a toppling world. He'd accepted long ago that he could live without sex and without everything that came with it, the powerful ties and commitments that seemed so important to others. It wasn't the only way to love, after all; and his life was rich enough already, as rich as he could handle. If that made him an emotional cripple in the eyes of the world, so be it. He had his own contentment; and the world didn't need to watch.

So he walked, and strove for balance, and found it; and

turned for home again. It was getting towards evening when he reached the refuge, and he went straight to the kitchen, to see if anyone had started dinner.

Walked in, and stopped dead, and felt that balance slip and slide away; because the first thing he saw was an orange cotton tote bag lying open on the table, with T-shirts and gaudy striped leggings tumbling out of it. It was the bag he'd watched Alex pack last night, the evidence of an intention to stay which had finally made him ask her to leave; the same bag he'd seen her carry off that afternoon.

Nina was peeling potatoes at the sink, but turning now to give him a knowing smirk.

"All right," he said. "Where is she?"

"Upstairs. In the attic."

"What the hell's she doing up there?"

"Painting, she said . . ."

Mark swore, and ran up the three flights to Jane's old room. Alex was there right enough, and obviously expecting his arrival; she waved a brush at him cheerfully, and went on splashing paint onto the wall.

"Alex, what's going on?"

"I told you before, I don't like leaving things half done. So I thought I'd get this finished. No need to thank me," she added graciously, "I'm enjoying myself."

"That much is obvious. But you haven't come back here to paint a wall."

"No. All right, I haven't. If you must know, my editor was so pleased with the story I bashed out for him this afternoon that he's decided to run it as a series over three days next week; so I told him I'd have to come back for some more material."

"What more? You've already talked to everyone here. There's nothing more I can tell you that I'd want you to print."

"I know that. It was a ruse. It occurred to me that you'd probably like to have a look at what I've done, and talk over the rest of it before it actually hits the street. Sort of an editorial veto, if you like, so that you can be sure I won't be doing you any damage. But I couldn't exactly tell my editor that, he'd hit the roof."

"Oh." As usual, she'd left him suddenly stranded, his suspicions and anger evaporating like puddles in sunlight.

"Well, thanks . . ."

"Pleasure." She perched the brush carefully on the up-turned paint-lid and came towards him, looking paradoxically thinner than ever in the vast, baggy overalls she was wearing. "Hullo, Mark."

"Hullo . . ."

"Did I ever say thank you, for coming out with me last night?"

"I, um, I don't know. You don't need to."

"Yes, I do. You really didn't want to, but you came anyway; and never mind that it was for your good as much as mine, I still appreciate it. I hate getting drunk on my own."

"That's all right, I enjoyed it."

"Educational, no doubt," she said. "Seeing how the other half gets by." That with a flashing smile; but when he didn't respond, she went on more quietly, "Seriously, Mark, what do you do, when things get rough? It's a reflex for me, I get pissed, and it helps. But I've often wondered about teetotallers. How do you cope?"

"By not drinking."

"God, you're a funny one. Don't give anything away, do you?"

He smiled, to fend her off. "Not if I can help it."

"No." She was close now, close enough to touch; and he didn't move, but it was as if she could sense his mind pulling back in a sudden scramble, because she cocked her head thoughtfully on one side, and asked, "Mark, are you gay?"

"No." *At least, I don't think so. Not as far as I know. Men don't scare me.*

"Okay. I just wondered."

"Why?"

She shrugged. "You keep yourself, I don't know, so carefully out of reach. Hands in pockets."

"I'm a careful man." *I have to be.* But as if to give her the lie, to prove something to her or to himself, he reached out and linked his hand loosely with hers, touching her of his own choice. Taking a chance, not sure whether it meant anything, or what he wanted it to mean. "Have you finished up here?"

"More or less."

"Well, hurry up, and we'll go and see how dinner's doing. Then we'll talk afterwards, about this bloody story of yours.

How's that?"

"That's fine. Mark . . ."

"Yes?"

"Can I stay tonight? I mean, you've got the space, and it's a long way back to my flat. And I've got my bag, all my gear . . ."

Again his decision, his risk; and he took it. "Yes, do. Stay. The kids'll be glad to have you."

*Damn the kids, what about you?*

But she didn't ask, so he didn't have to answer.

## 38   *Nothing for Nothing*

*Don't ever come here again,* he had said. *Ring this number at eight o'clock tomorrow evening, give them your name; they will have a job for you.*

She'd called the number as instructed, using a public call-box; the phone had been answered by a male voice speaking Bengali, who'd told her to go to a newsagent in Pimlico at ten the next morning, and ask for her reserved copy of *Nursing Today*.

Tia found the shop easily, and hung around until the clock in the estate agent on the corner said ten precisely; then she pushed open the newsagent's door, went inside and smiled at the young Asian man behind the counter.

"Can I help you?"

"Yes." The shop was empty, except for the two of them; she took a breath, and said, "You should have a copy of *Nursing Today* for me. It's reserved . . ."

"The name, please?"

"Tia Sharif."

He nodded, reached below the counter, and passed a magazine across. "Take this to Croughton Street, in Hackney. Number 57. Knock, and give it to Ali. He's expecting it."

"Croughton Street. Have you got a map or something? I don't know London."

"On the shelf behind you. The *A to Z*'s best. That'll be two quid."

She scowled. "Bastard."

The young man shrugged. "This is business, baby. You don't get nothing for nothing."

She paid him, and went outside; and made her way quickly to the nearest public lavatory. Locked into the privacy of a cubicle, she opened the magazine and found what she was expecting: three small plastic bags sellotaped securely to one of the pages, each containing a quantity of white powder.

She was careful not to touch the bags with her fingers, just in case; and was pleased with herself for remembering, until she remembered something else, that her fingerprints were all over the magazine in any case. And they'd come up great on this stiff, shiny paper. They should've used some cheap newspaper, that wouldn't hold a print . . .

Still, too late to worry now. Or maybe not; she pulled the scarf off her head and used it to wipe the magazine's cover where she'd gripped it, front and back. Then she put it into her shoulder-bag, holding it carefully through the scarf; took out the map-book, and looked for Croughton Street in the index.

It took her almost an hour to get there; and when she finally found the right door and knocked, it was opened by the same young Asian who'd given her the magazine in the shop.

Tia stared at him. "Are you Ali?"

"No. Come inside."

He led her into a curtained front room, and held out his hand. "The magazine. Please."

She fished it out of her bag without a word and passed it over, and never mind the fingerprints. He let it fall open, and ripped out one of the little bags, so carelessly that the plastic stretched and tore. Tia gasped, as white powder scattered across the dull carpet; but he only smiled, stuck his little finger into the bag and licked it.

"Bicarbonate of soda."

"What? I never –"

"No, we did. That's what it's meant to be."

"Oh." Understanding dawned in her at last. "I get it. It was a test, right?"

"Right. You were followed, every step of the way. What were you doing in the toilet?"

"What do you think?"

"I don't think you were pissing."

"No, I was looking. See what it was. Satisfied now?"

"No. You did this one right, but don't get cocky, girl. You'll be tested again. And again, and again. And you'll never know when you're being watched, or when what you've got is the real thing. So don't try to be clever, okay? Not ever. Just remember that we're smarter than you, and you'll do all right. Now take this," he handed over a strip of paper, "and call that number tomorrow. Six o'clock sharp. You'll be given instructions."

She put the paper into her purse, and waited with it open in her hand. He watched her, waited, finally said, "That's all. You can go."

"Not yet. I want paying."

"For what? Carrying bicarbonate of soda? Don't make me laugh. You'll get paid when you do something for real."

"I did this for real. It was you playing games, not me." And when he still hesitated, she added, "This is business, baby. You don't get nothing for nothing."

He scowled, reached into a back pocket and produced some folded notes. "Now get out of here."

She tucked the wad of money into her purse, not pushing her luck by counting it, and left.

"Mark, can I talk to you? Please?"

It took Mark a moment to understand his surprise at the question; then it dawned on him that as far as he could remember this was the first time Mandy had ever approached him or opened a conversation.

There was a touch of triumph in his smile, as he said, "Yes, of course. Come on through to the office, where we can be private." Maybe the atmosphere was getting through to her at last, coaxing her out of the shell

*(no, the womb)*

that she hid in.

He unlocked the office door, took her in and sat her down; and perched himself on her side of the desk, not to intimidate her. *Don't want to look like a headmaster, not with her.*

"So what's up, Mandy love? Got a problem?"

She nodded gravely. "I was watching telly, and there was this thing on about being pregnant, and smoking."

Mark sighed internally, careful not to let it show. It was still her baby, then. Maybe it was inevitable, maybe he shouldn't expect anything else; it must be hard for any girl not to be obsessed, with another life growing inside her. Doubly so when you were a teenager, when obsession was the ruling factor in everything you did; and double it again for a runaway with no friends or family around and little to do, nothing else to think about.

"Smoking's not a good idea," he said, "but you don't, do you? I've never seen you."

"No, but it isn't that, it's the others. This doctor was saying that it's bad for a baby, if its mother is even in the same room with people who are smoking; and they do it all the time."

She was right; between Colton and Davey, Nina and now Tia, it would be hard to escape a smoker. But, "I can't just tell them to stop, love. This isn't a prison."

"You could. I heard Davey saying Mrs Horsley didn't allow it."

"That's right, she didn't, except in the one room. But I'm not as strict as she was, and I can't clamp down on people now, that's not how I want this place to work. But I'll tell you what, Mandy. I've got to be fair to everyone; but how would it be if I made one room a no-smoking zone? Then you'd have somewhere to escape to, when they all lit up. And it wouldn't be fair to expect you to sit in the kitchen all day, so we'll say the games room, okay? That's where you spend most of your time anyway. You'll still have to eat in the kitchen, but I don't let them smoke during meals in any case. The boys'll howl if they're not allowed to smoke when they're playing pool, but they'll just have to put up with that. It won't kill them. Are you happy with that?"

Mandy thought about it, and nodded. "Yes."

"Good. I'll tell them at lunch. So how's life apart from that, any worries?"

"No."

"Have you thought any more about going home soon? They can't force you into an abortion, sweetheart, and it'll be too late anyway in a few weeks, you'll be too far along to do it."

But she shook her head hard at that. "I don't trust them. They'd do something to make me have a miscarriage."

That was pure paranoia, but Mark wasn't going to argue. He wasn't here to pressurise the kids into doing anything, even when it was easy and obvious. "Okay, love. You can stay here as long as you like, you know that. Just let me know if you change your mind. But as long as you are here, we'd better see about getting you some bigger clothes. Those jeans are starting to look too tight for comfort. And if you fancy a change of style any time, I'm sure Nina'd be glad to give you a haircut . . ."

Mandy just shrugged. Mark's private opinion was that her hair not only needed cutting, it could do with more regular washing as well. At the moment it hung lank and unattractive around her face, greasy and flecked with dandruff. But if peer pressure wasn't enough to make her care about her appearance, there was nothing he could do. Any suggestions from him would be either resented or ignored, and probably both.

## 40   *More than Shelter*

"What's this, then, hide and seek?"

Kez looked up and smiled, to see Colton coming along the corridor towards her. She shifted over without being asked, to make room for him on the narrow attic steps; his slim hips wedged in beside hers, his arm looped around her neck, she leaned comfortably into him, all of it native and inevitable, easy as smiling at the sight of him.

She felt his kiss on her hair, and the smile warmed, where he couldn't see it. "What took you so long? I've been here ten minutes."

"Bloody Nina skipped out on the washing up, didn't she? So I had to do it all." He hesitated, then went on, "You didn't want to be alone, did you? I could go away . . ."

"Stupid. We are alone, hadn't you noticed?"

"Oh. Yeah. That's all right, then." His forearm slipped under her chin and lifted her face up, to be confronted by his eyes at an inch's distance, huge and brown and worrying. "You okay?"

"Yes." With a sigh that said, no, not really. She watched him frown, and rubbed her nose against his to make him smile instead; and said, "I'm a bit bored, that's all. I want to *do* something, and there's nothing to do."

Colton grunted. "Yeah, it gets like that, sometimes. You know what you need, though?"

*Yes. I need my brother back, I need my* life *back the way it used to be. But even you can't do that for me, boy . . .*

"You need to get out for a bit," he said positively. "You ain't stuck your nose outside since you come here, and it ain't good for you. Fresh air, that's what you need."

She shook her head hard against his shoulder, gagged by the sudden taste of fear in her mouth.

"I got an idea," he went on, apparently oblivious. "How's about if we grab a couple of towels and go swimming? It won't be busy, this time of day. I can practise my diving, and you can give me points out of ten."

"Colton, I can't."

"'Course you can, it's easy. You just sit on the side and hold up little cards with numbers on, and then everybody claps."

"Not that," she hissed, fighting free of his grip. "And don't laugh at me. I can't go outside, you know I can't. He's *here* somewhere, in London . . ."

"Maybe he is," Colton said, pulling her casually back against his side, gripping her wrists with long brown fingers. "But so's millions of other people. He ain't gonna see you."

"He might. Alex found the refuge, didn't she?"

"Yeah, but she knew what she was looking for. He don't. And who says he's still here, anyway? He'll be long gone, if he's got any sense."

"You can't be sure of that," she muttered, sitting tight and still under the threat of a shadow that was cold, dark, bitingly real.

Colton sighed, and his breath was warm and damp in her hair. "Look, I'll be with you, right? He ain't gonna be there, no way; but I won't leave you alone for a second, I promise."

"I know. But – hell, he'd tear you apart. You haven't got the muscles to be a bodyguard."

She was afraid he'd be offended, but he only laughed. "Give me time, I'm working on that. And I've got a hell of a good scream, that'll scare him off."

She half smiled, didn't say anything; and he pressed her. "How's about it then, yeah?"

"No. I – Colton, I'm *frightened*."

"I know. And it's okay to be frightened, but you got to be a bit brave too. Look, do it for me, okay? I'm going crazy too, shut up in here all day. I need some sun, or I'll end up all pale and yuck."

She giggled, picturing him turned albino; and said, "You can go out without me, you know. I won't mind."

"No, I can't. I'd be scared then, not knowing what was

happening back here. So come on, eh? The pool's only just round the corner, ten minutes. Nothing to panic about."

"Well – what if someone recognises me?"

"They won't," he said positively. "You're too ordinary."

"Oh, thanks. Thanks a lot."

Colton grinned. "I mean you ain't got three legs, or purple hair, nothing weird like that. Nothing for people to remember. They might notice a black boy out with a white girl, but that's okay, it'll confuse 'em." He got to his feet, and held out a hand. "Coming?"

She started to nod, then stopped herself. "I still can't."

"What's wrong now?"

"I haven't got a costume."

He growled, snatched her wrist and yanked her up. "So we'll get some money off Mark, and go and buy one. There's a shop on the High Street."

They swam and splashed for an hour; he did spectacular belly-flops and called them dives while she floated on her back and laughed at him, and awarded him one out of ten for effort; he swam beneath her and blew bubbles that tickled all the way up her spine; and almost she managed to forget Seb, and the fear and distress that gripped her.

And afterwards, he met her coming out of the changing rooms and ran his hands through her wet hair, and groaned softly.

"Colton? What's wrong?"

"Nothing. Only, you're beautiful . . ."

"So are you, silly." She slipped her arms round his waist, and their bodies settled warmly against each other. She felt his hands on her back, pulling her closer, one sliding up under her hair to circle her neck; and the intensity, the sheer concentration on his face was something close to frightening as he bent to kiss her.

Not the usual shy touch of mouth on cheek, not this time. His lips nudged at hers, teasing them apart; she worked her hands up his long back and went with him, meeting him halfway as their tongues touched curiously. His breath tasted of tobacco, and she could picture him having a nervy cigarette while he waited for her to finish dressing; but that was superficial and not unpleasant. She could have stood like this for a long time, as long as he wanted, tasting and touching and sharing his air; it was Colton who broke first, pulling away with a gasp, panting as if he hadn't breathed at all.

"You . . ." He scowled, and shook his head. "You'll give yourself pneumonia, going out with your hair wet like that. Give us that towel."

"Get off! Not with all these people watching, don't you dare . . ."

He made a snatch at the towel, and she turned and ran, out of the door and down the steps. Colton came chasing after her, catching up halfway down the street. She grabbed his wrist and dragged him on; and they matched each other stride for stride all the way back to the refuge. He broke away then, sprinting off up the gravel drive to claim a victory at the door. She staggered up the steps behind him, laughing and gasping, clutching at his body for support. Again he drew her close and held her, his breath harsh in her ear and his ribs heaving as much as her own.

Kez could feel every muscle, every bone of his chest through his damp T-shirt. She knew them all already, from the long, shared nights in his bed, but it was different now. That was knowledge born of a need that he'd been able and glad to satisfy; and you couldn't call this need, not exactly, but she wanted to know them again, each separate muscle, bone, each stretch of skin, each hair, she wanted to *learn* them, and she wanted it now.

She turned her head to look at him, and saw his grin fading as if he could read her desire in her face – and maybe he could, at that. Or maybe he only felt it, sensed it in her body pressing against his; but whatever, he pushed the door open wordlessly and checked that the hall was empty before drawing her inside.

They hurried up the stairs, Kez hanging onto his free hand; she couldn't bear not to be touching him, not now, with the warmth he always woke inside her flickering into flame and the blood surging in her ears, making her head swim and her breath come short and hard, as if she were running again.

He hesitated outside the door of her room, but she pulled him past, down the corridor to his. She kicked the door open and almost had to drag him in, against a sudden nervousness.

"Kez . . ."

"Don't," she said sharply, urgently. "Don't talk."

"But . . ."

She grunted, and stood on tiptoe to kiss him, to silence him. Her hands tugged clumsily at his T-shirt, pulling it up his chest; and then he was helping, wriggling it over his head while she kicked her shoes off and struggled one-handed with her own top, while the other clung to the waistband of his jeans, slipped the button open and fumbled with the zip.

Time was a shy stranger, slipping out of the room to leave them naked and alone in a way they'd never been before, despite their nights together; and it didn't return until they were ready for it, until they were lying sweated and drained on the duvet, tangled together in more than body.

"Kez . . ."

"Mmm."

"Can we go swimming again tomorrow?"

She snorted and choked, fighting the surge of laughter; then she rolled over on top of him again and bit his neck. His arms closed around her, offering more than shelter, more than a place to hide; and he said, "Do us a favour, then."

"Sure."

"Call me Col."

## 41 Not for Shame

Davey carried the memory of that first night back
*(back at work)*
in his head like a sore, an evidence of sickness. It wasn't the pain that had made him cry, at the time or afterwards in the secrecy of his room; he didn't have the words to explain it even to himself, but he still shivered and felt close to vomiting every time his mind fed him pictures of what he'd done, what he'd let them do to him.

He'd do it again, though, for the money. He'd have to. But not tonight. Aspinall had promised him an easy one tonight, straight sex and nothing fancy. It was only worth a tenner, and Davey knew he could get more out on the street, turning tricks for himself; but there was danger in that, and not only the danger of Aspinall hearing about it and being angry. The police were still looking for him, and looking hard. It wasn't worth the risk.

So he'd come back to the house in Croydon, and sat waiting in one of the small back bedrooms, listening for the bell downstairs and trying not to think about the last time he was here. But the mind is a traitor to desire; it picks irresistibly at latent pain. And Davey was too close both in time and space to escape it, too weak to fight.

His head dropped into his hands, his body began to shudder as memories swamped and mocked him; and he never heard the bell chime, or the footsteps on the stairs. He didn't even hear the door open, looking up only as a shadow crossed the light. He saw a silhouette, broad shoulders and close-cropped hair, and felt a stab of recognition; then a voice shouted his name and strong hands seized his arms, pulling him up into a rough bear-hug.

"Davey, boy! Where in God's name did you spring from?"

"Hullo, Jesse." For a moment Davey almost resented the big American for surprising him, catching him in his self-disgust; but it didn't last, it couldn't. It didn't stand a chance, caught between Jesse's genuine pleasure and the warmth that rose inexorably in Davey himself to meet and match that pleasure.

Jesse sat on the bed and pulled Davey unselfconsciously onto his lap. "I thought you'd gone for good, kiddo."

"So did I."

"So how come?"

Davey shrugged awkwardly. "I need the money."

"Bad enough to work for old fat-gut?"

Davey just nodded.

"That's too bad," Jesse grunted. "I was glad, when I read about you in the papers. Don't get me wrong, I knew I'd miss you; but I figured you'd be looked after, in that refuge place."

There was nothing Davey could say to that, so he only shrugged again. Jesse whistled softly, the way he always did to fill an uncomfortable silence; then he stroked the short hair on Davey's neck with a finger, and said, "I like this. Very pretty."

It was what Aspinall had said, almost word for word; but the difference was strong enough to shake Davey, hard enough that he had to swallow against a sudden threat of tears. And Jesse felt it, and wouldn't let it pass. His arms tightened round Davey's waist, and he said, "Come on, then. Talk to me. What's the big hurry for cash?"

Davey wanted to lie, but couldn't think of anything that would convince him; and it was no good just ignoring the question, he'd tried that before with Jesse and it didn't work. So slowly, reluctantly, he said, "I need an Aids test, and it costs."

"Oh, shit." Jesse rocked Davey gently for a minute, kissed his ear, let his body speak for him; then he said, "How much?"

"A hundred."

"I'll pay. You can have it now, if you like."

"No!"

"Don't be stupid, kiddo."

"I can get it."

"Sure you can. You can sell your skinny little body to Larry Aspinall for a week or two, and let his sickos screw you up; and you'll end up hoping you have got it, and hoping they'll get it off you."

A flash of memory spun Davey back to that other room, that other night: to a moment when he'd lain sprawled on the bed, sobbing, silently praying that one of their vicious little canes would draw blood, that they'd get it into their mouths and swallow it, so that he might at least have the last laugh. And he twisted his head to stare at Jesse; but the American just met his gaze quietly, and said, "Or, you can just forget that foolish Irish pride of yours, and let your friends help you. So which is it to be, Davey?"

Davey shifted, chewed his lip, took one of Jesse's big hands in both of his, and said, "Would you, would you come with me? To the clinic?"

"Sure. If you want me to."

"I want you."

"Okay, you got me, boy. And thanks."

"For what?"

"For letting me help. Now, what do you want to do? We can sit here and talk if you like; or we can go to bed, if you'd like that. It's up to you, kid."

"Jesse, I – I've got Aids. I might have."

"So we'll use some of Larry's fancy condoms. That's what they're for." He paused, then slid his hands slowly down Davey's ribs. "It's your choice – but I said, I've missed you. And don't worry, I'll be careful."

"You do that."

So they undressed each other, no hurry, and went to bed – and for Davey, it wasn't like turning a trick at all. Jesse had always been a bit different, friendly and affectionate where most of them were urgent, embarrassed, anxious to get away; but tonight the whole game was new. Davey learned for the first time what it might be like to have a lover, even to be loved.

And when they were finished, when he rolled his head into Jesse's shoulder and cried again, he was crying for many things, some that were and some that might have been; but none of them was shame.

## 42  Questions and Answers

"We don't ask questions," Mark said. "Nor do we make judgements. The kids who come to us may be on the run from their families or from the police, from the courts, whatever. It doesn't matter to us. If we think they're making a mistake we tell them so, and we'll give them advice if they ask for it, but there's never any pressure on them to go back. That's not what we're for."

So what are they for?

"We're a refuge. A haven, a port in a storm. Shelter. That's all. Sometimes we don't even know why a kid has come to us. Not often, they're usually only too glad to have someone neutral to talk to; but we have had kids here who just couldn't talk about it. That's okay. It's their future that concerns us, not the past."

So what happens to the teenagers who do find themselves with nowhere else to turn? Where do they go from here?

"That depends." Mark shrugged, and smiled. "Some of them go home, after a week or a month here. Or if they're on the dodge from the law, they'll often give themselves up eventually. It's their choice. All we can give them here is time; but that's very often all they need. Situations sort themselves out, given time."

What about the youngsters who've been beaten up or sexually abused – the ones who are simply scared to go home?

"We do what we can. Talk to the Social Services, try to make other arrangements for them, foster homes or council care. Sometimes the older kids will simply stay with us till they're seventeen, when they can leave home legally. Again, it's their choice. We just take it day by day. At least while they're here, we know they're safe. And that's the main thing."

But for how long? The refuge can't stay hidden for ever; what happens when the authorities find it?

"That's up to them. I suppose they'll close us down; I can't see how they could do anything else. But we're here at the moment, that's the important thing. There are six kids eating and sleeping here right now, and that means there are six kids less out on the street getting sick, getting hurt, getting scared. That's what counts."

*Read more of Alex Holden's exclusive report tomorrow, when the kids themselves speak out about why they ran away, what are their hopes for the future and what life's really like at the refuge.*

Sebastian read through the feature twice, tapping a biro thoughtfully against his teeth; then he fished a scrap of paper out of his pocket and made a note of the reporter's name. It could well be worth having a word with him. Not that Kez would be hiding out at this refuge place, that was too much to hope for, but what was his name, Holden must have done a lot of digging before he found what he was looking for. He'd know the other places teenagers were likely to wind up in, in London; and Kez had to be somewhere.

And someone had to know where. She couldn't just go to ground in a strange city, not without help. Maybe this Holden man had heard something, maybe he'd even seen her; and he'd talk to Seb. Sure he would. With a little persuasion.

# PART SIX

*Less Than Sheltered*

When they came into the kitchen they found Alex there already, scowling at a cup of coffee.

"'Morning," Colton said cheerfully. "Kettle hot, is it?"

"Yeah, help yourselves." She shared her scowl impartially between them, and went on, "I know why I'm up this early, I've got to go to work. And I know why Mark's up, he likes to have a bit of peace before you lot start tearing things apart all over the place. But what the hell are you two doing out of bed at eight in the morning?"

"Couldn't sleep," Kez said quietly, slipping into a chair while Colton hunted for mugs.

"What, neither of you?"

Colton looked round quickly, and saw the scowl transformed into a wicked little grin.

"We're going for a swim," he said. "Early, before the crowds get there. We fixed it last night."

"That's nice." Alex glanced from one to the other, and giggled. "Oh, stop being so bloody cautious, you two. I'm not going to rat on you. It's none of my business, what you get up to. Just be careful, that's all."

Kez shifted uncertainly in her seat, and Colton changed the subject. "Is the doctor coming tonight, then?"

"That's right," Alex said, still chuckling. "It's regular now, Mondays and Thursdays. Gives Mark and me a chance to get away from you brats and remember that we're grown-ups."

Colton snorted cynically; Kez said, "I still don't think I understand about you, Alex. How long are you going to be around now?"

"Oh, until I get fed up with it," Alex replied lightly. "I'm a volunteer."

"Yes, but why?"

"I just don't think Mark should have to cope by himself, that's all. It's not fair on the boy. It's no skin off my nose, just to be here in the evenings and overnight; and it makes things a little easier for him."

Colton carried two coffees over to the table. "Yeah, but wouldn't it make more sense if you sat in on his evenings off, rather than both of you being off together, so's the doctor has to come round?"

"I suppose it would, in a way. But think a minute, Colton. You know Mark better than any of us, or you should do. If I just said, 'Go away, Mark, I'm in charge tonight,' what would he do?"

Colton scratched his head, and grunted. "He'd stick around. Not that he wouldn't trust you, exactly, but . . ."

"Precisely. But. He might pretend he was having the evening off, sit in his room or play with his car, but he'd be listening out all the time, just in case. Even if I chased him out, he wouldn't have anywhere to go. I don't think he's got any friends in London. Come to think of it, I don't think he's got any friends full stop. So the doctor and I made an arrangement, we do it this way, and I drag Mark out for a few hours. Do you two use condoms?"

Colton choked over a mouthful of coffee; it was Kez who smiled, with no trace of her earlier uncertainty. "Yes. But don't you dare tell Mark, or I'll let on about your real reason for being here."

"Oh, yes? What's that, then?"

"You fancy him like mad. Don't you?"

Alex chuckled. "Kez my love, you'd never make a black-mailer. He knows that. At least, I think he does . . ."

She fell silent then, as Mark himself came in with a hand-ful of mail. Colton saw him blink with surprise; then he said good-mornings all round, and added, "Colton, there's a letter for you."

"Eh?"

"Here."

Mark passed a pale blue envelope across the table. Colton took it blankly, sat looking at it, feeling Kez's eyes on him.

"Who's it from, then?" she asked.

"I dunno, do I? I mean, no one knows I'm here . . ."

"Someone does, obviously. Why don't you open it, and find out?"

"It's postmarked Ipswich," Mark said casually, "so I expect it's from Jane. The handwriting looks right, too, it's all over the place."

"Oh, right! Yeah, that'd be it. Good." Colton forced a grin onto his face, and pushed the envelope into the back pocket of his jeans.

"Aren't you going to read it?" Kez demanded.

"Yeah, later. No hurry, is there? It ain't going to go away. Now come on, let's go for that swim. Where's your stuff, upstairs? Don't bother, I'll get it . . ."

And he was on his feet and halfway out of the door before he'd stopped talking, *move, boy, move and just keep on moving . . .*

But it's easy to forget to move, when you're young and in love, and you just want to hold on to what you've got and stay where you are forever. And when they came out of the swimming baths, Colton felt the sun on his wet hair like a warm hand, and said, "There's a bit of a park round the corner. It ain't much, but it's got grass and trees and swings and stuff. Want to go and play?"

Kez shook her head nervously, not quite a refusal. "There'll be people there, someone might recognise me . . ."

"Not many, this time in the morning." She was wearing a baggy old shirt of Mark's, that she'd pinched out of the laundry pile; he untucked it from her jeans and started to undo the buttons, working from the bottom up.

"Col, stop it!" she hissed. "I'm not wearing anything under this, not even a bra . . ."

"I know," he said cheerfully. "I saw you put it on, remember?"

He tied the shirt into a neat knot over her midriff, and put his hands gently on her bare stomach. "There. Nobody's going to look at you like that and see a scared runaway, right? Just a girl getting a suntan with her boyfriend."

She chewed her lip, and nodded straight-faced. "Right. And you couldn't half use a suntan, boy."

"Right, then."

After they'd pushed each other on the swings, bounced on the seesaw and gone down the slide together, they sprawled contentedly on the grass. Colton pulled his sweatshirt off and lay on his stomach, folding his arms under his head and revelling in the feeling of the cool earth under his belly and the hot sun on his back. When Kez moved round to use his chest as a pillow, he closed his eyes and bit hard at the skin on his wrist with an overmastering delight.

And forgot that he was supposed to keep moving.

He remembered only when she pulled the envelope out of his pocket, and tossed it onto the grass in front of him.

"Forgot about that, didn't you, goofy?"

*Yeah, bloody right I forgot. I was going to dump it in my room when I was getting the towels and stuff.*

"Well, go on, open it."

"Later."

"No, now. I want to know what she says."

Colton sighed, and rolled over onto his back. "Leave it out, Kez. What's the hurry?"

"What's the delay?" she challenged. "You're being dead funny about that letter, Col boy. I'll start wondering about you and Jane in a minute, you're so keen to read it in private."

"You open it, if you're that bothered," he said, snatching at a sudden straw. "Read it to me."

"No, it's your letter. It might be personal, part of it."

"Yeah, it might; so why don't you just let it go, eh? I'll open it when I'm good and ready."

She was sitting up now, staring down at him with a puzzled curiosity. "Col, I don't believe this. We're not really going to fight over a letter from Jane, are we?"

He shrugged, *you're the one who's making it into a fight, girl* – but that was so dishonest he couldn't even say it. Instead he twisted away from her, turning onto his side so that he didn't have to look at either of them, Kez or that bloody letter; and felt her fingers picking grass-clippings off his skin as she whispered his name.

"Col. Don't do that, don't turn your back on me. I need you . . ."

"I know. It's all right, I'm here." He fumbled for her hand, and gripped it tight; but still kept his head turned away, as he said, "You're going to have to read that letter to me, private or not. You are or Mark is, and I'd rather have you."

"Why? I don't understand."

"I can't read, Kez."

He watched the trees, and listened to her slow, indrawn breath; then her fingers clenched and jerked hard, pulling him over onto his back again.

"Why didn't you just tell me?"

"I don't tell nobody." And he'd still rather not be looking at her, which was weird, when he'd thought he'd never be happy doing anything else. "Mark knows, and the doctor. No one else."

"You could've told me." That was an accusation, and a just one; but it wasn't true. She was the one he didn't dare tell. "So what is it, are you dyslexic?"

"No." He knew about that, he'd had tests for it at school, before he ran away. "I'm just stupid."

"No, you're not," she said angrily, "don't be stupid."

She checked herself, and looked like she wanted to bite the word back, too late. For a second everything seemed in the balance, and teetering for a fall; but then she giggled, and flung herself down on top of him, wrapping her arms and legs around him and nibbling tenderly at his neck.

"I do love you, Col . . ."

"Yeah," he said, "I know you do. Now are you going to read me that letter, or what? I want to know what Jane's up to . . ."

## 44   Rent Free

*Positive.*

Davey walked slowly down the corridor, through the doors and out into the street, seeing nothing, hearing nothing but the one word dancing a circle around him, cutting the world away.

*I'm very sorry, Michael, but I'm afraid the results are positive. You do have the virus.*

He'd listened to nothing after that, leaving it to Jesse to talk them out of there. It seemed to take forever, while he sat with his hands gripping the moulded plastic of his chair and their voices swam thickly around his head; but at last Jesse had stood up and touched his shoulder, and he was free to start walking, with the lino floor turning to concrete and then paving beneath his feet, looking different but feeling the same, soft and distant, out of touch. And then the paving was edged by a kerbstone with tarmac beyond, and he just kept on walking, the straight line of his passage something to cling to, to hold him in the world –

– and Jesse's hand grabbed his arm and pulled him roughly back onto the pavement as a taxi shot past just feet ahead of him, horn blaring.

"Jesus, kid . . ."

Adrenalin pulled him back, giving him a focus and something to grip, even if it were only someone else's fear; he shrugged, and almost managed to laugh. "What does it matter? At least that way'd be quick."

"It matters to me." Jesse shifted his grip to Davey's neck, the strong fingers closing painfully tight. "You can't just give up, Davey."

*Why not? Other people do, and with less reason.*

But that grip was still there, like an anchor to the world; and Jesse's face was only inches away from his, fighting to get through to him.

"Davey, you've got to promise me you won't do anything stupid. It could be years yet before you show any symptoms; and anything could happen in that time. They'll develop some new treatments, maybe find a cure – but we can't make plans how we're going to deal with this, if I can't even trust you not to throw yourself under a bus tomorrow!"

*Plans? What's to plan?* Davey looked away, shrugged, said, "Okay. I won't throw myself under a bus."

"Davey. Look at me."

Eye to eye again, and another anchor – and that wasn't fair, he didn't need Jesse's concern tangling him up like this, making things matter. But it was there, and he couldn't escape it. "I promise, Jesse. Okay?"

"Okay."

They stopped at the first cafe they came to; Jesse bought two coffees, then linked his fingers unselfconsciously with Davey's across the table and said, "I want you to come and live with me."

Davey jerked his head in a swift denial. "I'm all right where I am."

"For how long? That place can't stay hidden forever, someone's going to blow it. And they can't give you what you need now, Davey. I can."

"Oh, yeah? What's that, then?"

"A home."

"I had a home. I left it."

"That's different. Don't be difficult, Davey. I want you."

"I bet. Your own private little rent boy, right? Every night for nothing."

Jesse didn't speak, didn't flinch, didn't move except to turn his eyes away for a moment and then look back, calm and monumental. "You'll have your own room, with a lock on the door. Rent free."

"Oh, hell. I'm sorry, Jess. I didn't mean that."

"No, but it needed saying anyway. You don't have to sleep with me, that's not what this is about. But you don't have to sleep alone either. Your choice. And you don't have to make any decisions now. The offer's there, that's all I'm saying. Take your time. I'm not going to go away."

"Won't it make trouble for you, with your neighbours? Having me around?"

Jesse laughed. "Davey, I live in a gay cooperative. There are four apartments, and two of the others have permanent houseboys. You'll be welcome."

"I don't know, Jess. I can't think."

"Sure. I said, take all the time you want. There's a place for you, that's all I'm saying. Some place you can go."

But his hand said more, tightening on Davey's, offering something greater than comfort, and more needful.

"I'll smoke where I want to, you little git!"

"Not in here!"

"Listen, shit-head, I always have smoked in here, and I'm not going to stop just because you were too stupid to go on the pill, get it?"

"It's the rule, no smoking in here. Mark said so."

"Oh, yeah? And what's he going to do, throw me out for lighting up a fag in the games room? Fat chance. So why don't you just go and fuck yourself, Mandy?"

Nina slammed the door, and stormed across the hall to the kitchen. Davey was there, rolling a burning cigarette edgily around an ashtray, watching the smoke rise.

"*Christ!* Give us a fag, Davey."

He only shrugged; she picked his pack up from the table and helped herself.

"That little *shit* . . ."

"What?"

"Fucking Mandy. I was just having a quiet smoke in the games room, and she only grabbed the fag right out of my mouth and stamped on it, didn't she? I'll fucking kill her, I swear I will."

"You're not supposed to smoke in there any more. Mark said, last week."

"Yeah, and fuck Mark too. I'll bloody smoke if I want to. I mean, are you just going to sit there and take it?"

Davey shrugged again, and didn't bother to reply.

"Next time she tries it I'll put the fag out in her eye, that'll shut her up. I wish I'd just bloody left her in that bus-station now. I didn't have to bring her here; and she goes and pulls this on me . . . What's the matter with you, anyway?" And when he still didn't give her an answer, she found her own. "No, wait, I know. You've got it, haven't you?"

"Got what?" he demanded, suddenly alert.

"*You* know. Aids." And she stepped back a pace, while her mouth went on running. "I figured it out, see? What that message meant, from Secky. Your boyfriend had it; and that means you've got it too."

"He wasn't my boyfriend."

Which was no answer to the question, and at the same time all the answer she needed. "Just mind you keep away from me, hear? In fact, get right out of here, go into hospital or something. You're not staying here to give it to the rest of us."

Davey lifted his head, and said, "Since when have you been making the decisions who stays?"

"I'm just telling you, I'm not living with a guy with Aids, no way. You'd better bloody find somewhere else to go, mate."

"Or what?"

"Or I'll tell Mark and the doctor, and they'll have you out of here dead quick. It's not safe, you hanging around with the rest of us."

"And where else am I supposed to go, then?"

"That's your problem. You can go jump in the river, for all I care. That's probably the best idea anyway, it'd be quicker than dying of Aids."

Davey jerked to his feet, and Nina backed off quickly. She'd seen what happened when Davey lost his rag; and she wasn't scared of a weedy little creep like him, no, but she was scared of what he might be carrying round. Christ, she could give him a nosebleed and end up dying for it . . .

So she went out into the passageway and pulled the kitchen door shut behind her; and heard Colton and Kez coming in from outside, and stood still to listen.

". . . Bloody baby books," Colton was muttering sulkily.

Kez laughed. "Stop fussing, will you? We've ordered those others, they'll be more interesting for you; and these'll do to make a start with."

"Can't we just leave it, till the others come?"

"No, we can't."

"Well, for Christ's sake don't let Davey see them. Or Nina, she'd never let up about it . . ."

Nina arched an eyebrow, and walked innocently out of the shadows. Colton stiffened, and she smiled at him, all her temper melting away at the sight of his sullen, guarded face. She owed Colton for a dozen put-downs, and she'd been waiting a long time to catch him out. He thought he was so bloody important, just because he'd been here for ever . . .

"Been to the library, have you?" she said. "What have you got, then? Let's see . . ."

Kez was carrying three or four big, flat books under one arm. Her eyes flicked from Nina to Colton and back again, and she started to shake her head in a flat refusal; but then the front door swung open again behind them, and Kez turned automatically to see who was coming in.

*Thanks, Tia, lovely timing* – and Nina reached out calmly to twist the books out of Kez's grasp as the Asian girl hurried past them and up the stairs.

Nina read the titles out loud, giggling. "*Timmy's Special Day*, *Diana's Dragon*, *Mark Goes to the Market* – your little brother coming for a visit, is he, Kez? Oh, no, how silly of me, he's your *big* brother, isn't he?"

Kez went white, and Nina laughed. *Got you there, you cow.* "So, what, these must be for you, Colton, yeah? *The Little Kitten and the Big Dog*. You sure you're old enough for these? They sound a bit grown-up . . ."

"Can I have them back, please?" Kez said coldly. "If you must know, I got them out to look at the illustrations. I'm thinking of going in for that, after college."

"Bullshit." Nina passed the books back, with another giggle. "I bet you can't *wait* to get upstairs and start reading them, eh, Colton? They all sound dead exciting. Don't let me keep you."

He said nothing, just staring at her with a mute anguish; it was Kez who said, "Are you going to keep quiet about this, or what?"

"No chance."

"You bitch . . ."

"Yeah, and screw you too, dear," Nina said pleasantly. "Except Colton's doing that already, isn't he? And you want to watch your mouth, or I might not keep quiet about that, either."

And then Colton did move, jerking forward, one arm lashing out for her. Nina ducked and scuttled out of range, ready to scream if he came at her again; but Kez grabbed him round the waist.

"Leave it, Col. She's not worth it."

"Fucking little . . ."

"Leave it, I said. Let's go find Mark, he said to give him the library ticket back as soon as we got in, so's he knows where it is . . ."

"Yeah. Right . . ." And he went with her, down the passage to the office door; but his eyes found Nina's and held them, promising retribution. She brazened it out, giving him her best smirk; then went running upstairs after Tia, bursting to tell someone.

She was still laughing as she burst into the room she shared now with Tia; but the laugh died quickly, falling away forgotten, in company with the news she'd been so full of.

Because Tia was sitting on her bed, counting money. *Real* money, a thick pile of tens and twenties.

"Jesus fucking *Christ*, Tia . . ."

Tia's fist clenched on the notes, and for a second Nina almost felt afraid, seeing the cold anger and the colder distrust on the other girl's face.

## 46  Dead Weight

Alex still couldn't fathom Mark, but she was getting used to that; and it had its own attraction, even beyond the challenge. She'd get through to him eventually, she was determined on that. Whatever it was, that great secret that he hugged so jealously to himself, he'd share it with her sooner or later. And in the meantime she was enjoying the sense of struggle, of being out of her depth with a man she couldn't understand.

And he was getting better all the time, letting her closer. He looked forward to their evenings out as much as she did, she was sure of that; and he didn't shy away now either from her touch or from her questions. There were still some he wouldn't answer, but that was part of the game. It didn't embarrass either of them any more when he just said no. *Treat him gently, and take your time. He'll give in the end, he's got to. He wants to already, and that's the main thing.*

Walking back from the cinema tonight, she decided it was time for another little push against his barriers, see how strong they really were. It was a warm, sticky evening, and they were both in T-shirts; she linked one bare arm comfortably with his, slid the other hand up his bicep to be sure she had his attention, and said, "Girlfriends."

"What about them?"

"Don't be dense, it doesn't suit you. It's not the sort of question I expect to be asking a good-looking twenty-five-year-old, but there you go. Ever had any?"

She listened to his hesitation, and wondered if it was only the leading edge of a refusal; but the answer came at last, slow and careful. "Not since I was fourteen; and that was just a disco date and heavy breathing on her doorstep. Fulfilling obligations, I suppose. So no." *But don't ask me why not.*

She was used to those unspoken tags that marked the limits of where she was allowed. And, *I wasn't going to, fella. I'm getting good at this.*

Instead, she said, "Okay, now this is where I get *really* personal. Are you still a virgin?"

"Doesn't it follow?"

"Not necessarily."

"No, I suppose it doesn't. All right, I'm still a virgin. Are you?"

"Nah, not since ages. I gave it to my first-ever boyfriend, for his sixteenth birthday present." She grinned at the memory, then punched him. "Don't change the subject."

"I thought we were talking about sex?"

"We were talking about you, and your unwholesome burden of virginity. What I want to know is, are you holding onto it from choice, or has there simply been a lack of opportunity?"

This time he shook his head, which was deliberately not an answer.

"Ouch," she said; and when he lifted an enquiring eyebrow, "Just ran into that brick wall of yours again, didn't I? I was wondering where that had got to. So let me rephrase it. If I came tiptoeing into your room one night, just me and a packet of Mates, would you throw me out?"

"Is it likely to happen?"

"I'm not sure. It might. I've got the Mates."

"In that case, I'll put a bolt on the door."

"Don't bother, I can take a hint."

*But that wasn't really an answer, was it? That was a dodge.*

They walked on in an amiable silence, arm in arm, and came to the refuge around midnight. The doctor was in his usual seat in the kitchen, talking with Tia.

"Good evening," he greeted them gravely. "Good film?"

Alex watched Mark trying to remember, trying to push his mind back past their conversation; and giggled. "Very good film," she agreed. "How're things here?"

"All quiet. Nina wasn't feeling very well after dinner, so I chased her up to bed early; and I think it's probably time you joined her, isn't it, Tia? It's not fair to go in too late, when you're sharing a room."

"I suppose." Tia sighed, and got to her feet.

When she was gone, the doctor smiled thoughtfully, and said, "An interesting young lady, that. Very self-contained. I've been talking to her for an hour, and I can't remember the last time I've been kept so much at a distance."

Alex snorted. "You talked to Mark recently?"

The doctor laughed. "I have an advantage there. I've known him a long time."

Mark looked wary suddenly; and Alex thought, *Yes, and you know what it is about him, don't you? You know his secret. I don't suppose you'd tell me, though; and I'm not going to ask anyway. That'd be cheating both of us. I want him to tell me himself, because he wants me to know.*

"What about the rest of them?" Mark demanded abruptly, forcing a change of subject. "Anyone still up?"

"Davey is, he's watching television. The rest are all upstairs now, even Colton. That boy's becoming positively virtuous."

"It's not virtue," Mark chuckled, "it's love. He can't bear to be separated from Kez longer than he has to; so he goes to bed straight after she does, and gets up before. I think they're telepathic about that, unless he knocks on her door on his way down. He comes through here in the morning and makes two coffees, and she always appears before he's put the milk in."

Alex opened her mouth, hesitated, and closed it again firmly. If Mark wanted to believe it was telepathy, let him. No point stirring up trouble; they weren't doing anyone any harm, and it was probably the best thing that could happen for Kez at the moment, to have someone else to think about.

The doctor caught her eye then, with just the faintest suspicion of a wink; but all he said was, "Well, I'm glad Colton's taking on some responsibility here, even if it needed a romance to wake him up to it. He has a charmingly protective air about him, when you see the two of them together; and falling in love won't do him any serious damage either. It was high time he gave his glands some exercise. There's even the chance that it'll help to shift him out of here, if their mutual devotion can survive until Kez goes home."

"It wouldn't be the same here, without Colton," Mark murmured.

"No, but you can't expect him to stay for ever. I don't say that he's thought about moving, I don't suppose he has; but perhaps you should encourage him to start."

Any reply Mark might have made was forestalled by a sudden, urgent clatter of feet on the stairs, coming down. *Tia*, Alex thought, recognising the sound of high heels; and the girl followed the thought, bursting into the kitchen, nothing self-contained about her now.

"Doctor, can you come and look at Nina, quick? She doesn't, she doesn't look right. And I found this on the floor, I trod on it, that's why I noticed . . ."

She held out a small brown prescription-bottle. The doctor took it, read the label and glanced sharply at Mark.

"The sleeping pills I gave you, how many have you taken?"

"None. I'd forgotten about them. Christ, she hasn't . . ."

The doctor ran for the door, with Mark close behind. Alex jumped up and followed them, reaching out to take Tia's arm, to offer some spurious comfort as the distraught girl came with her.

When they reached the bedroom, the doctor was bending over Nina's bed, holding her wrist and peeling back an eyelid. A second later, he straightened and began to snap out orders.

"Mark – no, Alex. Here's the key to my car; run and open the doors. Mark, you wrap Nina in a blanket and carry her down, put her in the back seat. I'll phone the hospital. One of you had better come with me, Alex, I think . . ."

"No," Mark said flatly. "Me."

The doctor gazed at him for a moment, then nodded. "All right. You keep an eye on things here, then, Alex. Now move!"

It was three hours before Mark came back. Most of that time Alex spent trying to get Tia settled; she didn't waste any of it trying to settle herself, because intuition or something stronger

*(memories of his face, that frozen half-second as he stared at the pill-bottle and realised what it meant)*

was telling her that Tia would be the lesser of her problems tonight.

When she heard the front door, Alex went out into the hall, walking slowly; and found Mark halfway up the first flight of stairs already. She called his name, and he stood still, slowly turning to face her.

"Mark, how is she?"

"She's dead."

No attempt to break it to her gently, or to dilute the blunt finality of the words. He was beyond all that, seeing nothing but the fact of it, and his own part in it. Alex took a step up towards him, and had to watch him move the same distance in retreat.

"Mark, come down and talk to me. Please? I'll make us a drink, and . . ."

"No." That had the same dead weight to it, and carried the same unspoken message.

*No. What is there to say? She's dead, and it's my responsibility.*

They held each other's gaze across a gulf of more than distance; he rubbed a hand across his eyes, and said, "I'll see you in the morning."

*Leave me alone.*

But she had something to say too, in this silent conversation; and never mind that he'd already turned away and was trudging slowly away and out of sight. She hurled it violently at his back, and if he wasn't listening that was his problem.

*No. That's the last thing you need, boy, and the last thing you'll get from me. I'll see you up there. Not just yet, maybe, but I'll see you . . .*

## 47   Things in Balance

Under the sloping ceiling of the attic room, Mark was pacing. It was easier than sitting still, and lying down

*(aping death, aping Nina)*

was impossible. Moving was a goal in itself, even if he wasn't going anywhere; and it made no difference to his mind, nothing was going to shake that loose of the spirals, the coils and springs of too-fresh memory. So he paced, four steps and turn, four steps and turn: felt cold and clammy skin beneath his fingers, watched Nina's head lolling like one already dead, carried her weight in his arms like a body already emptied, counted her fluttering and helpless breaths like the final

*(dying)*

reflexes of muscles abandoned, no life to guide them.

Four steps and turn: and his thumb strayed across his fingertips and didn't touch them, touched Nina instead, cold and clammy . . .

Four steps and turn: and his arms swung free without his feeling them, too full they were of Nina's dragging weight . . .

Four steps and turn: and with his eyes so closely focused on Nina's twitching lips and the shallow breaths that lost ground with every minute, a tide turned too far, he didn't see the door open and close again, didn't realise he was no longer alone

*(with Nina)*

until two arms closed around his waist, tight enough to hold him still, to jerk him out of the relentless rhythms of movement and memory. There was a voice in his ear too, and that was close enough for him to hear even above Nina's blanketing silence.

"Mark, stop it, you hear? Just *stop* . . ."

It was Alex, of course; and of course, she didn't understand. He didn't have the option to stop. The only choice lay between walking and shaking, and he'd rather walk.

But she wrestled him over to the bed and pushed him down; and resisting wasn't an option either, so he simply let it happen, sitting on the edge of the mattress, feeling the shakes moving in on him.

But the arm that gripped his shoulders was strong and alive, nothing like Nina; there was warm skin against his, driving out the memories of cold, of fingers that could neither grip nor feel; and he could hear her breathing, slow and deep and patient. He lifted his head and turned to her with a need far beyond gratitude; and opened his eyes not to see Nina as she laid a palm against his cheek and kissed him lightly.

"Here," she said. "This'll help."

She put a long hand-rolled cigarette into her mouth, and let go of him for a moment to strike a match and light the twist of paper at the end. He watched it flame and char, and glow as she inhaled; then her arm came round his shoulders again, and her other hand offered him the cigarette.

"What is it?"

"Dope, what d'you think? Come on, it'll help you relax."

"No."

"Mark, trust me, will you? It's not a poison."

"For me it is."

"Shit. What makes you so different from the rest of us, eh?"

It wasn't a serious question; but he didn't hear it as a question at all, only as an invitation, offering him a choice at last; and he scrabbled for it, more desperate than grateful, stumbling the words out to get them said before the chance was lost under the weight of Nina's dying.

"I'm schizophrenic, Alex."

She breathed, once, twice, while the joint burned between her fingers; and said, "I don't understand."

"I'm schizophrenic," he said again, willing to repeat himself till dawn if he had to, willing to break down every wall his secrets sheltered under, if it would only keep him safe from Nina. "That's what makes me different."

"What, mad, you mean? You don't act mad." The naivety was deliberate, he knew that, hiding a genuine puzzlement; and he wanted to respond to that, but his mind was still
*(dead)*
numb, and his lips wouldn't support a smile.

"No," he said, taking it straight, all he could do. "We keep it under control. You can do that with drugs, but I stopped taking them five years ago. We've been doing it with diet since then. It works well for me, so long as I'm careful; but dope is a very bad idea for schizophrenics."

"Right." She inhaled, blew smoke out, watched it eddy around the room; then said, "Shit. Sorry . . ." and stubbed the joint out on a saucer.

"It's all right, I don't mind you smoking."

"Yeah, but you'll catch the backblast, won't you? The room's full of it already, you can't help breathing it; and this joint's strong enough to get you stoned just *looking* at it. Maybe I'd better open a window."

"No. Don't move."

She glanced at him, surprised; then nodded and shifted closer, her hip pressing against his. "So. You're schizophrenic, and dope's not good for you. Coffee too, maybe? And alcohol?"

"For me, no. It's all trial and error, but we've learned that much for sure."

"We, you keep saying we. Who's we?"

"The doctor and me, who else? He's been treating me since I got sick."

"He's a *psychiatrist*?"

"Yes, of course. Didn't you know?"

"No." She chewed her lip thoughtfully, and said, "I suppose I could've guessed. I never thought about it before, but it does make sense. You told me he was a friend of the family, you fibber."

"He is my family. Has been for ten years."

"From before you got ill, you mean?"

"No."

"Jesus, Mark, how old were you?"

"Fifteen. Nearly. It's his speciality, teenage schiz."

"Christ. You poor bugger . . . What's it like, do you mind

talking about it?"

"I don't mind." This was all relief to Mark; she could dig where she liked, probe at nerves with her fingernails, it would still be relief. "Only, it's hard to explain. It's like living on another planet. Everything goes weird . . . I'm sorry, I can't do this very well."

"You're doing fine. You need practice, that's all; so practise on me. Put your feet up, and go at it slowly. Here, kick your shoes off and we'll get comfy . . ."

She organised him quietly, so that he ended up leaning against the wall with his legs stretched out across the mattress and a pillow behind his back.

"You want to chuck us that other pillow?"

"No." He didn't want to break the contact, the touch of life that was all he had to set against the

*(cold and clammy)*

shadows; he reached out an arm in invitation, and she tucked herself up against him.

"So. Try it again, from the beginning. What *happens* to you?"

"You get . . . anxious. Upset about things. *Guilty.* At least I did, it's not compulsory; but everything that was going wrong with the world was my fault, and I knew how to fix it but I wasn't doing anything, and that doubled the guilt. Everyone else knew, too. Some days I kept apologising to people, total strangers, I couldn't help it. Or I'd sit and watch, and see them all talking about me. Even when they weren't talking. Every gesture, every movement was a code, and it was all about me. They knew how *significant* I was, you see. Everything that happened happened through me, and the responsibility all came back to me. It was like being God, if you can imagine a god riddled with guilt."

"Did you know you were ill?"

"No. I just thought I was special. Hell, I *was* special. Bright and beautiful and burning with it; but it's not just self-image, there are physical proofs. All your senses get magnified somehow, so that you're sensitised to everything around you. Eye-contact is electric; and if you'd met me I couldn't only have counted your pores from the other side of the room, I could've *smelt* you."

"Oh. Thanks."

"No, I mean it. Hearing too, you can listen to a whisper

twenty yards away and hear every word. Real words. You hear things as well, but that's different. Hallucinations, voices. Muttering sometimes, sometimes screaming at you, telling you to do things . . ."

"Christ, Mark . . ."

"Yeah. It's not fun. That's the worst of it, though – or it was for me. I was acute, you see. There's chronic schizophrenia as well, but that's something else again. I saw it when I was at Malmebury, a lot of it, but I never had it that way." He shifted, drawing her closer, catching his breath when she came without protest, with a soft sigh of contentment. "Sorry," he murmured. "Lecture over. I can get really boring on schiz, it's all I know about."

"I'm not bored. A bit scared, that's all. I never realised, I just thought it was that Jekyll and Hyde stuff, split personalities."

"Common misconception. That's something else, I forget the word. Schizos are the people who think they're Napoleon. The voices tell you so, see, and you believe them. You don't have the option."

"Right." Her hand moved, settling on his ribs, so that he could feel his own heartbeat echoing off it. "So okay, we've sorted out the coffee and the alcohol, and the dope. What about driving, that a bad idea?"

"Yeah. Can you imagine an uncontrolled schizophrenic behind the wheel of a car? It'd be murder. I don't know if I could get a licence or not with my history, I've never tried. I wouldn't trust myself."

"Uh-huh. And girls? Are they out too?"

"I don't know. I just, I'm afraid to take the chance. You have to try to keep things in balance, Alex, and to be safe, to be *sure*, that means keeping them flat. All stimulants are out, and, I don't know, any kind of emotional involvement . . ."

"Too exciting, you mean?"

"Yeah, that's it. It's dangerous. If I get too excited about something, some*one*, then the balance goes; and if I was really involved, I'd never see what was happening, till it was too late. And I won't, I *can't* go back to what I was ten years ago . . ."

She chuckled against his chest. "I think the doctor might have something to say, if you tried it. And I might not be too pleased myself, come to that. If you can't trust yourself, Mark, you might try trusting other people. Some of us do care about you, you know. We'd watch out for you, if you decided to chance your arm."

"I . . ."

"No, just listen, okay? And don't get excited. I don't want to scare you, I hadn't realised that you had, what, such good reason for being scared; but the point is, I don't want to leave you alone tonight. I know what'll happen if I do. You won't pace up and down any more, because you know I can hear that; but you won't sleep either, will you? You'll just sit here and shiver, like you were shivering before, before I got you talking; and you'll work yourself up into a right state, and that'll knock you more off balance than cuddling up to a friendly redhead. So that's what's going to happen, all right?"

He hadn't realised until she said it, that the shakes had left him; but she was right about one thing at any rate, they were only just around the corner, waiting shyly until he was alone again. But, "Alex . . ."

"Don't panic, stupe. I promise not to rape you. It's no fun anyway, if the boy's not willing. We'll just keep each other warm, and keep the shivers out. Tell the truth, I'm just a bit shivery myself, I don't want to be alone any more than you do."

And she was right about that too, he didn't want to be alone. Or more specifically, he didn't want her to go.

He nodded a nervous consent, and she smiled.

"Good, then. Let's get undressed, eh? We can keep on talking if you want to, but we might as well do it in situ."

"Mark?"

"Uh?"

"You still awake?"

"Yeah."

"Tell me about tonight. Please?"

"Now?"

"Yes, now. You're still churning it over, I can hear you; and it's on my mind too, I'm just as involved. Neither of us is going to sleep in this state, so we might as well talk. And . . . hell, imagination is worse than facts. I really do need to know."

"Well. They were all ready for us, at the hospital. They pumped her stomach out, gave her something, I don't know what. Rushed her through to intensive care. There wasn't anything for us to do, except wait. Then the police came. The doctor was brilliant, he had a story all pat, ready for them."

"What did he say?"

"That she'd broken into his flat a few days ago, he found her there; and she wouldn't say anything except that she was on the run, and if he turned her over to the authorities she'd just run again. He said he'd kept her, figuring that she'd be more forthcoming once she'd settled down, and she was better off with him than on the street. Only then this evening, he said he found her with a bottle of his own sleeping pills, that she must've pinched from his room. He didn't say so, but I think he knew already, that she wasn't going to contradict anything he said. About an hour later, they came through and told us she was dead."

"Is there any way they can trace her back to the refuge?"

"I don't see how. Unless it's through those articles of yours. You did talk about her, didn't you?"

"Only very generally, and under another name. The photos they used didn't show her, even in a back view. I think we must be safe there."

"Safe. Yeah. But she isn't, is she? And she should've been, that's what we're for. The way I feel at the moment, I wouldn't care if they did dig us out. Might be better that way. Let the doctor start again with someone else, if he wants to. Someone who doesn't let the kids die."

"Mark, that's stupid. You can't blame yourself."

"Can't I? They were my pills, I should've watched them like a hawk, in a place like this; but I forgot about 'em, I don't even know when they went missing . . ."

"Mark, listen. Whatever her reasons were, she obviously meant to do it. She went to a lot of trouble to be left alone long enough to be sure they worked. If she hadn't found the pills, she'd have used something else. You can't stop someone if they're determined enough."

"Maybe not, but you can talk 'em out of it sometimes. Or you can at least be aware that they've got problems, for God's sake! If I'd been doing my job properly, I would've known there was something wrong, I could've talked to her, or got the doctor to. And I just didn't, I hadn't got a clue. She was just a pain in the ass, most of the time; I never thought about her at all, if I could help it. And the poor kid goes and kills herself . . ."

"Mark . . . Mark, it's okay to cry if you want to. Don't fight it."

"I can't. I can't cry. It, it's another of those things I'm scared of. It's a *symptom*. I used to cry all the time."

"God, but you're an awkward fucker, aren't you? Well, all right, then – but you've got to relax somehow, or you really will make yourself ill again. You're so fucking tense, you're like wire, all the way through. Look, shift over this way . . . No, not like that, you idiot, you come underneath . . . That's it. Comfy? Right. Now, you don't have to do anything, okay? Well, not much. Just lie there, and let it happen . . . And don't be scared, right? . . . Right. That's a promise, mind."

*There are three species of mistake, the trivial, the dangerous and the fatal; and what we're watching here is the last of those three. They're all making assumptions – Mark, Alex, even the doctor – and that's fatal.*

*Because Nina didn't commit suicide, oh no. He killed her. Or rather, she killed her; but that comes to the same thing, because he told her to do it, and told her how. She's only a tool to him, an accessory before and after, during. That's her role and her raison d'être; and she can live with that.*

*Not like Nina . . .*

# PART SEVEN

*Things Sold, Things Given Away*

They met in a park this time, always somewhere different; and for a wonder he was there ahead of her, sitting on the grass with a carrier-bag, the top of a cornflakes packet poking out between the handles. As instructed, she had two carriers herself, stuffed with shopping.

She sat down beside him, dropped her bags next to his.

"Hullo, Ali."

"Don't call me that. Don't call me anything."

"You're the boss."

"That's right. Now listen, one of our couriers is sick and someone else has fucked up, so there's a lot of gear in this. And a lot of money for you, if you do it right. The stuff's all in bags, and there's a pile of envelopes and a list of how much has to go where, and when. What you do is you put the right number of bags into the right envelopes, and shove them through the right doors at the right times. The addresses are all over London, so we've spread the arrangements out over three days. You get paid at the shop on Saturday, after we've checked that it all arrived safely. Got that?"

"I'm not stupid."

"Keep it that way."

He moved to stand up, and she said, "Wait a sec. What happened to the one who fucked up?"

"We fucked him up. So don't go getting clever, right? We know where to find you."

*No, you don't. I'm not that stupid. I lied.*

"You don't have to threaten me," she said. "I couldn't sell this stuff on my own anyway, I haven't got the contacts. I don't know anyone in London."

He nodded. "That's why we gave you the job. Start tomorrow, with these; and don't fuck up. It's not a good idea."

This time she let him go without comment; and a few minutes later she headed off for the refuge, doubling back on herself several times just in case he'd set anyone to follow her, three carrier bags swinging heavily against her legs, their handles digging ridges into her fingers.

When Davey wanted to think, he climbed the fire-escape. The last time, he'd had a row about it with Mark; the guy had caught a glimpse of him moving past a window, and been spooked into thinking the sicko had come back, who'd broken into Jane's.

But Davey hadn't made any promises, and wouldn't have kept them now if he had. He wanted the wind and the height of it, and the sense of separation, sitting on cold cross-hatched cast-iron flooring with his legs dangling between the railings and a fag in his mouth, the world under the tree-tops under his feet. He wanted to get away.

(*Get away from the refuge, yeah, that's easy. Get away from Jesse, that'd be easy too, if it came to it. Tell him no, and goodbye. He wouldn't pester, even if he knew where to come. Too much Yankee pride in him. But blood's different, can't get away from blood, it comes with the package. And it's blood that kills you, that's for sure. That's positive.*)

But he walked up the fire-escape anyway, to be alone, *just me and my blood*; and looked through windows as he passed them, and saw Tia sitting on her bed, counting small white bags – no, counting small see-through bags, filled with white . . .

Tia was checking street names in her *A to Z*, trying to plan an easy route for tomorrow, when Colton pushed the door open and walked in. She glanced up angrily, said, "What the hell are you playing at, forgotten how to knock?"

"I want a word with you."

"What about?"

"I want to know what you're doing."

She waved the book at him. "Learning my way round London, okay? Now fuck off."

"Not that. You've got some stuff here, and I want to know what it is."

*He knows.* "None of your fucking business, is what it is.

Who told you, anyway?"

"Never mind that. What is it, heroin?"

*What the hell.* "Yeah, that's right. So what are you going to do about it?"

"Christ, Tia! You can't deal smack from here!"

"Why not? It's perfect."

"Jesus. We got enough bastards looking for us already, we don't need the Drug Squad on top . . ."

She shrugged calmly. "I'll chance that."

"What about the rest of us? If you get caught, we all do."

"That's tough, isn't it? You'll just have to hope I don't."

"You little shit. You just don't care, do you?"

"That's right."

"Suppose I tell Mark? Or the doctor? What then?"

Tia smiled. "They can't stop me."

"Want to bet? They can chuck you right out of here."

"They've got more sense. One phone-call from me, and the cops would be swarming all through this place." She laughed at his expression. "Get the picture now, Colton? I do what I like, while I'm here. And you don't say a word. Not one fucking word, right? And tell that to your spy too, whoever it was. Now get out of here."

## 49  Bargaining Power

"You see, Secky, it's like this. I've been looking for this bloody refuge for weeks now, ever since the *Evening Star* did their piece on it, and my editor's getting impatient."

"That's your problem, mate."

"Granted; but what I'm saying, it could be good for you. You're the only one I've found who'll actually admit to knowing where it is, so you've got a lot of bargaining power. You with me?"

"Yeah, I'm with you."

"Good. Now, what you've given me so far is all good stuff,

I can use it for a piece just about you; our readers'll be interested in your life-story, pure and simple. You're an interesting guy. But if you want to get big money out of it, you're going to have to give us the address. Why not? The way you tell it, you don't owe them anything."

"Bloody right, I don't. How much?"

"How does five hundred quid grab you?"

"Make it a thousand, and I might be interested."

"I don't know if I can do that, Secky. That's a lot of money."

"It's a big thing I'll be doing for you, right, Mr Riley? You said, you can't get it nowhere else."

"Jim, call me Jim. Well, I'll tell you what I'll do. I'll go back now and talk to my editor; and I'll meet you here tomorrow, same time, all right? I'll bring the cash with me, as much as I can talk him out of, and we'll take it from there."

"Yeah, all right. But you tell him, I want a thousand."

"I'm not promising. But I'll tell him. Trust me, kid. I'm on your side. I want to help you get out of this; and it's not my money. It's just up to the editor, that's all, how much he thinks the story's worth."

Secky watched the reporter out of sight, thinking, *I won't get the grand. Seven, seven fifty, maybe. It's nice, but it ain't enough to do anything with. There's a way to get more out of it, though. Maybe . . .*

He got off the bench and headed down the road, towards the bus-stop; and didn't look back, didn't notice a man following quietly, carefully, keeping him just in view.

The kids had been quieter since Nina's death, and Mark could have said the same about himself, though the causes were identifiably different. They were still half in shock, trying to adjust to a world where someone you were trading insults with yesterday can be dead today – and not just today, but dead tomorrow too, and tomorrow and tomorrow. For most of them it was their first direct encounter, and it lay on them like something tangible.

Mark was still trying to come to terms with his sense of responsibility, of guilt; and finding it hopelessly entangled with the knowledge of reality shifting, of new hope for the future. Memories of that night swung him perilously from bitter to sweet, from a body cold and slack in his arms to another warm and active. Death and life had seized and shaken him, both at once; but at the tail-end of that long night and in the nights since, he had found the quiet

*(the balance)*

he so urgently needed. There was a refuge from fear and distress both, in the slow time spent not thinking and not doing, only lying with his eyes open to the half-light of dawn while Alex slept against him. There could be no promises made at such a time, and no demands; for a while he need neither give nor take, and he did more than welcome, he cherished the insomnia that made him a gift of those silent, secret hours.

It all confused the hell out of him in daylight, of course; he didn't know what was happening or what was going to happen, and that insecurity had the power to rock him dangerously out of orbit, if ever he let it get a grip on his mind. But he'd learned long ago to take things a step at a time, fix his eyes on his feet and never look ahead. And the signs he watched for always and was most afraid of seeing, the sense

of strange but clear connections, of patterns building themselves around him like a net of interwoven truths – he could
almost afford to forget them in a world where nothing made
sense, where cause and effect seemed totally alien to each
other, where Nina could bring him Alex and disaster be
shadowed by delight.

Alex was working on another story, and she'd already
phoned to say that she'd be late back tonight. He hadn't
known what to say, except thanks and goodbye; it was an
almost overwhelming symptom of the changes that she was
bringing to him, that she'd felt it necessary to call. And had
been right: he would have worried, without. And he was
used to worrying about the kids, but to do it for an adult,
and for no reason – this was new, strange. Disconcerting,
like everything else about Alex.

But she had phoned, and he wasn't worried; and if he
didn't concentrate, he was going to lose another game of
pool. He'd issued a general challenge after dinner, expecting
the boys to be first in the queue, glad of something to occupy
their attention; but apparently they both had something else
on their minds, because Davey had shaken his head and left
the room with Colton only a breath behind, sketching only
the vaguest gesture of regret.

"Kez? Mandy doesn't play," with a smile over at the
younger girl, so she wouldn't think it a criticism. "You're my
last hope."

"Yeah. Sure . . ." She was still gazing at the open door,
with an air of puzzled indignation. Mark had laughed, and
poked her in the ribs with a pool cue.

"Don't worry, I'm sure it's only temporary."

"It had better be. He's hardly said a word to me since
Davey grabbed him before dinner. I asked him what was up,
and he wouldn't tell me . . ."

"Everyone's entitled to their secrets, love," Mark had said
lightly, trying to conceal his own quickening interest. Whatever it was, it would have to be important to make Colton
abandon and apparently almost forget his role as bodyguard,
servant and inseparable companion. And something that
important, Mark felt he ought to know about. But interrog-
ation had been Mrs Horsley's forte, never his. *Leave it;
they'll tell you when you need to know.*

He'd shaken the boys' preoccupations out of his head and tried to settle to the game, only to go drifting and dreaming into deeper waters. And now Kez was only one ball off the black, but she'd miscued her last shot and missed the pocket, and this was probably his last chance at a comeback, he couldn't count on her missing twice . . .

He potted two balls quickly, then saw the chance of a lovely snooker that would leave Kez sorry she'd ever picked up a pool cue. He was just lining up the shot when the front door banged, out in the hall.

*Alex*, he thought, straightening up and turning to greet her; and disappointment drove him back hard against the edge of the table as he saw and recognised a leather-jacketed silhouette in the doorway, right height, wrong sex, very much the wrong person.

"Hullo, Secky," he said, fighting to keep the dislike out of his voice and not altogether succeeding. "Come for a visit?"

"Not exactly."

"Do you want to come through to the office, then?"

"Nah, we're fine here. I ain't staying." He moved further into the games room, and glanced around. "Got some new girls in, eh? That's nice. Hey, did you ever get that kid I sent, the redhead?"

"Yes, she came here. But don't do that again, Secky. She was a reporter."

"Yeah?" Secky pursed his lips, whistled, and chased it with a broad smile. "Funny, that. 'S what I'm here about. I've got this other reporter on my neck, see? Badgering me for the address of this place."

"You wouldn't." *You would.*

"Well, I don't want to, do I? But he's offering me money, see? A thousand quid, he said. And I'm gonna need money, to get shot of what I'm doing now. I want to get right out of it, like you told me I should when I was here; but I've got to have something to live on, till I get a job. Ain't I? So I thought, maybe you could help. Solve my problem, should I or shouldn't I."

Mark's fists clenched on the pool cue he was holding, very slowly and very hard. "Let me get this straight. You're offering to sell us your silence, is that right?"

"Well, you could put it like that. I just need money, is all; and I'd rather not take it from the papers, but if I have to, then this place goes up the spout, don't it?"

"How much do you want?"

"I told you. A thousand."

"For God's sake, Secky!"

"It's what they offered me. And it's peanuts for the doctor, he'd never know it was gone."

Mark smiled slightly. "Try telling him that. It's him you'll have to talk to, in any case. He might be prepared to give you something, I don't know; but a thousand pounds is . . ."

Secky was shaking his head. "I ain't waiting to talk to the doctor. No time. I'm meeting this reporter guy tomorrow, see? And he'll have the money with him. So you got to come up with it tonight. All of it."

"That's ridiculous, Secky. Do you think I keep that kind of money here?"

"No, but I bet the doctor does, at his place. Phone him and see, why don't you? But tell him to hurry, I ain't waiting all night."

Mark pushed his hand through his hair, and said, "Suppose we did come up with some money –"

"Not some. A thousand quid."

"– what guarantee do we have that you won't go to this reporter of yours and sell him our address anyway? It's impossible, Secky, we can't trust you like that."

"That's tough. Maybe I will and maybe I won't, but you can be dead sure of one thing. If you don't come up with the money tonight, I'm going to meet that guy and give him what he wants. Then you'll all be in the shit. So what's it to be, eh?"

Just then there were footsteps loud on the stairs, and Colton appeared in the doorway behind Secky. The two boys tensed, eyeing each other warily; and Colton said, "What's going on?"

"Secky was just leaving," Mark said quietly. "Don't stand in his way, Colton." And as Secky looked round, startled, he added, "Nothing. Not a penny. Just get out."

"You'll be sorry."

"I'm sorry already, sorry we ever let you past the door. Now go."

And he went, angrily, pushing past Colton. The black boy half moved to follow him; but Mark called him back.

"Let him go, Colton. I don't need a fight. Besides, he'd

beat the shit out of you."

Colton grunted. "What did he want?"

"Danegeld."

"Eh?"

"Blackmail money," Kez translated, crossing the room to Colton's side, reaching for the comfort of his body. "He's going to shop us to the papers."

"Oh, Christ." Colton's eyes sought Mark's. "What are you going to do?"

"Phone the doctor, first; but there's not much we can do. Except be ready to move out of here bloody quick."

"Yeah? Where we gonna go?"

"I don't know. Malmebury first, maybe, if we have to. I'll talk to the doctor. Keep an ear open for Alex, will you?"

Secky paused briefly at the foot of the drive, to look back at the big house; then he spat and walked off, shoulders hunched, hands in pockets.

*Too bad, kid.* Jim Riley separated himself from the shadow of a tree, and watched the boy go. *They wouldn't play, am I right? But you shouldn't have been greedy. I'll try and get you something anyway, you did lead me here, and like I said, it's not my money. But the rate just dropped alarmingly . . .*

He turned and walked the other way, whistling cheerfully, looking for a cab; so he never saw the refuge door opening for a moment, and another dark figure slipping out.

## 51 Staring Without Seeing

*Mistakes, and fatal mistakes. They're easily made. What's not so easy is to tell between them, without benefit of hindsight. In the making, as it were.*

*Secky, for instance. His big mistake, his bad one – you could say it was going to the refuge at all, that night. You could say it was being greedy, two for the price of one. Or you could even say it was the can of Pils he drank on the way.*

*But let's keep it simple, and say it like this.*

*Secky's big mistake is nipping into a back alley to take a leak, before he catches the bus home. That's all.*

*He moves out of light into darkness, and still doesn't think to look behind him.*

*So he stands there against a wall; and he might as well have been bound and blindfolded for his execution, and stood against a wall. He listens to the hiss of his urine on the brickwork, watches the steam rise, and thinks about the seven, seven fifty he might get in the morning, and the thousand he didn't get tonight, thinks about spilling everything he knows about the refuge, address and all, and grins at the thought as he thinks it –*

*– and that's it for Secky, because the metal pipe in her hands (or is it in his hands? You could argue it that way, certainly you could) catches him across the back of the neck just then, crushing vertebrae and rupturing the spinal cord, and he stops thinking even before his head smashes into the brick wall, shattering his nose, the force of it sending splinters of bone deep into his brain.*

*He sticks there for a moment, as if perhaps his face had driven itself an inch into the wall, and he were hanging by his chin; but then his body starts the slow slide down, sliding and slipping and turning as it tumbles, to show that it has no face left to catch on, only eyes staring out of a torn wet ruin, staring without seeing.*

Tia came awake to the bite of cold on her arm, opened her eyes to a stinging pain, and jerked upright to a warm trickle of blood across her skin.

And found herself facing Davey in the darkness, Davey bare-chested, with something glinting in his fingers.

"What the hell . . ." She stared at him, at the thin dark cut on her forearm, at the razor-blade he made no effort to hide; and anger mixed with an odd fear to cut her voice off in her throat, and chase her into a confused silence.

"That's a warning," he said softly. "It's the only one you get."

Then he handed her a wad of tissues. She snatched at it, pressed it against the cut, and hitched up the shoulder of her night-dress with a furious shrug. "What, am I supposed to believe you'll be sneaking in here to cut my throat next time?"

"No. I don't need to. Next time I just cut myself first." He moved the blade slowly to rest against his own thin arm, never shifting his eyes from hers. "In fact I'll do it now, if you don't do what I tell you."

She shook her head, bewildered. "So fucking what? Cut your wrists, for all I care."

His answering smile was all threat, stirring that fear to life again. "I don't need that much. Just a drop'll do it, just a scratch. From me to you. Dirty razors is like dirty needles, Tia, you shouldn't share. Ask your customers, they'll tell you."

But she didn't need to ask anyone, she understood then, all too clearly; and her legs were already pushing her back into the corner, *keep away!*, even as she said, "You're lying. You're just trying to scare me . . ."

"I'm not lying." And just for a second there was an edge

of fear in his own voice, of panic barely controlled, which was utterly convincing.

"You're sick!"

He laughed thinly. "That's right. I've got Aids."

"What – what do you want?" But she knew already, and went on quickly, anything to get him out of here. "Look, I won't deal any more, I promise. Just let me get rid of what I've got, and I won't bring any more in . . ."

He shook his head. "Not enough, Tia. I don't know where you're hiding all that shit, but you're going to fish it out right now, and shove it all down the bog while I watch."

"I can't! It's worth thousands, they'll kill me . . ."

"You'll just have to keep out of their way, won't you? But that's what I want. Then I can be sure you're not still dealing behind my back, if your bosses are mad at you."

"You fucking shit! Why can't you just leave me alone? I'm not doing you any harm!"

"I don't like drugs. And I don't like you using this place to deal from, you could get us all busted."

"Christ, a puritan bum-boy . . ."

He didn't respond to that, he just jerked her duvet off the bed and said, "Get on with it, Tia. Now."

And the light played on the razor-blade, and the bare skin of his arm; and she shivered, and said, "Get away from me, then. Right away, over there."

He laughed, and backed to the other side of the room, leaning pointedly against the door; and with fear riding high in her chest, threatening to turn to hysteria as soon as she stopped moving, Tia got on with it.

Davey sat on the lowest of the front steps, cold stone beneath him and warm morning sunlight on his skin, sealing himself into his body and the moment, finding a temporary refuge in the world's touch. It wouldn't last, he knew that; but for this little time he could get away from the threats and promises of the future. Doing nothing, he could let others make his decisions for him, let the threats perhaps push him into the promises.

Inside, Mark was talking to the others, telling them that Davey had the Aids virus. That was the one decision that Davey had felt able to take for himself, that they had the right to know; it wasn't a knowledge that he wanted to leave like a weapon in Tia's hands, for her to use when the chance presented itself to hurt him. What happened now was up to them, but he was half hoping that they would react as she had. A common panic could pressurise Mark into asking him to leave; and then he could stop fretting about the right thing and do the only thing left, say yes to Jesse.

He heard voices in the house behind him, footsteps in the hall; and didn't turn his head to hear better, to wonder who was walking there, or what was being said. Instead he stared fixedly down the drive at a car parked in the road beyond, seeing the driver's window as a blaze of gold as the sun struck it, and only the vaguest shadow of movement behind to tell him that the car was occupied. As he watched, a line of darkness cut the gold and ate into it steadily from the top

## 54 Other Children, Other Shots

– and in the car Jim Riley focused a telephoto lens and waited, sucking air gently through his teeth like a man trying to attract the attention of a nervous cat; and the magic worked, the boy looked up, thin-faced and thoughtful, dark roots showing through the blond of his hair; and Jim took the shot and two more, and waited again for other children, other shots –

## 55 His Terror, Her Mind

*– and his terror numbs her mind, possesses her, moves her hands as though they were his own –*

– and Davey was still sitting, waiting, caught between promises and threats, as the slate sliced through the air and smashed itself to splinters on the step beside him.

Too shocked even to cry out, he stared at the shards of grey and the dust scattered across his jeans, and a shiver seized him as he turned his head slowly upwards. Overhead he saw what he knew was there, the gable of the roof to say that it was no accident, no loose slate sliding down by chance; and he saw the window of the upper landing standing open.

And he was on his feet with all the decisions made, ready to go inside and talk to Mark, when the front door opened. Colton and Kez came out hand in hand, and stopped when they saw him. It was Kez who moved first, Colton hanging back to give her the choice; and she came to Davey and hugged him wordlessly, cheek to cheek, a promise come too late.

"Yes, hullo?"

"Narfraz, this is Mudassar. I just had a call from the Anderson boy. He didn't get this morning's delivery."

"The courier was who?"

"That new girl, Tia Sharif."

"Your instructions were clear?"

"Yes. She had the address, and the time."

"Go and find her. Take someone with you. Take Sherman."

"Frighten her a little?"

"No. Frighten her a lot."

"Right."

Mudassar drove slowly down a street of terraced houses, checking the numbers from the car window.

"There it is. Fifty-seven." He pulled up by the kerb, and peered out. "It's strange, though . . ."

"What?" His passenger already had the door open, and one foot in the road.

"She's supposed to be living with a gang of runaways. It doesn't look right, a place like this."

"Well, let's find out."

"Yes."

They got out, and rang the bell of number fifty-seven. After a minute, a short, elderly man opened the door and blinked at them suspiciously.

"Yes?"

"We're looking for a girl, Tia Sharif, Asian kid . . ."

"Sorry, mate, can't help you. Never heard of her."

"This is the address she gave us."

"Well, she give you the wrong address, then, didn't she? She don't live here."

"I see. Thank you . . ."

The old man nodded, and shut the door firmly in their faces. Mudassar cursed; Sherman just smiled, shifting his shoulders in his leather jacket.

"What now, then?"

"You stay in the car and watch. He may have been lying. If they're sheltering runaways, they wouldn't admit it. But . . ." He looked up at the small house, and shook his head. "I'll phone Narfraz."

# GOOD NEWS FOR MRS HUGHES!

### *The Story The Star Didn't Print!*

We knew they had something to hide! At the beginning of this month, our so-called 'competition' (the Capital Con, we call it) gave its few readers what they called an 'exclusive', an 'in-depth' story from the secret teenage refuge in London. In fact, we'd said it all already; they had nothing to offer but a few blurred photos of the backs of kids' heads.

Today, *The Herald* prints the faces – and uncovers the truth they tried to hide! For months now, Mrs Angela Hughes has lived with fear and uncertainty about her two youngest children. Her son Sebastian is still being sought by police in connection with a series of rapes in Oxfordshire – but today *The Herald* can reveal the whereabouts of her missing daughter Keryn (16). The photograph on our front page shows her clearly, with her arm around the runaway rent boy Davey FitzAlan. She looks fit and well, and *The Herald* is delighted to be able to reassure Mrs Hughes about her daughter's welfare. It is not our job to wonder why the *Evening Star* refused to do this; but our readers will no doubt draw their own conclusions.

There's only one thing we agree with the *Star* about; and that is, that now is not the time to publish the address of the refuge. A newspaper has responsibilities to its readers, and to the society it serves; but it also has responsibilities to the people who make the stories. Our reporter Jim Riley describes on Page 2 how he found the refuge, with the help of seventeen-year-old Secky Viszinski; and readers will recognise that name, because Secky was found murdered in a back-alley just two days ago.

The refuge may defy the law and the courts, but at least it offers the kids a temporary safety that they cannot find on the street. We believe that some of them would only run again, if we told where they could be found; and for that reason alone, we will keep the address secret, against pressure from either the public or the police.

Other anxious parents worried about their runaway children should turn immediately to our centre pages, where we print more photographs of the kids at the refuge . . .

# PART EIGHT

*Getting There*

Jim Riley hustled down the steps of the *Herald* building, *hands in pockets and here I go. Young man in a hurry, and don't it feel great?*

There was a police car parked by the kerb; Jim's grin broadened, and he winked unseen at the waiting driver. *Must be what the big men came in. Lots of uniforms to impress the natives. Nice try, but it won't cut any ice with old Slimey. Or, of course, with me . . .*

Jim had just endured half an hour in Mr Slimson's office, with a Chief Superintendent and a sidekick, answering some questions and simply shaking his head at others, playing it the way his editor wanted, enjoying the game as both sides manoeuvred for position. The police were anxious to avoid the publicity of writs and a court case if they possibly could, but they were getting no change out of Slimson. The *Herald* would be quite happy with a day in the High Court, to keep the paper in the public eye. Not, of course, that he'd put it like that. The safety of the kids was naturally paramount, and as soon as the news broke that the police were going to court to get the address of the refuge, Mr Slimson was afraid that some at least would simply run for it, even before the judge came to a decision. And no, of course the *Herald* couldn't hand the address over quietly there and then, not after stating publicly that it would preserve the secrecy of the refuge. The paper had its integrity to maintain . . .

Integrity? Jim laughed aloud, as he hurried down the steps to the Underground. Slimson didn't know what the word meant; but he'd established a toehold on the moral high ground in his editorial this morning, and he'd cling to that as long as he could. If the police were to raid the refuge now, the *Star* would make hay out of the *Herald*'s broken promises . . .

Slimson had been in the middle of his spiel about integrity when he'd slipped Jim the high-sign to get the hell out of there. Jim had been watching for it; he'd have to act quickly, to make the first edition that afternoon. So he'd mumbled something about the toilet and slipped out while Slimson was still talking; and it would be a while before the police realised he wasn't coming back.

Meanwhile, he was on his way to the refuge again; and this time, he was going in. They wouldn't dare throw him out, and risk his exposing them; and if things went to plan, he should get a story out of Kez Hughes that would blow the *Star* right off the streets. He'd have to nip home first for his camera, though; he wasn't used to working without a photographer, and he'd forgotten the bloody thing this morning. But that would only cost him twenty minutes, it was more or less on the way, and he'd got time in the bank by ducking out of the meeting now.

Even so, he was almost running when he got home. He'd need as long as possible at the refuge – time to wheedle, threaten, promise, whatever he had to do to get the kids to talk. He unlocked the front door and hurried in, leaving it standing open; went through to the bedroom, picked up the camera bag from its place by the bookshelf; and was already turning to leave when he heard the front door slam.

Wind? Must've been wind. He walked out into the hallway, keys in one hand and bag in the other –

– and found two men standing waiting for him. One was white, the other Asian; and the white one looked about six foot six and twenty stone, and he was smiling,

*(with anticipation?)*

and the Asian was playing a knife between his fingers, and he wasn't smiling at all . . .

Sebastian saw the *Herald* at half past nine, Kez's face staring out at him from a newsagent's rack. He bought a copy, read it in the street and went on to the library anyway, to check the phone directories and steal a gazetteer of the capital's streets. He changed a five-pound note for coins at a bank, made a dozen calls, and had just enough money left for a one-way bus ticket to London.

*One way's all I'm going to need. This is it.*

He had a long walk waiting for him at Victoria, and it was more than an hour before he reached the first of two addresses he'd circled on his list.

*This was the only Riley J that didn't answer the phone, that didn't deny all knowledge of a Jim Riley. This must be it; a journalist's got to be in the phone-book. Too bad if I'm wrong, but I don't think I can be.*

He rang the bell, expecting no answer and getting none. There was a deadlock on the door, but he tested it just in case, and felt only the resistance of the Yale.

*Careless Mr Riley.*

He looked both ways, checked that the street was empty and no one was watching through a window, *so much for your Neighbourhood Watch sticker, Jim*; took a pace backwards and smashed his foot against the door, as close as he could get it to the Yale.

Nothing happened. He licked his lips, checked the street and the windows, did it again; and this time the door crashed open. Seb slipped inside, closed the door quickly behind him and looked around.

He was standing in a narrow hallway, with a door opening to his right into a bedroom. An empty bedroom. Satisfied of that, he walked cautiously down the hallway and round the angle. Two more doors: one leading to a spare room, empty again, the other to the living-room –

– and the living-room was empty only in a manner of speaking. Empty of life, to be sure; but not of Jim Riley. This morning's *Herald* had featured a photograph of the journalist, and the features were easy to identify, even under an obscuring mask of blood. He was on the floor, with his hands behind him and his legs stretched out wide, his back against the sofa and his head lolling on a cushion.

It wasn't necessary to touch him or even look closely at what had been done, to see that he was dead. His skin was a filthy white, and all the blood that should have given it colour seemed to be outside him now, soaking the slashed shirt that had been half cut from him, clotting in a pool between his legs.

Seb took a moment to close his eyes, not against the horror, only the shock of it; then opened them again, looked again, and felt something stir in him that was neither pleasure nor desire, but kin

*(blood-kin)*

to both.

*I could have done that. I think I could. To have heard him scream, and beg. To have laughed, cut the arteries in both legs, and watched him watch himself die. Yes, I could have done that. And enjoyed it.*

Which was odd, because it was another change of focus, perhaps of direction; but he had no time for it now. He had to get out of there (and thank God he'd thought to wear gloves), and he had to do it now – or in a minute. After he'd checked Riley's flat for money, and for an address-book, notebooks, anything like that. Checked his flat and, if he had to, checked his pockets . . .

Jesse was standing on the other side of the lake, looking around. Davey waved, not wanting to draw attention to himself by shouting; and after a second the American saw him, nodded, and started to make his way round.

Davey met him halfway, and was greeted with a warm hug, and fingers flicking at the long peak of his baseball cap. "What's this, then, kiddo, a factor ten sunblock?"

"They had my photo all over the front page today, with my hair this way; and with Nina, Nina dead, there's no one wants to mess around with it, so I thought, cover it up . . ."

"Yeah. I saw the paper. Regular publicity hound, aren't you? Can't get enough of it."

"Fuck off, it's not funny."

"No, I know. What's happening about it, anything?"

"Yeah, plenty. Mark's got the doctor coming round this afternoon, but he's talking about moving everyone out."

"And what, starting again somewhere else?"

"I suppose. I don't know."

"Uh-huh. And what about you, kid, what do you want?"

"Jess, I . . . What you said, can I come and stay with you?"

"You can live with me if it's what you want. You know that."

"Yeah. It's what I want. Something happened at the ref, there's this girl, she's out to get me. And, everyone knows about me now, and the rest of them are all right about it, but I don't know, I need . . ."

"You need looking after, kid. I know. And I want to do it, so that's settled, am I right?"

"Yeah. I guess . . ."

"Good. I'll take you to the house now if you like, show you around. We can talk there, make some plans for you.

You're going to need a doctor, but we can fix that. Pete upstairs'll know someone . . ."

## 61 Hell of a Time

"Kez is really in a bad way, but you'd expect that. The poor kid's so scared she hasn't been downstairs all day, she's just hiding up in Colton's room, watching the window in case there's anyone out there."

"Mmm." The doctor rubbed his long nose for a moment, and nodded. "And the others?"

"Colton's all right – or he would be, if he weren't so close to Kez. Her nerves are getting through to him a bit, he's starting to jitter. But I don't think you need worry about him."

"I'm not. Solid as a rock, that lad. And much to my credit that he is, I might add."

*The eagle preening himself – and he's only doing it for my benefit, so I suppose I'd better react. But if he wants a smile, he can whistle for it.*

Instead, Mark threw a pen-top at him, and smiled anyway as the doctor snapped it out of the air, pulled a ball-point from his pocket and fitted top to pen with an air of great satisfaction.

"Tia," Mark said firmly, and lost the smile with the word. "She's the odd one. She seems almost as scared as Kez, and I don't know why. She was another of the kids they photographed, of course, but it's not as if there was anyone actively looking for her. Except her family, I suppose, but she's never shown any sign of nerves before this."

"And Mandy?"

"Very quiet, as usual. Won't talk about it, but I think she's worried. At a guess, I'd say she doesn't feel safe here any more; and that's what she needs, more than anything."

"It's what they all need. How about Davey, how's he

taken it?"

Mark shook his head. "I'm not sure. I suppose it just doesn't seem that important, given what else has happened to him this week. He's gone out, anyway. I told him I thought it was stupid, with his face splashed across the front page like that, but he said he had to meet someone."

"Did he? Well, I'll have a word with him when he gets in. To be honest, I'm not sure what we should do about Davey. He won't go home, of course, and I wouldn't suggest it for a boy in his situation; but he's going to need a lot of support and counselling, and I don't think he should stay here."

"I don't think any of them should. Mandy's right, it isn't safe any more. Alex phoned after she saw the paper, and she says we can't trust the *Herald*. The police are going to the High Court tomorrow; and she reckons the paper'll make a great play for the freedom of the press, but if they lose, and they will, they'll probably appeal at once and then hand over the address and follow the police out here to get a nice exclusive story of the raid."

"Yes. So that would give us what, a couple of weeks before the appeal's heard?"

"At most. They could hustle it through in days rather than weeks, and they'll certainly try. We can't just sit and wait for it, doctor. We've got to evacuate."

"Yes, I believe you're right, it's probably come to that. We'll watch what happens in court tomorrow, and hope the *Herald* doesn't cave in immediately; if it does, you'll have to move the kids out there and then. I'm sure Alex can get herself assigned to the story, so she can phone the news through straight away, whichever way it goes. Assuming the *Herald* does appeal, I'll organise transport for the weekend, and bring you all down to Malmebury." He frowned then, and scratched irritably at his nose. "What puzzles me is why the *Herald* hasn't sent a reporter back today, to bully his way in and get a follow-up story for this evening's edition."

"I know. I've been waiting for it all day, but there's been no sign. And there's no one out in the street either."

"Let's hope it stays that way. I don't want anyone following us down to Malmebury."

"Christ, no. What about this house, you're sure the police can't trace it back to you?"

"Positive." The doctor smiled thinly. "If they get past the

solicitors and the dummy company, they'll find themselves confronted by three very good friends of mine, two barristers and a highly influential financier. Given the choice, I'd rather squeeze blood from a stone."

"That's good. But what are we going to *do*, doctor? Buy another house and start again?"

"We'll talk about that later, Mark. There's no point in trying to make long-term plans at the moment. Just live for the day, yes?"

"Sure." *I've had enough practice, God knows.* "But . . ."

"But nothing, lad. Sufficient unto the day is the evil thereof. Speaking of which, what variety of evil are you intending to perform with young Alex this evening?"

Mark stared. "I wasn't. We called it off. I mean, with all this happening, I can't just . . ."

"Yes, you can. Or do you doubt my competence to take care of your charges?"

"No, of course not, but . . ."

"You two children are going to be very busy over the next few days; it'll do you good to run out and play tonight. Have you got any money?"

"Not much, no."

"All right." The doctor took a wallet from his jacket, and peeled out some twenties. "Take this, and enjoy yourselves. Buy the girl dinner somewhere smart, and tell her from me I expect her to dress outrageously."

"Doctor . . ." Mark looked at the money, but didn't reach for it. "I don't think she's in the mood. She said on the phone, she was feeling really guilty. It was her story in the *Star* that started all this . . ."

"That," the doctor said patiently, "is the point. Call it a gesture of confidence, if you like; but I don't think you'll need to explain it to her, she'll understand."

"I don't know, doctor . . ."

"No, but I do. Tell her it's doctor's orders, if she cuts up rough. Now take the money, have a bath, spend some time making yourself look halfway respectable, and go. I recommend a shave, some flowers, and a taxi to Soho. The restaurant I leave to your discretion, but do the thing properly, Mark. And try not to be scared of the waiters, they're only doing their job."

"I bet you were a terrible bully at school."

"On the contrary, I was a very good bully at school. And I've been getting better ever since."

Baths were one of the few indulgences Mark had felt it safe to allow himself, at least until Alex appeared on the scene and started rewriting his laboriously assembled rulebook. He liked them deep and hot and unhurried; and he'd missed them since Mrs Horsley's accident had left him in sole charge at the refuge, unable to afford the time for a slow, sybaritic soak. Even the doctor's stepping in as babysitter hadn't changed that, because Alex had annexed all those free evenings as soon as they became available. He'd been reduced to quick splashes in the morning, before the kids were up; and now, with official sanction

*(doctor's orders)*

and plenty of time in hand before Alex got off work, he bolted the door, started the bath running, and undressed slowly in a room that filled with steam.

Of course, he hadn't entirely missed out on pleasant experiences in bathrooms; there had been that evening ten days ago when Alex took him to her flat and dragged him in under the shower with her . . . He grinned at the memory, and then at himself for being so blasé about it, for being able to grin. She'd stayed in the flat that night, as she still did two or three times a week; but she'd given him her keys as he left, and told him to come back "any time you feel dirty. And you can take that any way you like, mate . . ."

But still, a shared shower was a long way from a proper bath: something to be cherished (and repeated?), but no substitute. He lowered himself carefully into the scorching tub, slid down until the water lapped at the corners of his mouth, and let his eyes fall shut.

And whether it was the magic that there is in a bath, or whether it was simply the doctor's efficient bullying, he contrived to forget about the kids, the refuge and the future; and spent the next hour worrying pleasantly about the evening ahead – what to wear, where to go, whether he ought to book a table or just take pot luck, whether he could give their order to a waiter without stammering and feeling a fool.

Bathed and shaved, after-shaved and dressed with all the

care he could contrive, he went back downstairs and searched out the doctor in the games room, practising trick shots on the pool table.

"Are you still here?"

"I need some advice."

"More?"

"It's your own fault, you started this. And I don't know where to take her. She'd have her own ideas if I asked, but I'd like to surprise her; and I don't know my way around. You know that I never eat out."

"Ah, the innocent abroad." The doctor chuckled, then said, "All right, lad. You go and find your lady; I'll book you a table for two at Spiridion's, in Dean Street. For nine o'clock, so that you don't have to rush. They know me there, you'll get a good table; and you can dance afterwards. I don't want to see you back before two, understood?"

"I don't dance."

"Tell that to Alex. Goodbye."

Mark checked his watch as he hopped off the bus. Six thirty, and perfect timing. Alex should be in by now, but only just; she'd be shifting gear after work, winding down, wondering what was happening at the refuge, thinking of fixing herself something to eat before going round to find out. Thinking about him, maybe – and that was a warm idea, still curious and alien, still able to shake him. But she wouldn't be expecting him, that was for sure.

He grinned, and hurried along the street and around the corner. He could see the block she lived in now, and the windows of her flat; anticipation slowed his feet for a moment and tightened his grip on the roses he held in his hand, before spurring him into a run, unwilling to lose even the few minutes he would waste walking.

He was breathing hard when he reached the entrance to the block, but his legs drove him straight in and up the stairs two at a time. There'd be time enough inside to get his breath back, with her laughing against him and her lips nuzzling his ear, telling him things he wouldn't even hear through the pounding of his heart and the gasp of air into his aching lungs . . .

He had her keys

*(his keys)*

in his hand as he took the final flight at a sprint, leant against the door while he fumbled the right one into the lock and twisted, almost tumbling in as the door fell open under his weight –

– and felt his dreams and desires twist and fall away from him, too fragile to survive this. He snatched at his balance and could catch only a physical shadow of it, jamming an arm out to hold his body upright while his mind slipped and screamed above the sudden darkness, and scrabbled for something solid to cling to in a loose and sliding world.

He was panting hard, fighting for more than breath and struggling to think, to make sense of it, while his eyes jerked around the chaos in the hallway

*(the table overturned and the phone lying in the middle of the carpet, half buried under a pile of directories and a scatter of scribbled notes, a coat-hook ripped from the wall)*

and the noises, the christless noises thudded through ears and mind, their strangeness giving him no pictures

*(dark, heavy sounds of breaking and falling, grunts and small high cries)*

and nothing to grab onto.

He pushed himself away from the wall with fear scratching and biting at him like something small and living, unutterably vicious; and pushed open the living-room door, with Alex's name tentative and fearful on his lips.

At first he was conscious only of movement, writhing shapes on the floor – but that was Alex, her hair like a clear beacon to draw his eye, dragging herself across the carpet on her elbows with her shirt half ripped from her and her breasts hanging free; and the other was a weird and faceless figure pulling away and scrambling to its feet as Mark floundered, took a pace into the room, let the flowers fall and lifted his open hands in a gesture nothing stronger than rebuttal.

Time snagged them and held them staring;

*(and no, not faceless, it was just a dark and woollen mask, a balaclava pulled down to leave only a slit for sharp blue eyes; and that was better than faceless, but what the hell . . .)*

and it was the other that moved first, panic or desperation or some motive force more potent than Mark's confusion breaking him free of that frozen moment. He charged forward, one hand slamming against Mark's chest and sending him staggering back against the wall as the man ran into the hallway and out of the flat.

His footsteps sounded flat and fading on the concrete stairs; Mark half turned to follow, but a sound behind him
*(Alex . . .)*
brought him turning back again, to see her pushing herself half upright, then dropping back against the kitchen door, her eyes wild and blind.

"Alex . . ."

Mark walked slowly and uncertainly across the room, crouched beside her, reached out a hand and watched her jerk away as his skin touched hers. He listened to the breath catching and tearing in her throat, watched her ribs judder with it, saw her fists clenching helplessly against the carpet, and couldn't bear it.

"Alex, this is me, Mark, right? And you can fight me if you like, you can break every bloody bone in my body so long as you know it's me you're doing it to; but I can't just sit here and look at you, so . . ."

So he sat on the floor beside her and reached out again, and this time didn't let her pull away. He put an arm firmly round her shoulders and tugged her close against him. She shivered, and lifted a hand to shove him off; he grabbed the wrist quickly and guided the arm up around his neck instead, where it clung suddenly, savagely tight as she thrust her head against his chest with an odd little moan.

He shifted cautiously, so that he could hold her with both arms and support her weight as long as she needed; then he rested his cheek against her stiff hair, and settled down simply to wait.

She made no noise, and she'd been shaking from the first, so it was only the dampness soaking through his shirt that told Mark when she started to cry. He gave her another five minutes, then slipped a hand underneath her chin and nudged it gently upwards, lifting her face till her eyes met his.

"Enough?" he asked quietly, rubbing his thumb across her wet cheek.

"No." But she hitched herself a little higher, and let her head drop onto his shoulder. "Oh, Christ. Mark . . ."

"Yeah. I know."

"No, you don't. You *don't* know."

"That's what I meant. I know I don't, but at least I know that much."

"Unh." She pushed a hand through her hair, then stood up suddenly and looked down at her ripped shirt. "Oh, God . . ."

She tried to pull it shut, but her fingers were shaking too badly to manage even the few buttons that hadn't been torn off. Mark got to his feet quickly and reached to do it for her, but she shook her head and yanked the shirt off, threw it onto the floor.

"What now, love? Want to talk about it?"

"*No.*" She looked round the room, down at herself, shuddered. "I want a shower."

"Sure. What do you want me to do?"

"Just wait. But – make noises, yeah? Nice friendly Mark-type noises. So I know I'm not alone in there." And then she looked up at him, lifted a hand to his cheek briefly, tried to smile. "That was, that was some entrance, fella. Great timing. You should be in the bloody cavalry . . ."

And her lips touched his and stayed for a moment, less than a kiss but more meaningful, sharing his air.

Mark put a record on loud, to fill the flat with sounds that couldn't possibly be threatening; then he went through to the bedroom. There was no bed, only a double mattress on the floor. He built a nest out of pillows and quilt, and left it waiting while he unhooked her ancient towelling dressing-gown from the door and took it into the bathroom. Looked at her quiet and easy, neither staring nor shying away; hung the dressing-gown over the door handle and said, "When you're ready, Alex. No hurry. I'm in the bedroom, okay?"

She nodded, one jerk of the head, and stepped back under the steaming jet of water, and reached for the soap again.

Finally she came to him, damp and vulnerable, swathed in the vast gown. He kissed her cheek and took her over to the nest, pushed her gently down into it; then he settled himself behind her, easing her back against his body as he got to work on her wet head with hair-dryer and fingers.

She sighed softly, and squirmed as he sent a blast of hot air down her neck.

"You could make a profession of this. Lady's maid."

"So long as you're the lady." He kissed her ear, then said, "Come on, tell me. What happened?"

"You saw."

"Before I got here, I mean. How did he get in?"

"I let him in, didn't I? Opened the bloody door . . ." She grunted and reached up for his hand, pulling it down into her lap and holding it with both of hers. "He was on the next landing up, when I got home. Looking out of the window. He was just a bloke, that was all, I figured he was waiting for someone. He was staring at me, though, when I unlocked the door. Like he was surprised, or something. Maybe I should've known, but . . ."

"Hang on, you mean you saw his face? He wasn't wearing the balaclava?"

"Not then, no."

"What did he look like?"

"I don't know. A bloke. Twenties, good looking. Brown hair, but there was something about that – blond roots, that was it. I remember thinking, I wouldn't dye my hair brown if it was naturally blonde, most people do it the other way round. Anyway, I let myself in, and I was just putting the kettle on when the doorbell rang. I hadn't been in a minute. And I didn't think, I went to answer it and he was there, with that thing on, the balaclava. I didn't get a chance to do anything, as soon as the door was open he came barging in, grabbing at me, pushing me down the hall. I suppose I could've fought back somehow, I've done self-defence classes and all that, only I couldn't think, he never gave me time. I just tried to hang onto something, but he was too strong; and next thing I knew we were down on the floor, and he had his, his hands on me . . . And then you came. Cavalry time."

She tried to laugh, and he heard it lose itself somewhere between throat and lips.

"So what do we do now? Police?"

"I – I guess so. Yeah."

"It's your decision, love."

"Yeah. I don't want to, it'll be awful; but, hell, I wrote a piece last month about rape, saying it was important to report it, didn't matter how you felt. So I'd better do it, really. As long as you come with me . . ."

"Of course."

"Hey."

"What?"

"This is a hell of a time to say it, but I love you."

## 62  *Waiting, Seeing*

There was a bus terminal opposite the police station; and Seb stood by the window in the waiting-room, watching through the dirty glass. He didn't know who the man was, who'd disturbed him before he'd got anything out of the girl, either pleasure or information; but Seb had recognised his face. He'd been in one of the *Herald*'s photographs, pictured in the refuge doorway. Maybe he was Alex Holden, and the girl was his lover; or maybe it was the other way around. Either way, it didn't matter. They could still lead him where he wanted to go.

So he'd taken a chance, and hung around outside the block of flats; and finally, the two of them had come out together. He'd trailed them to the police station, and almost lost his nerve when they went inside. She'd seen his face, she might have recognised him.

But she might not; and there was nothing left for him anyway, except to play his luck and hope it led him to Kez. He could think about the girl later, he knew where to find her. So he was waiting again, watching again, thinking and hoping.

If the girl was Alex Holden, and her boyfriend worked at the refuge; if she didn't want to go home that night, and went back with him instead; if they refused a lift from the police (and they'd have to do that, surely, they couldn't take a chance on that), and if he could follow them without being spotted . . .

Too many ifs, too much uncertainty. He shook his head abruptly, and settled for watching. Wait and see, that was all he could do now.

So he waited; and he saw.

*He's angry; and that anger is bright enough to mask even his fear, his vulnerability. It burns in him like a flame behind glass, lighting both his power and his weakness. She is neither of those, only his tool, his willing tool; and her it burns, because she it was who failed him. He spits it at her, into her like poison, and she can't hide from it, can't deny it, can't do anything but open her veins and take it in like heroin, like poison.*

*Because he's right, she did fail him; and failure is poison too. Failure is death, or could be. So she goes to the kitchen and takes a knife, hugs it to her like a promise of safety; and takes the rubber gloves from the sink, and hurries upstairs to hide with him until the early morning, when danger sleeps.*

*Hoping only that steel will do what slate did not, and make him safe again.*

# PART NINE

*A Little Blood, a Little Love*

". . . So we made statements and that, but I've got to go back some time, to look at mug-shots and see if I can identify him. They want a look at the flat, too, but I just left them the keys and told them to go in when they wanted, I didn't want to watch. Then we got away as quick as we could, and walked back. And look," Alex held up a hand, fingers splayed, and backed it with a weak smile. "I've stopped shaking, isn't that good?"

"That's excellent."

But the hand ducked quickly down out of the doctor's sight, below the level of the desk, and clenched itself around Mark's; and Mark thought, *You're not fooling him, girl, not for a moment. Stiff upper lip notwithstanding.*

"It's very broad-minded of you," the doctor went on easily, "leaving your keys with the police."

Alex laughed, short and high-pitched. "They can strip the place out, for all I care. I don't, the way I feel at the moment, I just don't want to go back there. I wouldn't care if I never saw it again. Or any of the stuff in it."

"Well. Take a few days, you may feel differently then. But moving might not be a bad idea, at that. You can join the club, we'll all be doing it. Which reminds me." He shifted his gaze to Mark. "Davey came in a couple of hours ago, and he's taking himself off our hands."

"How?"

"Apparently he's going to live with a friend. He didn't want to say too much, but I gathered it's a man he met when he was working the streets. It seems to be more than a commercial relationship, though; the man knows about Davey's Aids test – he paid for it – and he's already taking steps to see that the lad gets medical supervision. It's what Davey wants, and I think that's good enough in these circumstances, so long as we keep in touch with him. It'll be as well to get him out of the refuge, in any case. Some of the kids aren't reacting well."

"You mean Tia."

"And Mandy. I've noticed that she's very wary of him. It's fair enough, given her condition, and the way she's responding to it." He turned back to Alex then, and said, "Listen, young lady, I'm not going to suggest tranquillisers for you; you're fit and sensible, you shouldn't need them. Particularly as you've stopped shaking on your own account, without chemical assistance. But I can give you something to help you sleep tonight, if you like."

Alex shook her head. "No, thanks. I don't mind not sleeping. So long as I've got someone nice to be not sleeping with."

Mark ducked her sideways glance, and concentrated on working her fingers gently between his hands as he heard the doctor laugh.

"Hush, you'll embarrass the boy. But I'm content with that. I'd prescribe Mark sooner than a sleeping pill myself. Now, would you like me to stay here overnight, so that you don't have to concern yourself with the kids?"

Mark left that to Alex's decision, and she shook her head again. "No, it's okay. We can cope, thanks. And you'll have things to fix at Malmebury in the morning, if we're moving the kids down there. Mark and me can organise the evacuation from this end."

"You won't be going to work?"

"No. I've decided, I can't face it tomorrow. They'll know by then, about the, about me. Hell, they probably know already, they've got enough contacts in the police. And they'll want the story from me, and splash it over the front page, and I, I just *can't* . . ."

Which was the closest she'd come to breaking since it happened; and in a moment of clear sight, Mark realised that this was almost the worst of it for Alex now, that she should feel threatened by her own colleagues, and almost afraid of the job that meant so much to her. He eased an arm round her shoulders, and felt her starting to tremble again; and wondered afterwards if it was only to shock her out of that line of thought that the doctor made his next suggestion.

"I wonder, Alex. I'm drawing a bow at a venture, but I'm

no great believer in coincidence, and you did say that the man who attacked you was wearing a balaclava to hide his face. I know he's not the only one who does that, but Kez's brother Sebastian always wore a balaclava . . ."

Shivering muscles stiffened suddenly beneath Mark's touch. She lifted her head, and whispered, "Shit. Yes, of course. Of *course*, why didn't I . . .?"

"You weren't in any condition to think straight," Mark said, hoping that the same excuse could apply to him, because of course he should have seen the possibility too, it was so obvious now . . .

"Don't make excuses for me," she said savagely. "I even saw his *face*, for God's sake! Only in shadow, sure, but enough to see that he'd dyed his hair. It could be him, from what I remember of the photos. And I'm a journalist, I'm supposed to make connections . . ."

*Me too, I'm a schizophrenic, we do it all the time.* But it was the wrong time to be flippant, so instead, he said, "It is a hell of a coincidence, though, isn't it? If it was him?"

"Don't be stupid," Alex snapped. "It's not a coincidence at all. If he reads the papers, he knows that I know where the refuge is; and we've got to assume that that's what he's after in London, that he's looking for Kez. As far as we know, she's still the only witness against him."

"Or was, until tonight," the doctor put in quietly.

"Yeah, right. There's me too, now. The guy fucked up . . ." Something touched her face then, a thought she didn't share with them and didn't need to. *He meant to kill me, afterwards. He must have done.* But there wasn't time to assimilate that or react to it, as Alex went on, "I guess him – Christ, why can't I say it? – him trying to *rape* me, was just incidental. A spur of the moment thing, when he saw the chance, a girl alone. It must have been this address he really wanted."

"How would he have found you in the first place, though? Your paper wouldn't have given your address out, surely."

"Not unless he was clever about it. But he wouldn't need to be, there aren't many Holdens in the phone-book. *Shit.* I don't know what to do, now."

"Phone the police. Now." The doctor gestured with his head, towards the wall-mounted telephone. "And stick to what you said earlier, don't go home for any reason. He knows where you work too, so you'd better keep away from there until this is sorted out."

"Suits me. I'll come to Malmebury with the rest of you." She went to the phone, managing a smile that looked almost unforced. "You can even put me on the pay-roll if you like, doctor. Sod my brilliant career, I think I'd rather work for you."

"One thing at a time, young lady. But we might talk about that, if you still feel the same way after this is over."

Alex told the police most of the truth, that she thought her attacker might have been Sebastian Hughes, after the address of the refuge; and she just managed to avoid admitting that she was actually speaking from the refuge, or that Mark worked there.

After that Mark left her with the doctor for an hour, while he mingled with the kids and told each of them that they would be moving temporarily down to Malmebury, hopefully the following day. Davey he extracted a promise from, for a long talk in the morning about his friend and his plans for the future.

Then he went back to Alex, leaving them to absorb the news in their individual ways, grateful that they all recognised the necessity of moving. Indeed, they seemed to welcome it; life at the refuge had turned sour and unsafe since Nina's death and the threat of disclosure in the newspapers, and there was a general feeling that they would be glad to get away.

A little before midnight, a short, elderly man came out of the house and drove away in the black BMW that had been parked on the drive all evening. Seb watched from where he lay with his long body stretched out in the shadows of the shrubbery, dropping his head into his arms as the headlights swept across the lawn, so that the man shouldn't see a pale face shining in the darkness.

When the car was gone, he turned his eyes back to the house and watched the lights going out, one by one.

There was no hurry now; he had the whole night to act in. And his luck was back with him, he would never have found this place without it. He could feel the surge of it in his body, coupling with the familiar sensation of time slowing, holding its breath, waiting for him to act. He was confident, full of power, riding with the night.

He moved when it felt good to move, when the world was ready for it. He ran doubled over across the grass, and light-footedly over the gravel, only a soft whisper of sound marking his passage. He spared the front door one glance, and turned away from it; no hope of getting in through there. But there were two other chances. He could break in through a window, either on the ground floor or up the fire-escape; or, if he were lucky,

*(and oh, he was lucky; it surged and sang in his bones, his luck, with the voice and strength of the sea)*

he could find a way in from the cellar. He'd try that way first, in any case; it was further from the sleepers inside, and hopefully quieter.

So he turned to his left and followed the concrete steps down between walls of brick to the cellar door. It was old and weak, rotting at the bottom; one sharp kick broke the lock and let him in.

It was pitch black inside, with only the one small window
below ground level, but Seb was sure enough to risk turning
on the light. He fumbled on either side of the door frame for
the switch, and couldn't find it; so he stepped cautiously in,
turned to shut the door, and cracked his head on wood. He
swore softly, reached up to find the beam with his hand and
duck under it, and felt the round shape of a switch beneath
his fingers. He smiled,

*(luck, you're a lady)*

masked the window with a sheet of cardboard he found
underfoot and flicked on the light.

Five minutes' exploring, picking his way between ancient
pieces of furniture and clambering over piles of junk, as-
sured him that there was no way up into the house from
here; but by then another idea was seeding itself in his mind,
feeding on what he saw around him, the plywood tea-chests
and the oily rags, the half-full bottles of white spirit and the
foam-filled sofa cushions heaped in one corner. It was
chancy, but no more so than breaking into the house and
creeping from room to room, looking for Kez. And it was a
night for taking chances, for playing his luck. If he played it
well, this way he could get rid of Kez and the other girl both,
without having to lay a finger on either of them . . .

So he cleared a space in the middle of the concrete floor,
and built another bonfire. He pictured the blaze in his mind,
sending soft messengers of smoke up through two floors to
the sleepers overhead, lulling them into a deeper unconsciousness while the fire spread undisturbed below –

– and was startled out of his imaginings by the sudden
clamour of a bell above, bright and fatal as a searchlight.

Davey's light was off, but he wasn't asleep, or even undressed. He was sitting on the bed, arms around his knees
and his eyes not seeing the darkness he sat in. Two thoughts
filled his head, two words and two sensations, ice and fire;
and one was Aids and the other was Jesse, and he skidded
between them with no control and no hope of control,
nothing to do but skid and slip, let it happen and only trust
that at the last he would be caught and held by the fire, and
go down burning.

He hadn't wanted to come back to the refuge tonight.
He'd spent the afternoon and evening with Jesse, and there
was a terror in parting, in coming back to a house where fire
was only a memory and a promise, ice

*(and the grip of it deeper than his bones, his blood sharp
with it, killing-sharp)*

the present reality. But Jesse had insisted; he wouldn't let
Davey quit the refuge with just a phone-call to say he wasn't
coming back. *You're not running away this time, kiddo.
You're walking out of there with your things packed and your
head up high, you get me?*

And it wasn't the memory of the words that made Davey
smile suddenly in the darkness,

*(skidding close to the fire again, and the warmth of it)*

it was how they'd been said, murmured into his ear while
Jesse's finger traced a line across his stomach, dipped for a
second into his navel and went on down . . .

So he'd come back, just for the night; and tomorrow the
rest of them could go to Malmebury, they could go to hell if
they wanted, Davey knew where he was going.

And for tonight he sat on his bed alone and afraid and
hopeful, skidding and sliding in his head; and the sudden
strange clamour of the doorbell was something to be grateful

for, jerking him back into a life he understood.

It was probably only one of the others back late, forgotten their key and wanting in. He rolled off his bed and padded downstairs in his socks, turning lights on as he went, wondering who. Not Colton, that was sure: he wouldn't go anywhere now without Kez, and she was never out after dark. And Mandy never went out at all, so chances were it'd be Tia. He scowled, but went on down anyway; she was leaning on the bell now, and Mark'd raise hell if she roused the house.

When he reached the front door, he twisted the catch on the lock and pulled; it opened six inches and stuck, and it was only then that he realised the chain was on. Davey grunted, and would have pushed the door shut, taken the chain off and opened it again without even looking to see who was outside.

But he never got the chance, because the door shook suddenly as someone threw their weight against it; and a moment later he saw a dull steel beak close around the stiff chain, and bite it through.

He backed off one pace, two, and turned to run; but the door slammed back against its hinges, he heard feet coming after him light and fast, and there was no time to get away, no time even to change his mind and yell for help. He hadn't reached the foot of the stairs before an arm closed tight around his throat and jerked him to a standstill, while a big hand clamped itself over his mouth.

He tried to squirm free, jabbing backwards with elbows and feet, but the man who was holding him only laughed softly, and crushed his nostrils together between finger and thumb. Black mists threatened the corners of Davey's sight, while his chest fought for air and found none; and a voice in his ear said, "Just stand still, kid, and do what you're told. It's not you we're after."

Then the grip on his nose relaxed, to let him breathe again; and the arm under his chin forced his head up. He could see two other men; there was a white guy by the door, holding it almost closed and looking out, but closer to Davey a tough-looking Asian stood watching him, swinging a pair of heavy wire-cutters loosely in one hand.

"Tia Sharif," he said. "Where is she? Just point, we'll go that way."

And he could have done it, he could've led them straight
to her. Christ, he didn't care what happened to Tia, why
should he? Only, *they'll kill me*, he remembered the fear on
her face and thought maybe it was true, maybe they would;
and Jesse was still strongly in his mind, and Jesse wouldn't
tell them anything, wouldn't like it if he did . . .

So he lifted his hand and didn't point, just gave the guy a
savage V-sign without stopping to think what it might mean.
And the guy looked at him a moment, then lifted the wire-
cutters and laid the steel blades cold against Davey's cheek.

"Last chance. Where is she?"

Davey's eyes twisted away to stare up the stairs, *someone
else must've heard the fucking bell, where the hell are they?*
But there was no one there, no one coming, and a simpler
fear was chewing at his gut now, but he couldn't just cave in.
Someone would come soon, they'd have to . . .

So he lashed out one foot for answer, and caught the guy
on the shin with a soft, awkward kick that wouldn't have
hurt a child.

"Hold him still."

Davey's head was pulled back against the chest of the man
who held him, and clamped there with arm and hand; and
this time the cutters' blades were open as they approached
his face.

It wasn't reason pulling Davey's strings now, or at any rate
not alone; cold terror had a hand in there too, jerking his
hands up to grab the Asian's wrists, trying to force them
away. No squirming or struggling now, there was only the
one sharp focus, and the one intent; his feet were fixed and
still, his body rigid, every muscle straining to keep those
glittering edges off; and he might as well have been pushing
against

(ice)

a glacier.

Sweat pricked his skin like sandpaper, blood rushed and
ebbed in his ears like a tide – and it was as if the blades could
hear it as loud as he did, because they turned hungrily
towards his left ear, turned and closed, closed and bit,

(*and Christ! the cold, the ice winning and the fire forgotten*)

and pain stabbed and swirled and spun him almost out of
his body. A scream built deep in his belly, and arched his
back with the force of it as it ripped acid from his stomach to

his throat. His jaw spasmed against the hand that held it closed, the scream filled his mouth like vomit; and finding no way out, it turned black and sour inside his head. It was a thick cloud behind his eyes, flecked with dazzle; it was the sweat turning to stink on his forehead, the saliva flooding his tongue, making him swallow and swallow again, the hot acrid taste at the back of his throat, and . . .

And the bloke who held him jerked his hands away with a mutter of disgust and let Davey drop; and he held himself on trembling arms while the vomit gouted from his mouth and splashed onto the floor, seasoned with the blood that dripped off his cheek and jaw.

He gasped and retched until his heaving stomach had nothing more to throw out, until the violence of his sickness receded and left him swimming in the dark whirlpool of pain again. Then he felt cold metal under his chin, forcing his head up; and he stared numbly along the length of the cutters' handles at the hand that held them, and the arm and face beyond.

"That's only a start, you understand me? Take us to Tia Sharif."

Davey pushed himself slowly, awkwardly to his feet, and staggered, and might have fallen again if his interrogator hadn't grabbed his arm and twisted it savagely up to his shoulder-blade, giving him another sharp pain to lean into, to focus his mind. There was no fight in him now, no hope of rescue; it was only a sullen resistance that whispered to him through the raw agony of torn flesh that used to be his ear, that said, *Mark. Take them to Mark* . . .

He stumbled towards the stairs, the grip on his arm pushing him along while warm blood ran down his neck and soaked into the shoulder of his T-shirt. His breath was coming in sobs, short and hard, too weak to cry out and warn the others even if he'd thought of it; but the blood was putting another thought into his head, one that brought a twisted smile to his mouth. Never mind how warm it felt, there was ice in that blood, sharp and deadly and a slow death – and blood's gregarious, it likes to share itself around. It must be all over their hands by now, both of them. On the cutters' blades, too – and all it'd need was a nick, a little scratch on the skin, to get in there and start mixing . . .

He shook his head suddenly, to flick a few more drops towards the men behind him, splash it about a bit more; then they'd reached the passage on the first floor, and he led them along to Mark's door and pushed it open with his free hand, hit the light-switch and called, "*Mark!*" with all the strength he could find, give the guy a second's warning –

– and saw Mandy already sitting up in bed, staring at him, and realised Christ, he'd fucked it, he'd forgotten, Mark was up in the attic now –

– and there was a sudden curse behind him, and a shove that sent him staggering into the room; and he turned his head, scrabbling for something to say, an appeal losing itself in terror as he saw the heavy cutters blurred above his head, moving too fast to focus, barely time enough to feel the ice close in –

## 66   Awful Clarity

Mandy had been listening ever since the doorbell rang; she'd heard soft voices and movement in the hall below, and footsteps coming up the stairs. She'd been scared then, scared already, hugging her arms around her swelling belly, *they're coming for me, for us. For you. But I won't go, I won't let them take you . . .*

Then the door had swung open and the light had blazed, and she'd seen Davey with his face smeared and darkly streaked, and the men behind him. She'd heard his voice, "*Mark!*", hoarse and urgent, and seen him check at the sight of her, seen and understood his mistake with an awful clarity.

The man behind him moved suddenly, pushing Davey into the room, and lifting his hand with something in it, a giant pair of pliers. Davey twisted round too slow, and the pliers swung down, straight at his head. There was a soft thudding sound, and Davey fell sideways onto her bed, onto her, with

a deep hollow the size of her fist on one side of his head, and
blood gushing from somewhere, blood that spattered and
stained her, blood that she could taste on her lips and feel
trickling across her face –

## 67   *And He Screams*

*– and he screams –*

## 68   *Death, All Death*

– and she screamed and screamed again, screaming for him
who had no mouth to the world and could only scream to
her; and it was death, all death, in his scream and hers, in
Davey's blood, in Davey; and she saw a face coming towards
her, a moustache curling back above bared teeth and those
pliers lifting again, and that was death too, and she snatched
   *(for him, it was all for him, to keep death from him)*
beneath her pillow –

– and Mudassar felt it all slipping away out of his control as the girl screamed loud enough to raise

   *(the boy)*

the dead; and he rushed into the room to silence her, never mind how, the cutters' weight in his lifting hand, the only way he could think of; and as he got close he saw her hand come out from under her pillow with something in it, something that caught the light and gleamed with danger; and he hesitated only a moment, because she was only a kid and maybe he didn't have to do it, maybe he could scare her into silence; but even that moment was too much, because she moved the wrong way, hurling herself towards him with that gleaming thing held two-handed before her, and his mind said *knife* too late, as he felt the blade punching through shirt and skin and driving deep; and his body was suddenly too heavy to hold itself together, and he felt himself falling, falling apart . . .

## 70   Whichever Way She Came

Seb had his fire already burning when he heard the screams, shrill and piercing. He cursed, wondering what the hell was going on up there. No hope now of its catching them asleep, killing them quietly; but he couldn't have counted on that anyway, and at least he could still be sure of its forcing them out.. With the house ablaze, they wouldn't be looking for danger in the dark outside . . .

He picked up his weapons, a two-foot length of lead piping and an old rusty chisel with a chipped and broken blade, and slipped cautiously out of the cellar, pulling the door to behind him. Making his way softly up the steps, he saw windows lit on all three floors of the house, and more light laying a path down the stairs from the open front door, marking out the shadow of a man. Seb froze; but the watcher was inside the hall, and the angles would prevent him from spotting any movement on the cellar steps, or this side of the house.

So Seb moved again, going very slowly up to the head of the steps and then back across the gravel until he could slip around the corner. From here he could watch both the door and the fire-escape, and meet his sister whichever way she came . . .

## 71   The Worst Of It

Mark had learned, or discovered, or invented a whole new way of sleeping, since Alex had come to him. In some ways he slept better than he had since he was a child, he certainly felt more rested; but it was as if he tucked himself just under the edge of sleep, keeping a finger's-hold of awareness on the night. He didn't know if it happened to everyone who shared a bed, or if it was only him; but he could sleep and dream and still be conscious of Alex beside him as he slept, as he dreamed. When she moved, he knew it; and often he would let himself drift out of dreaming, put a hold on it, to open his eyes for a moment and see if she'd woken up or simply shifted in her sleep. If she was awake, then so was he; and if not, he'd just have time and thought enough to move an arm or a leg, to give her a little more room or to hold her more closely, before he slipped away into his dream again.

Tonight, though, it wasn't Alex who pulled him up out of sleep; and it wasn't that gentle stirring of consciousness that could subside again without disturbing his dream. This time it was an invasion, something alien, a noise dragging at his mind. He heard it in his dream, and knew it didn't belong there; so he opened his eyes and found it there too, a scream punching through the house like a fist through glass.

He rolled out of bed with a muttered curse, and fumbled for his trousers in the dark. There was a soft murmur of springs behind him, and Alex's voice, anxiety fighting through the slur of sleep.

"Mark? What's going on?"

"God knows. You stay there, I'll see to it."

"No," as another scream cut through the echoes of the first. "I'm coming too."

He heard what she didn't say, *I don't want to be alone,* and accepted it; was glad of it, indeed, because whatever was happening downstairs to cause those screams and the running footsteps, he didn't want to be alone either as he faced it. It wasn't only teenage hysteria, he was confident of that. And with memories of the evening still fresh and frightening, his imagination gave him pictures of a man in a balaclava running rampant through the house; and his mind gave a name, however reluctantly, to that man.

*Seb Hughes. If Seb's found us, if he's found Kez . . .*

It was the fear of that chance that sent Mark suddenly running out of the room and down the stairs without waiting for Alex. Alone or not, he had to get there.

He took the last three steps at a leap and plunged round the corner into the first-floor corridor; and a momentary relief clubbed him to a standstill, as he saw Colton in the doorway of his room, fumbling with the buttons of his jeans. The boy was looking back over his shoulder, saying something Mark couldn't catch. But the words didn't matter, because it couldn't be anyone but Kez he was talking to, and never mind what the hell she was doing in there . . . Mark killed his worst fantasies quickly, and turned his head as movement caught his eye further down the passage.

He saw Tia pressing herself back against the wall as a man, a stranger, ran past her and out of sight down the stairs. Tia's door was open, and so was Davey's, and Mark's old room too, where Mandy was now. That was where the screams were coming from, changing now to a strange, cracked sobbing. Mark and Colton hurried down the passage together, and met Tia in Mandy's doorway.

As the three of them looked inside, Tia gave an unvoiced little scream, Colton moaned slightly; Mark couldn't make even so much noise as that, he couldn't do anything but look, as his dead fantasies were exchanged for a worse reality.

There were two still figures in that small room, Davey lying across the bed and another stranger, an Asian man, crumpled on the floor. Both were soaked in blood, both surely dead, and no fantasies; but they weren't the worst of it. It was the living horror standing over them that chilled Mark in both mind and body, the sight of Mandy

*(quiet, frightened little Mandy)*

with her hair and skin and nightie spattered with blood and a kitchen-knife clutched in both hands, the blade showing streaked as it caught the light. More even than that, it was her face distorted beyond all sense or knowledge, and the terrible animal noises that broke from her throat, and her eyes darting in a frenzy from Davey to the stranger and back, and now towards them as they stood in a huddled group in the doorway.

She pointed the knife in their direction and scuttled two awkward scorpion steps towards them, two back. Tia shrieked; Mark pushed her aside, and forced himself slowly into the room. He held his hands out and open, knowing that the gesture was futile, would mean nothing to Mandy now; and watched the blade lifting towards him, and wondered if he could move fast enough

*(faster than Davey, or the other man, the stranger?)*

to dodge it.

"Mark, be careful . . ."

That was Alex. He didn't dare look round, but Mandy's gaze shifted to stare wildly over his shoulder, and he thought, *Now, do it now, grab the wrist –*

– and couldn't move as fast as thought, but it didn't matter anyway, because another cry ripped itself living from Mandy's twisting mouth, a scream of simple pain; and the knife dropped unregarded to the carpet as she snatched at her stomach with both hands.

Mark stepped forward
*(and one leg brushed the body on the floor, and he almost screamed himself as a sticky hand dropped dully down onto his bare foot)*
and took her uncertainly by the shoulders.

"Mandy? Mandy love, what's hurting?"

And she lifted her head and gave him more than an answer, gave him another nightmare to add to the horrors of the night.

"He's coming. He says, he's coming out . . ."

## 72    Growing Tighter

The dead man on Mandy's floor was no stranger to Tia. She didn't know his name,
*("Don't call me Ali. Don't call me anything.")*
but she knew his face all right, and she could guess what he wanted. Which was why she didn't resent it, when Mark pushed her aside, away from the door; she was just glad to be forced into movement. The grip of fear was still on her, and growing tighter; but thank Christ he had somehow gone into the wrong room and died there, never mind how. And never mind Davey either, or Mandy, or any of it. Get the hell out of here, that was all that mattered now. Even if she ended up back at home, at least she'd be safe . . .

She hurried, almost ran back down the corridor to her room, and slammed the door; grabbed her shoulder-bag from the floor and stuffed a few clothes into it at random; and thought, *Maybe he wasn't alone, no, he wouldn't have come alone. And maybe they were waiting outside, watching the door, waiting for her . . .*

And turned to the window, with the fire-escape beyond. She could get out that way, slip down in the shadows and they'd never see her, she could go round the back and get out into the alley, walk to King's Cross and catch the first train going north . . .

## 73   *The Wrong Thing*

Seb heard her before he saw her, a heavy clatter on the iron staircase; he spun round and saw a girl climbing out of a first-floor window, silhouetted against moon-pale clouds. A slim figure, long hair blowing in the breeze: he caught his breath and ducked quickly out of sight, crouching below the stairs, tightening his grip on the old chisel.

She came down slowly, quietly, and turned at the bottom to hurry straight past him with tense little paces, looking back over her shoulder as she went. He could hear her breathing, louder than his own; and, *I don't know what's scared you so bad, Kez, but it's the wrong thing. I'm not in there, I'm right here*, and he rose up behind her and let it happen quick and easy, one hand tight over her mouth and the other driving the chisel deep in under her ribs, twisting and thrusting upwards to find the heart.

She stiffened and sagged, and slid down his body onto the ground, *so long, sis*; and her face lolled towards him as she lay in the light of an upper window, and it was the wrong face, some Pakistani girl, not Kez, holy *Christ* it wasn't Kez . . .

Mark came out into the passage with Mandy in his arms, sobbing and clinging to him, her mouth babbling and running foul with delirium.

"Mark . . ." Mandy screamed, and Alex swallowed, tried again. "Mark, what's *wrong* with her?"

"She's having a miscarriage." His face, his voice were clamped and stiff, holding something, maybe everything back. *That's not all, is it? That's not enough to make her like this, to hurl her into madness.* But there was no time to ask questions, or even to wonder what the hell had happened in that room, as Mark went on, crisp and commanding. "Alex, fish the keys out of my pocket, I can't get at them. Got them? Right. Run down and get the Morris started. You'll need to get into the office first, for the car keys. Wait – Colton, you go with her and open the garage doors. Hurry."

Colton hesitated only a moment, to look back at Kez and get a nod of permission; then he was sprinting away down the stairs, and Alex was happy to follow, to have something to do that took her away from the questions, the sounds of Mandy's living nightmare and the smells of blood and death.

She fumbled the keys from their hook in the office and went through to the garage, where Colton was already fighting with the stiff bolts on the double doors, swearing under his breath.

The car wheezed twice, coughed, and caught. Alex flicked the lights on, and saw Colton throwing a bare brown arm across his eyes as he folded the second door against the wall and stood back to let her out.

She drove onto the forecourt and stopped, seeing Colton automatically closing the garage doors behind her, shutting himself inside. As she got out of the car, Kez came uncertainly down the steps from the house, flinching as the gravel cut into her bare feet.

"Mark . . . Mark'll be down in a minute, he's just getting a blanket for Mandy . . ."

"Okay, love. That's fine. Did he say where we're going?"

"Malmebury, he said. All of us. He said, there's time enough to get there, and Mandy needs more than an ordinary hospital, he said she needs the doctor . . ."

"He's probably right, at that. But I hope he knows the way, because I don't."

"Alex, what's going on?"

Alex sighed, and shoved a hand through her hair. "Wish I knew, kid. Are you scared?"

Kez nodded mutely.

"Yeah, me too." She slipped an arm round the younger girl's waist and hugged her gently. "But it'll be over soon. I reckon Mark's got the best idea, just getting us all out of here. Look, you get in the car, okay? Colton'll be out in a minute, so don't worry. I'm just going to run in and find Tia."

She waited for another nod, and got it; and jogged away up to the door. She glanced back then, and saw Kez still standing, hugging herself for comfort. Alex thought, *you need more than that, kid, we all do*, and went inside yelling for Colton.


## 75  *Here Comes the Luck*


Seb had been pushing the Pakistani girl's body out of sight under the fire-escape when he heard the roar of a car's engine, and saw its headlights cutting past the corner of the house. He gave the corpse one last kick to drive it deep into the shadows, snatched up his weapons and ran to peer around the brickwork.

He saw the rounded jelly-mould shape of an old Morris, and a girl getting out of it, the girl from the flat; and then

*(here comes the luck)*

he saw Kez, really Kez this time, coming down from the house.

They stood together for a minute, speaking just loud enough for him to hear; then the reporter went back inside, leaving Kez alone and unprotected.

And Seb moved in that moment, knowing he wouldn't get a chance like this again. He sprinted across the gravel towards her, with the lead pipe in one hand and the already-blooded chisel in the other; and he was halfway to her before she looked and saw, closer still before she screamed, practically there and already swinging the pipe at her head before she moved.

She half ducked, half fell behind the shelter of the open car door, and the pipe missed her skull by half an inch. Kez screamed again, and scrabbled stupidly into the car as Seb reached over the door and grazed her shoulder with a lunge of the chisel.

No room to swing in there, so he threw the pipe down onto the gravel, dodged her kicking feet and bent low to slash at her, grabbed one ankle to pull her out where he could finish her off quickly and get the hell away . . .

## 76   *No Movement, No Threat*

Colton was still struggling with the bolts on the garage doors – and studiously ignoring the little voice whispering in the back of his head, saying there was no point, they wouldn't be coming back here – when he heard the screams.

Sick and muddled as he was, it took a second to place them, *outside the house, not Mandy, Christ what now?*, and another to recognise the voice.

*Kez!*

He fought the door open and stared out into the night. There was a man by the car, crouching low, and –

– and Jesus, he was trying to drag someone out, and she screamed again, and –

*Christ!* –

twenty yards to cover, and Colton plunged out onto the gravel, barely aware of its bite on the soles of his feet as he ran;

fifteen yards, and the guy had Kez half out of the car, her legs flailing wildly as she clung to the back of the seat inside;

ten yards, and it was Seb, it had to be, lifting his hand with some kind of dull knife in it, and God he was going to kill her;

five yards, and Seb doubled up suddenly as Kez's heel caught him in the groin. She scrambled back into the temporary safety of the Morris, and Colton saw a shadow-shape on the ground just ahead of him, long and straight, and

*(let it be a weapon, please, something I can fight with)*

snatched it up. It felt cold and heavy, steel or lead under the flaking paint; he gripped it two-handed and desperate, and scythed it at Seb as he straightened.

It caught him in the neck, with a sound softer than it should have been. Seb's head jerked away from the impact, his legs skidded towards Colton, and he fell in an awkward, crumpled mass against the car's front wheel.

Colton watched him for a moment, saw no movement and no threat, and let the pipe slip from numb fingers. He turned to the open car door, and put his head in; and Kez screamed again.

"Kez, don't, it's all right, it's me . . ."

She lifted her head and stared at him, drew a slow, hacking breath that was something close to a moan, and whispered his name.

"Yeah, it's me. And it's okay, it's safe now, honest . . ."

"Has . . . Has he gone?"

Colton glanced sideways at the slumped body. "Well, no – but he ain't going to hurt you. He's well out of it. Come on, now . . ."

He took her hands and tugged her gently out. She snatched at him, and he clung to her no less gratefully, each leaning on the other as footsteps sounded urgently behind them, coming down from the house.

"Who screamed?"

"Are you two all right?"

Mark, and Alex – Mark with Mandy still in his arms, but quiet now, wrapped in a blanket with her eyes wide open and empty, her lips moving around words with no shape or sound to them, no sense.

"Yeah. We're okay. But . . ." His eyes pointed them where his voice couldn't; Alex gave a little groan, as if this were one crisis too many, and moved reluctantly over to the sprawled body.

"Who's that?" Mark demanded wearily, inching past the teenagers to lay Mandy along the back seat of the car.

"Seb. I think . . ."

"Yes," Kez said, her voice dry and dead. "It's Seb. Is, is he all right?"

"He's still breathing," Alex said, which wasn't quite an answer. "What happened?"

"He was going for Kez. I – I hit him. With that." Colton's foot nudged the pipe.

Mark's hand closed on his arm, offering a tired comfort. "It all happens at once, doesn't it?"

Alex stood up, her eyes still fixed on the unconscious Seb. "So what do we do now?"

They all turned to Mark, and Colton could sense the struggle in him, the fight to be decisive. "What I said. We'll carry him inside, lock up and just go. Call the police from Malmebury, tell them to come here. We don't need to tell them where we are."

"But, Davey . . .?"

"We can't take him with us, love. I don't like to leave him either, but . . ." Mark shrugged helplessly, then looked around. "Where's Tia?"

"I don't know," Alex said. "I yelled, but she didn't answer."

"Unh. Well, she'll have to look after herself, that's all. Kez, can you manage on Colton's lap, in the front? I'll be in the back here, with Mandy. But let's get Seb into the house first. Give us a hand, Colton. And move it," as Mandy cried out weakly. "We're running out of time."

So they picked Seb up and hustled his limp body into the hall, laid him on the floor and left him; and neither of them noticed the smell of smoke rising through the floor.

. . . Two bodies have so far been recovered from the gutted ruins of the house. One has not yet been identified; the other is believed to be Davey FitzAlan (15), the former rent boy. A third body, that of a teenage Asian girl, was found in the grounds. She had been stabbed with a sharp instrument; police say that causes of death have not been established for the other two, but neither is believed to have died in the fire. Post-mortems will be held this afternoon.

Police have refused to confirm or deny the rumour that they are expecting to find yet another body in the ruins of the still-smouldering house. Nor will they speculate about the cause of this tragedy; but anyone with information is asked to come forward as a matter of urgency.

# Envoi

*Running in Circles*

## (i)  Sick and Dreaming

"It was him, see, Mark, all the time. My – my baby, he kept talking to me, telling me what to do; and I couldn't just ignore him, he went on and on, and I, I don't know, everything he said was *right* . . ."

"I know, love. Believe me, I do know. I've been there."

"How d'you mean?"

"You were ill, Mandy, that's all. It's called schizophrenia, it's something that happens in your head, that turns the whole world crazy. I had it too, when I was your age; but the doctor pulled me through it, and he'll do it for you, too." *I hope.* "We'll talk about it more later, when you're feeling better. Meantime, just do what he tells you, and don't worry, okay? Forget what happened before, it's over, and you're safe now. Really safe."

"It, it feels like a bad dream now, all of it; but it wasn't, when it was happening. It all felt so *real*, his voice and everything. Like, he was my baby, of course he could talk to me . . ."

"Yes, but listen, love, that's what I came in to tell you. It wasn't real, and I can prove it to you."

"How?"

"Your baby would have been a girl. The doctor told me so."

"Is that true?"

*I don't know, sweetheart, he's a good liar and I didn't ask. But it's what you need right now, so,* "Yes, it's true. I promise. You were sick and dreaming, that's all. I'm going to leave you now, so get some sleep, okay? It'll do you more good than any of the doctor's pills. Only don't tell him I said that, or you'll get me in trouble . . ."

## (ii)   The Circle of his Distress

"Mark . . ."

   "Mmm?"

   "You know what I'd really like?"

   "What?"

   "Well, I'm not greedy for your time, and I'm not possess-ive, and I know you've got a lot on your mind; but I have too, and most of it's same stuff, and what I'd really like would be for you to stop forgetting that I exist, you know? I mean, you don't have to talk to me if you don't want to, but it would be kind of nice if I could feel confident that you did actually remember that I was here . . ."

   She screwed a finger slowly into his ribs, to underline the point. He slapped her hand away, then reached for it again and held it loosely, turning the focus of his eyes from the distant trees to the loose skin on her knuckles, the focus of his mind to her.

   "I'm sorry, Alex. It's just . . ." He gestured helplessly, stranded on a dry shore with no words, left as inarticulate as any of the kids; and touched a brief smile to her face.

   "I know. Too much happened too quickly, and you don't understand half of it either, right? And you're not used to talking things through, except with the doctor. You're too used to keeping your problems to yourself, you are. You have the habit of solitude," with another smile, pleased with the phrase. And slipped in as an afterthought, in an effort to bring an answering smile, "You know, I could be helluva jealous of the doctor, if I had a mind to. He's the only guy you ever talk to."

   "Used to be." He put an arm round her shoulders, and that was as good as the smile she'd been working for, or better.

   "So okay, talk to me."

"You just said I didn't have to."

"Changed my mind. It's compulsory. Tell me about Mandy."

A shadow touched him, almost took him away again; but she hung on tight, laid her free hand against the stubble on his cheek, and at last he said, "That's what cuts me, more than any of the rest of it. That's what I could have stopped, if I'd only seen it. She didn't have to go through all that. And Christ, I've seen enough of it, I should have *known* . . ."

"The doctor didn't spot it either, Mark. And he's the expert."

"He wasn't living on top of her, like I was. The poor kid was just sitting there, right under my eyes, with all the classic symptoms – Jesus, she spent all her time just *listening*, and I was so tied up with fretting about myself, watching myself for the slightest sign of a crack-up, I never saw what was obvious in her."

"So, what, you're going to spend the rest of your life wishing you'd been smarter, is that it? It *happened*, Mark, and you can't change that. And Mandy's okay now, or she will be."

"Maybe she will. It's not certain."

"Nothing's certain, mate. So leave it out, will you? I've got trouble enough nursing you through the terrors of your first girlfriend, I don't need you with a heavy guilt trip on top. Believe me, any time you deserve a kick up the arse, you can rely on me to deliver it. You don't have to do it to yourself."

He glanced at her wearily. "It's not funny, Alex."

"I'm not laughing. Or not at Mandy. And if you stopped making yourself ridiculous, I might stop laughing at you."

He identified the game then, he'd have to; neither of them had laughed since that long, terrible night, and each was too well aware of it, feeling the lack in the other. He grimaced and nodded, *point to you*, and stuck his tongue out. She smiled, and kissed him.

"That's better. But seriously, how much of, of what went on was down to Mandy? What did that voice of hers actually make her *do*?"

He shook his head. "I'm not sure. No one's asked, and no one's going to. I think she's forgotten half of it, and with any luck she'll forget the rest; but you can work some of it out, if you want to. That's the thing about schiz, it's very logical; and she said enough to give us the clue. Imagine you're a paranoid foetus – only hell, it's not paranoia, you *know* they're out to get you, they want to abort you. And your own safety is the only thing that concerns you, right? So you start by getting Mandy to run away, because you're not safe so long as she's at home; and you go on from there."

Alex looked back to her first day at the refuge, and said, "Jane's rats."

"Right. Rats are a health hazard, so you get rid of them. And you do it flashy, do it big, so you can be sure no one's going to bring any more in. Then make it look like it was an outsider, and that's that."

Alex nodded unhappily. "Mark, health hazards – Nina? I know Mandy got pretty hysterical, about the way she kept on smoking in the games room after you banned it."

"I'm not sure. I've been wondering about that, too. You can be pretty confident that if Mandy was hysterical, she was only echoing the voice in her head; and yeah, it might have driven her to do something. Grind the pills up, dissolve them in a cup of coffee – Nina wouldn't have noticed, she drank it so sweet. It could have happened that way. I don't think I want to know."

"Me neither. Tell you what I would like to know, though – what happened to Tia. And who those men were, who broke in."

"You can have a guess, for what it's worth. Colton says she was dealing drugs, and Davey stopped her, he doesn't know how. It could have been something to do with that; and if she was scared, made a run for it and ran into Seb . . ."

"Seb again. Yeah. You know, that, that's the only thing I'm glad about, in the whole fucking mess – that Seb was in that house when it burned. I bet he set the fire, too, so he deserved it. I hope he was bloody conscious, and all . . ."

Her voice broke strangely, and she turned her head quickly away; but just the touch of Mark's fingers on her neck brought her back again, pressing her face against the warmth of his jumper.

"I'm not," she muttered. "I'm not going to cry, not again."

"Why not?"

"Done it enough for one lifetime."

"Which lifetime was that, then?" he asked bleakly, above her head. "Davey's, or Tia's? Nina's? Mandy's baby?"

"Don't. Don't be a shit."

She felt herself lifted suddenly onto his lap, and nestled there like a tearful child; but she was right, she didn't cry. She only sat and listened while he cried, held in the circle of his arms, of his distress.

## (iii)   *Kez Lvs Colton OK*

They came slowly down through the gardens to the river; and turned to follow the water till they came to a copse of trees. Letters scratched in the bare ground gave testimony that they had been here before, and more than once: BEASTIE BOYS RULE, and I GOT A CRUSH ON MY TEACHER, and an area scuffed clean for the next lesson; and larger than any, carved in the earth with a fallen branch, COLTON LVS KEZ OK.

He sat with a sigh on the felled trunk they used as a school-bench, and stretched his long legs out. She dropped onto the ground beside him, curled an arm round his knee and let her head fall against his thigh.

His fingers played in her hair, brushing it back from her cheek. "You okay?"

"Yes. No. What are we going to do, Col?"

"Work on my spelling, you said."

"Not that. I mean really. It's nice here, but we can't just hide forever."

"What, you mean you want to go home?"

"No. I don't want to. It terrifies me. I don't know how I'm going to face Mum, what can I *say* to her? But I have to do it, sooner or later."

"Make it later, eh? I don't, I dunno what I'd do, with you gone."

"That's what I'm saying, stupid. I want you to come too. I *need* you, Col. And you could get a job in Oxford . . ."

"Oh yeah, sure. Lots of jobs for a black kid who can't even read."

"You can read."

"Not without you to hold my hand and whisper the difficult words, I can't."

"You'd find something. And it wouldn't matter anyway, even if you didn't get a job. You can live with us."

"You're dreaming, girl. Your mum ain't gonna want nothing to do with me." *I'm the guy who killed your brother.* And he was just wondering whether to say it aloud, whether she could take it, when the bushes rustled on the other side of the copse. Kez's hands clenched tight on his leg, he lifted his head –

– and saw a shadow-figure rising from shadows, thrusting itself to its feet. Colton rose slowly to meet it, hearing Kez's fear in the scream she tried to swallow, tasting his own, bitter at the back of his throat.

It shambled forward into the light, breathing harsh and dry and heavy. Colton saw filthy, baggy clothes over skin tight and pink with healing blisters, a head carried strangely awry; and he almost laughed, almost said, *It's all right, Kez, I didn't kill your brother*, in the half-second he had left before Seb rushed him.

The weight of that charge sent Colton crashing down onto his back, with Seb on top of him. He tried to push him off, tried to squirm free; but strong, clammy hands were already hard on his throat and digging deeper, digging for breath and life and all. Colton arched his spine, lifted his own weight and Seb's both – and fell back again, and flailed weakly against the rigid arms that gripped him, and reached up in despair – *go for the eyes* – as his vision blurred and his chest heaved and hurt, and

*Kez, get away, get help, get Mark, get the doctor, get away* . . .

– and behind them, above them, Kez lifted the branch that Colton had carved his love with; and sobbed, and swung it with both eyes open and a deliberate aim.

It caught Seb across his twisted neck, with a dull thud and a sharp snapping sound. She watched him fall, and waited till Colton pushed himself out from under the slumped body, till she saw him shakily on his feet; then she dropped the branch from dead fingers, turned with only one thought in a dying mind, and started to run.

## Author's Note

There is in fact a *sub rosa* refuge in London where teenagers can find shelter, no questions asked. It has perhaps similar intentions to the Harlborough Institute, but no other connection. It is organised and financed not as a private enterprise but under the aegis of a highly respected charity; and any resemblance between the kids and adults who live and work there and the equivalent characters in my novel is entirely coincidental, and deeply regretted.

All other characters in this book are equally fictitious, and should not be taken to represent any real person living or dead.

Meanwhile, the following very real people are owed something more than thanks, for their help and encouragement over the last year:

Carol Smith, of course; Nick Sayers and Amanda Stewart; Jay and Lellie (once is not enough); and almost everyone in Newcastle, but particularly Ian and Mary, Nick, Rik, Philippa and Mike, Simon, Jane, Harry and Steve. And of course Sara, and Sara's jacket, and Carein, Sue, Robin, Alasdair, *everyone* at Mosaic; and the Bats as they were, for music and cigarettes and general mayhem. Under which latter heading Pat and Jon are not forgotten; nor Geoff and David, for hospitality and friendship above and beyond everything.